APPALACHIAN WEDDINGS

APPALACHIAN WEDDINGS

THREE-IN-ONE COLLECTION

DEBBY MAYNE

BARBOUR
PUBLISHING

Noah's Ark © 2009 by Debby Mayne
Special Mission © 2010 by Debby Mayne
Portrait of Love © 2011 by Debby Mayne

ISBN 978-1-61626-476-5

Cover design: Kirk DouPonce, DogEared Design

Published by Barbour Publishing, Inc., P.O. Box 719, Uhrichsville, Ohio 44683, www.barbourbooks.com

Our mission is to publish and distribute inspirational products offering exceptional value and biblical encouragement to the masses.

ecpa Member of the
Evangelical Christian
Publishers Association

Printed in the United States of America.

Dear Readers,

I'm delighted to have the opportunity to share the highly emotional experiences of three very different couples in the gorgeous state of West Virginia. I believe it's my responsibility as a writer to show God's truth, even in the fiction I write.

The Lord has provided us with the comfort of eternal salvation, so as we go through life, we need to be grateful for His mercy and enduring love. This doesn't mean we won't have challenges. In fact, it's in the challenges where we often find the deepest truths. As Emily in *Noah's Ark* struggles to find her way in life, the Lord presents options she's never even dreamed of. In *Portrait of Love*, Mandy initially fails to see that the Lord's path is much better than the one she would have chosen for herself. Kim in *Special Mission* is faced with the dilemma of following her heart versus doing what is honorable.

I hope you enjoy the journey with the characters in these three stories as they experience frustration, confusion, and challenges—things we all have to face. Falling in love is never easy, but those of us who know the Lord understand that the reward is worth the risk.

I enjoy hearing from my readers, so please let me know what you think about *Appalachian Weddings*. You may contact me through Barbour Publishing or my website at www.debbymayne.com.

NOAH'S ARK

Dedication

*Thanks to Kathleen Lamb who works with her husband,
Dr. Scott Lamb, at the Trinity Animal Hospital in
New Port Richey, Florida, for answering my animal questions.
I'd like to thank Brenda Holley, Member Relations coordinator
with the Huntington, West Virginia, Chamber of Commerce,
for providing information specific to the area.
Also, thanks to Byron Clercx, chairman of the Department
of Art and Design at Marshall University, Huntington.*

Chapter 1

Emily Kimball opened the sunroof on her nearly ten-year-old Nissan as she hummed to a country tune on the radio. Free from the constraints of a schedule, she felt a slight sense of freedom—something she'd never experienced in her life. After quitting her job at an art supply company and selling everything she didn't absolutely need, there was nothing left to hold her back.

Sunlight flickered as the sugar maples and oaks thickened on either side of the West Virginia country road. The hills provided a wall of foliage in varying shades of green. Although Emily had never lived in Huntington, she'd visited enough for the familiarity of it to feel like home.

The old farmhouse came into view, giving her a fluttery sensation in her chest. She blinked but not in time to hold back a tear that slipped down her cheek. Last time she'd been here had been a celebration—a family reunion. Her aunt and uncle had a way of making her forget her mother was no longer around. This visit was different. She needed to figure out what she wanted out of life, and she needed the strength of someone who loved her nearby.

Aunt Sherry sat on the swing that Uncle Mel had suspended from the front porch ceiling when Emily was a little girl—back when her parents were still together and her father was still alive. She remembered the sensation of floating as she and one of the adults in her life swayed to the rhythm of the night birds chirping. Back then, she had no idea her mother would decide she wasn't cut out for family life and abandon her and her father as soon as Emily hit puberty.

Her aunt glanced up right before Emily turned onto the narrow, paved driveway leading to the house. Emily turned off the radio, slowed down as she approached, and stopped in the exact same spot where her parents always parked whenever they came to West Virginia to visit.

"Mel!" Aunt Sherry hollered. "Emily's here!"

"Be right out!" Uncle Mel's husky voice flooded Emily with even more nostalgia.

Aunt Sherry didn't waste another second before heading straight to the driver's side. As soon as Emily opened the door and stood up, Aunt Sherry pulled her into an embrace that smelled of apple dumplings and cinnamon.

"I can't believe you're really here." Her aunt held her at arm's length and looked her over, smiling the entire time. "It's been years since we've seen you."

Emily cast a glance down at the ground, embarrassed that she'd let so much time lapse since her last visit. "I—uh, I missed you."

Aunt Sherry flipped her hand from the wrist. "Don't you worry about it. You're here now and that's all that matters." She gave Emily another hug. "Come on in, sugar. I've been cooking up a storm, ever since I heard you were coming." She put her arm around Emily's waist and guided her toward the house. "I bet you're starving."

"I am a little hungry."

"Well, I'll be. . ."

Emily glanced up and saw Uncle Mel coming out of the house, arms open wide. "Uncle Mel!"

Ignoring the steps, he hopped down off the side of the porch and strode toward her. "You sure have grown up, young lady. In fact, you look just like your mama when she was your age."

Aunt Sherry shot him a warning glance. "Mel, this isn't the time."

He snorted and winked at Emily before turning to his wife. "It's not a secret that her mama was a looker, and there's definitely no hiding that our little Emily is just as pretty." He focused his attention back on Emily. "You look just like a movie star. All the boys in church will be gawking at you."

Emily's cheeks heated with embarrassment, and she allowed her aunt to take control. "Mel, the poor girl has just arrived. Where are your manners? At least show some hospitality and give her time to rest before you start in on her."

"I'm just sayin'. . ."

"Emily, sugar, why don't you give your uncle your car keys, and he can bring your things in?"

As soon as Emily handed her uncle the keys, he left the two women alone. Aunt Sherry led her the rest of the way to the kitchen, which Emily could have found with her eyes closed. All she had to do was follow the aroma that grew stronger with each step.

"Have a seat, sugar, and I'll cut you a slice of pie. We have apple, custard, and chocolate. Which one do you want to start with?"

Emily laughed. "You're still determined to make me fat, aren't you?"

"You never did have much of an appetite. It's no wonder you've always had a hard time keeping meat on those bones." She pulled a knife from the kitchen drawer and turned to face Emily. "Is custard still your favorite?"

"I think I'd like chocolate today."

Aunt Sherry chuckled. "Chocolate's always been my favorite. That's what I'll have, too." She cut each of them a generous slice and added a dollop of whipped cream before setting the plates on the table and lowering herself into the chair adjacent to Emily. "I'm glad you're here. It's been getting mighty lonely with just Mel and me."

"I don't know how to thank you for letting me stay here until I figure out what I want to do with my life." Emily cut the tip of the pie and raised it to her mouth to savor the taste. "This is delicious."

Aunt Sherry took a bite and nodded. "It was your grandma's recipe. While you're here, I'll teach you how to make it."

Emily didn't plan to be there long enough, but since she didn't want to rattle any cages, she just smiled and cut another bite of pie.

"Tell me all about what you've been up to since you graduated from college." Aunt Sherry paused for a moment, her fork suspended over her pie. "Last I heard before your call was you had a great job. What happened?"

Emily crinkled her face and scrunched her nose. "The job wasn't what I thought. I wanted to do customer service, and they had me making sales, complete with quotas."

Her aunt offered a sympathetic look. "Isn't that the way it goes sometimes? Why, those people ought to be ashamed of themselves for telling you one thing then doing another."

"I'm afraid I'll have to take some of the blame. I was so desperate for a job I didn't pay much attention to the full job description until I accepted the position. When I realized what I was about to do, I tried to make the most of it." She paused as she traced her fork over what was left of her pie, and then she looked her aunt in the eye. "But with all the things happening in my life, I couldn't focus on something I didn't have my heart in, especially after a new manager came in and acted like I didn't have a brain in my head. That only lasted a few weeks. I just wish I knew what I wanted to do."

"If it's any consolation, sugar, I didn't have any idea what I wanted when I was your age. Mel and I had been married a year, so I stayed in my dead-end job because I didn't know what else to do."

"Then we had kids." The sound of Uncle Mel's voice by the kitchen door instantly caught their attention. "It's amazing how babies can change your life." He chuckled. "Then they grow up, and you find yourself wondering what happened."

Emily smiled. "I'd like to have children someday but not until I figure out who I am first."

"And you need to meet the right man," Aunt Sherry reminded her. "A man who loves the Lord as much as you do."

"Absolutely." Emily wasn't even sure if such a man existed, at least one who would love her for who she was—a very confused daughter of a mother who took off at the first sign of teenage angst.

Aunt Sherry gestured to one of the empty chairs. "Have a seat, Mel, and I'll cut you a piece of pie."

"Maybe later. I'm waiting for the chickens. Noah should be here any minute."

Emily turned to her uncle. "Chickens? Who's Noah?"

"Noah's the vet we brought in a little more than a year ago. We renamed the old animal clinic Noah's Ark."

"With a name like Noah, what else could you have done?" Emily asked with a grin.

Her aunt and uncle both laughed, and then Uncle Mel turned serious. "Anyway, after that last flood in the valley, a bunch of livestock had to be rescued. Noah and some of the other fellas got there just in time."

"So. . .the chickens were rescued from the farms?" Emily was still confused.

"Yep. And Noah's bringing a whole bunch of 'em here."

Aunt Sherry made a clicking sound with her tongue. "We haven't had chickens in quite a while. It'll take some getting used to, having them around here again."

"Better get used to it, Sherry," Mel said. "Noah can't handle all the animals without a little help from friends."

"And the Lord," Aunt Sherry added.

Mel cupped his ear with his hand. "I think I hear the truck comin' now. Y'all wanna go help?" He took a quick glance at Emily. "You might wanna change out of those nice clothes. Chickens can get you pretty dirty."

"What are you trying to do to our guest, Mel? She just got here. Give her a chance to relax."

Emily stood and carried her plate over to the sink. "I don't mind helping. I'll be right out."

Uncle Mel had already gone outside, but Aunt Sherry paused by the door, a look of consternation on her weathered face. "You really don't have to, but I'm not one to turn down an offer of help."

"Just let me find my jeans, and I'll join you all in a few minutes."

Aunt Sherry took off outside to help Uncle Mel, leaving Emily alone in the old farmhouse. Nothing had changed much. The wood-paneled walls provided warmth and welcome. The only rooms not lined with wood were the bedrooms and bathrooms, all painted in soft pastel colors to add a hint of cheer. Emily walked down the wide hallway with the locked gun closet on one side and bedrooms on the other. She peeked in every room looking for her things. When she got to the end of the hallway, she smiled. Emily was delighted that Uncle Mel had put her bags in the creamy yellow bedroom, her favorite.

She walked around the trunk filled with memorabilia, opened the bigger of the two suitcases, and found jeans and a T-shirt. As soon as she changed, she pulled her hair up into a ponytail and headed outside to lend a hand.

Uncle Mel stood beside an old pickup, taking crates from a dark-haired man bent over in the bed of the truck. He grinned and motioned for her to join them.

"Where's Aunt Sherry?"

The squawking chickens drowned out Uncle Mel's answer as he bent over and picked up another crate.

✁

At the sound of a different voice, Noah straightened and found himself looking at the prettiest woman he'd seen since he'd been in West Virginia. Her eyes widened as they stared at each other.

"Noah Blake, meet my niece, Emily Kimball." Mel turned and faced Emily. "Noah's the veterinarian we told you about earlier."

Just as Noah was about to jump off the back of the truck to shake Emily's hand, Sherry came out of the barn. "I thought I heard Emily out here. Why don't you come help me get these chickens situated?"

Noah turned to see Emily shade her eyes with her hand. "I'll be right there, Aunt Sherry." Then she swung back around and faced him with her cornflower blue eyes focused directly on him. "Nice to meet you, Dr. Blake."

He smiled back at her. "Just call me Noah."

She blinked. "Okay, Noah." Then she took off and disappeared into the barn before he had a chance to say another word.

Mel belted out a chuckle. "Her mama had that kind of impact on men. Too bad she wasn't half the woman Emily is."

"Huh?" Noah was dumbstruck, first by his own reaction to Mel and Sherry's niece, then by Mel's comment.

"Emily is a sweet Christian girl—takes after her daddy. Her mama never stepped foot inside a church after the wedding. It's no wonder she didn't stick around when the goin' got tough."

Noah still hadn't gotten used to the openness of these West Virginia folks. He'd just learned more about Emily Kimball than he knew about his housemates from college.

"How many more loads of chickens you got?" Mel asked.

"Um. . .let's see." Noah forced his thoughts back on the task at hand. "Two more?"

Mel lifted his eyebrows and let out a snort. "I reckon you better head out and get 'em before it gets dark. Suppertime will be here before you know it."

"I don't have to bring all of them here," Noah said. "Clayton said he could make room in his barn."

"Nah, better not do that. He has enough of his own cacklers to deal with. No sense in getting them all mixed up."

Noah hoisted the last crate from the truck, handed it off to Mel, and brushed his hands together. "I wasn't sure if you had time for this, with your niece being here and all. I figure you don't want to miss a minute of precious time you can spend with her." What he wanted to know was how long pretty Emily with the gorgeous blue eyes and wavy, honey-colored hair would be staying, but he didn't want to come right out and ask.

Mel's eyes squinted as he cast a long look at Noah. "That girl's been around barnyard animals before. I reckon she doesn't mind."

"She likes animals?"

"Yes, of course she likes animals," Mel said. "She's related to me, isn't she?"

Noah laughed. "She's been living in the city, so I wasn't sure."

Mel planted his fists on his hips and looked him squarely in the eye. "How would you know she's been living in the city?"

Busted. Noah glanced down then back up at Mel. "Sherry told me."

"I figured as much." Mel motioned for Noah to join him.

They finished unloading the truck and getting the chickens situated in half the time Noah expected. "I don't know how to thank you, Mel."

Mel made a face. "You don't have to keep thanking me for what I offered to do. C'mon, let's help the ladies and get the rest of these chickens in the barn so we can be done before dark. You're stayin' for supper."

"I can't—"

"Nonsense. It's the least we can do."

Noah appreciated the values of these rural West Virginia people—how they did favors yet considered it a privilege and insisted on paying people for allowing them to do favors by feeding them. This was something he wasn't used to.

A half hour later, Noah was on his way to pick up the next batch of chickens. A year ago he never would have pictured himself working at the outskirts of Huntington, West Virginia, with his clients' livestock on family-owned farms. When he first got into vet school, he assumed he'd take over for his father, who had a small-animal practice in a ritzy area of Atlanta. However, when he heard about the need for someone in West Virginia, he decided to check it out. The moment he crossed the line into some of the most beautiful, mountainous countryside, he knew he'd come home.

The people were amazing, too. From the farmers to the businesspeople in town, he felt like he'd run into old friends whose sole purpose in life was to welcome weary people who didn't know what they were looking for. To top it all off, Noah now knew exactly what he wanted, and this was it.

Every day something new awaited him. One day he might get an emergency call that Mrs. Crowley's pampered poodle, Precious, had something in her paw. The next day he could find himself in Junior Whitmore's barn delivering a brand-new foal.

And on another day he could be up to his elbows in chickens, only to look up and see the most beautiful woman he'd ever laid eyes on. Emily was even more gorgeous than the picture on the Kimballs' mantel. To top it off, she was a Christian—couldn't ask for better than that.

"Need me for anything else?" Emily said.

"Noah went to get the rest of the chickens. But you can go on inside if you're tired."

"He's bringing more?"

Uncle Mel nodded. "Yup. Two more loads, in fact."

"Then I'm staying out here and helping until the last chicken is taken care of."

Aunt Sherry grinned, and she joined Uncle Mel as he closed the gap between himself and Emily. "You're a good girl, Emily. I don't know how it happened with all you went through, but we're mighty blessed to have you in our family."

"Daddy raised me right." Emily's eyes stung as she thought about how shocked her father had been when her mother—his wife—had chosen to take off when Emily needed her the most.

"You miss him, don't you?" Aunt Sherry asked.

Emily nodded. "More than you can ever imagine."

Her aunt tilted her head forward and raised her eyebrows. "So does Mel. Those two were closer than any brothers I've ever known."

"Daddy always talked about how much he appreciated both you and Uncle Mel."

"Don't go gettin' all sappy on me," Uncle Mel said. "We got work to do. No point in cryin' over something we can't do a thing about."

Before Emily had a chance to say another word, they heard the rumbling of Noah's truck on the bumpy road. "Let's go get those chickens so we can eat at a decent time."

They worked hard until the last chicken was securely in the barn. Aunt Sherry placed her hand in the middle of Emily's back. "Why don't you get cleaned up and rest for a few minutes before supper?"

"I can help," Emily argued.

"No, do what I said. Tomorrow you can help with meals. You've already done more than enough for today."

An hour later, the four of them—Aunt Sherry, Uncle Mel, Noah, and Emily—bowed their heads to thank the Lord for the meal in front of them. When Emily opened her eyes and saw Noah staring at her, she felt the blood rush to her cheeks. She offered a nervous smile, and he grinned right back at her.

She'd been through a long day, so after supper Noah left, and Emily excused herself to unpack. Her muscles ached from all the lifting, but she didn't mind. It sure beat being alone and in a dead-end job.

The next morning, Emily awoke to the sound of a rooster crowing. She blinked a couple of times before she remembered where she was. Then she smiled. As long as she was here with Aunt Sherry and Uncle Mel, all was good in her world. She slowly got out of bed and slipped on a fresh pair of jeans and a button-down shirt.

As she headed toward the kitchen, she took a deep breath and inhaled the aroma of fresh coffee brewing. Aunt Sherry turned around and held out a cup. "I hope you slept well."

"Like a baby," Emily replied. "How are the chickens?"

Aunt Sherry chuckled. "I trust you heard the crowing?"

"Yes."

"It's been awhile since we had roosters. I'd almost forgotten how much I enjoyed that sound."

Emily nodded. There was something comforting about a rooster crowing, and it sure beat the jolting ring of an alarm clock. She sat down at the table and stirred some sugar into her coffee.

"I told Noah we'd stop by his office on the way into town."

"How long has he been practicing here?"

"A little over a year." Aunt Sherry joined her. "That's long enough for all of us to appreciate what a hardworking young man he is." She smiled. "He goes to our church, too."

"That's nice." Emily squirmed and tried to think of a different subject. "I need to do a little shopping while I'm here."

After a quick bowl of cereal, the two of them took off in Aunt Sherry's station wagon. Emily appreciated how Aunt Sherry chattered nonstop. It kept her from having to make conversation. When they pulled into the parking lot of a strip mall with mostly vacant space, Emily turned to her aunt.

"What's this?"

Aunt Sherry pointed to the end of the shopping center. "That's Noah's clinic at the end. I like to park here, in case one of his elderly clients needs a closer spot."

Emily was surprised as she glanced around. She wasn't sure what she expected, but this wasn't it.

"He has some chicken feed that should tide us over until we can have some delivered," Aunt Sherry explained.

As soon as Emily opened the front door, she was accosted by a menagerie of farm animals—a goat, a couple of chickens, and the squealiest pig she'd ever heard.

Chapter 2

Noah came around from behind the wall and tugged on the pig. "Sorry about that. Peewee likes visitors."

"Peewee?" Emily couldn't help but laugh.

"That's his name. Excuse me a minute while I tie him and Billy up in the back." He snapped his fingers. "C'mon, guys, you can't attack our friends." As Noah led the pig and goat to the back, his fingers tucked beneath both of their collars, the chickens scurried along right behind him.

Aunt Sherry winked at Emily. "Looks like Noah could use some help."

"Doesn't he have a receptionist?"

"Yes, Jillian comes in the afternoons, but she only works part-time."

Noah came back out, brushing his hands together. "Some of my patients are too nosy for their own good."

A clucking sound drew closer, capturing Emily's attention. "Looks like they can't stay away."

He snorted. "That's Helen. She hid when I put the other chickens in the cages. I know y'all are busy, so let's go get the feed, and you can be on your way."

The three of them piled up some sacks of chicken feed by the back door. Aunt Sherry held up a finger. "Let me drive around so we don't have to carry them so far. Why don't you stay here, Emily?"

Emily nodded. After Aunt Sherry left, Noah bent over, picked up Helen, walked across the room, and unlocked the back door.

"They have interesting names," Emily said. "Any of them belong to you?"

Noah shook his head. "No, they're all flood rescues, and I'm waiting for some folks to come pick them up. These aren't from the same farm as the ones I brought over to your aunt and uncle's yesterday."

"I wondered about that." She looked down at the chicken, who'd made herself comfortable in Noah's arms. "Helen obviously likes you."

"Of course she does. Animals have a sense of who they can trust."

As if on cue, Helen belted out a loud squawk and flapped her wings. Noah laughed as he gently put her on the floor.

Emily squatted to get a better look at Helen. "Uncle Mel let me adopt a baby chick one summer when I stayed on their farm."

"That's what happened with Helen. After she fell out of the nest, the farmer's little girl found her and brought her inside, thinking the chicken might be hurt. At first she managed to hide her under the bed, but then she started making all kinds of noise. According to the child's mother, they tried putting her back with the other chickens, but she couldn't make it socially."

"I guess she must not have fit into their pecking order," Emily quipped.

Noah rolled his eyes. "That's pretty lame, but I like it."

"Oh, it gets better."

The back door slowly opened, and Aunt Sherry stepped gingerly inside. "Let's get the feed and head on home." She looked down at the chicken. "Is that Helen?"

"Yes. The Stantons had to be evacuated, and Chip Morris can't come until tomorrow, so I offered to take her until then."

Aunt Sherry leaned over and made some clucking noises before standing back up. "I bet she misses her family."

"I'm trying to keep her mind off them so she won't get homesick."

After they loaded the feed into the back of the station wagon, Emily and Aunt Sherry said good-bye to Noah and headed back to the farm. Emily suddenly found the whole situation hilarious, and she started laughing—softly at first, then in an uncontrollable fit.

"What's that all about?"

"A homesick chicken." She snorted through her giggles. "I've never heard of such a thing."

With that, Aunt Sherry started laughing so hard tears started falling, and she had to pull over to wipe her eyes. "It is funny."

"I wonder where she got the name Helen," Emily said between guffaws.

"That's a question for Noah." Aunt Sherry maneuvered the car back onto the highway leading to the farm. "But I'm not sure he knows."

"He fits in here pretty well, doesn't he?"

Aunt Sherry nodded. "We went through three different vets, all right out of college, and none of them could handle all the livestock. We're fortunate to have Noah. He spent some time working on farms around Georgia, and he discovered how much he enjoyed it."

"How did you find him?" Emily thought for a moment then amended her question. "Or should I say, how did he find you?"

"His family goes to church in Atlanta with one of Pastor Chuck's former classmates."

"I wonder why he wanted to get away from Atlanta."

Aunt Sherry shrugged but kept her focus on her driving. "Sometimes kids just need to find their own way out from under the shadow of their parents—especially after they've been adults for a while."

That made sense to Emily.

As soon as they got to the house, they fed the chickens. Emily offered to help with the other animals, but Aunt Sherry said she preferred to do it alone. "Why don't you go through that box of pictures I have on the coffee table and see if there's anything you want copies of?"

Emily spent a few minutes looking through the pictures, but the memories were too painful. All the snapshots of her before she hit her teens included her mother—the woman she hadn't seen for years until her father died. By then they'd become strangers who could barely look at each other.

When Aunt Sherry came inside to start dinner, Emily stepped in with an offer of help and wouldn't take no for an answer. "Why don't you drive into town tomorrow?" Aunt Sherry said. "There's no point in hanging around here all day."

"I might do that."

"On your way back, you can stop by and pick up some medicine for Francine. She's gotten into something that's making her sick."

Emily grinned as she remembered how Francine the goat always had something wrong with her because she couldn't stay out of trouble. Last time Emily saw the goat—a couple of years earlier—she'd gotten tangled in some barbed wire. "What did she get into this time?"

"She's been getting into everything lately. Mel's been trying to figure out how to keep her contained, but Francine's an escape artist." She snickered. "We even tried tying her up, but she always manages to get loose."

Francine was one of Emily's favorite animals, mostly because she was such a rebel. While the other goats seemed satisfied hanging out inside the barn and playing in the small fenced yard beside it, Francine was a wanderer. Last time Emily visited, Francine actually made her way into the house—and no one had any idea how she'd gotten in.

The next morning, Emily got up and had breakfast before heading off toward town. She slowed down as she passed Pullman Square. Then she meandered through town until she found Ritter Park, wishing she'd brought her sketch pad. Her stomach started growling around noon, so she stopped for fast food. She'd have to investigate the little town's art galleries on her next trip.

Aunt Sherry had said she'd call the clinic for the medicine, so all Emily would need to do was pick it up. When she opened the door, a young woman with curly blond hair who sat behind the reception desk greeted her.

"I'm here to pick up some medicine for my aunt's goat," Emily said.

The girl frowned. "Goat medicine?"

Emily nodded. "My aunt, Sherry Kimball, was supposed to call this morning."

"Oh, I just got here." She jumped up and came around from behind the counter. "Let me see if Dr. Blake knows anything about it. What's the name again?"

"Sherry Kimball."

Emily shifted her weight from one foot to the other and looked at the pictures on the wall, until she spotted movement in the doorway from the corner of her eye. When she looked up, Noah smiled at her.

"Hi, Emily. Did you need something?"

"Did Aunt Sherry get in touch with you about medicine for the goat?"

Noah frowned for a second then slowly shook his head. "I've been in surgery all morning, so if she called then, I wasn't available. Jillian has morning classes, so she doesn't get here until the afternoon. I assume you need something for Francine. Did Sherry tell you what kind of medicine she needed?"

"Something for her stomach. Aunt Sherry said she'd call," Emily replied.

Noah groaned. "Oh no, not again. I don't know why she likes to escape. She has it made there."

"I think she likes to do anything she's not supposed to."

Noah smiled and motioned for her to follow. "I'll fix you right up. Maybe I can come out there next weekend and help Mel build a special pen that'll hold her."

Suddenly, a squealing grunt sounded from one of the examining rooms. Emily cast a questioning glance toward Noah.

He smiled. "That's Peewee. He hasn't gotten much attention lately."

"What's the deal with that pig? Why is he still here? I thought—"

Noah looked like he was ready to burst into laughter, but he managed to control himself with a half smile. "He wasn't one of the flood victims. They left yesterday afternoon. I'm waiting for the new owners to come pick Peewee up. He's part of the Vietnamese potbellied pig revolution."

Emily tilted her head. "The what?"

"Potbellied pigs. Their popularity surged until people realized there was no guarantee they'd stay small."

Small was the last word she would use to describe Peewee. "Do you ever rest?" she asked.

The squeals grew more frantic, so Noah crossed the room and opened the door. Peewee came trotting in, his belly swaying with each step. Emily bent over and scratched behind Peewee's ears, eliciting delightful pig sounds.

Noah glanced down at her and laughed. "What do you mean by that? I rest."

"You're always working."

"I like what I do, so it doesn't seem like work." He pulled a bottle off the shelf and pointed to the directions taped on the side of it. "Give this to her as directed. It might take two of you—one to hold Francine still and the other to get her to swallow it."

"Thanks." Emily took the bottle without moving her gaze from Noah. "I'm really sorry about what I said. It was out of line."

"No offense taken. In fact, I think it's sweet that you noticed. I love animals, and I feel blessed that the Lord has allowed me to follow my dream of becoming a vet."

Emily offered a slight grin. "That must be nice—to know what you want and then be able to do it."

Noah tilted his head and studied her. "What do you want to do with your life, Emily Kimball?"

She glanced down then slowly lifted her gaze back to his. "I sure wish I knew. It seems there's not much of a demand for an art history major."

"You can teach."

"I'm not really qualified to teach." She shifted her focus away from him. "Besides, I'm not sure if that's what I really want."

"Why don't you try different things?" he asked.

"Like what?"

He glanced around the room. "Like maybe work with animals?"

"Work with animals?" she repeated.

He nodded. "Why not?"

"But where?"

Something electric sizzled between them. Noah looked up at the ceiling as he folded his arms and widened his stance. "How about right here? I could use some help in the mornings."

"Doing what?"

Noah gestured toward the reception area. "Answer phones, let me know when clients arrive, escort patients to the examining rooms, soothe upset pet owners, help bathe animals, take payments—"

"Are you serious?"

"Yep."

She squinted to get a different perspective. When he didn't budge, she finally nodded. "I think I just might consider it."

His eyebrows shot up in a look of pleasant surprise. He opened his mouth then shut it.

Maybe he didn't mean what he said. Sometimes people said things or made offers just to be polite. She was about to let him off the hook when a broad grin took over his face, crinkling the area around his dark brown eyes, melting her from the inside out.

"That would be awesome," he said, now with conviction. "When can you start?"

Emily let out a nervous chuckle. "I think I need to talk to Aunt Sherry and Uncle Mel first. I'm only supposed to be here for a few weeks."

"Even a few weeks would help." He gestured toward the reception desk. "I'm sure Jillian would appreciate not having a huge to-do stack waiting for her when she comes in every day." His expression grew more serious. "She has a lot going on in her life, and I don't want to add to her stress."

After Emily had paid for Francine's medicine and left, Jillian snapped her fingers in front of his face. "Earth to Dr. Blake."

He jumped. "Oh, sorry. Did you say something?"

She smiled as she shook her head and sat back down at her desk. "You've got it bad."

"Huh?"

"You really like that girl, don't you?"

Noah blinked and turned to face her. "Yes, she seems very nice. Why?"

"She's more than nice. I saw how the two of you looked at each other." Jillian held up a stack of paperwork she hadn't yet filed. "You were right about needing some help around here. I sure hope she decides to take you up on your job offer."

"Yeah, me, too."

As Noah headed back to tend to one of the animals, he heard her mumble. It sounded strangely like, "Yeah, I bet you do."

He had a simple neutering surgery to do before his next appointment, so he prepped the table. As he scrubbed it down, Noah thought about how he'd blurted his offer to Emily before thinking about it. Yes, he needed more help, but he hadn't planned to add another person to the office for at least another month or so. It wasn't that he couldn't afford the help. He just didn't have the time to train anyone.

But now that he'd made the offer, he knew it was the right move. Since meeting Emily, he'd thought about her more than he should, something that hadn't happened since he and Tiffany had broken their engagement shortly after she moved to West Virginia. She'd rented an apartment in Huntington, and they'd spent quite a bit of time together at first. Then his new practice had taken so much of his energy, and she whined about feeling neglected. Suddenly she stopped complaining, so he thought everything was fine. Then he was blindsided when she announced that she'd met someone new and they were moving to Charleston. What surprised him most was that he wasn't all that disappointed. After he thought about how different life was between the posh Atlanta suburb of Dunwoody and the rural area he served in West Virginia, he knew she'd be miserable. But he loved every minute of his new life.

At first, he felt free from worrying about how Tiffany would adapt to the new life. He saw the split-up as a sign that he and Tiffany weren't meant to be together. However, there were times when he got lonely, and he wondered if he'd made a mistake.

Until now, he hadn't given much thought to a love life, but there was something about Emily that sent his senses reeling—something he couldn't quite put his finger on. Sure she was pretty, but there were plenty of attractive women in town. She was smart and funny, too. But that wasn't all.

Noah had felt an unexpected zing in his heart when she didn't hesitate to pitch in with the chickens. Her genuine ease with the animals reminded him of how he'd always been. And it made her beyond attractive. Sometimes when their gazes met, he felt as though she was looking into the windows of his own soul. They had some kind of unspoken connection he'd never experienced with anyone.

The bell on the front door jolted him from his thoughts, so he turned around and glanced at the clock. *Whew.* It wasn't too late to start on the neutering before his appointment. He wanted to leave at a decent time so he could check on some of the animals he'd placed in the care of nearby farmers. His schedule had been turned upside down since the flood.

He was about to pull Festus, the Yorkie who'd been patiently waiting for his surgery, from the cage, when he heard a woman's voice and a little girl's wail. Noah patted Festus on the head, said, "Be a good boy. I'll be right back," and placed him back in the cage.

Jillian had her arms around the little girl, who held tight to a half-grown chicken. "I promise we'll take good care of her," the receptionist told her.

"No!" The little girl yanked the chicken away and started sobbing. "You can't have Pinky."

Chapter 3

Noah assumed the woman next to the child was her mother, so he gestured for her to follow him. Once they were out of hearing distance, he stopped. "Why is Pinky here?"

The woman looked distraught. "We had no idea the baby chick would get so big. Gina wanted a pink Easter chicken, so we got her one." She swiped at the tear on her cheek. "The chicken isn't pink anymore, and she's obviously not a baby, and—I don't know what to do. We live in town, and we're not allowed to have farm animals in our apartment. The manager told us to get rid of the chicken, or else."

Noah groaned. The very thought of animals being sold as Easter presents had always been a sore spot with him.

"So you brought the chicken here for me to find it a home?"

She nodded. "If you can." After a sniffle, she added, "I heard you like chickens."

His jaw tightened, so he took a deep breath and slowly let it out. "I think I can find someone who'll take the chicken, but you need to understand that it's not okay to buy dyed baby chickens—no matter how much your child wants one."

"Yes, I know." She offered a slight smile of apology. "Gina was a very sick little girl, so we're guilty of spoiling her."

Although Noah didn't have children, he had been guilty of spoiling a few of his animals, so he nodded. "I know how that can happen. Let's go see if we can convince Gina to let go of her little friend."

When they got back to the reception area, Noah was pleasantly surprised to see that Emily had returned. She sat on one side of Gina while Jillian sat on the other. They all had their hands on Pinky, who had started clucking in annoyance. Emily looked up at him as she stifled a smile.

"I think she's lonely," Emily offered as she turned back to the little girl.

Gina shrugged. "She's not lonely, 'cuz she has me."

Emily glanced over Gina at Jillian, who smiled and nodded. "Do you have any friends besides Pinky?"

The little girl frowned for a moment then nodded. "Lacy is my friend, and sometimes I play with Brooke in the next building."

Emily stroked the chicken then placed her hand on Gina's shoulder. "I think Pinky would like other chickens to play with."

Gina didn't waste any time shaking her head. "She can't. The manager of our apartment won't let us have chickens."

"I have an idea," Emily said. "Why don't you bring Pinky to my aunt and uncle's farm, and she can play with the chickens there?" She glanced up for reassurance from Noah.

He nodded and took the cue to join them. "That's a great idea. They have a whole barn full of chickens. Pinky will have all kinds of playmates there."

Everyone in the room held their breath while Gina pondered this idea. Finally she said, "Okay, we can see if Pinky likes any of those chickens. But I don't want to give her away."

Noah wasn't sure exactly what to do next, so he turned to Emily, hopeful that she'd have a suggestion. Once again the room grew quiet.

Finally Emily's shoulders relaxed. "I understand. Let's just give Pinky a chance to play with the chickens and see how things go, okay?"

Gina's face lit up. "Can I watch?"

"Yes, of course you can watch." Emily turned to Gina's mother. "Would you like to follow me to the farm?"

"Sure. We'll be glad to." The woman extended her hand to her daughter. "Come on, Gina." She turned back to Emily. "We'll wait in the car. Take your time."

After they left, Noah looked relieved. "You just saved me. I had no idea how to handle the little girl."

"The only reason I knew what to do was because I had to give up a chicken when I was younger." His heart melted at the look of sympathy on her face. "Oh, I almost forgot. I think I left my cell phone on the counter when I paid for Francine's medicine."

Jillian walked over to the reception counter, got the phone, and brought it back to Emily. "Here ya go. I was so busy I didn't even see it."

"Thanks," Emily said as she pocketed the phone. "I guess I better head on out so Pinky can meet her new friends in the barn."

"Want me to call your uncle and let him know you're bringing a guest?" Noah offered.

Emily grinned. "That would be nice. Thanks! I'll give you my cell number, just in case."

As soon as Emily left, Noah picked up the phone and punched in Mel's number. It rang five times before the voice mail came on. He left a message and hung up.

"I'll be in surgery for a little while," he said. "If Mel calls back, tell him about the chicken."

Jillian gave him the thumbs-up sign. "Sure thing."

Festus was so happy to see Noah when he returned to the holding area that he licked all over Noah's hand and looked up at him, his tongue still hanging out of his mouth. Noah chuckled. "Sorry, little buddy. The things we do for the ladies."

Festus pulled his tongue into his mouth and cocked his head to one side. After a couple of seconds, he resumed his licking until the anesthesia kicked in.

After the surgery was over, Noah gently put Festus in the recovery room then went back out to the reception area. "Have you heard from Mel yet?"

Jillian shook her head. "Not yet."

Noah tried again but to no avail. "Mel needs to carry a cell phone."

"I'm sure it'll be fine. After all, it's only one chicken we're talking about."

"Yeah, what's one more when you have a barn full of them?" Noah picked up the phone again. "I need to let Emily know I couldn't get hold of Mel."

The instant Emily made the last turn toward the farm, she saw all the commotion. Aunt Sherry was running around the area by the barn, a pot in one hand and a spoon in the other, banging them together. Uncle Mel stood off to the side, one hand on his hip, the other rubbing the back of his neck.

And chickens were everywhere! Something had obviously happened, and the chickens were loose. She slowed down to try to figure out what to do about the little girl and her mother who'd followed her home.

Suddenly her phone chirped, so she flipped it open and said, "Hello?"

"I couldn't get in touch with Mel," Noah said. "I'm sure he won't mind taking on another chicken."

"He might not mind, but I'm not so sure about little Gina." Then she told Noah what she saw.

"Is there any way you can hold them off? I don't want to scare the child."

Emily glanced in her rearview mirror and saw Gina's mother pointing toward the barn. "No, I don't think so."

She heard Noah exhale. "Call me back if you need me."

"I think I can handle this, Noah. I understand that you feel responsible for all the animals in the county, but you need to let go. There are some things out of your control." The instant those words left her mouth, Emily couldn't believe she'd said them.

"Um—okay," he said. "I'll check with Mel later."

Emily felt bad about the brashness of her words, but she knew what it was like to worry about something out of her control. "Let me give you a call in a little while—after I find out what's going on and everything is settled."

He hesitated for a couple of seconds before he finally said, "Okay."

She pulled into the driveway with the car behind her still in her line of vision. At least Gina's mother hadn't freaked out and given up.

Aunt Sherry ran right over to her the instant she opened her car door. "Francine let the chickens out."

Emily looked at the barn then back at Aunt Sherry. "How did she do that?"

Her aunt shook her head. "To make a long story short, back when we still had chickens Francine used to follow Mel when he went to the barn to check on them. Since she seemed harmless and she didn't bother them, we didn't think anything about it when she wandered into the barn this afternoon."

"But how did she let the chickens out?"

By this time, Gina and her mother had joined them. Pinky rested in Gina's arms like a fashion accessory. Emily's mind instantly went into artist mode and imagined what a great portrait that would make.

Aunt Sherry glanced over at Gina then her mother before settling her gaze on Emily. "Would you like to introduce me to your friends before I go back and help Mel get the chickens back in the barn?"

Emily briefly told her aunt about Pinky. Gina held her chicken out so Aunt Sherry could see her better.

"She looks like a very nice chicken, Gina," Aunt Sherry said. "If you'd like to go on into the house, there's some fresh cobbler on the kitchen counter. It should be cool by now." Aunt Sherry nodded toward Emily. "Why don't you get them settled at the kitchen table, and I'll be in there in a few minutes. This won't take long."

Emily gestured for Gina and her mother to follow her. They'd gone about twenty feet when Francine the goat joined them.

"Mommy!" Gina shrieked, still holding on to Pinky.

"Francine is a nice goat," Emily said as she reached for one of Gina's hands and managed to gently wrest it free from Pinky. She guided the little girl's fingertips to Francine's back and slowly stroked the goat. "See? She's just like any other animal."

"Will she hurt Pinky?" Gina asked.

Since Emily wasn't sure about anything anymore, she didn't want to take a chance. "I've never seen her hurt chickens before, but why don't you hold on to Pinky until my aunt gets all the other chickens rounded up and back in the barn?"

They went inside, where Emily scooped some cobbler for Gina and her mother. When she turned around, she saw Noah standing at the kitchen door. Her heart made a flip.

"I couldn't stay away after I spoke to you on the phone," he said. "Let me go help Mel and Sherry, and I'll be right back."

He disappeared without another comment. As Emily set the bowls of cobbler down in front of her guests, Gina's mother grinned at her. "He seems like such a nice man. How long have you two been together?"

"Huh?"

"You and the vet? You *are* dating aren't you?"

Emily shook her head. "No, I'm sorry if I gave you the wrong impression. He takes care of all the animals around here, and my aunt sent me to Noah's

Ark to pick up some medication for Francine."

Pinky let out a loud squawk then flapped her wings, nearly toppling the bowl in front of Gina. The girl's mother reached out and grabbed it in the nick of time.

And Emily was relieved that she didn't have to answer the question, but it shouldn't have bothered her at all. Somehow it seemed intrusive on her innermost thoughts.

Emily hopped up and put everyone's bowls in the sink. By the time she finished rinsing and putting them in the dishwasher, Aunt Sherry had come inside.

"We got 'em all back into the barn, thanks to Noah," she said as she stuck her hands under the faucet and washed them. "He and Mel are out there working up a solution to keep Francine out of the barn. We can't have her deciding to set the chickens free just because she likes the attention."

Gina held up Pinky. "My chicken likes attention."

Aunt Sherry grinned down at the little girl. "I think most animals do."

Gina's mother stood up. "I'm afraid we're imposing. If we can come back at another—"

"Nonsense," Aunt Sherry said. "You're definitely not imposing. We welcome guests. I just hate that y'all had to see us in such a flap."

Emily had to stifle a giggle. Gina looked at her and blinked.

Aunt Sherry spoke up again. "I understand you're looking for accommodations for Pinky." She dried her hands and crossed the room to where Gina and her mother stood. "Forgive my manners. I'm Sherry Kimball. I know your daughter is Gina, but I didn't catch your name."

The woman smiled. "Maria. Nice to meet you, Sherry. And yes, we'd like to find a nice home for Pinky. Our apartment complex isn't set up for farm animals."

Emily held her breath as all of them looked down at the little girl whose grip on Pinky had only tightened since they'd been there. Aunt Sherry reached out and stroked the bird on the head. "Pinky seems like such a nice chicken. Would you like to take her out to the barn and let her meet some other chickens?"

Gina glanced up at her mother, who nodded, then turned to face Aunt Sherry. "Can I meet them, too?"

"Of course you can. We have some mighty friendly chickens."

"Do they play together?" Gina asked.

"Sometimes. But mostly they sit around and cackle while they lay eggs."

Gina's eyes widened. "They lay eggs? Real eggs?"

Aunt Sherry reached down, placed her arm around Gina, and gently guided her to the door. "Yes, real eggs. In fact, there might even be some now. Wanna go out there and see if they left us any?"

Gina grinned. "Can I get them?"

Emily stood watching in amazement as Aunt Sherry led the little girl, still holding Pinky—only not so close as before—outside to the barn. She turned to Maria. "My aunt is wonderful with children. I used to love coming here when I was Gina's age."

"I'm so happy there's a place for Pinky," Maria said. "The apartment manager threatened to send her to a chicken-packing plant. That scared Gina half to death."

Emily shuddered. She couldn't imagine what must have gone through Gina's mind when he said that. "He sounds like a cruel man."

"You don't know the half of it."

They got outside in time to see Aunt Sherry and Gina disappearing into the barn. "Would you like to see the chickens, too?"

Maria looked skeptically at the wooden structure. "Do they bite? I mean, I'm used to Pinky and all, but she's the only chicken I've ever been around."

"No. Some of them make a little noise, but I've never seen one bite anyone."

"I guess," Maria said softly. "It would be nice to see where Pinky will be living."

A single bulb hanging in the middle of the massive structure lit the center of the barn and cast a gentle glow around the walls, leaving darkened corners. Chicken crates and coops covered one wall of the barn, while the other side was lined with hay.

"What do you think?" Emily asked. "Is this what you expected?"

Maria's nose crinkled. "It smells weird. Kind of earthy."

"That's the hay." Emily took a deep breath. "I've always loved that smell." She laughed. "It would stink if Uncle Mel didn't keep it so clean."

"Mommy, look! Pinky has her own bed and she likes it!"

Maria flashed a smile at Emily before scurrying over to her daughter, who stood beside a coop. Pinky had settled down and seemed perfectly content.

"That's so sweet!" Maria said.

Aunt Sherry reached for Gina's hand. "Now let's go gather some eggs. You want to take some home with you?"

"Can we, Mommy?"

"If Mrs. Kimball doesn't mind, it's fine with me."

Aunt Sherry found a basket and helped Gina check the coops for eggs while Emily chatted with Maria.

"Your aunt is a very sweet woman," Maria whispered. "I'm glad Pinky has a nice place to stay."

Emily nodded. "She'll be just fine."

A few minutes later, Gina headed toward the door of the barn carrying a basket filled with eggs. She stopped off at Pinky's coop, leaned over, and whispered something then caught up with the adults. "I told her to behave and not run away, even if the goat tells her to."

After Gina and her mother left, Emily hugged Aunt Sherry. "Thanks so much. Oh by the way, do you mind if I hang out here for a few extra weeks? Noah needs some help at the clinic, and I sort of—well. . ."

Sherry smiled and nodded. "He already told me he wants you to work mornings. And I'd love to have you here as long as you want to stay."

"Thank you so much!"

"We have everything under control." The booming voice made both women jump.

Emily turned around and saw the look of amusement in Noah's eyes and the slight grin on his lips, and she felt the heat rush to her face. Why did he have to be so attractive? "You startled me!"

He shoved his hands into his pockets but kept smiling. "At least you're still breathing."

The combination of his rugged good looks, the way he cared about his work, and the mischievous look on his face made her wonder if he could hear her raspy breath. She swallowed hard and forced herself to deeply inhale then slowly let it out.

"Yes, I'm still breathing." She mimicked his stance and put her hands in the pockets of her own jeans then stared directly into his eyes. "By the way, when did you want me to start working at the clinic?"

Chapter 4

Noah stifled the temptation to tell her *now*. Immediately. He didn't want to spend another minute away from her.

"How about tomorrow?" he blurted.

Sherry didn't give Emily a chance to speak. "Isn't that a little soon?"

"Yeah, don't rush the girl," Mel piped up as he joined them in the kitchen. "She probably has a dozen things to do to get ready for this job."

"Like what?" Sherry asked.

Mel tilted his head back and belted out a hearty laugh. "Exactly. Why can't she start tomorrow?"

Noah couldn't hide his amusement. He rubbed his chin for a moment then looked at Emily. "When would you like to start?"

All eyes were on her as she stood there trying to figure out what to do. Finally she held out her hands and shrugged. "There's really no reason I can't start tomorrow, unless Aunt Sherry has something she wants me to do around here."

"We're good," Sherry said. "Do you need her, Mel?"

"Nah, not really." Mel turned and faced Noah. "If she wants to start tomorrow, I think it's a fine idea. It'll keep her from being bored."

"I'm not bored," she said. "There's always something to do around here."

Noah couldn't help comparing Emily to Tiffany. Emily was the type of woman who could find something to do no matter where she was, while Tiffany had to have her hair stylist, manicurist, and favorite designer shops to keep her entertained.

"Since you're starting right away," Sherry said, "why don't the two of you go somewhere and discuss everything?"

Emily cast a questioning glance toward her aunt. Then she turned to Noah. "Do we need to discuss anything?"

Sherry jumped in again. "Sure you do. Things like hours, salary, and dress code."

Noah smiled. "This is strictly part-time—at least for now. Jillian comes in around one most afternoons, and she really needs the work, so any morning hours would be appreciated." He made an apologetic face. "I can't afford more hours than that."

"I understand. Is it okay if I wear jeans?" Emily asked. "I mean, since I'll be working around animals and all."

"Sure." Noah gestured toward his own clothes. "That's what I wear most of the time." He paused for a moment before adding, "I haven't thought about salary yet. Why don't we discuss that tomorrow when you come in?"

"Okay, that's fine," Emily said. "It's not like I expect to get rich or anything."

Quite unlike Tiffany, he thought. He extended his hand. "Shake on it?"

As she reached out and placed her hand in his, he felt the soft warmth in her slender fingers. She had quite a firm handshake, but there was no question about her femininity, which caused a stir in his heart.

Mel rubbed his hands together and turned to his wife. "Looks like this will work out for everyone. We get to have our niece here with us, Noah gets help at the clinic, and Emily will have something to do while she's here and some money in her pocket."

Noah took a step back. "Hey folks, I need to get back to the clinic. Anything else I can do while I'm here?"

"Let me walk you to your truck," Mel said. "I have something I'd like to discuss before you leave."

The instant the men left the house, Aunt Sherry turned to Emily. "Are you sure you want to do this? We didn't expect you to work while you were here."

Emily nodded. "I really don't mind."

"I didn't think you did. I just wanted to make sure." The twinkle in her eye was a giveaway she was up to something.

"Is there something you're not telling me, Aunt Sherry?"

"Whatever do you mean?"

"Are you plotting something?"

Aunt Sherry flipped her hand at the wrist and clicked her tongue. "Must you always be so suspicious of me?"

Emily giggled. "You have a way of making things happen."

"Yes I do, don't I?" Her smug expression left no doubt in Emily's mind something was going on, and she wouldn't find out until her aunt was good and ready to let her know.

"I guess you probably wouldn't tell me if you had something up your sleeve."

"That's right," Aunt Sherry replied, grinning. "But there is one thing I want you to think about, since you're planning to take a job. You love art so much that you might want to consider applying at one of the art galleries in Huntington."

"I'm just doing this to help Noah."

"Good girl."

"Besides," Emily added. "I really do love animals, and I think it'll be fun working with them."

"Let's start supper. We've had a big day, and I don't want you doing everything by yourself."

As they worked in the kitchen, they discussed how little their schedule would change. "With you working mornings, you can run errands on your way home—that is, if you don't mind."

"Of course I don't mind. And I can still help out with chores in the afternoon."

Aunt Sherry stopped chopping and looked up at Emily. "You've always enjoyed farm chores."

Emily nodded. "It doesn't seem like work to take care of animals and tend to the garden. It's more fun than anything."

"That's the way your uncle and I feel. Unfortunately your father didn't like farming. He hated getting his hands dirty, and so did your mama."

The mention of her mother made Emily pause. "Mama didn't like much of anything."

"I'm sorry I brought her up, sweetie. If you'd rather not talk about her—"

"No, that's okay. It's been long enough—it doesn't hurt as much."

"Maybe one of these days she'll come around," Aunt Sherry said. "I hope you find it in your heart to forgive her when she does."

"I've already forgiven her." Emily cleared her throat and thought for a moment, trying to remember exactly when she'd taken that major step. Her daddy had told her that when he and her mama first got married, they'd dreamed of having a little girl just like her mama. When Emily came along, they were elated. Her mama dressed her up in the frilliest dresses and took her along on shopping trips. But Emily hadn't truly found joy until she was old enough to spend summers on the farm with Aunt Sherry and Uncle Mel. "It really hurt when she first left, but Daddy was always there for me, no matter what. I think Mama's the one who's suffering the most," she said softly. "At least that's what Daddy once said."

"He's right, you know. I just hope what your mother did won't keep you from falling in love one of these days."

Emily let out a nervous chuckle. "It's not like the men are lining up to be with me."

"All it takes is one," Aunt Sherry reminded her. "One good man who loves the Lord."

Emily's thoughts instantly went to Noah. She already knew he went to church, but based on experience, she also knew that going to church didn't make a man a Christian.

She opened her mouth to ask Aunt Sherry, but she quickly clamped it shut. She didn't want to make her aunt think she had a desire for anything but employment from Noah.

"In spite of his privileged upbringing, Noah's one of the humblest Christian men I've ever met," Aunt Sherry said.

Now when she heard that, Emily's curiosity got the best of her. "What do you mean *privileged*?"

"He lived in one of the swankiest neighborhoods in a suburb of Atlanta. His father still has a veterinary practice there, and he treats cats and dogs worth more than some people's monthly salary around here."

Emily frowned. "How do you know all this?"

Aunt Sherry smiled and placed her hand on Emily's shoulder. "A group of us spent quite a bit of time getting to know Noah. We wanted the best vet to take care of our animals—from our livestock to our pets. We liked the fact that Noah not only helped his dad for a while but that he worked on different farms around Atlanta."

"How did y'all convince him to come?"

"We didn't. After the interview process, he brought his dad and showed him around to get a different perspective. His father said he wished it was him instead of Noah."

"But I thought—"

Aunt Sherry nodded. "Noah's father told Mel that all the money in the world can't make a man happy. His pampered patients are treated better than humans in some parts. The man has integrity, and he won't abandon his practice, but he encouraged his son to follow what he knew was right." She clicked her tongue. "He wanted Noah to work with him, but he also wanted his son to be happy."

Emily admired Noah even more. "I'm glad it all worked out so well."

"There's only one thing that saddened us at the time though," Aunt Sherry said, the corners of her mouth turning down. "He had a very pretty young woman with him, and we all thought they'd be getting married and settling here."

Emily's heart landed with a thud. "A pretty woman?"

"Yes, but she didn't like it here. Seems we don't have enough of the finer things in life that she's used to."

"So what happened to her?"

"She sort of faded away." Aunt Sherry resumed her task and continued talking. "If you ask me, it was all for the better. Noah didn't seem too fazed by her decision. Mel thinks he might have even been relieved. Some women require so much upkeep it's hard to do anything worthwhile."

Emily tried hard to imagine Noah with a high-maintenance woman, but she couldn't wrap her mind around it. That didn't seem like his type. He was handsome and obviously committed to what he did, but she pictured him as more of a rugged sort.

Aunt Sherry coughed and got her attention. "I think he's lonely."

"Why do you think that?"

"I don't know. Maybe because all he ever does is work and go to church.

I don't think the man has gone out just for fun since he's lived here."

Emily knew what that was like. But Aunt Sherry didn't need to know that.

"What time is church on Sunday?"

Aunt Sherry grinned. "Changing the subject, huh? That's fine. I understand. Church is at ten."

Later that night, Emily got out her outfit for the next day. She decided on dark-washed jeans because they looked nicer than her everyday jeans. Then she hung her coral-colored, collared T-shirt on the closet door. A lightweight khaki jacket and her newer sneakers would complete the ensemble.

As she stepped back for a good look at her clothes, she couldn't help but wonder if Noah would even notice what she wore. And if he did, would he compare her to his former girlfriend? She shook herself and forced different thoughts. It didn't do a bit of good to harbor notions of her boss that were totally inappropriate.

The next morning she awoke to the sounds of her aunt and uncle milling around the house. They'd always been early risers—most of the time before dawn. She flung her legs over the side of the bed and got up, rubbing the sleep from her eyes.

She showered, got dressed, and applied a light touch of makeup before sauntering into the kitchen, where the aroma of fresh coffee welcomed her. Uncle Mel had just sat down at the table with his coffee mug and a newspaper in front of him.

"Good morning, sunshine," Aunt Sherry said. "Eggs and bacon or cereal and fruit?"

"I'll just pour myself a bowl of cereal, thanks."

Uncle Mel looked up from his paper. "Nervous?"

She wanted to say "no, not at all," but that would be lying. Instead she shrugged and scrunched her face. "Just a little."

"That's normal." He patted the table. "Grab some coffee and have a seat."

A half hour later Emily was on her way to town for her first day on the job at the vet clinic. Throughout school, she'd had no idea what she wanted to do with her life, but she never would have imagined being a receptionist for a veterinarian.

The light was on in the clinic when she arrived, but it was still half an hour before the posted opening time. Emily shoved on the door, but since it was locked, she cupped her hands and looked to see if anyone was there.

The moving shadows beyond the reception area let her know someone was there, so she knocked and waited. Noah appeared and let her in.

"I'll get you a key later." Noah gestured toward the reception desk. "After you put your things down, we can take a tour."

Emily was impressed with Noah's organization and his obvious compassion for animals. All the smaller animals had toys and blankets from home in their cages to comfort them with a sense of familiarity.

"I try not to keep them in cages any longer than necessary," he said.

Emily looked behind the door. "Where's the rest of the greeting committee?"

Noah tilted his head and frowned. "Greeting committee?"

"Peewee."

"Oh, him." He glanced at the clock behind her then laughed. "He's been picked up."

Noah continued with his tour, working his way from the back of the clinic to the front. "C'mon, let me show you what to do when someone comes in. We have all our files on the computer, and it's a simple program with easy-to-navigate screens."

It took all of ten minutes for her to understand how to pull up a patient's file and do what she needed. Noah explained how he had a tight schedule of caring for smaller animals in the clinic and visiting the nearby farms. No wonder he didn't have much of a social life. There wasn't a spare moment in his day.

"Jillian should be a few minutes early today. You can stick around until one, or you can leave."

"Why don't I run out and have a key made when she gets here?" Emily offered. "That way you won't have to take the time."

"That'll be great, if you don't mind."

As their gazes locked, Emily felt as though the bottom had fallen out of her stomach. The chemistry between them was so strong that she wondered if he felt it, too.

He backed up. "I have to prep one of the rooms for my first patient. If you need me, just let me know."

She went around behind the counter to put some distance between them and sat down in the chair. "I'm sure I'll be fine."

Over the next four hours that morning, Emily met a half dozen dogs, a pair of vocal cats who obviously wanted to be anywhere but where they were, a ferret, a baby squirrel monkey named Punky, and a miniature pony named Razzle Dazzle. She didn't have a chance to look at the clock all morning.

Jillian walked in shortly after noon and dropped her handbag beside Emily's. "How was your first day on the job?"

"Busy." Emily stood up so Jillian could take over. "Where's the best place to have a key made? I told Noah I'd do that before I left for the day."

Jillian handed Emily her key to the clinic and told her where to go. Emily stepped outside and offered a quick prayer of thanks. The morning had gone by much too quickly, and she'd enjoyed every moment of it.

After she had a copy of the key, she returned Jillian's. Noah thanked her and asked if she planned to return the next day.

"Of course," she replied. "Why wouldn't I?"

Noah laughed. "This place can be a little crazy sometimes. I'm glad Punky didn't scare you away."

Jillian's eyes lit up. "Punky was here? He is so adorable!"

Emily agreed. "His expressions are priceless. You should have seen his face when he saw Noah."

"I can imagine," Jillian said. "Last time he was here, he didn't want to leave. He wrapped his arms around Noah, and we had to pry his little fingers loose."

"I heard he pitched a temper tantrum in the parking lot," Noah added, shaking his head. "Monkeys can be a handful."

Jillian turned to Emily. "In case you haven't already figured it out, Noah prefers farm animals."

As cute as Punky was, Emily agreed with Noah. She wasn't sure how to act with Punky.

The phone rang and Jillian answered it. She listened, mumbled a few words, and hung up. Noah and Emily exchanged a glance, then Noah turned to Jillian.

"Who was that?"

Jillian shrugged. "Wrong number."

Emily thought that was odd because, although Jillian had only been on the phone a few moments, it was longer than she should have spent with a wrong number.

※

The next couple of days at the clinic went by just as quickly as the first. Each night during dinner she entertained Aunt Sherry and Uncle Mel with tales of the animals' antics.

"You like working there, don't you?" Uncle Mel asked.

She nodded. "I love it, but I also know it's temporary."

Her aunt and uncle exchanged a quick glance before Aunt Sherry turned back to her. "You know everything in this life is temporary, but the Lord wants us to enjoy our work. We want you to know that you're welcome to stay with us as long as you feel comfortable here."

A lump formed in Emily's throat. "I appreciate that."

Noah had told her she didn't need to go in to work on Saturday, but she didn't want to miss anything; she went for a couple of hours, and he told her he was glad she had. When Sunday morning arrived, Emily slept an extra hour, until it was time to get up and get ready for church.

As they pulled into the parking lot, she spotted Noah standing on the church steps. Her heart skipped a beat.

"I told him to sit with us," Uncle Mel said. "I hope you don't mind."

Emily didn't have a chance to respond, since her aunt and uncle were out of the car and halfway across the parking lot by the time she got out of the car. Noah shook Uncle Mel's hand and hugged Aunt Sherry before meeting Emily's gaze with a wide grin.

Throughout the service, Emily couldn't forget Noah's presence beside her. He held the hymnal so she could see the words, which gave them a physical closeness that made her tingle. During the sermon, Noah casually draped an arm over the back of the pew, making her feel protected and warm.

Once church ended, Noah walked them to their car. "You've been a huge help at the clinic. I'm glad you agreed to work with me."

"I don't mind."

Uncle Mel laughed out loud. "That's an understatement. I've never seen my niece this happy since she was a little girl."

Emily felt the heat rise to her cheeks. She glanced over at Noah, and he winked.

"Why don't you come on over to the house in an hour or so?" Aunt Sherry asked. "I have a big dinner planned."

Noah appeared conflicted as he glanced around at the three of them. Emily wasn't sure what was going on in his mind as his chest rose and fell with each breath.

The sound of a car approaching captured their attention. A sheriff's department cruiser came to a stop not far from where they stood.

When the officer got out and headed straight toward them, Emily saw Noah's forehead scrunch. "Who's that?" Emily asked.

"My buddy Dwayne, but I don't think this is a personal visit." Noah turned toward the police officer. "Everything okay, Dwayne?"

"Nah, not really. Your alarm triggered a call that someone was breaking into your clinic. By the time I got there, they were gone, but the door was wide open. Alarm from the controlled substance cabinet must've scared 'em off."

Chapter 5

I better get on over there then." Noah turned to Emily. "Looks like I have an emergency to attend to."

Emily's heart raced as she glanced back and forth between Noah and Dwayne the police officer. Noah's clinic had been broken into, yet both men moved at their standard pace.

"Want me to go with you?" she asked.

When Noah shook his head, she saw the lines that had instantly formed on his face. She felt a combination of relief that he was worried and concerned about the break-in.

Uncle Mel grabbed her hand and tugged her back. "We better let them handle it. Let's get on home." He turned to Noah. "Stop by the house after you finish dealing with this."

On the way to the farm, Uncle Mel and Aunt Sherry discussed all the possibilities of why someone would want to break into Noah's Ark. "Could be all the fancy equipment he has," Aunt Sherry speculated.

Uncle Mel snorted. "I suspect it's worse than that. I bet it's the drugs."

"But those are for the animals," Emily said. "Why would someone steal animal drugs?"

Her uncle glanced at her in the rearview mirror. "Animal narcotics are powerful. Put those in the hands of a serious drug user or dealer, and you've got a dangerous situation."

The thought of a person breaking into a vet's office for drugs had never crossed Emily's mind before. "I sure hope they catch whoever did it."

Aunt Sherry turned and faced Emily. "This isn't the first time we've seen this."

Emily didn't miss Uncle Mel's eye signal. "What happened before?"

"We might as well tell her, Mel. It's not like it affects her or anything."

Her uncle thought it over for a couple of seconds before he finally bobbed his head. "Okay Sherry, go ahead."

Aunt Sherry took a deep breath before she began. "The last vet we had was excellent—but not quite as good as Noah, of course. He was wonderful with the animals, and he worked tirelessly. Then something snapped, and he started showing up late. Once when he came out here to help deliver one of the goats, I thought he was drunk."

"That's terrible."

Her aunt nodded. "Yes, it was rather frightening because Daisy needed help that we couldn't give her. The only reason we called him was because the kid was breech."

"Daisy seems okay now."

"She's fine, and the kid is fine. But that's only because Pastor Chuck just happened to stop by for a visit. He helped Mel deliver it, while Marvin—that's the vet—slept in the corner of the barn."

"So what happened then?"

Uncle Mel and Aunt Sherry exchanged a glance. "We found out later he wasn't drunk. Mel called the police and told them Marvin had driven drunk to our house, so they sent someone out to pick him up. When they did the blood test, they found a high level of narcotics in his blood."

Emily's face tightened as her eyebrows shot up. "He was taking the animals' drugs? That's insane."

"That's one of the reasons the community got involved in the search for a new vet. We all agreed that we needed to do a background check on the prospects."

Uncle Mel snorted. "That didn't sit too well with some of them. We lost a couple who said they didn't appreciate their privacy being invaded. In fact, one of them threatened to sue. But we stuck to our guns and didn't let them bully us."

Aunt Sherry touched Uncle Mel's arm before she took over. "When we heard about Noah through the pastor, we actually went to visit him. I guess I told you most of this already. Thankfully everyone agreed that this was a good fit for Noah."

"Everyone," her uncle added, "but that prissy girlfriend of his." He made a face. "After she left, Noah seemed miserable, but I think he sees that he's better off without her. All she cared about was the money he could make so she could gallivant around town in her fancy clothes and uppity ways."

"Now Mel, you know it's not right to judge people."

In spite of the seriousness of the conversation, Emily couldn't help but smile. Aunt Sherry was the quintessential Christian woman. She stood behind her faith in actions and thoughts.

Uncle Mel cringed and ducked. "I'm just sayin'. . ."

They rode most of the rest of the way home in silence, until they reached the road right before the last turn. Aunt Sherry looked at Uncle Mel. "I hope Noah plans to stop by later for dinner."

"Oh I'm sure he will. When was the last time that boy turned us down for Sunday dinner?"

Aunt Sherry turned around and winked at Emily. "He has good taste in food."

Ten minutes later, the three of them had changed out of their church clothes and headed outside to tend to the animals. After all the chickens, goats, and cows were fed, Aunt Sherry swiped her sleeve across her forehead. "I need to go in and take a shower before I start cooking."

"Need any help?" Emily asked.

Aunt Sherry glanced at Uncle Mel then shook her head. "Why don't you help Mel finish up out here? I'll put you to work after you're done and cleaned up."

As soon as she went inside, Uncle Mel stopped working and got her attention. "Any chance you'll stick around here?"

"You mean permanently?"

Uncle Mel paused, narrowed his eyes, then shook his head. "Well nothing's permanent, but for a while."

"I might," Emily replied without hesitation. "But I don't want to impose on you and Aunt Sherry."

"Don't go gettin' the notion you're imposing. We already told you to stay with us as long as you want. This house is plenty big."

"You miss having the family all here, don't you?"

He gave her a sad look that melted her heart. "Yeah, that's the thing about kids growing up. They start new lives, and it's not always close to home. We never expected Saul to move halfway across the country. Meredith and Jennifer, yes, but not the baby."

"At least they're happy, and you know they love you."

Uncle Mel pondered that for a moment. "I think your mama loved you. She just didn't know how to cope with the stress of having a teenager."

"I might have been a little trouble, but I really wasn't all that bad."

"I know you weren't, Emily. In fact, you were the best-behaved kid we knew—including your three cousins." He grinned. "Sherry and I always suspected you went overboard in trying to please all the adults in your life because you were afraid of running them off."

He was so right! Emily had always blamed herself for her mama leaving, and sometimes she had lay awake at night, watching the door, praying that her daddy wouldn't take off in the dark.

"Here, take this rake and finish strewing the straw, and then go on in and help Sherry. She's goin' all out on today's dinner, and I'm sure she could use an extra pair of hands to finish up."

Emily did as she was told. As soon as she stepped out of the shower adjoining her bedroom, she heard voices from down the hall—Aunt Sherry's, Uncle Mel's, and. . .she was pretty sure that was Noah talking, but the tone was so soft she wasn't positive.

Fortunately her aunt and uncle had always been casual, including during special meals. She pulled on a pair of her newest jeans and a knit baby-doll shirt. For an extrafeminine touch, she added a necklace with a butterfly pendant.

By the time she got to the kitchen, Uncle Mel had gone to clean up. Aunt Sherry stood at the counter rolling out dough for biscuits, and Noah was stirring the gravy. They both glanced up when she entered the room.

"Was it bad?" Emily asked. "Did they take anything?"

Noah shook his head. "No, but not for lack of trying. It's illegal to leave certain medications out. I have them under lock and key—and behind that, another security lock with an extra alarm."

"Good thinking," she replied. "How did they get in?"

"That's a good question. Either someone is very good at picking locks, or they had access to a key."

"Who else has a key?"

"That's where I'm puzzled. Right now, there are only four of us who have a key—you, Jillian, Jeffrey the maintenance man, and me. You and I were in church when this happened, and Jeffrey is out of the country."

Emily felt the blood drain from her face. "You don't think Jillian—"

"No," he said, interrupting her. "At least I hope Jillian wouldn't do something like that, but I do need to find out if she gave the key to someone else."

"Why would she do that?"

"Maybe she was busy and asked a friend to feed the kittens."

"Kittens?"

Noah pursed his lips as he laid the spoon on the plate. Then he turned around, folded his arms, and leaned against the counter. "I guess she must not have told you about the stray cat and kittens we feed. The mother cat started coming around a couple of months ago, and we felt sorry for her because she was obviously homeless and hungry. I've tried to catch her to spay her, but she runs off when I get near her. Next thing we knew, she had a litter in one of the bushes behind the clinic. We've been waiting for their mother to wean them so we can find homes for them."

"Why don't you bring them all over here?" Aunt Sherry asked.

Noah chuckled. "That might have been an option before the flood, but I don't think it's a good idea with all those chickens you're taking care of. Besides, this cat's very skittish, and although she'll come close, she keeps a distance of about ten feet."

Aunt Sherry put the last biscuit on the pan and brushed her hands together. "If you have trouble placing any of those kittens, we'll take them."

"Oh we will, will we?"

The sound of Uncle Mel's voice made Aunt Sherry turn. "I miss having a house pet."

Uncle Mel laughed. "I know you do. That's fine. We can have one kitten."

"Two?" Aunt Sherry made a puppy dog face.

"Okay, two." He rolled his eyes then turned to Noah. "I'm too easy."

After the biscuits were done, they sat down and said a blessing before

42

filling their plates. Emily expected talk to be all about the break-in at the animal clinic, but the subject never even came up again.

Emily looked around the table after they finished eating. She couldn't believe how much they had left.

"I like having leftovers," Aunt Sherry explained.

"Sherry, there's enough food for a family of five to have leftovers for a week." Uncle Mel looked at Noah. "She likes to keep us well fed."

Aunt Sherry grinned at Noah. "I'll just send some home with you. I'm sure you'll be hungry later."

He pushed back from the table and carried his plate to the sink. "I'd love to take you up on that, but I'm afraid I can't. I have to go back to the police station and talk to Dwayne before he goes off duty."

"Want Emily to come along?" Uncle Mel asked.

Noah glanced at Emily, making her heart skip a beat. "Would you like to join me?"

She thought for a few seconds and realized he'd have to drive her all the way back to the farm, so she slowly shook her head. "I better not. I have to do some laundry and get ready for the week."

Aunt Sherry cast a stern glance her way, but Emily turned her head. She didn't need matchmaking at the moment, and Noah had more important things on his mind.

The next morning, Emily went off to work with no idea what she'd find. Hopefully the perpetrator had been caught, but she was fairly certain if that were the case, she would have heard something by now.

Emily turned into the parking lot and drove past the spaces near the front door, leaving them for patients. As she got out of her car, she inhaled deeply, closed her eyes, and said a silent prayer as she slowly released her breath.

Every light in the clinic was on as she pushed the door open. About a second and a half later, Noah popped around from behind the wall. When he saw that it was her, he grinned.

"I'd like you to meet Kingston," he said as he led a black, full-grown, floppy-eared, flap-jawed Great Dane on a short red leash. "He's going to hang out with us until we find out who tried to get in."

Emily knelt beside the dog, making him taller than her. She scratched behind his ear as she glanced up at Noah. "Who does Kingston belong to?"

"Joel Zimmerman. He's been trying to find someone to take care of him while he travels to Europe. When he first asked me if I knew of anyone, I couldn't think of a soul, but I said I'd take Kingston if nobody else would." He grinned. "After what happened..." His voice trailed off.

"I thought you had the drugs under lock and key." Emily stood, folded her arms, and waited for an answer.

"That's right, but since I don't know who came in here, I don't know what they'd be willing to do to get the drugs. What if they come back?" He snapped his fingers to beckon Kingston, and the dog eagerly obeyed.

"Good point," Emily agreed as she smiled at the dog. "Kingston seems like a sweet dog, but I don't think anyone will mess with us as long as he's here."

Noah glanced at his watch. "I have two annual checkups first thing this morning, and then I have to go out for some farm visits. Kingston can stay here with you."

"Will you be back before I leave?" she asked.

He nodded. "I should be. If not I'll call you." After a short pause, he added, "I'll call you anyway. I'm concerned about leaving you here alone."

Emily pointed to Kingston. "I won't be alone."

As if on cue, the dog left Noah's side and plopped his rear beside Emily's feet. She placed her hand on his shoulder, and he leaned against her hip, looking up at her with the most soulful, adoring eyes, his jaw flapping open. He let out a long sigh that sounded like that of an old man. Both Emily and Noah laughed.

"I don't think he'll let anything happen to you," Noah said. "He's already enamored."

"Yes, I do have a way with animals." She leaned over and cupped Kingston's face in her hands. "You'll protect me, won't you, boy? You'll chase anyone who comes after me, and you'll lick 'em to death."

The door opened, signaling the beginning of Noah's busy day. After Noah left for his farm visits, Emily worked steadily, filing, answering the phone, scheduling appointments, and processing client bills that were long overdue. She could see that Noah made a good living, but he could do much better if people would pay on time. He didn't seem to worry about it, so she didn't need to concern herself with it either.

Noah called her midmorning and shortly before lunch. The second time, he said he wouldn't be back until midafternoon, but she could go ahead and tell Jillian what had happened. Disappointment flooded her as she hung up. It wasn't likely she'd see him again until the next morning, and that wouldn't be for long since he was booked with farm visits most of the week.

A few minutes before one o'clock, she started clearing away the desk, getting it ready for Jillian. But one o'clock came and went, and Emily's replacement still hadn't arrived. That was strange. Jillian was early most days, and the one time she ran late, she'd called. She tried Jillian's cell phone, but it went directly to voice mail without ringing. Emily didn't want to call and alert Noah because he was so busy.

At two thirty Noah walked in and did a double take then smiled. "Can't stay away, huh? Where's Jillian?"

Emily shrugged. "She didn't come in."

"Did you call her?" He frowned.

"I tried her cell phone, but it didn't even ring. Want me to try again?"

"No, let me see if I can find her mother's number. I'll see if she knows where Jillian is." Noah pointed to the computer. "Can you pull up my address book in Outlook?"

Emily got the information Noah needed, and he called Jillian's mother. As he chatted with the woman, Emily saw his look of concern deepen. Then he hung up and ran his fingers through his hair.

"That's odd. She said her daughter hasn't been home in several days, but she doesn't seem worried at all. In fact, she hasn't seen Jillian since Thursday night."

"She was here Friday."

"Yeah, I know," he said. "So she left here and didn't go home. Something's not right."

Chapter 6

Emily studied Noah and wondered if he'd made any connection between Jillian being missing and the break-in. After all, there were only a few keys to the front door, and it had been established that entry wasn't forced.

Noah frowned as he pondered what to do. Emily had to come up with something—a way to help.

"Tell you what," she said. "Why don't I call around and see if anyone has seen her?"

He slowly nodded. "I'll call her mother back and get the numbers of some of her friends."

"Do you have any idea where she likes to go when she's not here or in class?"

He shook his head. "No idea whatsoever. I hired her because she was in college and needed some money. The pastor brought her to me." The worry etched on his face tugged at her heart.

Emily smiled to try to soothe him. "I'm sure everything will be okay. If something bad happened, we would have heard by now."

"I hope you're right."

They devoted the next hour to getting contact information. After Emily assured him she'd be fine at the clinic with Kingston by her side, Noah took off looking for Jillian in all the places her mother said she might be. What puzzled Emily was why the woman wasn't more worried about her own daughter.

As soon as Noah left, Emily called her aunt to let her know she'd be late. "Jillian didn't come in, so I'm filling in for her."

"Oh dear," Aunt Sherry said. "I hope she's not sick. Something awful's going around. I bet she caught it at school. If you talk to her, tell her I hope she feels better soon."

Rather than let her aunt know what she suspected, Emily simply said, "I'll tell her if I talk to her."

Emily called all the numbers she had and left messages for Jillian to call Dr. Blake. No one had seen or heard from Jillian. After Emily hung up from the last number she called, she turned to Kingston.

"Looks like this is turning into a real mystery."

The dog sat up, tilted his head, and let out a soft, "Mmff."

In spite of the situation, Emily couldn't help but laugh. No doubt

Kingston could hold his own if trouble came at him, but he sure was a sweet, comical creature—and excellent company.

When the bell on the door jingled, Emily expectantly looked up, hoping it was Jillian. But it wasn't. It was Aunt Sherry, holding a box.

"This is heavy," her aunt said as she carried it toward the counter, where she plopped it with a gentle thud. "I promised Noah he could have some leftovers, and here they are."

"He'll appreciate that." Emily got up, put the leftovers in the fridge, and grabbed a chair to pull it closer to her own. "Do you have time to chat?"

"No, not today. I'm heading over to the hospital to see one of the people in my small group from church." She backed toward the door. "Oh, before I forget—I put a can of disinfectant spray in the box so you can clean your work area. I figured that since you and Jillian share the computer, it might be a good idea. I read somewhere about how many germs are on keyboards."

Emily smiled at her thoughtful aunt. "Thanks, I'll do that."

After Aunt Sherry left, Emily rummaged through the box and found the spray. She figured she might as well clean, since she still had nervous energy after doing everything she could to find Jillian. Besides, like her aunt said, there was something going around.

Noah finally returned a little after five, looking dejected. "No one has seen her since Thursday night, except us when she came in on Friday." He glanced around the office then blinked when his gaze settled on the box from Aunt Sherry. "What's that?"

"Leftovers from my aunt. I just pulled them back out of the refrigerator so you wouldn't forget to take them home."

He laughed. "Thank her for me. I certainly appreciate being fed by one of the best cooks in the county."

"I'll tell her you said that." She hesitated before asking, "Do you think we should call the police about Jillian?"

"Probably," he replied. "I would have thought her mother might do that, but when I asked her, she acted like it was no big deal. That surprised me."

"I've been thinking. . . ," Emily began. "Remember that phone call Jillian said was a wrong number?"

Noah's forehead crinkled as he thought about it. He nodded. "Yes, as a matter of fact, I do remember. Why?"

"If it really had been a wrong number, I don't think she would have spent more than a couple of seconds confirming it. From what I remember, she was on longer than that."

"Have you deleted anything from caller ID since then?" he asked.

"No, I didn't think about that."

Noah came around behind the counter and started scrolling through the numbers until they came to the date and time the allegedly wrong number had come through. He grabbed a slip of paper and jotted down the number. "I don't know if this will get us any closer to Jillian, but it's worth a try. I sure hope she's okay."

Emily offered a sympathetic smile. His compassion never stopped.

"Want me to call?" she offered.

"No, it's probably nothing. I'll call and see if someone needed veterinary care. I think playing dumb is probably the way to handle this."

"Oh I can play as dumb as the next person," Emily said with a chuckle.

"Not as well as me, I'm afraid."

Emily sat and waited as Noah placed the call. The first thing he did was introduce himself, and then he was obviously cut off. He barely had half of his next sentence spoken when he reared back, and his eyebrows shot up. Then he blinked and shook his head as he held the phone out.

"What happened?" she asked.

Noah put the phone back on the cradle. "I just got told to mind my own business and never to call back."

"That's rude."

"Not only is it rude, but it worries me. Since we don't have anything else to go on, I think I need to call this number in to Dwayne and have the sheriff's office check into it." Noah fumbled with some papers and pulled out the police report from the break-in. "We need to pray that they can get to the bottom of this and find Jillian."

He closed his eyes for a moment, so Emily shut hers and said a silent prayer. When she opened them and caught him staring at her, he blinked and cleared his throat.

"I bet Jillian is fine, Noah. She's young. I bet she just decided to take a vacation at the last minute."

Noah pursed his lips and shook his head. "It's still not like her to do this. She knows I'll give her some time off if she needs it."

Emily didn't know what else to say. Something was definitely wrong, and it looked more and more like Jillian's disappearance was somehow related to the break-in. She couldn't imagine how, and she certainly hoped that wasn't the case.

After Noah called Dwayne and gave him the information, he picked up the box of food and asked her to lock up behind them. "There's nothing else we can do now, and it's getting late. I bet you're exhausted after working here all day."

"I'm fine," she replied, although she felt like a bulldozer had run over her.

"Would you like to take Kingston home with you?" he asked. "Mel already said it's okay with him and Sherry."

She nodded. "Sure. Kingston and I get along great."

At the sound of his name, the dog looked up at Emily and panted. She patted him on the head.

They walked out to the parking lot on the side of the strip mall, and Noah put the box inside the cab of his truck before turning back to face Emily. "I appreciate everything you're doing."

She smiled back at him. "I know you do, which makes me want to do more."

For a few seconds they stood there staring at each other, silence interrupted only by the humming sound of insects in the nearby wooded area behind the clinic. Even Kingston remained quiet. Emily was transfixed by the unspoken message between them—a chemistry she could no longer deny, no matter how much she tried.

"Emily." His voice cracked, so he lifted his hand to his mouth and cleared his throat.

She took a step back and turned slightly. "I really need to leave now."

"Tell your aunt I said thanks for the food."

Emily turned, smiled, held the door for Kingston, then got into her car. She didn't trust herself to speak, so she just waved.

Noah felt as though he was swirling in a cyclone of feelings and events that were out of his control. So much had happened in such a short time. The flood had sent everyone scurrying around, trying to find a way to protect their animals. Emily had arrived and quickly filled his mind with thoughts of confused joy. His clinic had been broken into—obviously for the narcotics that he kept double locked. And now Jillian was missing.

He didn't want to expose what he knew about her past, but if she didn't show up soon, he'd be forced to let the authorities know that Jillian hadn't been to work since the break-in. The last thing he needed to do was impede their investigation. Before this, there was no indication that Jillian had fallen back into her old ways, but there was always that possibility, which was why he'd added another lock to the controlled drug cabinet at the clinic and had it connected to an alarm.

After Noah got to his apartment and put the food away, he jumped into the shower. He'd barely dried off when the phone rang. He contemplated not answering it, but he couldn't resist.

It was Dwayne calling to let him know they'd found Jillian. Noah let out a whistle of relief.

"Good. Now maybe we can get back to normal around the office."

"I don't think so," Dwayne said. "We have her locked up."

"Wha—"

"Can't say right now, but she's asking for you."

Noah didn't hesitate. "I'll be right there."

"I haven't known you all that long, Noah, but I think I know you well enough to give you some advice. This is a troubled young woman, and you took a chance hiring her."

"Yes, I realize that, but I think she's a good girl who got in with the wrong crowd."

Dwayne made a sniffing noise. "Yeah, I can see why you feel that way. Ever think she might be *part* of the wrong crowd?"

Noah understood why Dwayne said that, but he refused to give up on any injured creature—especially a person who had so much potential. "We don't need to talk on the phone right now, Dwayne. I'll be there in a few minutes."

"Gotcha. See ya."

The walls seemed to be closing in around Noah as he sat down on the edge of his bed. He lowered his head, stared at the floor before shutting his eyes, and prayed. He wanted Jillian to understand that God loved her, in spite of her past. And He loved her now, even though she'd fallen. Or at least it appeared she'd fallen. Sometimes things weren't as they seemed. Noah had enough life experience to know this.

He arrived at the small jail, and Dwayne led him back to a room. "Her court-appointed attorney will be here any minute, so you don't have long."

"Okay, I just wanted to let her know I care enough to come down here."

Dwayne cast a pitying glance his way then shook his head and mumbled something as he walked down the hall to get Jillian. Noah liked the deputy, and he understood why the man was so cynical.

When Jillian walked into the room, she looked about ten years older than she was. Her hair hung in strings around her face, and her clothes looked like she'd slept in them for days. Maybe she had.

"What happened, Jillian?" he asked as he leaned forward.

She looked him in the eye for a split second then looked down. "I don't know."

"You were doing so well. You never gave me any reason not to trust you."

"I know. It's just that. . ." Her voice trailed off, and she let out a tiny whimper.

Noah wanted to assure her that she wasn't in this situation alone. He'd been around her enough to know she was a good person deep down. "I'm praying for you. And I want you to know that when you get out, you can have your job back."

She glanced up at him and glared, an uncharacteristic frown contorting her face. "Why? I don't want people feeling sorry for me."

"I don't feel sorry for you, Jillian," he said firmly. "I just happen to be someone who believes in a smart, personable woman who used to have some friends who are very bad for her."

"How do you know all this?"

He smiled. "Just a good guess."

They sat in silence for a few more seconds before she buried her face in her hands and started crying. "I told him to leave me alone, but he wouldn't. When he called me and said he just wanted to see me to say good-bye, I really thought that's what he wanted."

"Are you talking about your old boyfriend who got you into the mess last year?"

Jillian nodded. "He called me at the clinic and asked me to meet him. I told him that would be the last time, and he said fine because he was leaving town." She blinked back another tear. "Then after we started talking, he told me I was worthless and no one would want me—and no amount of college will make me any better than I am."

"That's not true and you know it."

She tightened her lips and her chin began to quiver. Noah reached over and pulled a tissue out of the box on the table. "Where is he?"

"He's in jail, too. After we left the clinic—yeah, I let him in, but he couldn't get the drug cabinet open. Those locks are strong."

"You knew the locks were there, right?"

"Yeah, I've seen you double-check them enough. I was counting on them keeping him out of the cabinet."

Noah nodded. "So what happened after you left the clinic?"

"We went to another friend's place. They'd just scored some stuff from the emergency room at the hospital."

"I won't even ask how," Noah said. "So where did the police pick you up?"

"They found us at his mother's house."

That must have been the woman Noah had spoken to—the one who hung up when he'd asked about Jillian. "What does she have to do with all this?"

Jillian shuddered. "That woman is evil. She took off after you called."

"So you knew about my call, huh?"

A tap came at the door, and Noah stood up. "I won't give up on you, Jillian. I want you to know that we'll be praying for you."

"Is Emily going to keep working for you?"

Noah nodded. "Yes, and I'm going to ask her to work full-time until you get out. Take care, Jillian."

He was all the way to the door before he heard her soft "Good-bye, Noah. I'm really sorry I messed up." Her voice cracked as she added, "Tell Emily—you can tell her everything, and tell her I'm sorry."

Noah didn't look back at her. He focused straight ahead as he left the station and headed toward his apartment. Although he didn't have a bit of an appetite, he fixed a small plate with some of Sherry's leftovers. He needed to keep up his strength.

Emily got to work early the next morning, hoping that there would be some development in finding Jillian. Noah hadn't arrived yet, so she got Kingston's bed ready, turned on the computer, and set up the front desk for the day.

She loved being there in the mornings, but working all day made it difficult to do what she came here for—to find herself. The best therapy for Emily was working outdoors, helping Aunt Sherry with her garden and Uncle Mel with the animals. She'd discuss it with Noah and let him know she couldn't continue working full-time for more than a few days.

Noah walked in a half hour later, bags under his eyes, his shoulders sloping downward. When he looked at her, she melted. Then he looked away and continued toward the examining area. It was unlike Noah to walk by without greeting her, so she panicked and jumped up from her chair.

"What's wrong, Noah?"

He stopped and turned to face her. "Jillian's in jail."

"She's what?"

Noah took a deep breath and slowly let it out. "There's some stuff I haven't told you about Jillian, but since all this has happened, I guess you ought to know."

"Yeah." She planted her hands on her hips and glared at him.

"Check when the first appointment is coming in. This'll take awhile."

She looked on the computer and saw that the first appointment wasn't due for almost an hour. "Is that enough time?" she asked.

"Yes, that should be enough time."

He pulled a chair from the waiting area to the reception desk then unfolded the whole story about how Jillian had been caught up with the wrong crowd after high school and gotten into some trouble. Pastor Chuck had counseled her and encouraged her to go to college. Then he asked Noah to hire her part-time. Everything was going smoothly, so there didn't seem to be any reason to talk about her past.

Emily listened to every word Noah said as she sat there stunned. "I had no idea about any of this, Noah. Jillian seems like such a sweet girl."

"I know. And she is when she's not with that loser exboyfriend of hers. She also asked me to tell you she's sorry."

Noah obviously wanted to save the world, but Emily felt the same way. Jillian had a tremendous amount of potential. She was smart, wonderful with customers, and she loved animals. In Emily's book, that made her pretty special.

"I'm going to do whatever I can to help her," Noah said. "In the meantime, would you consider working full-time? That is, until Jillian can come back?"

"How long do you think it'll be?" she asked.

Noah shrugged. "Who knows? The court system can be slow, or she could be back in a couple of weeks."

Emily glanced down at the floor as she thought about the conversation she'd planned to have with him. On the one hand, she was justified in telling him she couldn't do it. However, she liked Jillian, Noah really needed her, and she didn't have anywhere else to be. So how could she turn him down?

"I guess I can for a little while," she replied. "How about you, Kingston? Are you okay with that?"

He looked up at her and expressed his approval. "Mmff."

When Noah smiled at her, the skin around his eyes crinkled. The accompanying flutter in her chest caught her off guard.

"Thank you, Emily. I owe you one." Noah got up and replaced the chair where it belonged. "I have some prep work to do, so just let me know when the first appointment arrives."

The bell sounded, so Emily glanced up, fully expecting a standard-size poodle and its owner, but instead, Aunt Sherry came bounding through the door, grinning from ear to ear. "I have a surprise for you and Noah! Where is he?"

Chapter 7

He's prepping for a patient," Emily said. "Whatcha got?"

Aunt Sherry grinned. "Just something I know both of you like."

"You're not gonna tell me, are you?"

"Nope." Her aunt patted her oversized tote. "It's right here. I'll sit in this chair and wait until Noah's finished with whatever he's doing."

"That might be awhile. His patient should be here any minute." A big white SUV pulled into the space out front. "In fact here he is right now."

Within a minute, Seymour the poodle and his exuberant owner came walking in. Kingston got up and walked around to see who'd just entered. Emily pointed to the floor beside her. "Sit." Kingston sat.

"Wait right here, Seymour," the woman said to her dog. "I have to check you in."

"Hi, Mrs. Whitley." Emily grinned at the woman then turned to Seymour. "Hey, Seymour. Ready to see Dr. Blake?"

The poodle got excited at the sound of his name, so he forgot his order and came around the counter. Emily held her breath for a moment before she realized Kingston wasn't about to disobey her, no matter what Seymour did.

Emily had been warned about Mrs. Whitley's dog who'd been through a couple of obedience classes but still couldn't control his urges. All the pampering his owner gave him spoiled the dog and made him a pest around other animals.

The two dogs sniffed each other, but the Great Dane remained planted in his spot. After a few seconds of not getting a reaction, Seymour lost interest and headed back to his master. However, he suddenly stopped, sniffed the air, and instantly bounded toward Aunt Sherry, whose eyes widened at the surprise.

"No-no, Seymour, honey," Mrs. Whitley said in the voice she obviously reserved for her precious poodle.

Seymour wasn't listening. He knew Aunt Sherry had something good in her tote, and with one sweeping swipe of the paw, he'd knocked her tote off the chair next to her. Suddenly there was a mad scramble for the bag.

"No, Seymour!" Aunt Sherry hollered. "Down!"

The poodle jumped back at the sound of her harsh tone, but that didn't stop him from diving back toward the bag a second later. By now Emily had no doubt Seymour wouldn't stop until he got whatever he wanted, so she went around to the waiting area with the leash she kept beside her.

She counted on him remembering some of the commands from obedience training.

"Sit, Seymour," Emily said. The second he obeyed the command, she snapped the leash on his collar before he had a chance to think about what was in Aunt Sherry's bag. "C'mon, boy, I have a treat for you."

"Oh, he can't have a treat," Mrs. Whitley said. "I have him on a very special diet."

Emily cast a glance at Aunt Sherry, who still looked shell-shocked, and turned back to face the dog's owner. "He's going to get a treat, whether I give him one or he gets it from her bag. It's just a little piece of dog food anyway, so don't worry."

Mrs. Whitley swallowed hard and looked over at Aunt Sherry. "I—I guess it's okay if he has a treat at the doctor's office."

Noah chose that moment to come out for the dog. "Hey, Mrs. Whitley, how's Seymour?"

The poodle forgot all about the treat, jumped toward Noah before Emily snapped the leash, and the dog landed on his rear. He let out a whimper, but Noah didn't let him get too distressed before taking the leash from Emily. "I've got him." He squatted down next to Seymour. "How's my big buddy?"

Seymour licked him across the face in response.

Noah wiped his face with his sleeve and grinned at Mrs. Whitley. "He looks healthy. How's the obedience training coming along?"

His poor owner looked frazzled as she shook her head. "Not so well, I'm afraid. I still can't make him behave."

"You just have to stick with it. He's still young. His attention span will grow as he gets older."

Emily thought about the Great Dane who remained behind the counter. She could only imagine how curious he must have been, yet he was so well trained he didn't budge.

"Perhaps you should consider going through the training with him," Noah advised. "Sometimes all it takes is for him to see that you mean business. They can teach you how to be firm."

The woman flipped her hand at the wrist. "Oh, I couldn't do that. I'd hate to break his spirit."

Emily and her aunt exchanged a knowing glance. She'd seen plenty of disobedient animals, and almost every one of them would have been easy to train if their owners had been willing to spend more time working with them.

Noah tugged on Seymour's leash. "C'mon, boy, let's go see how you're doing." He cast a look over to Mrs. Whitley. "Would you like to join us?"

She scrunched her face. "I can't bear watching him get his shots."

"Then you better stay out here. We won't be long."

Emily and her aunt chatted with Mrs. Whitley until Seymour was finished with his checkup and shots. As soon as Noah opened the door from the examining area, the proud poodle pranced out into the waiting room like he owned the place. Kingston whimpered, but after a stern glance from Emily, he remained in his spot.

Noah found himself continuing to lose his heart to Emily, a piece at a time. As he watched her handle each situation that came her way, he knew she could do anything she set her mind to. Not only was she organized, friendly, and professional, she had a knack with animals and for putting people at ease.

After Seymour and Mrs. Whitley left, Sherry carried her tote across the room and hoisted it onto the reception counter. "I brought you some sustenance," she announced with pride. "Emily's favorite blueberry oatmeal muffins." He watched her pull out a plastic bag filled to capacity with treats he knew would be tasty. When she opened the bag, a delicious aroma filled the clinic.

"You didn't have to do that, Aunt Sherry." Emily's cheeks were pink, and she wouldn't look him in the eye.

"Oh but I'm glad she did." Noah reached into the bag and pulled out a muffin. One taste and he felt like he was floating on clouds. "This is absolutely delicious."

Sherry fastened her tote and grinned. "I'm glad you like it." She edged toward the door and waved. "I know you're busy, so I'll leave the two of you to your work." Then she winked at Emily. "See you when you get home, sugar."

As soon as the door closed behind her, Noah looked at her and smiled. "Sherry is amazing. You're fortunate to have her."

"Yes I know." Emily still didn't look him in the eye, so he turned back toward the examining rooms. "I need to clean up then call on a couple of farms before my afternoon appointments."

He took his time cleaning since he wasn't expected at the first farm for another hour. For once he wasn't slammed. He would have loved to spend a little time with Emily, but since she seemed flustered and unsure this morning, he figured it might be better to leave her alone until she worked through whatever was bothering her.

Soon it was time for him to leave. "These are short visits, so I'll see you in a couple of hours."

Emily glanced up, and then her gaze quickly darted to something on the floor. He glanced down and spotted a fifty-dollar bill beside his feet, so he picked it up. "Any idea whose this is?"

She nodded. "It has to be Mrs. Whitley's."

"Are you sure it doesn't belong to your aunt?"

"I'm pretty sure it wouldn't be my aunt's because she was sitting over there." Emily pointed to another row of chairs. "Besides, she's not likely to walk around with a fifty."

On top of everything else, she had to be the most honest woman he'd ever met. "Why don't you call Mrs. Whitley and ask if she wants us to send her a check or if she'd rather pick up the money next time she's out."

"I'll do that right now."

Noah walked out of the clinic, headed to his truck, and tossed a few things into the back before getting in. Emily's image played in his mind as he drove to the first farm.

He knew it wasn't right to compare, but he couldn't help holding her next to Tiffany in his mind. If Tiffany had seen the fifty-dollar bill, he wasn't sure she would have mentioned it to him. Instead, she would have considered the finders-keepers rule and spent the money on herself.

There were too many differences between the two women to count. What he saw in Tiffany back a few years ago was now a mystery to Noah. Sure she was pretty, but lots of girls were. She was smart, but her goal in life was to marry well and have her days free to hang out at the country club and get her nails done. Not that he expected her to be a career woman, but he at least wished she had some purpose outside her own personal circle that seemed to get smaller as time went on.

When Noah arrived at the first farm, all he had to do was check a couple of the goats and administer medication to a horse with an infected foot. He was back in his truck less than an hour later.

His second stop was even shorter. A year earlier this farmer had to sell off some of his land to pay his taxes, so Noah didn't expect to see the payment for his services—at least not any time soon.

As he got back in the truck, his thoughts drifted to the business side of his practice. He made enough to survive and pay the bills on the clinic. However, what he considered a decent income would have been debatable with his father, whose practice had flourished over the years simply because his clientele was more upscale than any of the ones Noah served.

There were times when Noah thought about calling his delinquent clients to see if they could arrange a payment plan, but the staggering amount some of them owed might freak them out. Most of the people who brought smaller animals into the clinic paid as they went, but he billed the farmers. When he had time, he actually mailed the bills. Lately he'd been so busy he'd let it slip. In fact, he couldn't remember the last billing he'd mailed. He'd intended to get Jillian on that project soon, but he hadn't even had time for that.

Emily finished all the daily work and started looking around for something else to do. When she was sure she'd covered everything Noah had asked her to do, she pulled her sketch pad from her tote and doodled.

After a few minutes she felt guilty because she was on Noah's clock, so she put down the sketch pad and clicked through the files on the computer to see if any loose ends needed to be tied up.

When she got to the Blalock farm account, she stopped and stared at the screen, stunned by what she saw. The farmer owed Noah more than a thousand dollars, and he hadn't even shown an attempt to pay a dime of it.

This prompted her to check all the other farm accounts, and she quickly saw that the Blalock account was the norm, not the exception. After clicking through every account in the Noah's Ark system, she realized that the only people who paid were customers who brought their patients into the clinic and a very small handful of farmers, including her aunt and uncle.

She jotted down some of the larger accounts and came up with a staggering total. If everyone paid what they owed, Noah would be able to hire a full office staff and never have to bat an eye.

Emily knew this was a ministry of sorts for Noah, but it was also his livelihood. He wouldn't be able to stay in business if he didn't collect some of the money he was owed. She'd have to figure out a way to talk to him without sounding like she was nosing into his business.

The phone rang and it was Noah. "I'm stopping off at a deli on my way back. What are you in the mood for?"

"Turkey on wheat with lettuce and tomato," she replied. "I'll pay you when you get here."

He laughed. "That's not necessary. You're doing so much for me, I wouldn't even think about asking for money from you."

"We'll discuss that later," she said.

After they got off the phone, she brainstormed ways to collect some of the money Noah was owed. No matter what she came up with, she knew he'd balk, but she couldn't just sit back and do nothing. He obviously made enough money to stay in business, but she knew he had so much more potential if he collected what was owed.

Noah arrived a half hour later. "Here's the food. I need to put this stuff away and wash up. You don't have to wait for me."

"That's okay," she mumbled. "I'll wait."

They could discuss the billing issue after lunch, since there wasn't anything on the schedule for another hour. Emily dreaded bringing it up because she had no idea what Noah's reaction would be. One thing she was fairly certain of, though, was that he wouldn't even consider strong-arm tactics. And that was one of the things she found most attractive about him. Noah was a strong man with a gentle spirit. His generosity was a major bonus but also his biggest flaw. A giving nature was an admirable trait, but he didn't know when to stop.

At the sound of Noah's footsteps drawing closer, Emily shoved her scratch paper into the pencil drawer. He opened the bag, pulled out a wrapped sandwich, and handed it to her. "I got both of us the same thing," he said. "I got chips, too, but I had no idea what kind you liked, so I got a bag of each."

Emily laughed. "You don't have to do that, Noah."

He put his sandwich down and let his gaze settle on her. "I know I don't have to, but I want to. No amount of money can repay you for all you're doing for me and this clinic."

She let out a nervous chuckle. "You're paying me for my time here, and it's all part of my job."

"It's more than that." Noah broke his gaze and reached for the sandwich. As he slowly unwrapped it, Emily could tell by the set of his jaw that his mind was somewhere else.

Emily took a bite of her sandwich and let silence prevail. She'd been around Noah enough to know he didn't always have to have conversation filling every moment.

After she swallowed her second bite, she put down her sandwich. "So how was the Jenkins clan?"

Noah shook his head as he finished chewing. "I feel so bad for Patrick Jenkins. After he sold that last piece of land, his heart doesn't seem to be in his farming anymore."

Emily had already heard about the hard times that had fallen on many of her aunt and uncle's friends and fellow farmers. "Maybe things will turn around." This definitely wasn't the time to bring up billing.

The phone rang and this time it was Jillian. "Want to talk to Noah?" Emily asked.

"No."

Her answer was so abrupt Emily was startled. "Okay, so what's going on?"

"Can you come to my mom's place after work? I need to talk to someone, and I'm not allowed to go anywhere."

"Um. . ." Emily glanced at Noah, who sat there watching, waiting. "I guess so. Want me to bring you anything?"

Jillian coughed. "Just a listening ear and the willingness to believe me."

"I can do that," Emily promised. "Now I need your mother's address."

After Emily hung up, Noah cocked his head and stared at her. "Well?"

Her throat tightened. "That was Jillian. She asked me to come over after work."

"I'll go with you."

Emily glanced down then looked Noah squarely in the eye. "She wants me to come alone."

The look of concern on his face touched Emily. "I don't want to put you in jeopardy," he said.

She smiled. "I'll be fine."

"Call me the second you leave so I won't worry."

Chapter 8

Emily hadn't even sat down before Jillian blurted out, "I don't deserve to live after what I did."

"What exactly did you do?"

She and Jillian were now at the kitchen table in her mother's tiny cottage. Emily couldn't help but notice the peeling paint and timeworn furniture.

Jillian folded her hands and stared at them for what seemed like an eternity before she looked Emily in the eye. "Did Noah tell you anything about my past?"

Emily nodded.

"When Brad told me he wanted to stop off at the clinic, I told him no because it was closed."

"After all the things I heard about him, why would you even be with him?" Emily asked.

The younger woman shrugged. "Just lonely, I guess. Mom comes and goes, and I haven't made friends with anyone at school. The few people I knew in high school moved away."

Emily reached for Jillian's hand. "I'm your friend. And Noah really cares about you."

"Yes, I know he does. That's why I feel so awful."

This Brad guy must have something Jillian needed. "You're a very smart woman, Jillian. Why do you let Brad do this to you?"

Jillian blinked but not in time to stop a tear that trickled down her cheek. "He told me he loved me and that he'd do anything to make me happy." She sniffled. "And I've been so sad lately it sounded good."

"I didn't realize you were sad," Emily said. "And I don't think Noah knew either."

"There was no point in burdening you and Noah with my feelings. I figured both of you had enough on your minds."

Emily smiled and squeezed Jillian's hand. "So tell me why he said he wanted to go to the clinic."

Jillian pursed her lips and shuddered. "It's really stupid."

"That's okay. Tell me anyway." Emily squeezed her hand.

Jillian sucked in a deep breath and slowly blew it out. "His cat eats this expensive food, and Brad was broke, and we carry it at the clinic. I told him we didn't sell much of it, so he convinced me it would be good to go get some since it would go bad anyway, and he'd write a check after he got paid."

Emily could tell how heartbroken Jillian was, so she refrained from asking again why she'd trust Brad. "Why didn't you call Noah when you realized what Brad was really there for—or at any time? He could have stopped Brad from getting you into trouble."

"I—I couldn't. Noah's the last person I'd want to upset. I begged Brad to get out of there, but he just laughed at me." She pulled her hand away from Emily's and held it out. "Now I've completely blown any chance of having Noah's trust."

"It's not that he doesn't trust you, Jillian. I think we're both concerned about your judgment at this very difficult time in your life."

Jillian shook her head. "No one can understand what it feels like to be in my shoes. I never knew my father, and my mother only wants me around when she needs something."

"You're right," Emily replied. She pondered how much she should say before finally deciding it was best to come out with it. Even if it hurt to talk about it, she might be able to relate to Jillian on her level. "I don't know what it feels like to be in your shoes, but I do know what it feels like to have a mother who doesn't want you."

Jillian snorted. "How would you know?"

"My own mother abandoned me at one of the worst times of my life. I spent all of my teenage years wondering what I'd done wrong."

The younger woman's eyes widened. "What did you do? Where did you go?"

Emily closed her eyes and said a silent prayer for guidance. "Fortunately for me, my father was still there. He did the best he could, but there were times he was clueless."

"At least you had someone."

"Yes," she admitted. "I also had Aunt Sherry and Uncle Mel who have given me unconditional love all my life. There was never any doubt I had someone who cared."

"I don't—well, besides Noah—and you."

"There's someone else," Emily said softly. "I know you've spoken to Pastor Chuck about this, and I don't want to preach at you."

Jillian bobbed her head. "Yeah, we've talked several times, and he keeps talking about how much Jesus loves me. But where was He when my mother told me I was good for nothing?"

"He's right there with you all the time," Emily replied. "I don't have all the answers about why things like this happen, but remember that you never have to walk alone in life. Just understand that sometimes people you care about will disappoint you."

With a half smile, Jillian nodded. "Yeah, like I disappointed Noah."

Emily leaned back in her chair. "Noah will trust you again someday. It'll take time, but believe me, he's a forgiving man."

"I know he is."

"Good. Now tell me what's going on with your court date."

They discussed when she had to report to court. "I'd like to come back to work for Noah after this is all over—that is, if he'll have me." She grew pensive as she flicked a bread crumb off the table. "But I'll understand if he won't."

"I'm not a hundred percent sure what he'll do, but I bet he'll give you another chance." Emily paused until she caught Jillian's gaze. "Especially if you promise not to see Brad again."

Jillian opened her mouth then closed it without uttering a sound. Emily realized how difficult this was for Jillian, but ultimately she was responsible for her own actions. After all, she was an adult. Too bad she didn't have the coping skills she needed.

"Is there anything you'd like for me to tell Noah?" Emily asked as she stood up to leave.

"Tell him I'm really sorry and that I'll do anything to make it up to him."

Suddenly an idea popped into Emily's head. "Why don't you start going to church with us? You know Pastor Chuck. He preaches great sermons."

"I know. I heard one once on a CD he gave me." She followed Emily to the door. "But I'm not sure I'm ready to go to church. Let me think about it."

"Just remember that you don't have to be ready. Jesus will accept you as you are."

Jillian nodded then smiled. "So how are things between you and Noah?"

"Huh?"

"I've seen the way you two look at each other. There are definitely sparks."

Was she that obvious? Emily didn't want to take any chances on people jumping to conclusions just because she was so easy to read, so she shook her head. "Noah and I have a lot of respect for each other. That's all."

"Right," Jillian said with a smirk.

"I'll call you about church, okay?" Emily had reached the front porch, so she turned around to wait for an answer.

With a slight hesitation, Jillian nodded. "Fine."

After she gave Jillian a hug, Emily headed out to her car. All the way home she rehashed her conversation with the hurting young woman. She remembered wondering where God was when her mother left. How could He have put her through something like that when she needed her mother the most? She'd searched scripture, trying to figure out what the whole Christianity thing was all about. The magnitude of what people endured in biblical times made her feel that her problems were small next to some of theirs. However, it still hadn't made her pain go away. Now that she was an adult, she understood that God hadn't made it happen, but He'd used the bad situation to help her grow as a Christian.

Then there was the issue of her feelings for Noah. Yes, she did have what she used to call a crush on him, but wouldn't anyone in her shoes? After all, he was a smart, sweet man with a heart for Christ that spilled over into everything else he did.

Emily slowed down as she drove past the clinic on the way home, and she noticed that the lights were still on. Noah worked such long hours, it was amazing he had any energy left.

She was tempted to stop and give him a full report about her meeting with Jillian, but she decided not to. That could wait until tomorrow. It was time to go home and see what she could do to help Uncle Mel and Aunt Sherry. They'd been awesome about everything.

As soon as she walked into the kitchen, Aunt Sherry pointed to the hallway. "Why don't you kick off your shoes and take a rest? Dinner will be ready in about half an hour."

"I want to help."

"No need. I threw a bunch of stuff in a casserole dish and made a salad before I left to run errands this morning. All I had to do was stick the dish in the oven, and I'll toss the salad right before we eat."

"Then I'll go back outside and see if Uncle Mel can use some help."

Aunt Sherry gave her a puzzled look. "Was he out there when you got home?"

"No, I didn't see him. Why?"

"He probably isn't back yet, then. He finished all his chores and headed into town to meet with a bunch of men from the church. They're banding together to help some of the farmers who aren't as fortunate as we are."

Emily smiled. One of the things she loved about farm life here in West Virginia was how everyone worked together for the good of all.

When Uncle Mel got home, they sat down to eat. Aunt Sherry asked him one question after another, but Emily only heard a fraction of his answers. She'd drifted into a world of her own thoughts when she realized it had suddenly grown quiet and that her aunt and uncle were staring at her.

She cast a sheepish glance down then forced a smile as she looked back up. "Sorry, but today has been kind of insane."

Uncle Mel stretched both arms over the table and nodded. "I heard. Wanna talk about it?"

"What did you hear?" Emily hadn't said a word about her conversation with Jillian to anyone.

"Well," he began slowly, "I know about Noah's assistant being involved in the break-in and that you went to visit her after work."

Aunt Sherry obviously knew, too, because she didn't look the least bit surprised. "Did she explain why she did it?"

"Sort of." Emily wasn't sure how much to tell or if she should keep everything to herself.

"Did she ask you not to discuss it with anyone?"

Emily shook her head. "No, not really. It's just that—well. . ."

"That's okay," Aunt Sherry said. "You don't have to tell us. We can still pray for her. I do know enough about the girl to know she can use all the prayers we can give."

"Ain't that the truth," Uncle Mel agreed. He looked at his wife. "Did you fix dessert?"

"No, I did something better. When I stopped off at the bakery this morning, I picked up a dozen of your favorite peanut butter cookies."

The grin on Uncle Mel's face said it all. He definitely approved.

After Emily helped Aunt Sherry clean the kitchen, she headed to her room and pulled out her cell phone to see if she had any messages. There were three—one from Jillian and two from Noah. She called Jillian first.

"Hey look, Emily, I've been thinking. . . ."

When she didn't speak for a few seconds, Emily urged her. "About what?"

"You said God was with me all the time. I have some questions about that."

"Would you like for me to come over tomorrow during lunch? We can talk about it then."

"Do you mind?" Jillian's voice squeaked with uncertainty.

"Of course I don't mind. There's nothing I love talking about more than the Lord. He's walked with me for as long as I can remember. Without Him, I wouldn't be here today."

Next Emily called Noah. "Hey, I wondered how your visit with Jillian went."

"It was good. She told me what happened."

"You do believe her, don't you?" Noah asked.

"Yes, I do. Have you spoken with her?"

Noah hesitated for a couple of seconds before speaking. "I have."

"That's good. Did she tell you what all she and I talked about?"

"She said you mentioned something about going to church on Sunday. I told her that was an excellent idea. I'll see if I can get permission from the court for her to leave the house."

"Oh, I didn't think about that," Emily admitted. "But now I understand why she called a little while ago. I guess she just needed that little extra encouragement you gave her."

"That's not a bad thing. We all need encouragement."

The way he said that made Emily feel like he'd left something unsaid. "I'll be in early in the morning because I told Jillian I'd come over to her place for lunch. There's something I'd like to discuss with you."

"You're not leaving us, are you?"

"Leaving? No, of course not. It has nothing to do with me."

A nervous chuckle escaped his lips. "Sorry, I'm not being paranoid or anything. It's just that I like having you at the clinic. You have such a calming effect on my clients."

Emily laughed. "I'm glad I'm good for something."

The next morning Noah arrived about five minutes before Emily. When she pulled up, his pulse quickened, but he managed to hide his excitement when she walked in. His feelings for her had advanced beyond the professional stage, and he didn't want to let her know—at least not yet. Not until he had some idea of how she felt about him. "Have a seat. I'll get you some coffee."

"You don't have to wait on me, Noah. I can get my own coffee."

He picked up his mug, went around behind the counter, and sat down in the extra chair he'd brought back there. Emily joined him in less than a minute, a steaming cup of coffee in one fist and a couple of bagels in the other. "Aunt Sherry sent these, so I brought you one."

"So what was so important that you needed to come in early?"

The strain on Emily's face was apparent as she braced herself to break some news. That made him nervous, but he'd learned to take deep breaths and loosen his jaw.

"I noticed that some of your clients have owed you money since you've been here," she blurted as her face turned bright crimson. "And they haven't even made an attempt to pay."

"Yeah, that's true. I'm not sure what I can do about it though." He studied her face and watched her expression change.

"You can't let people take advantage of you, Noah. You're such a nice guy, people will run all over you."

Noah had to smile at that. "Trust me, Emily. No one's running all over me. I don't do anything I don't want to do."

She calmed down. "Maybe it's none of my business, but I worked up a plan that might help you get some of that money." When he didn't say anything, she added, "I think most people want to pay their bills, but they only see the full amount, which in some cases is staggering."

He tilted his head to one side. "Oh yeah? So let's say I was interested in some sort of recovery plan. What would we do?"

"Well, first," she said as she held up one finger and touched it with the index finger of her other hand, "we can send a letter reminding people what they owe."

"They get a monthly bill as it is," he said. "I think they know what they owe."

"But this would be different. We could write a letter explaining why you need to collect the money. They can work on a payment plan if they can't afford the entire balance, which I'm sure many of them can't."

"You're right about that," he agreed. He shoved the last of the bagel into his mouth, folded his arms, and stretched out his legs to hear the rest of her plan.

"All they need to pay is a small amount for you to continue rendering services." She slowed down and cast a wary glance toward him at the tail end of that sentence, as if checking to see his reaction.

"So what we're saying, in essence, is that if they don't pay something, they can find another vet?"

She shrugged, held up her hands, and let them fall with a slap onto her jeans-clad thighs. "In a roundabout way, I guess."

"I don't know," he said. "I'll have to think about that one. The thought of an animal needing medical care and not getting it just because of money doesn't sit well with me." He snickered. "I guess I must take after my dad. When he first opened his practice, some of his clients didn't pay on time. That stopped when he hired Hazel, a woman who turned things around for him within a month. His clients could certainly afford his services though. Some of mine might not be able to."

From the look on her face, he knew she understood. She was trying to be pragmatic and help him but not at the risk of his animal patients not getting the care they needed.

"Do you have any other ideas how we can do this?" he asked.

She shook her head. "Not really. But I can draft a letter, and we can discuss it before it goes out."

"Okay, why don't you do that?" he said. "Just don't send it out until I give you the go-ahead."

She smiled and nodded. "Of course."

They talked about Jillian next. He'd already spoken to Dwayne, who offered to help get permission for the girl to go to church, as long as someone trustworthy accompanied her. Noah offered to be that person. Dwayne said he'd be happy to help as well, since someone had done the same thing for him when he was searching.

The phone rang so Emily stopped to answer it. He could tell it was her aunt as soon as she started talking. She laughed then held the phone out to Noah.

"She wants to talk to you."

He took the phone and answered a few questions. Then Sherry asked him to come to dinner that night and then again Sunday after church. She even said if he had time he could come over on Friday night and Saturday, too. With a chuckle, he said he could probably swing one or two times. After he got off the phone, he told Emily, hoping she'd give some indication of her feelings about him being around so much during her personal time.

"I'm so sorry, Noah. My aunt means well, but I need to talk to her and let her know it's awkward."

"Awkward? How so?"

"There's nothing but a professional friendship between us. I don't want her putting you on the spot like that."

A sinking feeling flooded Noah. He needed to protect his heart, or he'd be an emotional wreck.

Chapter 9

The expression on Noah's face confused Emily. He looked hurt. Had she misread him?

His appearance quickly changed to one of fierce determination. "I can handle it, but if it makes you uncomfortable, please, by all means talk to her."

She sensed that something between them had shifted. "I will."

He put a few more feet of distance between them then paused. "If you want to draft a letter for my nonpaying clients, you may. I'll take a look at whatever you have and make adjustments if necessary."

Noah left Emily sitting there in silence with nothing but her thoughts rumbling through her head. His tone was sharp and edgy, without the warm friendliness she was accustomed to.

Between patients, Emily worked on a letter, but it didn't come easy. She typed a paragraph and deleted most of it then started over. No matter what she put on the page, it sounded harsh or trite. It was much more difficult than she thought it would be. Maybe she should leave things as they were. After all, this wasn't a permanent job for her. As soon as Jillian got back and she figured out what she wanted to do with her life, she'd be gone.

Emily's stomach knotted at the very thought of moving on. She liked it here. Aunt Sherry and Uncle Mel made her feel like she was home. Their farm felt safe. West Virginia was beautiful. Now that she thought about it, working at Noah's Ark gave her a sense of purpose. This was nothing like what she'd expected when she first arrived.

Okay, now that she had those thoughts behind her, she'd write a killer letter. She turned back to face the computer and cranked out a letter in half an hour. It would have been done sooner if she hadn't had to answer the phone a dozen times. She typed Noah's name at the end then sat back and read it. Not bad. A few minor tweaks and it came across friendly but firm.

The next time Noah stuck his head out the door to see if his patient had arrived, Emily motioned for him to come and take a look at the letter. She'd printed it and had it on the counter, waiting.

He picked it up and slowly read it before looking up. "Not bad. Would you mind handing me a pen? I want to make a couple of changes, but you did a very nice job."

When he handed the paper back to her, she saw that he'd only changed a couple of insignificant things, but he didn't alter a single major point. She caught him staring at her.

"You did a very nice job, Emily." His voice had softened a little, but it still wasn't back to the same friendly tone he'd had before their talk. "I think this might get some results without insulting anyone."

"Thank you." Emily swallowed hard. "Would you like for me to print it and get it out this week?"

"Sure, if you can. I don't want you stressing over it though."

"It's not stressful."

"Okay, good. Let me know when the next patient arrives."

One of the farmers who'd managed to escape the flood stopped by with a box of kittens. Noah didn't normally board animals, but he kept cages and pens for emergencies.

"I sure hope you can find them good homes," he said. "We already have enough barn cats. Any more and the ones we've got will starve to death."

Emily wasn't sure what to do, so she went back and got Noah, who was lecturing the owner of a very temperamental Doberman puppy that he needed to get control over the dog or he'd regret it. It was hard for Emily to imagine the frisky, friendly little puppy turning out bad, but she'd seen all kinds of dogs who hadn't gotten the training they needed.

Bruiser put his front paws on her as she walked into the room, and he bounced around on his hind legs. She started to reach down and pet him, but when Noah gave her a sign and shook his head, she pulled her hand back.

"Sorry to bother you, Noah," she said, "but there's someone here with a box of kittens."

Noah's shoulders slumped. "Barn kittens?"

Emily nodded. "He says he already has too many cats. What should I tell him?"

"I was just about to finish up here. Why don't you ask if he can wait about five minutes?"

"Okay." Emily headed back to the front, leaving Noah to the rest of his lecture about obedience training.

The farmer had already made himself comfortable in one of the chairs, with the box of mewing kittens at his feet. Emily had to resist the urge to go over and peek inside the box. She was such a pushover for baby animals that she knew she wouldn't be able to keep her emotions in check.

The man with the puppy came out and paid his bill. Noah followed shortly afterward. His face lit up when he saw who the farmer was.

"Hey, Barry! I hear you have some kittens to give away."

"I reckon I do." Farmer Barry picked up the box and set it on the chair. "They're mighty cute little things, but it wouldn't be right to keep 'em."

"You know how I feel about spaying and neutering," Noah said as he looked down into the box then lifted his gaze to the other man's. "I'll give you a discount if you let me take care of all your cats."

The farmer pursed his lips then let his head drop forward. "I know I ought to do that. Maybe after we get this crop in."

"Don't wait too much longer, or you'll have another box of kittens. It's gotten harder to place them since the flooding."

"Yeah, I know. Maybe in a couple of weeks, okay?"

"Sounds good," Noah said.

With that, the farmer left empty-handed. Noah lifted the box, turned to Emily, and shook his head laughing. "I'll take a picture with my digital camera this afternoon, and maybe we can send out a few e-mails to church members."

Another farmer, Mack Pierce, brought in some chickens. "Something's wrong with these hens," he said. "They used to be some of my best layers, and I haven't gotten any eggs from them in a while."

"Why didn't you just call? I could have come out to your farm."

"I know how busy you are, and I had some business in town, so I figured it was just as easy for me to bring 'em here."

"Thanks. I'll take a look at them," Noah assured him. "Can you leave them overnight?"

"Yeah," Mack said as he placed his hand on his hip. "I'll come back first thing tomorrow and pick them up. I hope there's nothing serious."

"Probably not," Noah said. "I'll let you know in the morning."

The animal shelter called with a couple of dogs that needed neutering, and since the regular vet who did that was swamped, Noah agreed to take them. The shelter folks arrived fifteen minutes later and dropped off the dogs.

"I don't think we can take in any more animals, no matter what the circumstances are," Noah informed her. "I sure hope no one else comes or calls with an emergency."

The remainder of the morning was busy enough to keep Emily occupied but not crazy like some days had been. Shortly after noon, Emily went to the back and told Noah she was leaving for lunch at Jillian's.

"Want me to bring you something back?" she asked.

"No thanks. I brought my lunch. Give Jillian my best, and tell her we're all praying for her."

"Okay," she said as she backed out of the room. She started to close the door behind her when she decided to address their discussion earlier. "I don't know what I said to upset you, Noah, but whatever it was, I'm sorry."

The instant she said that, a pained expression popped back onto his face. "Don't worry about it."

After Emily left, Noah sank down on the bench in the examining room. He wanted to kick himself for falling in love with Emily. Any normal guy would have learned his lesson by now and known not to trust his own heart.

Tiffany and Emily couldn't have been any more different. Tiffany's gold digging mind-set had been obvious to everyone but Noah. After they parted ways, his heart was bruised but not completely broken. However, when Emily eventually moved, he knew she'd break his heart completely. The very thought of not seeing her sent him into a state of depression.

No matter how hard he tried, he couldn't find anything about her that would make him want to go the other way. It was obvious to other people as well. Pastor Chuck had said something about how love makes a man smile more—and that was when Noah was grinning from ear to ear. Sherry and Mel weren't matchmaking without encouragement from him. In fact, he'd given Mel a hint of how he felt about Emily. Mel had warned him that Emily had some abandonment issues to work through. Even her father's death felt like rejection.

Noah knew that Emily had planned her stay to be temporary—that she was there to figure out what to do with the rest of her life. He liked her right where she was—in his office, helping him build his business in the right kind of way, with a Christian attitude. Even her letter showed a gentle, caring spirit.

He ate his lunch alone. Well, maybe not alone but without human companionship. Chickens, dogs, and cats didn't count.

"What are you looking at?" he asked in the direction of the cage holding one of the eggless chickens. "Haven't you ever seen a man feel sorry for himself before?"

The chicken squawked, and he laughed. He was either losing his mind, or he had it worse than he thought. In Noah's experience, being in love was painful.

Jillian was back to her old self, so lunch was relaxing. They chatted about some of the clinic patients and had a good laugh over the variety of farm animals they saw.

"We have a full house as of this morning," Emily said. "You should see all the critters in that office."

Jillian giggled. "I always get a kick out of the animals that come through the door. Did I ever tell you about the choking snake?"

Emily shuddered. "I love all animals except snakes. They give me the creeps."

"This one was funny. Some guy had gotten a snake and fed him a mouse."

That mental image was disgusting, but Emily didn't want to interrupt her friend. "So what happened?"

"Have you ever watched a snake digest its food?"

Emily shook her head. "No, that's one thing I've never seen."

"You can see the form of the animal as it moves through the snake. The guy was certain his snake was choking because it didn't chew its food well enough."

That made Emily laugh. "I don't know much about snakes, but even I know better than that."

"Noah had to give the guy a talk on the care and feeding of a snake," Jillian said, still laughing. "I think he might have gotten rid of it after realizing he couldn't handle it."

"Do a lot of people bring in snakes?" Emily asked. "That's one creature I'm not fond of."

"No, fortunately that was the only one. I really don't like them much either."

That was a relief. "Right now we have a litter of barn kittens we need to find homes for. Know anyone who might want one?"

"I might," Jillian replied.

"Who?"

"Me. I have to give up Brad and all my old friends who might get me into more trouble. I'm getting lonelier by the minute. You're the only person who bothers with me."

"Don't forget about Noah."

Jillian smiled. "Yes, and Noah. But I might take one of the kittens. Are they cute?"

Emily nodded. "Yes. Very cute. In fact, I'm thinking about taking one, too. Aunt Sherry is anxious to have a house pet, and I think this might make her happy."

"Would that make us related?" Jillian asked. "Sort of?"

"Yes, I think we can claim a family tie there."

"So what else is going on?"

"We've been super busy," Emily said. "I've been working full-time, and when I leave every day, I'm exhausted."

"I'm really sorry." A sad expression fell over Jillian's face. "I messed things up for everyone."

"We believe in you, Jillian." Emily reached for her friend's hands. "The only advice I can give you is to keep your focus on straightening up your life and don't give Brad a chance to ruin anything. You have way too much going for you."

"You really think so?"

Emily nodded. "I know so. If this hadn't happened, I never would have known you had anything but a perfect past. You impressed me from the very beginning."

Jillian's eyes instantly misted. "Thank you so much for telling me that. I've never had anyone who believed in me before."

"We believe in you. Not only that, we need you." Emily paused for emphasis. "I need you."

"You'd think Noah would at least hire one more person to help him in the back," Jillian said. "But I'm glad you're there in the mornings to help out. I always felt so bad about not being able to get there until the afternoon."

Emily thought about that for a moment. If Jillian had felt so bad leaving the reception area of the clinic unattended in the mornings, she should have thought about the impact of letting her boyfriend into the clinic when it was closed. If it hadn't been for the powerful locks and alarm system Noah had on the controlled-drug cabinet, Jillian would have been in a whole lot more trouble than she was now.

Suddenly Jillian broke into a grin as she clapped her hands together. "I finally have my court date!"

"Good." Emily leaned forward and gave Jillian a hug. "How long do you have to wait?"

Jillian shook her head. "For some reason I don't understand, Dwayne managed to get me in next week."

"Wow! That's fast."

"I know. If everything comes out all right—and Dwayne seems to think it will—I might be able to go back to work the week after next. I'll have to be supervised. . . ." She cast her glance downward then looked up with a smile. "But that's probably for the best. My judgment obviously stinks."

"Give yourself some time, Jillian." Emily stood up to go. "I need to get back to the clinic. Call me when you hear any more news."

They hugged again at the door. "See you at church Sunday," Jillian said as Emily walked across the yard to the driveway.

Emily waved back and got into her car. She used the time driving to the clinic to reflect and pray. So much had happened in such a short time that she felt as though her head were spinning.

When she pulled into the parking lot, she saw a couple of cars in front of the clinic, so she hurried inside. Noah stood talking to one of the men by the front desk. He saw her and smiled.

"I'm glad you're back, Emily." His tone was more professional than usual.

She moved around behind the counter and settled into her chair beside Kingston, who appeared to be in the exact same spot where she'd left him. He lifted his head to greet her with one of his throaty sounds but quickly lay back down. "Is there something I can do?"

Noah offered a clipped nod. "Emily, I'd like you to meet Jerry and Gary, brothers who just moved into their parents' house to run the family farm."

Emily extended her hand. "Nice to meet you." She wasn't sure what was expected of her, so she let Noah take the lead.

"Would you set up a farm account for them?"

"Oh, yes of course." She felt stupid, but she'd never done this before.

Noah pointed to a box. "There are some cards in there that they can fill out." He turned to one of the men. "I'll come out to your place on whatever schedule is convenient for you. If there's an emergency, just call my cell phone and I'll be there as quickly as I can. We bill monthly."

The men exchanged a glance then turned to Noah. "Fine," Gary said. "Jerry will be out of town the rest of this week, but he'll be back on Monday. Why don't you come out next week?"

"Sounds good. Just give me a call and let me know what day."

After the men left, Noah answered questions from the lady who'd been waiting. He even told her how much he charged to examine dogs. Once everyone was gone, Noah turned and grinned at Emily, looking proud of himself. "Did I do okay?"

She tilted her head and looked at him in confusion. "What do you mean by that?"

"I mentioned billing and fees. I figured that way they wouldn't be surprised when they got one of your letters."

Emily laughed. "I think most people expect to pay for veterinary services."

Noah did an about-face. "I need to head on back and see about those chickens."

After he left, Emily began to work on getting the mailing list for the new billing letter, when suddenly Kingston scrambled to his feet and started growling. That was weird.

"Kingston, what's wrong?"

He ran over to the supply closet and barked a couple of times before glancing back at Emily as if he wanted something. A low growl vibrated from his throat before he started barking again.

Noah stuck his head out. "What's going on out there?"

"I don't know. He just started this random barking."

Kingston stared at the door, still growling, so Emily got up and opened the supply closet door. That was when she caught a whiff of an awful smell.

As calmly as she could, Emily turned to Noah. "Either we have a gas leak, or someone's trying to burn the place down."

Chapter 10

Quick! We need to get the animals out!" Noah shouted. "Grab the leash and take Kingston first. You can hook him on that tree out back." The urgency in his voice startled Emily into quick action.

The two of them ran back and forth, carrying cages of animals, the smell of the gas growing stronger as the minutes passed. Chickens squawked, the kittens mewed, but Kingston stood guard over them until all of them were under the tree—including Emily and Noah.

"Got your personal belongings?" Noah asked.

Her eyebrows shot up. "My purse is inside."

"I'll go get it." Noah ran back in before she had a chance to tell him not to worry about it.

When he didn't come out after a couple of minutes, Emily panicked. She ran toward the building and opened the front door. The odor of gas was so pungent she had to close it. By now she could smell it outside. Where was Noah?

She took a couple of steps back and deeply inhaled. Then she opened the door again and hollered Noah's name. No answer.

What if something happened to him? What if he fell? Her purse had been behind the reception counter near the front door, so he should have been out by now.

Emily started to bolt back in, but the next thing she knew, Noah was running toward her, handbag slung over one arm and a tiny kitten in the other hand. She ran out of the way, and he bolted out the door right behind her.

"I heard a noise when I went in for your purse," he said as he handed it to her. "I couldn't leave this innocent little creature behind." He rubbed the top of her head with one finger. "She'd somehow gotten out of the box and crawled beneath one of the cabinets. I had a hard time getting her out."

That was one fortunate kitten. "You scared me half to death, Noah."

"Sorry." He walked around the animals and checked to make sure they were okay. Kingston sat there watching every move Noah made.

Emily opened her handbag and pulled out her cell phone to call 911. The dispatcher told her not to go back inside for any reason—not even something valuable—because the building could blow up. She knew that, but hearing it come from an authority figure made her dizzy.

When Emily reached out and touched Noah's arm for comfort, he immediately pulled her into his arms for an embrace. It felt natural to be there.

Emily allowed herself to bask in his warmth for a moment, but then she came to her senses and pulled away.

Noah gave her a puzzled look. "Emily. . ."

As the sound of sirens drew near, Emily turned to Noah. "What do you think happened?"

"Who knows? I guess we'll find out soon enough."

It took more than an hour before the fire department had an answer for them. They had to be cautious as they approached the building. Eventually one of the firefighters came over to where Noah and Emily waited with the animals.

"The line to the water heater in the closet had burst. We had to turn off the gas." He rubbed his neck. "That was some gas leak. Y'all were fortunate the place didn't blow up." He looked around at the animals. "You got all of them out? Man, you took a huge chance with your lives."

"We had to," Emily replied. "We couldn't just leave them in there."

"That was mighty risky. There was so much gas in there, another five minutes and this place would most likely have blown to bits."

⚜

Noah inwardly shuddered as he considered what could have happened. Emily hadn't hesitated to run back into the building—not only for the animals but to look for him. That had to mean something. But then he remembered her reaction when he'd pulled her close. He'd acted on instinct—something he'd have to control in the future.

After the firefighter gave them the go-ahead to carry all the animals back inside, Noah told Emily to sit down and let him do it. "You've done enough already."

She cast a you've-got-to-be-kidding look in his direction. "No way. I'm not letting you do all this by yourself."

An image of Tiffany sitting and watching him move all her furniture into her new apartment while she supervised flitted through his mind.

"I appreciate all this, Emily. You've been amazing."

"Anyone would do this," she shot back. "Now let's get all those chickens back inside." She turned to the Great Dane. "I'll be right back for you, buddy."

It took them longer to get the animals back inside than it had to carry them out. Noah realized they must have been operating on adrenaline.

On the firefighter's advice, he called a plumber to replace the water heater. They promised to be there that afternoon.

Once the animals were all back in their rightful places, Emily looked up at Noah. "Never a dull moment around here, is there?"

He let out a chuckle. "You could say that."

She grinned. "I just did."

Noah felt an emotional tug as Emily positioned herself back behind the reception counter. He went about his business, with her and her bravery on his mind. Despite the danger, he suspected she would do it all over again.

After examining the first chicken, he put her back then picked up the next one. A glimmer of something white caught his eye. He reached his hand into the cage and pulled out an egg.

Holding the chicken in front of his face, he smiled. "So it takes a little excitement to get you to do your job, huh?"

The chicken made a few jerky movements with her head, but she refused to look him in the eye. He put her back in her cage and got the next one. He was happy to learn there was absolutely nothing wrong with any of the chickens.

He went out and told Emily to get Mack on the phone.

"Are the chickens okay?" she asked.

"They're fine. I suspect they're just molting. It's natural, and they generally take a break from laying because they have to put all their energy into feather growth."

Emily laughed as she picked up the phone. "We wouldn't want a naked chicken, would we?"

"No," Noah agreed. "That would be scandalous."

"Hopefully Mack can pick up the chickens before I leave today."

"Yeah, I don't want to have to worry about them after the scare we had."

"Me either."

The rest of the day was fairly routine, which was just fine with Noah. He didn't need any more excitement for a while. The plumber installed a new water heater and attached a gizmo that would detect a gas leak and sound an alarm.

On Sunday morning, Aunt Sherry beamed at Emily from her normal spot by the stove. "We've been blessed with the task of picking up Jillian for church."

Emily grinned back. She loved how her aunt saw everything as a blessing. "It'll be fun."

"I have to admit, when Dwayne first called and identified himself, I was worried something else had happened."

"That's understandable, considering how much crazy news we've had lately."

Aunt Sherry laughed as she turned back to the stove to tend to the eggs. "I'm just glad Kingston was at the clinic to sniff out the gas before it was too late."

At the sound of his name, Kingston rounded the corner and came to a sliding halt at the entrance of the kitchen. He tilted his head, as if to ask if someone had called for him. Both women laughed.

"Good boy," Aunt Sherry said as she reached into a container and pulled out a jerky treat. He looked at Emily, who nodded, and then he didn't waste another minute before getting his treat. "I've heard that a dog's sense of smell is hundreds of times greater than a human's."

"I'm sure we would have smelled it eventually," Emily said. "It was pretty strong once we opened the closet door. I'm just glad Kingston caught it soon enough for us to get all the animals out."

"That's good. You just never know about things like that. I'm thankful it turned out okay."

They ate breakfast and left for church as soon as Mel was ready. "Do you know where this girl lives?" he asked.

Emily gave him directions. Jillian was waiting by the door, so she ran out to the car as soon as they got there.

"You look nice, Jillian," Aunt Sherry said. "I love your dress."

A look of panic shot across Jillian's face as she glanced around at everyone else. "Did I overdress?"

"No," Aunt Sherry said. "Most of the time I dress up, but I figured I'd wear slacks today. You'll see people in everything from frilly frocks to jeans."

Frilly frocks. Now that's funny.

When Jillian looked at her with a half smile, it took everything Emily had not to crack up. Uncle Mel caught her gaze in the rearview mirror, and she could see the smile playing in his eyes, too.

Noah stood at the church entrance waiting, so when they walked up, he shook Uncle Mel's hand and gave the rest of them a hug. Since Emily was last, he kept his hand on her shoulder as they went inside. Emily felt like part of a couple—which she enjoyed much more than she should have, considering Noah was her boss.

It felt natural to be with him, yet she tingled at his touch. She never wanted him to remove his hand, but once Uncle Mel found a pew with enough room for all of them, he let go and gestured for her to move ahead of him.

Since Jillian hadn't been to church much, Emily helped familiarize her with the order of service. She showed her the hymnals they'd use and pointed to the large overhead screen at the front of the church. "That's for the words of the more contemporary songs," she explained. "I don't know all of them, so I usually listen to the first verse. Then I join in after I know the tune."

Jillian nodded. "That makes sense."

Emily could see Jillian's hands shaking, so she reached over and gave her a squeeze. Hopefully Jillian would agree to return—that is, if she didn't get into more trouble.

When Emily turned back, she saw that someone had joined them on the other side of Noah. "Oh hi, Dwayne."

He grinned and lifted his hand in a wave. Then when he leaned forward and made eye contact with Jillian, she saw Dwayne's compassion and that instantly made her heart melt.

After the service, Noah asked if she and Jillian would like to join him and Dwayne for a walk around Pullman Square.

She turned to Aunt Sherry, who waved her hand. "Y'all go and have a good time. If you get hungry, there's always plenty of food at our place."

Noah chuckled. "I just finished the leftovers you brought from last week."

"You can come by and pick up some more for next week," Mel said with a snort. "Sherry cooks up a storm on Sundays. She doesn't know when to stop."

"Why, Mel, this is the first time I've ever heard you complain!"

He winked at his wife. "Oh, I'm not complaining. I'm just sayin'. . . ."

Emily gave her aunt and uncle a hug before returning to her friends. Noah used his eyes and a tilt of his head to turn her attention to Dwayne and Jillian, who were chatting. Emily suspected Dwayne was giving his testimony and she relaxed. Jillian was in good hands with these wonderful people.

"Do you think there's something going on between them?" Emily whispered.

Noah slowly smiled and shrugged. "Not overtly, but maybe on a subconscious level. Wouldn't that be an interesting twist?" A more pensive look covered his face. "He needs to be careful. We've gotten close, and he admitted that he's attracted to vulnerable women. Maybe it's his protective instincts."

"Yes," Emily agreed, "he does need to be very careful." Emily grinned back. "You can't find a finer man than Dwayne. He's a deputy for all the right reasons. He wants to help this community."

They walked around Pullman Square then left to have lunch at a diner not far away. The entire time, Jillian and Dwayne chatted nonstop. Emily overheard Dwayne witnessing to Jillian.

"Wanna go for a little walk?" Noah asked.

"Sure."

After letting Dwayne and Jillian know that they were heading off on their own and assuring Dwayne they wouldn't be long, Noah took Emily's hand and led her down a different path. She pointed out some flowers and trees that she'd love to paint.

"You ought to come up here sometime and set up your easel," Noah said.

"I'd like to do that." When she turned to face Noah, she saw his features softening. "What are you thinking about?"

"Really wanna know?" His bottom lip twitched.

"Yeah."

He took her hands in his, forcing her to turn to face him. "I really like you, Emily."

"I like you, too, Noah."

"I mean I *really* like you. I think we're good together."

Emily swallowed hard. She didn't know what to do, so she blinked a couple of times then pointed in the direction they'd come from. "I think we need to head on back."

"I guess I know how you feel now."

"Noah, I have strong feelings for you, too, but I'm still going back and forth on what to do with my life. It wouldn't be fair to you if we allowed our feelings to develop into more than what they are."

He snickered. "I guess you're right. Let's get on back. They're probably wondering where we are anyway."

By the time they got back to Dwayne's car, Emily's heart had slowed to a more normal pace. Dwayne gave them an odd look then chuckled and shook his head.

"Any idea when you'll be able to come back to work?" Noah asked Jillian.

"Are you sure you want me back?"

Noah didn't hesitate to nod. "Absolutely, yes. You made a mistake that will affect you for a long time, but I don't think you intended to hurt me. Hopefully you learned to stay away from bad dudes."

"You got that right."

Noah couldn't help but notice Dwayne's protective gaze toward Jillian. "So back to my question. Any idea when?"

She glanced at Dwayne before shaking her head. "Not sure yet. If everything goes like I hope, I'll be able to finish out the semester at school and go back to work soon."

Emily figured it was time for her to say something. "I'll be able to fill in until you can return."

"I appreciate that," Jillian said. "How much longer do you think you'll be around?"

All eyes were now on Emily, forcing her to answer a question that had been playing in her mind since she arrived. "That's a tough one to call," she said slowly. "I still don't know what the Lord wants me to do."

Noah's eyes narrowed and an odd expression crossed his face. Was it a look of concern, or was it disapproval? She suddenly felt self-conscious.

Dwayne held up his hands. "We'll pray about it then," he said. "I've seen Him answer my prayers in ways that I never would have imagined." He looked down at Jillian, who nodded.

There was no doubt in Emily's mind that Dwayne wanted to do everything in his power to help Jillian. However, it was hard to tell what was going on with Jillian, other than the fact that she'd royally messed up her life and needed to spend every waking moment getting it back in order. At least she'd agreed to go to church.

As they settled into Dwayne's car and buckled their seat belts, Emily thought about how everyone's lives seemed to be in a state of turmoil. She'd once thought she was the only person who didn't have her act together, but as she looked around the car, she realized she'd been mistaken.

Jillian's chaos was obvious. She was still in school but not even certain about whether or not she could continue with the semester. Her former boyfriend was a drug dealer, and he didn't mind using her to get what he wanted. And now the attraction between her and Dwayne cast a whole new light on her life.

Dwayne had been a sheriff's deputy for four years, and today Emily had learned that he aspired to move up to a detective position with the child services department. He wanted to save kids from suffering as he had in foster care.

Even Noah had issues that she suspected had something to do with his former fiancée. Maybe one of these days she'd get him to open up.

"Do y'all mind if I take Jillian home first?" Dwayne asked, jolting her from her thoughts. "I managed to get permission for her to go to church and out to lunch afterward. I don't want to push things." He glanced at his watch. "We're close to her curfew."

"No, of course we don't mind," Noah replied. He looked at Emily.

Emily shook her head. "I don't mind."

Jillian turned around toward Emily and Noah. "I had the best time today. After hanging out with Brad, I almost forgot what it was like to be a normal person."

"How did you and Brad meet?" Emily asked. "I can't imagine someone like you getting involved with someone like him."

"He came by one day with a friend who needed to discuss something with my mom. Mom and that other guy left for a while, so Brad and I started talking. I thought he was pretty nice, and to be honest, I was a little attracted to his bad-boy image." Jillian paused for a moment.

Emily nodded. She'd known other girls who liked guys who lived on the edge.

"Anyway, one thing led to another, and the next thing you know, he and I were hanging out every weekend."

"Did you have any idea he sold drugs?" Emily asked.

"No, but I did know he used them." She licked her lips and grimaced. "That's the main reason I broke up with him. It created a big mess."

Noah cleared his throat and gave her a firm look. "I hope you stay broken up with him this time."

Jillian offered a half smile. "Trust me, I will. I don't need someone like Brad in my life. If he ever gets out of jail, I'll be more prepared for something like this. He caught me off guard."

Dwayne turned to her and nodded. "There are plenty of nice guys to pick from."

After they made the last turn onto Jillian's road, she gasped as she reached out and grabbed Dwayne's arm. "Don't stop."

"Huh?"

She pointed to the car parked in front of her house. "That's Brad's car."

Chapter 11

Emily's throat constricted as she glanced at Noah then Dwayne. He tightened his jaw. "We can't run from him."

Noah leaned forward. "But I thought he was still in jail."

"Someone probably posted bond." Dwayne's shoulders sagged as he slowed down. "We didn't think anyone would."

Jillian shook her head. "He has some friends with money. I'm just surprised any of them came through for him."

"Are you afraid?" Dwayne asked as he glanced over toward Jillian.

She hesitated then nodded. "A little."

Dwayne pulled up in front of her house. "I'll go up with you and make sure everything's okay."

"Want me to come with you?" Noah asked.

"Nah, I don't think that would be such a good idea." Dwayne patted his pocket. "I have my cell phone right here. If I don't come out in five minutes, call me."

As soon as she and Noah were alone, Emily let out the breath she'd been holding. "This is too weird."

"Yes, I know. I feel sorry for Jillian." Noah leaned over and looked at her house. "She's a nice girl who stumbled over the wrong guy. I've seen it happen before."

"Yeah, me, too," Emily whispered. She looked down at her watch. "How long has it been now?"

Noah smiled and patted her arm. "About two minutes."

Emily turned and looked directly into Noah's eyes. Something strange but wonderful flashed between them, and her stomach felt like it was on a free fall. His tenderness and concern stirred the chemistry between them. She cleared her throat.

"Waiting is never fun, is it?" Noah asked.

Emily swallowed hard as she thought how she'd waited for her mother, who never returned. Based on her experience, waiting was always miserable.

"Emily?" He gently touched her face.

She turned to face him. "No, waiting isn't fun. Not when we're worried about someone we like." She straightened her shoulders then paused before adding, "Want to call Dwayne, or do you want me to?"

Noah took her hand in his and squeezed it. "Let's say a prayer, and then I'll make the call."

As they bowed their heads in prayer, Emily felt a warm tenderness as it surged through her. Noah consistently ignited something in her that she'd never before experienced. There was no doubt in her mind that he genuinely cared for her. But he cared about Jillian, too, so maybe he saw her as nothing more than another friend in need.

Noah finished his prayer for guidance and safety. As they said "Amen," Emily slowly lifted her head and opened her eyes, only to catch him staring at her.

"You okay?" he asked, a new softness in his voice. "I don't want you to be afraid."

As long as Noah was by her side, she didn't feel an ounce of fear. She smiled back. "I'm fine."

Noah punched in Dwayne's number and held the phone to his ear. After several rings and no answer, he frowned. "This isn't good."

"You don't think. . . ?" Emily's voice trailed off as she tried to block out the possibility of something bad happening.

"I don't know," he replied. "Let me try once more before I do anything."

He called Dwayne's number again. After a few seconds his face lit up and he winked before talking. "Hey, man, I was worried about you when you didn't answer."

Emily watched Noah's face as he listened to Dwayne. As his smile faded to concern, her heart sank. Noah clicked his phone shut and pursed his lips.

"What happened?"

Noah lowered his head then turned and looked at her. "Dwayne says he's not leaving until Brad leaves."

"Why doesn't he just tell Brad to get out?"

"Apparently Jillian's mother is in there complicating matters." His forehead crinkled. "He acted like he couldn't talk."

"Should we do something?" Emily asked. "I mean, we can't just sit here."

Noah chewed on his bottom lip for a moment before nodding. "I'm not sure yet."

"Want me to. . ." The sight of Jillian's front door opening caught her attention.

Noah turned, and they both saw a strange man coming out of the house, with Dwayne close behind. As they got closer, Emily noticed the flash of handcuffs on the man's wrists.

"Uh-oh." Emily turned to Noah. "Looks like we have a situation."

"You stay here while I go find out what's going on." Noah looked at her with his head tilted forward. "I don't want to take a chance on anything happening to you."

Her heart pounded as she pulled her lips between her teeth and nodded. "I'll be right here."

Emily forced herself to remain calm as she watched Noah get out of the car and walk toward Dwayne, who still hadn't let go of the man she assumed was Brad. The situation seemed dangerous, and Noah had no idea what he was getting into. Jillian hadn't shown her face, which seemed odd to Emily.

She watched as Noah and Dwayne discussed something that caused Brad to scowl. All her attention focused on the one hand Dwayne had on Brad, whose arms were hidden behind his back.

Finally, after what seemed like forever, Noah issued a clipped nod then headed back to the car. "Looks like Brad's going back to jail. Dwayne said he'll be able to take us home as soon as his backup arrives."

Emily felt a surge of relief as the squad car arrived, lights flashing but silent. A couple of police officers hopped out, relieving Dwayne so he could go back to his car.

As soon as he got in and closed the car door, Dwayne shook his head. "That guy is bad news. Everything would have been okay if he'd stayed away, but he's a time bomb."

"What happened?" Emily asked. "Can you talk about it?"

"He threatened Jillian and her mother in front of me. That's all I can say right now. We have some people on their way here to see about Jillian and her mother."

Emily turned to Noah and shook her head before refocusing her attention on Dwayne. "Is Jillian okay?"

"A little shaken," Dwayne replied, "but otherwise okay. I told her I'd call later and maybe stop by if she didn't mind." He cleared his throat before adding, "Just to make sure she's not scared."

"I'm just glad no one was hurt," Noah said.

Dwayne snickered. "You and me both."

Noah changed the subject and chatted about the message during church. Emily could tell he did that on purpose to relieve Dwayne of the stress from the confrontation.

After they dropped Emily off at Mel and Sherry's place, Noah turned to Dwayne. "So what really happened in there?"

Dwayne flinched. "Do you really wanna know?"

"Yes, of course."

"He had a knife at Jillian's mother's throat."

Noah shuddered. "I figured it was worse than you let on. Thanks for not giving the details in front of Emily. She's worried about Jillian enough as it is."

Dwayne shook his head. "I don't know what Jillian ever saw in that guy. She's cute and smart. He's dark and dangerous."

"I understand he's an actor, too. Jillian said she had no idea how bad of a guy he was until after she was involved."

"Yeah," Dwayne agreed. "Guys like that are con artists. That's how they get what they want, but it eventually catches up with them."

"Do you think Jillian will be safe coming back to work at the clinic?" Noah asked.

"She will be as long as Brad stays in jail."

"I don't want to do anything that'll endanger her life." Noah folded his arms as he thought for a moment. "I'll ask Emily if she can stay on full-time until we know what's going on with Brad."

As they approached the stop sign, Dwayne turned to Noah and grinned. "I have a feeling she won't mind staying as long as you want her."

Noah felt a rush of joy, but he quickly squelched it. "She's a nice woman, but I don't want her to think I'm taking advantage of her."

"Any idea what she plans to do?" Dwayne asked. "Mel said she's having a hard time finding herself."

"She doesn't say much about it. All I know is what she told me—that she's trying to figure out what to do with her life."

"It's tough." Dwayne paused for a few seconds. "I've known all my life I wanted to be a cop." He cast a quick glance Noah's way. "How about you?"

"I've always wanted to take care of animals. I went through a short period when I thought I might want to be a rancher, but it's tough to make a living at that on a small scale these days."

"Tell me about it," Dwayne groused. "My folks have been trying to sell their ranch for a fraction of what it was worth ten years ago. So far the only possibility is the man who owns the land next to them. Dad doesn't want to sell to him because the guy hasn't always been honest, but he might not have a choice."

"All we can do is pray about it and leave it in the Lord's hands."

"Amen to that, brother."

After Noah got home, he thought about a plan to discuss with Emily. Having her full-time worked out well for him, but she couldn't go on indefinitely. He needed to find out when Jillian might be able to return and have a backup plan in case she couldn't.

He was the first to arrive at the clinic early the next morning. Emily walked in a half hour later, Kingston at her heels.

"Kingston." Noah patted the dog on the head and got a slurp on the arm in return. Then he turned to Emily. "Hey there."

"Good morning," she said. "How's Jillian?"

"I don't know yet. I figured I'd call later on if we don't hear something soon."

"Did Dwayne have any idea when she'd be safe from Brad?"

Noah leaned against the counter. "They're trying to push up his court date. If he's convicted, he'll go to prison for a while, since this isn't his first offense. Then Jillian can breathe easy—at least until he gets out."

"He won't stay out long, I'm sure," Emily said. "Unless he has a major life conversion, I can't see someone like that changing."

"As hard as it is, we need to pray for him."

"Any appointments this morning?" Emily asked.

"Not until ten. But there's something I'd like to discuss with you."

Emily's heart pounded as she met Noah's expectant gaze. She licked her lips and forced a smile. "Sure. Discuss away."

"I know you've been trying to figure out what you want to do, so I hate to ask you this favor. Since Jillian obviously can't come back until she's safe from Brad, would you consider staying on full-time—at least for a little while longer?"

She slowly nodded. "I can do that. After all, they're trying to schedule the court date soon, so it shouldn't be too long."

Noah frowned but quickly recovered. "Yeah, it shouldn't be too long." He straightened up and stepped away from the counter before he stopped and steadied his gaze on her. "Any idea yet what you might do after you leave here?"

"I'd like to do something with my degree, but most of the jobs I've applied for want a master's, and I only have my bachelor's."

"Why don't you go back to school?"

Emily made a face. "To be honest, I'm sick of school. I worked hard to finish so I could get a good job, but with the economy like it is, that isn't enough anymore."

"Did you know what you wanted to do when you first started college?" he asked. "When you told me you majored in art history, I wasn't sure what kind of job you could get with that."

She closed her eyes then opened them as she offered a dreamy grin. "I thought it would be fun to work as a curator at an art museum in New York or Chicago."

"So you want to move to the big city, huh?"

Once upon a time that was exactly what she wanted, but she wasn't so sure anymore. "I really don't know what I want." She held up her hands and shrugged. "And without my master's, well. . ." Her voice trailed off.

"We have some decent colleges around here," Noah said. "If you decide to go for your master's, I'm sure Mel and Sherry would love for you to stay with them." He paused before adding, "And as long as you're in town, I'll always have a job for you."

That actually sounded good, but if she went back to school, it would have to be one with a better-known art program. Then there was the fact that Emily loved working with Noah, in spite of the fact that she wasn't using her education.

"I'll think about it. Thank you."

Noah flashed a full smile her way. "I mean it. Just let me know. Hopefully Jillian will be back soon, so you can go back to being part-time and not have to spend your whole day here."

Emily felt a flash of annoyance with herself for thinking it wouldn't be so bad to spend entire days at the clinic. After all, she didn't need her degree for that.

"Let me know if you change your mind," he said softly. "I'm never sure what you're thinking—or if you're just doing things because you're trying to be nice."

"What's wrong with trying to be nice?" The instant the words came out, she realized she'd snapped. "Sorry."

He held her gaze for several seconds before blinking. "I'm the one who should apologize."

As soon as Noah left her and Kingston alone, Emily got right to work on pulling up the files of people who owed Noah's Ark money. Starting with the highest dollar amount first, she generated a billing plan that would enable people to at least knock out some of what they owed.

After she had a large stack of envelopes ready to take to the post office, she boxed them up and stuck them in a corner so Noah could take a look at them. The next few hours flew by.

As soon as the last morning appointment left, Emily ducked into the room where she knew Noah would be cleaning. "Got a minute?"

He glanced up and nodded. "Sure. Be right there."

Emily paused and watched his strong shoulders as he wiped down the surfaces with care. Noah was good at what he did, and his clients were fortunate to have him. She hated that some of them might be taking advantage of his generosity.

After he looked at her and grinned, she smiled back and headed back to her desk. A few minutes later he joined her. "What's up?"

She pulled the envelopes toward her. "I'd like to send out the bills this afternoon, but I wanted you to glance at them first."

Noah's jaw pulsed as he stared at the stack. Even after agreeing to do it, she knew it grated on him to pursue collection on the accounts.

"This is just a subtle prompt to jog their memory about the money they owe you," she reminded him, "and I offered a payment plan so it shouldn't be too hard for any of them, and. . ." She caught herself rambling. "Here," she said as she lifted the top envelope and handed it to him. "See for yourself."

He opened it and pulled out the paper. As his gaze raked over the paper, Emily held her breath, hoping he'd give her the go-ahead to mail it.

"You didn't change anything, right?" he asked.

She nodded. "The smaller amounts are on a six-month plan. The higher amounts are broken down into one-year and two-year payback plans. And the first due date gives folks a few weeks to work it into their monthly budget."

After a short pause, he finally agreed. "I hate strong-arming people, but you're right—they do owe me for services. I should have done this sooner."

"It's not like you're threatening them or anything," she added.

Finally he chuckled. "Yeah, let's send them out and see what happens. If anyone can't pay, I'm sure we'll either hear from them or they'll just stop calling."

"I don't think that'll happen," Emily said. "If they have animals, they obviously need a vet."

"You're right." Noah stood and continued staring at her, making her feel very uncomfortable.

She reached up and tucked her hair behind her ear. "I'll mail these during lunch."

"I appreciate it, Emily." He pulled his lips between his teeth then opened his mouth to say something else when the phone rang.

With a smile, she lifted the receiver. "Good morning. Noah's Ark. May I help you?"

Noah waved good-bye then headed for the door. He'd switched his schedule for the day to meet the needs of his clients, which was why he needed someone at the clinic all the time. Emily felt an internal tug, watching him leave.

⚜

Given everything he had to work with, Noah was doing the best he could to keep his feelings for Emily in check. For the past several years he'd watched friends he'd grown up with fall in love, one by one, until he was the last bachelor left. He didn't understand what they meant when they said they couldn't imagine life without the women they chose to spend the rest of their lives with—until now. Even with Tiffany he hadn't felt that all-consuming need.

Emily was special. She cared about everyone she was around—him, Jillian, the animals, her aunt and uncle. It was almost like she thought she was solely responsible for their happiness.

On his way out to the first farm visit, he decided to stop by and see Dwayne at the sheriff's department. He needed to find out if Brad's court date had been set yet.

As Noah pulled into the parking lot, he noticed the tiny red Subaru. He found a spot then walked past the car he thought might be Jillian's and looked in. Yep, those were her textbooks. It was hers. What was she doing at the sheriff's department?

Chapter 12

Noah spotted Dwayne the second he walked into the lobby of the station. Jillian stood in front of Dwayne with her back to the door.

"What are you doing here?" Noah asked. "I thought you weren't allowed to go anywhere without permission."

Jillian tilted her head and gave him a you're-kidding look. "I obviously have permission to be here."

Noah snickered. "Good point. Any word yet?"

Jillian turned around and smiled. "They're still working on the court date."

"It won't be long though." Dwayne glanced at Jillian then quickly looked up at Noah.

"I'll sure be glad when everything's back to normal," Noah said. "Emily agreed to work full-time until Brad's behind bars for good and Jillian can return."

Jillian offered a sympathetic grin. "I'm really sorry, Noah. It's all my fault."

Dwayne narrowed his eyes. "Guys like Brad are con artists. They prey on nice people—especially nice, vulnerable girls. You had no way of knowing that."

Noah found it charming that Dwayne was defensive toward Jillian. Under different circumstances, he could see the two of them in a more romantic relationship. It could still happen, but Jillian needed to work through some serious issues first.

"Tell Emily I'll call her later," Jillian said before she turned back to Dwayne. "I have to run to class now. They're letting me sit in on a later class to catch up."

After Jillian left, Noah turned back to Dwayne. "She's a sweet girl."

"Yeah." Dwayne stared at the door, as though her image were still there.

"Too bad you met her at such a difficult time."

He slowly turned to Noah and nodded. "Yeah, I thought that, too. But I have time. I'm still in my twenties." Dwayne paused for a moment. "So, what brings you here?"

"I just wanted to see when I could get Jillian back. As long as there's a chance Brad will get out, I can't let her have the key to the clinic."

"Yeah, the temptation for Brad to come after her is too great as long as he thinks she can open the door to the narcotics," Dwayne agreed.

Noah took a step toward the door then stopped. "After this thing is all behind us and Brad's safely locked away in the penitentiary, the four of us need to celebrate."

"So I was right," Dwayne said, a smug look on his face as he crossed his arms.

"Right about what?"

"You and Emily." He grinned. "You like her a lot, don't you?"

"Emily and I are friends, if that's what you're saying." Noah couldn't look Dwayne in the eye, but he didn't want to create a problem for Emily. Besides, what was the point in starting a rumor about even a hint of a relationship between him and Emily when she was likely to leave after she figured out where she wanted to go?

"Right." Dwayne snickered.

Noah lifted his hands. "Okay, so I think she's cute."

Dwayne lifted an eyebrow and pursed his lips. "And?"

"Well..." Noah pondered what else to say. "She's smart and fun."

"That's what I thought. You can't deny it," Dwayne said, a wide grin spread across his face. "You're smitten."

"Smitten." Noah shook his head. "Now that's a word I haven't heard in a while." He snickered. "Well, okay, so what if I am?"

"At least you're finally admitting it."

"Yeah." Noah shoved his hands in his pockets and looked around before settling his look on Dwayne. "It must've been rough seeing Jillian behind bars. I can't picture it."

Dwayne shook his head. "You don't know the half of it. I stood on one side of the bars with her on the other, and I didn't know what to say. She looked so fragile and helpless, and there wasn't a thing I could do about it." He chewed his bottom lip as the lines in his forehead deepened. "I've seen a lot of people in jail, but this one really got me."

Noah felt terrible for Jillian. She didn't deserve many of the things she'd experienced in life. He had no doubt that the Lord had crossed their paths for a reason, and he didn't want to miss an opportunity to be a gentle, loving witness. Obviously Dwayne felt the same way.

"At least she knows she has us on her side."

Dwayne tightened his lips across his teeth, showing his continued frustration. "We talked a few times, and she was very open about her past. Her problems started early. She's been through a lot, and her mother was never a good one to give her direction."

"Not everyone has good parents. Thankfully Jesus has given us grace and the opportunity to change things through faith."

"You're so right." Dwayne hooked his thumbs through the belt loops of his uniform. "Jillian seemed to like church."

Noah smiled and nodded. "I think so."

"Like you said, the four of us will have to get together." Dwayne looked at Noah with expectation.

"Sounds good." Noah had run out of things to say, and he suddenly felt awkward. "Emily and Jillian get along great, so we might even hang out for a whole day."

"After this thing with Brad is settled," Dwayne reminded him.

"That goes without saying." Noah took a step toward the door. "I have a few farm calls to make, and then I want to get back to the clinic."

"At least you get to see Emily every day."

"True," Noah agreed, "but I'm not sure she's all that happy about it."

"She might not realize it, but I think she's very happy to see you. I can see it on her face."

On that note, Noah chuckled and waved good-bye to his buddy. He was glad to have a Christian friend he could talk to.

After she dropped off the bills at the post office, Emily stopped at a deli and grabbed a sandwich to take back to work with her. She couldn't take Kingston inside, and she wasn't about to leave him in the car.

Between the constantly ringing phone and the paperwork that needed filing, Emily stayed busy, and the afternoon flew. When Noah returned, she glanced up at the clock. It was almost closing time already.

She handed him his messages then turned back to her computer. He didn't move away from the counter, so she glanced up at him, only to catch him staring back at her. Suddenly he seemed flustered.

"Did you need something?" she asked.

"Um. . .oh, no, I just. . ." He chewed his bottom lip as he flipped through the messages. "If you're done for the day, why don't you go on home? I don't have any more appointments today."

"Are you sure?"

He nodded. "Positive. In fact, I think I might leave in a few minutes. I'm pretty booked tomorrow."

"Okay," she said as she slowly reached for her handbag beneath the counter. "I got the bills in the mail today."

Noah smiled through a groan. "Maybe you should plan to stay late for a few days—that is, if you don't have to be somewhere."

"I don't think it'll be too bad," she said.

"I should have been firm about it from the beginning. I guess I was so busy with my clients' needs that I neglected my business."

"It'll be fine," Emily assured him. "If they balk, I'll do what I can to work it out." She glanced down then looked back up at him, feeling a little bit embarrassed. "Of course, that's only if you trust me enough to let me handle it. I didn't mean to be presumptuous."

"I do trust you, Emily." His look said more, but she couldn't hold his gaze too long without feeling an uncomfortable flutter inside.

"C'mon, Kingston," she said as she leaned over toward the dog. "Ready to go home?"

His ears perked up as he scrambled to his feet. Kingston's legs were long, and they seemed to tangle every time he lay down. The dog was so comical she had to smile.

"How's he been?" Noah asked. "Giving you any trouble?"

"No, not at all." Emily tucked her hair behind her ear with one hand and snapped the leash on Kinston's collar with the other. "In fact, I'll be sad when Mr. Zimmerman comes back and takes him away."

"I feel like you're safe as long as he's with you," Noah said.

"Yeah, me, too."

She felt Noah's gaze as she and Kingston walked toward the door. After one last good-bye wave, she guided the dog toward her car and got in. All the way to the farm, she alternated between praying and talking to Kingston, who listened with rapt attention.

The next morning, Emily and Kingston arrived at the clinic a half hour early. She wanted to get all her daily work done before the bills she'd sent arrived at Noah's clients' houses.

By midafternoon the calls had begun to trickle in, but none of them were bad. So far, all they wanted to know was if they could still continue using Noah's services before they'd paid in full. Emily assured them that they could, and she reminded them to read the entire message at the top of their bill. "We just wanted to make sure we were in agreement on your outstanding balance," she said.

Occasionally she caught Noah standing nearby, listening as she spoke to clients. After she hung up, he always gave her a thumbs-up and a heart-warming grin.

The next several weeks were busy for both Noah and Emily. The floodwaters had continued to recede, and he spent quite a bit of his time helping the farmers clean up the mess then moving their animals back. Soon Emily was up to her elbows in accounts receivable payments. Her hunch had proven to be correct—people didn't mind paying their bills; they just weren't sure what they owed, and they needed a nudge.

❦

As Noah's account grew, he saw what a valuable asset Emily was to his business. Back home, his father had always talked about how important the right front office help could be. Now he understood that. He'd never expected Jillian to do more than schedule appointments and greet clients when they came in for their appointments—and she was very good at that. However, Emily gave his office a more professional atmosphere, without making it seem stuffy. She was the perfect balance for his office.

"Noah."

He glanced up at the sound of his name. "Everything okay?"

Emily tilted her head and slowly moved it side to side. "Mrs. Anderson's cat fell out of a tree, and she thinks something's wrong with her."

"Bring her on back."

"I would, but we can't catch her."

Noah frowned. "Didn't she bring her in a cat carrier?"

"No, she had her in a box. As soon as she put the box on the floor, Muffin hopped out and ran."

"Let me see if I can catch her," Noah said as he put down the manual he'd been reading. "I've told Mrs. Anderson she really needs to invest in a carrier for Muffin. Poor kitty is scared half to death every time she comes here."

"Can you blame her?" Emily asked. "The only time Muffin ever goes out, she comes here and gets a shot. I'd be scared, too."

"Good point."

Emily led the way back out to the reception room. As soon as Emily opened the door, she spotted Mrs. Anderson leaning over the reception counter, looking panic-stricken.

"Th–that beast is going to eat my little Muffin." She pointed. "Get her away from him."

When Emily rounded the corner and saw Kingston cuddling with the tiny cat, she smiled. "He won't hurt her, Mrs. Anderson. I think he's protecting her."

Noah came up from behind. "Great Danes are known as gentle giants," he explained. "They get along with other species quite well."

"B–but he's so big." Mrs. Anderson's eyes were still wide, and her face was drained of color. "He could hurt her."

"Kingston wouldn't want to hurt her." Noah bent over and picked up the cat then lifted her to his face so he could look her in the eye. "Did you make a new friend, Muffin?" He glanced up at Mrs. Anderson. "She seems fine, but I'll check her out anyway."

The cat's meow elicited a worried look from her owner. "I can't believe you let such a big dog run loose in here like that."

Emily smiled as she gently took Mrs. Anderson by the arm and led her around the counter over to Kingston. "Look at that sweet face. He's a very friendly dog. Would you like to pet him?"

The older woman pondered that and frowned. "What if he doesn't like me?"

As if on cue, Kingston stood up and licked Mrs. Anderson's hand. She pulled back and giggled.

"See? He's very nice."

Mrs. Anderson carefully extended her hand for another lick, and she giggled again. Then she ran her hand over his head. "He does seem to be a friendly dog."

"He's very protective," Noah explained. "Dogs can sense fear in other animals, and since Muffin was afraid when she came in here, he wanted to look after her."

Mrs. Anderson's eyes glistened as she looked at Emily. "That's so sweet."

Emily felt ready to burst with pride, even though Kingston wasn't officially her dog. He was the sweetest animal she'd ever been around.

"Ready to go in for your checkup, Muffin?" Noah asked. He turned to her owner. "Would you like to come back with us?"

Mrs. Anderson looked over at Kingston and pointed. "Can he come with us?"

Emily turned to Noah, who nodded. "Sure, if that would make you feel better."

"I think it'll make Muffin feel better," Mrs. Anderson replied. As Noah, Muffin, Mrs. Anderson, and Kingston went back to the examining room, Emily heard the woman chattering, "Do you think I should get a dog for Muffin? How much do they eat? Where can I find a dog like this one?"

Emily smiled as she tried to imagine Mrs. Anderson having a dog the size of Kingston. Surely Noah would talk her out of it.

Fifteen minutes later the door opened and out walked Kingston, followed by Muffin. Emily could tell that Kingston was annoyed by the look on his face, but he didn't growl or snap. Instead, he headed straight for his bed behind the reception counter. Muffin plopped her little self down beside him. Kingston gave her a lick across the face, which got her motor purring. Within seconds Muffin's eyes closed and Kingston rested his chin on his front paw.

Mrs. Anderson still hadn't come out, and this concerned Emily. She waited a few minutes before she finally got up and went toward the examining room, where she heard Noah's voice. So she hunkered behind the wall and listened.

"I really don't think you need a dog the size of Kingston," Noah said. "In fact, getting a dog isn't the answer."

"But I've never seen her so happy," Mrs. Anderson argued.

"How much time do you spend with her?"

"As much as I can, but I still have things to do. Last time I came home from my bowling league, she'd shredded the curtains in the guest room."

"We can clip her nails," Noah said.

"I really want to get her a dog—"

Suddenly a sharp crashing sound jolted Emily from her perch behind the wall. She took off running toward the reception area to see what it was.

Chapter 13

"Uh-oh."

Emily stood at the door and surveyed the scene before her. Muffin was sprawled in the middle of a pile of dirt on the floor, with shards of a ceramic pot that had hung from the ceiling scattered around, green leaves peeking out from beneath her. Kingston stood about five feet away, looking back and forth between Muffin and Emily, as though wondering what to do next.

"What happened?" Mrs. Anderson's voice was shrill with panic. "What did that beast do to my little Muffin?"

Noah came up right behind them. "Looks like Muffin decided to go for a ride on my plant." He squatted down beside the cat and stroked her fur. "She seems to be okay."

"My sweet little Muffin." Mrs. Anderson pointed at Kingston. "I'm sure it's his fault."

With a crooked grin, Noah stood up and planted his hands on his hips. "Still want to get her a dog?"

Muffin finally stood and shook the dirt off her fur, her ears cocked back in annoyance. Mrs. Anderson stepped back. "She's so dirty. Do something."

Emily spoke up. "I can give her a quick bath before you leave."

"She hates baths," Mrs. Anderson said.

"We have the right equipment." Noah lifted Muffin and handed her to Emily, who took her to the examining room with the deep sink. "It won't take her long," he added. "She's fast."

Fifteen minutes later, Mrs. Anderson and a much cleaner Muffin were out the door. The remains of the pot, plant, and dirt had been swept up and disposed of. Emily was glad Noah kept extra T-shirts in the supply closet because after Muffin's bath, she was a muddy mess.

Noah laughed. "I'm sort of glad that happened. I was concerned about her getting Muffin a dog, since she can barely care for the cat. I don't think we have to worry about that now."

Emily looked at Noah and felt her heart flutter. "There's definitely a silver lining to this."

His smile faded as he gazed at her. "I don't know what I would have done without you, Emily."

She opened her mouth to speak, but it was impossible with her heart pounding so hard she could hear it echoing in her head. Instead she forced a smile and nodded.

"Would you like a soda?" Noah asked. "I filled the fridge with a variety."

"Sounds good," she managed to squeak. A soda was just the thing for her parched mouth.

After he left the reception area, Emily took a seat behind the counter and buried her face in her hands. She really needed to focus on what she was there for and stop harboring romantic thoughts about Noah. Neither of them needed a relationship—not Noah who was still trying to build his business and certainly not her, since she needed to figure out what she wanted before getting involved with a man.

He came back and handed her a can of Dr. Pepper. "How did you know this was what I'd want?"

Noah grinned. "Mel said he has to keep them in stock when you visit."

For the remainder of the day, Emily fielded calls that continued to straggle in about the bills. Then the mail came. A whole sack of it.

"Hang on to the bag, and I'll pick it up tomorrow," the mail carrier said.

"Thanks, Charlie."

After Charlie left, Emily started the task of opening each envelope and clipping each check to the bill. Noah wasn't in, so she entered the information in each client's file then prepared the deposit for Noah to drop off on his way home. Until now he'd made enough money to pay the bills and salaries from clients who paid at the time of service, but now there would be more, which would enable him to expand and hire additional assistants.

He finally arrived about fifteen minutes before she was due to leave. His eyes widened when he saw the deposit.

"Whoa." He picked up the stack and shook his head. "That's double the normal deposit. I see it, but I almost don't believe it."

"Believe it," she said. "All we had to do was ask."

"To be honest, I've never been good at collecting money people owed me." He plopped down in one of the chairs in the waiting room and stretched out his legs. "One of the guys I shared a house with in college once borrowed money to fix his car engine. I assumed he'd pay me back as soon as he got his next check, but the weeks went by, and he didn't hand over a dime."

"Why didn't you just ask him for it?"

"So much time had passed, and I couldn't find a way to do it."

"So how did you get your money back?" Emily asked.

"I didn't. He moved out at the end of the semester and left his furniture for the rest of us. I guess he figured that was his payment." Noah shrugged. "I knew he'd struggled with money all his life, and he went to school on student loans. It's especially hard for me to ask people for money that I know they don't have."

Emily liked that about Noah—his generous spirit. However, she also knew that some people would see it and take advantage of him if he didn't make an effort to collect.

Noah stood up and pointed to the deposit. "I'm grateful for all your hard work in getting this, Emily."

"I figure since I'm here anyway, I might as well earn my paycheck."

Noah was definitely indebted to Emily. Not only had she boosted his income, she'd managed to soothe nervous clients and patients when he felt frazzled. Emily wasn't just an employee; she was a valuable asset to his clinic. But he had to remind himself that he couldn't expect her to stick around much longer. She had her own dreams and aspirations, which certainly didn't include being a receptionist in a country vet clinic.

"Have you decided what to do about school?" he asked.

She averted her gaze. "Not really."

"Just remember, you can stay here as long as you want." He now knew that he wanted her forever, but he didn't want to confuse her even more.

When she turned back to face him, her eyes glistened with tears. Had he said something wrong?

"No pressure, okay?"

Emily swallowed hard and nodded. "I just feel like—I don't know—like I should know more about what I want out of life."

Noah bridged the gap between them and rested his elbows on the counter. The close proximity brought a sizzle to his nerves. "I know how difficult it can be. The only reason I knew what I wanted was that I loved hanging out in my dad's clinic ever since I can remember." He chuckled. "However, my favorite animals were the ones he hardly ever saw, which is why I'm here with the chickens, goats, and pigs."

Kingston stood up and audibly yawned. Emily laughed. "And Great Danes, right?"

Noah walked over to Kingston and rubbed behind his ears. "Absolutely. Great Danes and whatever else walks, flies, or slithers through that door."

Emily shuddered. "Thankfully I haven't seen much slithering since I've been here."

"Just wait," Noah said with a grin. "If you're here long enough, you'll see some slithering."

The instant those words were out of his mouth, he regretted saying them. He shouldn't have quantified her time with him—even with such a subtle reference to the future.

Emily offered a closed-mouth smile and quickly looked down. He wished he knew what she was thinking.

Kingston stood up, turned around, and sat down next to him. Then he leaned his body against Noah's side. One side of the dog's jowl flopped open as he looked up at Noah.

"Whatcha thinkin', boy?" Noah asked as he scratched Kingston's head.

The dog sighed, which made Emily laugh. "He's in doggy heaven."

"I've never met a dog who didn't like having his ears or head scratched." Noah gently nudged Kingston away so he could go back to work. "But Kingston is probably the easiest one to please."

"He is absolutely the best dog I've ever been around," Emily admitted.

"Maybe you can talk Mr. Zimmerman into handing him over for good. He could be your companion until you leave. I'm sure Mel would love to have a dog like this." Noah looked her in the eye. "I've heard Mr. Zimmerman's thinking about selling his farm and moving to Florida."

"Why wouldn't he take Kingston with him?"

"He's too big to live in a condo."

"I can't imagine owning a farm all these years then moving to a condo," Emily said.

"It happens." Noah took a few more steps toward the examining area. "Maybe we'll know something when he gets back from Europe."

After Noah left her alone in the reception area, Emily looked at Kingston, who stared at her with soulful eyes. She'd love to have Kingston for her own, but how would the dog feel about that? No doubt he was a loyal friend to Mr. Zimmerman.

Emily patted her leg. "C'mere, Kingston."

He dutifully closed the distance between them. Emily started to pat his head then decided to give him a hug instead. She leaned forward and pulled him toward her, allowing him to rest his chin on her shoulder. She didn't care if he slobbered down her back. All she knew was that it felt good to have the companionship she'd missed for so much of her life.

No matter how hard her dad had tried to be both a father and a mother to her, he was stretched so thin between his full-time and part-time jobs to keep a roof over their heads and food on the table that she rarely saw him. She'd spent many nights longing for her mother, knowing she'd been abandoned for a life of excitement. It still hurt and probably always would.

Emily would never forget when her dad came to her to break the news that her mother had left and wasn't coming back. At first she blamed her dad, thinking he'd done something to make her mother leave. But over time she realized that her father had nothing to do with it. If anything, his stability and faith in God had been what kept his wife there as long as she was.

"Your mother is a very confused woman," Aunt Sherry told her. "We pray for her every day, and you should, too."

At first Emily had a difficult time praying for someone who wanted nothing to do with her, but over time she realized how pitiful her mother's existence was. As an adult, Emily saw things differently. She'd learned more about her mother and understood that the woman had always teetered on the brink of disaster, and her father had pulled her out of a mess shortly after they met.

Emily's earliest memories of her mother were good. She and her dad went to church most Sundays, but her mother begged off due to a headache or some other malady. Then one Sunday, a few weeks after Emily's fourteenth birthday, she and her dad came home to an empty house. She'd always remember her father's loud gasp when he picked up the note on the kitchen table. He never let her see it, but he told her it would just be the two of them from then on.

For months Emily alternately blamed her dad and herself for her mother leaving. If only she hadn't gotten so upset when she was told she couldn't wear makeup to school or told her parents she wanted to run away. At times she thought she'd given her mother the idea.

No matter what her dad did to console her, she still felt responsible, until he finally took her to a Christian counselor, who eventually convinced her she wasn't to blame. She was being a normal teenager, but her mother wasn't equipped to deal with everyday life.

"You have a choice," the counselor had said. "Life can be difficult, but you don't have to let it keep you down. You can wallow in the past, or you can look forward to the future, knowing that your faith in Christ reserves you a place with Him for eternity." She'd paused to let Emily digest that before adding, "You have an earthly father who can only do so much, but your heavenly Father is with you for eternity—no matter what happens."

Those words had stuck in Emily's mind and gotten her through the most difficult of times. Her counselor was right. Life was extremely difficult. Fortunately, the people from church were loving, caring folks who never wavered in their commitment to help her and her father. And every summer she got to stay with Aunt Sherry and Uncle Mel and her cousins, where she felt like she was part of a happy family.

Kingston sighed again, pulling her back to the moment. She loved this dog. Maybe it wouldn't be such a bad thing for Mr. Zimmerman to move to a condo in Florida. She'd love to keep Kingston—or at least have him with Uncle Mel and Aunt Sherry so she could visit him. She just wished she wasn't so confused.

"What am I gonna do, Kingston?" she asked softly.

"Anything I can help with?"

The voice by the counter startled her. She glanced up and saw Noah standing there looking concerned.

Emily was tempted to brush him off, but what was the point? She figured she might as well be open.

"I'm frustrated about my future." She looked back at Kingston who continued staring at her with adoring eyes then turned back to Noah. "Now that I've been out of school for a while and had some time to think, going back sounds pretty good—at least sometimes—but I don't want to do it without a goal in mind."

Noah nodded but didn't say anything. He appeared to be mulling over her comment.

"I mean, I don't want to stall for time with school being my excuse. I've seen other people do that."

"Yeah, I have, too." Noah gestured to the desk. "Just remember that you always have a place here as long as you need it."

"Thank you."

"Why don't you go on home now? We've had a busy day, and Kingston and I don't want to wear you out." He smiled.

Kingston seemed to understand what Noah said. He walked over to the counter, picked up the leash in his mouth, and brought it to Emily.

"Sometimes it's hard to remember he's a dog."

Noah laughed. "I know what you mean. He's in tune to you." Suddenly his smile faded, and he looked at her as though he saw something he'd missed before.

Emily felt a familiar internal fluttering—something that had been happening more often lately when Noah looked at her that way. "I—I guess you're right. It has been a long day, and Kingston is obviously ready to go home—I mean to Uncle Mel and Aunt Sherry's."

Noah patted Kingston's head as they walked past him to the door. Emily stopped, turned to face Noah, and blinked. "I appreciate everything you're doing, Noah."

"And I feel the same about you."

Her mouth grew dry as she waved and said good-bye. Kingston looked up at her as if he wanted to acknowledge what she was thinking. For the first time in her life, she felt like she truly belonged—yet she didn't have a permanent home, a career that seemed ideal for her, or a clue about her future. What was up with that?

All the way to her aunt and uncle's, Emily chatted with Kingston. He gave her occasional understanding glances, but most of the time he focused straight ahead on the road. Their afternoon routine was basically the same, but her feelings had escalated; she felt like she might burst if something didn't happen soon. It was all up to her now.

When they pulled onto the dirt road, the dog's ears perked up. There was no doubt he knew where he was.

"We're home, Kingston."

The instant she stopped the car, Kingston pawed at the door. She hopped out of the driver's side and looked at him, which was all the encouragement he needed to hop over her seat and out the door. He ran around in circles for a few seconds, until Uncle Mel hollered that he was in the barn.

Kingston took off running toward the sound of Uncle Mel's voice. Emily went into the house to put down her handbag. Aunt Sherry greeted her as she walked into the kitchen.

"Mel has some news from town," Aunt Sherry said.

"News?" Emily lifted a carrot stick off the platter on the island and munched the edge. "What happened?"

Aunt Sherry frowned for a moment then shook her head. "I better let Mel tell you. Why don't you go on out to the barn?"

Panic rose in Emily as she followed her aunt's orders. When she got to the barn door, she paused to let her eyes adjust.

"Hey, Emily girl, come on over here. I gotta tell you something." Uncle Mel patted a bale of hay next to him. "Have a seat."

Chapter 14

I talked to Dwayne this afternoon," Uncle Mel said. "Apparently there's a whole list of warrants out for Brad's arrest—some from other states."

"So what happens now?" Emily asked.

Uncle Mel shrugged. "We're not sure yet. Looks like he might be extradited, but they have a bunch of paperwork to handle first."

"What does that mean for Jillian?"

Uncle Mel offered a half smile. "Looks like Jillian won't have to worry about Brad coming after her. He'll be in jail somewhere for a very long time."

So that meant Jillian could go back to work soon. Emily had mixed feelings about that. Having Jillian back at the office would free Emily up to pursue other things—and give her time to figure out what she wanted to do with her life.

"What's wrong?" Uncle Mel asked as he paused, folded his arms, and leaned against a post. "Are you unhappy about something?"

"No." Emily slowly shook her head. "I just don't know what to do yet."

"It's tough having to make decisions," he agreed. "I remember trying to decide whether I should seek my fortune in the big city or stay on the farm where I'd always been."

"What was the turning point for you?"

He snickered. "I tried the city for about a year and quickly learned that it's not for me."

Emily couldn't imagine Uncle Mel in the city. "I could have told you that."

"If you'd been around then, I might have asked you." With a grin he added, "But there are some things we have to figure out for ourselves."

"So do you think I should consider farm life?"

Uncle Mel shrugged. "Everyone's different. Some people know what they want all their lives."

Emily thought for a few seconds. "Ever since I went to an art museum with my middle school class, I've wanted to work in one."

"Is that what you still want to do?"

She frowned. "I think so."

"Well, then do it. You're young and you have your whole life ahead of you."

"Thanks, Uncle Mel."

Emily felt the warmth of his smile as he nodded. "I didn't do anything but encourage you to do what you said you wanted."

"That's exactly what I needed." She fought an unsettled feeling that kept creeping up.

"I'm glad I could help." He reached over and picked up the rake. "I better get back to work. Sherry doesn't like me being late for supper."

Aunt Sherry glanced at her as she walked in through the kitchen door. "So what do you think about what's going on?"

Emily forced a smile. "I'm just glad Jillian will be free to come back to work. I know she misses working at the clinic."

"She's a good girl but a little naive. Maybe this experience will help her become more discerning."

"I'm sure she will," Emily said. "Need some help with that?"

"Thanks, but no. I'm almost done here. Why don't you go get washed up and come help me set the table?"

The next couple of weeks went by quickly. Jillian had to go to court, but she didn't have to testify in front of Brad. Emily and Noah were in the courtroom to offer their support, so when Brad was led away the last time, they let out a collective sigh of relief. Emily felt a surge of protectiveness as she met Jillian's gaze.

"She's holding up quite well," Noah acknowledged. "To be honest, I wasn't sure how this would turn out."

"I was concerned, too." Emily glanced back and forth between Noah and Jillian who stood about twenty feet away. "Why don't we go see how she feels?"

Jillian met them halfway. "I am so glad that's over with."

Emily put her arm around Jillian. "So how are you feeling now?"

"Beyond relieved." She cast a quick glance toward Noah. "And ready to go back to work, if that's all right with you."

"Of course it is," he said. "When would you like to return?"

Emily felt her insides tighten as she turned back to Jillian. Until now she hadn't really thought about how her own life would be affected by another change. Would she still be needed at the clinic? She knew she couldn't continue working part-time forever. Maybe this was the push she needed.

Jillian glanced at her, smiled, and turned back to Noah. "How about next week?"

"Perfect," Noah said. "I'm sure Emily will be glad to have you back."

Noah couldn't tell what was going on with Emily, but she didn't seem herself. Outwardly she appeared happy, but he could tell there was something behind that smile. Something that he'd spotted a few times since he'd known her.

As soon as Jillian left, he gently placed his hand in the small of her back and leaned over to whisper. "Are you okay?"

She hesitated for a split second then nodded. "I'm fine."

"Wanna go somewhere and talk?"

Noah's chest constricted as she looked him in the eye and nodded. "Sure."

Since they'd driven together from the clinic, he helped her into the passenger seat then went around to his side of the truck and got in. "It's nice out. How about a park?"

"Sounds good."

Since he knew she loved roses, he drove to Ritter Park where they could sit and chat in the rose garden. She smiled as he took her hand and led her to a quiet place.

"This is so beautiful." Emily looked around at the rows and rows of flowers in various colors.

Warmth flooded him. "I thought you might like it."

After they found a place to sit, a comfortable silence fell between them. The only sound was the chirping of birds.

Finally Emily turned to him. "I'm relieved that Jillian won't have to worry about Brad anymore."

Noah nodded. "Yeah, me, too."

"That was quite a scare we had when Dwayne had to go inside and get Brad out of her house."

Noah met her gaze. "Dwayne is trying to witness to Jillian, ya know. He feels like she just needs to be surrounded by Christian love to stay strong against the evil nature of people like Brad."

Her smile added even more sparkle to the beauty surrounding them. "That's a no-brainer."

He chuckled. "As much as I don't understand it, all the things that happened with Jillian turned out to be a blessing." He paused for a moment then added, "We need to continue praying for Brad. Something terrible must have happened to him in the past."

"I'm sure." Emily cleared her throat. "So what did you want to talk about?"

Noah wasn't sure how to begin, so he figured he might as well just come out with it. He looked her in the eye and held her gaze for a few seconds before he finally said, "You."

She instantly frowned. "Me?"

He nodded. "Yes. I could tell something was bothering you in the courtroom, and I thought you might want to talk about it."

Emily swallowed as she looked around before locking gazes with him again. "I'm really happy for Jillian, and I want her to come back to work. It's just. . ." Her voice trailed off as she seemed to gather her thoughts. "It's just that now I need to make a decision about what I need to do next."

"What you *need* to do?" he challenged.

She snickered. "Okay, what I *want* to do. I still don't know."

"You once mentioned that you wanted to become a curator in an art museum. How about that?"

"I'm not so sure I can do it."

When she looked down, he gently turned her face toward his. "Of course you can. I have a feeling that you can do almost anything you set your mind to." She'd already proven that after nearly doubling his accounts receivable deposits in the short time she'd been working for him.

"To get what I need, I'll have to go to New York."

"New York? There's a graduate art program at Marshall University."

She offered a sad smile. "Yes, but if I want to work in a bigger city, I'll need to go to NYU."

He pondered that for a moment. As much as Noah wanted to keep her in West Virginia, he cared enough to want what was best for her. "If that's what you really want, just do it. I've seen people who don't pursue their dreams, and they go through life wondering 'what if?'" As he spoke, he shuddered at the very idea of her leaving town for the big city and the possibility of not seeing her again.

Once again they fell silent. A slight breeze had picked up the scent of the roses and carried it toward them. After several minutes, Emily stood. "I'll think about it, okay?"

He nodded. "Just let me know if there's anything I can do to help you." But what he really wanted to do was tell her he loved her and beg her not to go.

❧

Early the next morning, Emily got up and started the process of applying to NYU for their art history graduate program. Noah's words about people wondering 'what if?'" kept flowing through her mind. She knew her mother was one of those unhappy people, and she certainly didn't want to end up like the woman who'd abandoned the people who needed her most.

When Emily saw the cost of the program, she nearly choked. However, she'd made it through four years of college on grants and scholarships, so her next step was to find as many of those as she could.

When she had the last form filled out and in the mail, she shut her eyes and said a prayer. This wasn't easy, but nothing in her life ever had been. From the earliest she could remember, anything she wanted had been a struggle to attain. And the one thing she used to want more than anything—her mother by her side—had always been beyond her reach.

Once Jillian came back to work and got into a routine, Emily went back to part-time—mostly mornings. That gave her quite a bit of free time to help Uncle Mel or Aunt Sherry around the farm and house. It also gave them plenty of opportunities to talk and try to get her to open up. As much as she wanted to share her deepest feelings, it was impossible—and she was well aware that they knew. Each time Aunt Sherry looked at her with understanding, Emily had to turn away or risk bursting into tears. She'd learned to be strong—to not let anything get her down. At least, that was how she appeared on the outside. Inside she was a jumbled-up mess.

Kingston was the perfect companion. He never left her side, and he knew when she needed a hug. Mr. Zimmerman had extended his stay in Europe, so Noah had asked if she could keep Kingston for a little while longer. Some days she hung around the clinic to help Jillian manage the paperwork, now that they had a workable billing routine in place.

"How about a raise for both of you?" Noah asked as he walked in after one of his daily deposits. "We're all in this together, so we should share the prosperity."

Noah wore a smile, but she missed seeing that old sparkle in his eye and spring in his step. Something was definitely bothering him, but she knew him well enough to know he wouldn't tell anyone what it was.

Emily shrugged. "A raise is nice, but since I probably won't be here much longer, why don't you give my share to Jillian?"

"No," Jillian said with a flick of her hand. "That's silly. If anything, you should have all of it. You're the one who got everyone paying their bills."

Noah laughed out loud. "I've never heard of employees turning down raises. Should I call the news station, or do y'all need a doctor?"

Emily grinned at Noah. "I'm just happy to be here. If it weren't for you, I don't know that I would have applied to NYU."

"You would have eventually—that is, if it's what you really want." His smile faded, and he tilted his head forward as he looked at her with an intensity that made her uncomfortable.

"Maybe so, but I still appreciate you giving me that nudge."

Jillian stood and backed out of the room, leaving Noah and Emily alone. "I'll be in the break room if you need me."

As soon as she left, Noah stepped closer to Emily. "Any idea when you'll hear something?"

Her heart pounded harder as he drew closer. "Should be any day now. I barely made the deadline for next semester."

Noah stopped and glanced down at the floor then looked back at her, frowning. "Just let me know so I can make arrangements. You've not only gotten my clients paying, but you're responsible for bringing in more business than I can handle with one part-time employee."

"I can't take credit for any of that, Noah. Your business was growing, and I just happened to be here."

He continued gazing at her, his frown gradually softening. "You have no idea how valuable you've been around here."

Emily sensed that his words held more than one meaning. She held his gaze for as long as she could, until she felt like flinging herself into his arms. The combination of his kindness, his love of animals, and his commitment to the Lord had warmed her heart, and she knew that if she weren't careful, she could easily fall in love with Noah.

After her experience with loving her mother who wasn't capable of loving her back, she needed to leave as soon as possible—or she'd risk another heartbreak. Emily and her father had loved her mother, and look where that got both of them. She loved her father, but he'd worked himself into an early grave to support her and help supplement the scholarships she'd gotten for college. There was no way she'd be able to endure another heartbreak this soon.

Emily was glad when Jillian returned to the desk and Noah's appointment arrived. He'd asked her to stick around for a little while, so she busied herself with finishing the paperwork she'd committed to then left for the day.

"C'mon, Kingston. Maybe we still have time to help Uncle Mel in the barn."

The dog trotted alongside Emily to her car. He knew the routine. He hopped over the driver's side and settled into the passenger's seat. All the way to the farm, Emily chatted to Kingston, who gave her an occasional glance as if to let her know he understood. When she pointed to another dog on the side of the road, he let out a *woof* then turned to her with a pleased expression.

As soon as she pulled onto the long driveway leading to the house, Kingston's eyes focused on the barn and his ears stood a little higher. Not only had she grown attached to Kingston, he and Uncle Mel had a special bond. She wished they didn't have to give him up when Mr. Zimmerman came home.

Kingston waited patiently as she put the car in PARK, took her handbag off the floor, and got out. The second she patted her thigh, he bounded out of the car and gave her a quick glance for approval. As soon as he got the nod, he took off for the barn in his lopsided gallop. Emily hung back, laughed, and watched the pure joy as Uncle Mel greeted him at the door. Every day their return to the farm was basically the same, but each time her attachment felt stronger. She was afraid that if she stuck around much longer, she'd never be able to pull herself away.

When she joined them, Uncle Mel was still smiling. "This is the nicest dog I've ever known, and I've been around quite a few dogs in my life."

"I know. Sometimes I forget he's not human."

Uncle Mel gave Kingston a final rub behind the ears before turning his attention to Emily. "So how was your day at the clinic?"

She shrugged. "The usual for me, but Noah's business is taking off. After I leave, he might have to hire someone else."

He studied her for several seconds before he nodded. "I'm sure you'll be a hard one to replace."

"Anyone can do what I do there," Emily said. "It's no big deal."

"Not according to what Noah said."

Emily wanted to change the subject—get it off Noah. "Anything I can do out here before I go in?"

Uncle Mel looked over at Kingston, who sat waiting for some interaction with the other animals. "Why don't you grab one of those baskets and get the eggs from the chickens on the east side and take them in to Sherry? We didn't finish getting them earlier."

As soon as Emily filled the basket with eggs, she waved to let Uncle Mel know she was done then headed inside. Aunt Sherry glanced over her shoulder and grinned.

"There's an envelope for you on the table by the door," Aunt Sherry said. "I think it's what you've been waiting for."

Chapter 15

Emily didn't waste a second. She quickly picked up the envelope with the NYU logo but paused. *What if it's a rejection?* She closed her eyes and said a prayer. When she looked at the envelope again, she forced herself to remember that if they turned her down, she hadn't lost anything.

She spotted Aunt Sherry out of the corner of her eye and let out a nervous giggle. "I might as well open it and see the verdict."

Aunt Sherry folded her arms and offered a sympathetic smile. "I can't imagine why they'd turn you down."

The second she pulled the paper out and read the first line, her heart thudded. It was an acceptance! Her mind instantly raced with all sorts of thoughts—from the thrill of having the honor of going to NYU to concern about how she'd do it. She lowered her head once again.

"Are you okay?" Aunt Sherry asked as she bridged the gap between them. "They didn't turn you down, did they?"

Emily shook her head and tried to force her voice, but her throat felt scratchy. "No, I've been accepted, but I have no idea how I can afford it."

"Did you read the entire letter?" Her aunt nodded toward the envelope still gripped in Emily's hand.

Emily took a deep breath and held it up to finish reading what the registrar had to say. "They're asking me to go there and talk to some people about money."

"Then do it." Aunt Sherry gave her a hug. "I'm so proud of you I could squeal. Imagine my niece being smart enough to go to NYU."

"A lot of people go there, but thanks, Aunt Sherry. Let me go put this away, and I'll come help you in the kitchen."

Her aunt opened her mouth then quickly closed it. "Okay. I understand that you need some time to digest the news. Just remember that Mel and I will support you in anything you decide to do. We'll even buy your plane ticket if you need us to."

Tears stung the backs of Emily's eyes. "Thank you so much. I don't know what I'd do without you."

"So go on and do what you have to do. I'll see you in the kitchen in a few minutes."

Emily didn't waste any time putting the letter in the folder with her transcripts and other related paperwork. She took a few minutes to regroup then went to help Aunt Sherry. Fortunately they were too busy putting dinner on the table to discuss NYU.

Uncle Mel came inside just in time to say the blessing. After he finished, Aunt Sherry blurted, "Emily has some wonderful news she'd like to share."

He turned to face her with a wide grin. "I knew you didn't have a thing to worry about, Emily. So tell me when you start."

She explained that they wanted her to come up to visit before everything was final, but if everything went well in the interview, she was that much closer to getting into the master's program. "Then all I'll have to do is figure out a way to pay for it."

Uncle Mel frowned. "I thought you filled out all those forms for that."

Emily shrugged. "It might take awhile for them to come through. In the meantime—"

Uncle Mel interrupted her. "In the meantime, your aunt and I will do everything we can to make this happen for you. If the money comes through, you can pay us back. If it doesn't, then don't worry about it. We want to invest in your future."

Suddenly Emily couldn't hold back the tears. They sprang out of her eyes before she had a chance to catch herself.

"Look what you've gone and done, Mel." Aunt Sherry stood up and came around to hug Emily. "I want you to relax about this, honey. We're just doing what a loving family does. I know you've had a difficult time of it, but there's no point in that anymore. We have more than we need, and it's an honor for us to share it with you."

Emily's bottom lip quivered as she nodded. "Th–thank you."

"Now let's eat," Uncle Mel said as he winked at Aunt Sherry. "Since we suspected that letter might be good news, your aunt made a special dessert to celebrate."

She had to fight the tears once again. Having this much support was almost more than she could handle. Even as much as her father loved her, he'd argued about her going to college, letting her know that she'd be wasting four years of having no income, and she wouldn't be able to stand on her own two feet for a long time. Guilt had overcome her when her father passed away during her freshman year, and at times she wondered if he'd still be alive if she'd taken his advice.

"When people have dreams as big as yours," Uncle Mel said, "it's just wrong for other people to get in their way. Our dream was to have this farm, and we've been blessed, thanks to the people who helped us get started."

Emily frowned. "I thought this was a family farm. Dad said you inherited it."

Uncle Mel cut his glance over to Aunt Sherry, who nodded. Then he turned back to Emily. "Your dad and I inherited it together, but he wasn't interested. He sold his share to me. Not only did I have to get the money to buy him out, I had to update the barn and all the equipment."

"You paid Dad for his share? He never mentioned that."

"He most likely didn't want you to know."

Emily sat back and wondered what her dad had done with the money. It must not have been much because he'd struggled financially for as long as she could remember. Finally she had to ask. "My parents always struggled and acted like they were flat broke. In fact Mom used to make snide remarks about how worthless Dad was because all he knew was what he learned from being raised on a farm."

Uncle Mel's eyebrows shot up. "She said that, huh?"

Emily nodded. "I never understood that. Dad always had a job—sometimes two. I wonder what he did with the money you paid him for the farm."

Her aunt and uncle exchanged a glance, and Aunt Sherry nodded. Uncle Mel squared his jaw as he put down his fork. "He spent most of that money trying his dead-level best to keep your mother happy. When he ran out of money, she lost interest and found someone else who could buy her what she wanted."

Emily looked down at the table as she processed all that. She knew her mother constantly harangued her father about not making enough money, and she often wondered why her mother didn't go out and get a job after Emily was old enough to be home alone after school.

"I'm really sorry I had to be the one to tell you all this, but it's obvious your dad didn't want you to know what happened. Sherry and I have been talking, and since you kept blaming yourself for everything, we figured it was time for you to know the truth."

Aunt Sherry reached out for Emily's hand and squeezed it. "You've always been a good girl—the kind of child any parent should feel honored to have. We're just thankful your dad continued taking you to church. He had his flaws, but deep down he was a good man. Some men might've caved in and denounced their faith."

Armed with all this information, Emily had quite a bit to think about. "Is it okay with y'all if I don't have my celebration dessert now?"

"Sure, honey." Aunt Sherry stood and started clearing the table. "We can do it later or even tomorrow night if that's better for you."

Emily started helping with the dishes, until Uncle Mel nudged her out of the way. "Let me take over for you here, Emily. I'd like to spend some time with my wife. Why don't you go on to your room and figure out when you can go to New York to check out that school?"

※

Noah was surprised to see Emily's car in the parking lot, since he'd arrived an hour early. He pulled some of the new equipment off the back of his truck, placed it on a dolly, and rolled it to the entrance. She saw him and jumped to her feet to hold the door for him.

"Whatcha got there?" she asked.

"Some equipment that I couldn't afford until our clients started paying, thanks to you."

"Need some help setting it up?" she asked.

"I need to wait until the technician gets here." He rolled the equipment to the back then joined her in the reception area. "So why are you here so early?"

She turned away from the computer screen and looked him in the eye. "I've been accepted to NYU."

Noah froze in place as a strange feeling of dread washed over him. He was happy for her. Really, he was. Well, at least he wanted to be.

He forced a grin. "Congratulations, Emily! That's a big deal! When do you have to leave?"

Emily flashed an odd expression. "Not until next semester—but if you don't mind, I'd like to take a few days off so I can go up there for a short visit."

Noah choked back the words he wanted to say—that he needed her and didn't want her to leave—and nodded. "Yes, of course you can take off all the time you need."

Her half smile warmed his heart. "Thank you, Noah. You've been wonderful to me."

He wanted to kick himself in the backside for wishing she hadn't been accepted. Everything was running so smoothly at the clinic, and all the clients adored her. Though Jillian was sweet and did a good job, Emily added a spark to the office.

And being truthful with himself, he felt the spark all the way to his heart. At some point along the journey of getting to know her and growing his business, Noah had fallen in love with Emily. Thoughts of *ever after* had even flickered through his mind. That fact made him take a physical step back.

"Don't forget, Emily, you've helped me quite a bit around here. We'll certainly miss you." He couldn't hold back his businesslike tone.

"I know you'll probably need help training someone new, so maybe I can do that after I get back from my visit?"

He gave her a clipped nod. "That's fine." If he didn't get to work soon, he knew he risked begging her to stay. "What time is my first appointment?"

"Ten." She didn't even have to glance at the calendar.

"I'll go prep the examining room and start positioning the new equipment to make it easy for the technician to set up."

"Need help with that?" she asked.

"No." His voice was brusque, so he started over and tried for a softer approach. "No thanks."

"Okay," she said as she tucked her hair behind her ear. "Just let me know if you need me."

Oh he needed her all right—way more than he'd ever admit. Over the past few months he'd felt the change as she worked her way under his skin. The only thing he could do right now was pray—at least if he didn't want to lose his mind.

Lord, I don't know what's going on with this feeling I have for Emily, but I pray that I don't act like a jerk about her leaving. She's wonderful—everything I've always wanted in a woman. Not only does she brighten up every room she enters, she has a heart for You. She's beautiful and smart and interesting. He opened his eyes for a moment then added, *I pray for her success in anything she does. Amen.*

The morning went by more slowly than usual, in spite of the fact that Noah was as busy as ever. Emily occasionally came back to tell him something, and he made it a point to keep their contact brief. He didn't want to run the risk of saying the wrong thing—not when she was about to embark on the journey of her dreams.

But one thing kept playing in his mind. What if there was some chance that she felt the same way about him? He decided to take a chance and let her know how he felt.

"We need to talk," he said.

Emily looked at him and tilted her head. "Sure. Now?"

He hesitated then nodded. "Yes, now."

She leaned back in her chair. "Okay."

"This probably isn't the best place to do this, but I don't see that I have a choice. Emily, I've fallen in love with you."

Her eyes widened, and she opened her mouth. Nothing came out.

"I almost didn't tell you because I didn't want to confuse you. But the more I thought about it, I realized it wouldn't be fair not to let you know how I felt." He glanced down at the floor then slowly looked back at her. "Sorry if I upset you."

She shook her head. "I think I'm falling in love with you, too, Noah, but that's not enough. I don't want to risk letting go of something I might later regret."

"I understand," he replied. "I'm just glad we got this out in the open. We should always be honest with each other."

Did he dare to hope she might stay? Nah. At least not until she had a chance to check out New York.

❧

The following week, Aunt Sherry stood in the doorway as Emily zipped her suitcase. "Got everything?"

Emily nodded. "I'm pretty sure I do."

"Plane ticket, identification, toothbrush?"

"It's all here." She patted her shoulder bag. "And I have enough clothes for a week."

"Do you have the Carsons' address?"

Emily double-checked to make sure she had the slip of paper with the address of Aunt Sherry's cousin who lived in Manhattan. "It's here."

Aunt Sherry looked at her with sad eyes. "Okay, I reckon it's time for us to take you to the airport. Ready?"

Six hours later, Emily was in the taxi on her way to Todd and Bonnie Carson's apartment in the city. As the driver whisked her through the streets of Manhattan, she felt an overwhelming surge of fear.

What am I doing, Lord? Is this what You want for me? Or should I act on my feelings for Noah and stay in West Virginia? Please make that clear before I make a huge mistake.

"That'll be forty-five dollars." The taxi driver turned around and held out his hand.

Once she paid him and had her luggage on the sidewalk beside her, she stood in front of the building, cupped her hand over her eyes, and looked up. It sure was tall—much higher than any building in West Virginia.

She said another prayer—this time for strength—before forging ahead. Once she pushed the button to ring the Carsons' apartment, she was on her way.

Bonnie greeted her as the elevator opened. She'd met Aunt Sherry's cousin once, but she instantly felt close to her as they hugged.

"Look at you, Emily! You look wonderful!" Bonnie held her at arm's length and looked her up and down. "There's something about that West Virginia air that makes people glow. I miss it more than you can ever imagine." She took control of Emily's rolling suitcase and led the way to her apartment. "The guest room is tiny, but I fixed it up for you. There's some space in the closet, and the bathroom is right outside your door."

The building showed its age on the outside, but once they'd entered Bonnie's apartment, Emily felt as though she'd been transported into the future. Everything was so modern and sleek—quite unlike the country home of Uncle Mel and Aunt Sherry.

"This is beautiful," Emily said.

Bonnie laughed. "I guess it's okay, but it's not my taste. I prefer more traditional, but Todd likes contemporary, so we compromised. He decorated the living room, and I got everything else."

Once again Emily was amazed at the change when she got to the guest room. The walls were painted in a warm peach. The four-poster double bed, covered in a Double Wedding Ring quilt, took up most of the space in the room. There was a braided rug beside the bed, and an old-fashioned water pitcher sat on the tiny dressing table.

"Why don't you take a few minutes and put your things away?" Bonnie said as she backed out of the room. "I'm working on something in the kitchen, so when you're ready, why don't you join me?"

As soon as she was alone, Emily sat down on the edge of the bed and sighed. She'd never felt so overwhelmed in her life.

She opened her suitcase and hung up the few nice things she'd brought. Then she powdered her nose and freshened her lipstick.

When she opened her bedroom door, the smell of cinnamon overwelmed her, and she allowed her nose to lead her to the kitchen. Bonnie pointed to the baking sheet on the counter.

"Sherry said you love pastries, so I pulled out our grandmother's old recipe and baked some cinnamon buns."

Emily's heart instantly warmed. "You didn't have to do that." She took a deep whiff and grinned. "But I sure do like the way they smell. It's almost like I never left Aunt Sherry's."

Bonnie chuckled. "Have a seat, and I'll bring it to you. Coffee?"

A few minutes later, as they munched on cinnamon buns and sipped coffee, Emily almost forgot that she was in one of the largest cities in the world. It felt almost as cozy as being in Aunt Sherry's kitchen.

"What's on the agenda for your trip?" Bonnie asked. "We don't have a car, so you'll have to take the subway or taxi, but that's really the easiest way to get around."

"I can't even imagine trying to drive here," Emily said.

Bonnie laughed. "That was the first thing I gave up when I moved here."

Emily told her what all she planned to do while in the city, and Bonnie gave her some pointers about getting around to the various places. She explained the subway system in detail and even gave her a metro card.

"You didn't have to do that," Emily said. "I brought money."

"This will save you from having to deal with buying tickets. This is good for the rest of the week." She stood up and carried the plates to the sink then turned to face Emily. "Since you don't have anything else to do today, why don't we take a little walking tour of the area? We might even get a little shopping in while we're at it."

They spent the remainder of the day going into shops and giggling like best friends. Bonnie had the energy and youthful spirit of a woman half her age. On the way home, they stopped off at a deli and picked up some prepared food.

Todd arrived just in time for dinner. When they sat down, Bonnie reached for their hands and Todd said the blessing.

Throughout dinner, Todd talked about his ministry in the city. He was the pastor of a large congregation that had four services each Sunday, due to space limitations. At least Emily knew she'd have a church home once she moved to New York, but that didn't still the uneasy feeling about what lay ahead.

The next day, she set out for her first meeting with a few members of the university faculty. All three of them were cordial but aloof. They asked questions, and she answered them to the best of her ability. She had a list of her own questions, but she was too uncomfortable to ask any of them.

Finally, as they stood at the end of the meeting, one of the men smiled, extended a hand, and said they'd let her know very soon. "The grant you applied for should cover all your expenses for the semester—that is, if it comes through."

The woman beside him nodded. "You'll have to reapply for the next semester, but that shouldn't be a problem."

Emily blinked. "All expenses?"

"Yes," the woman said. "Including living expenses. Assuming you don't mind living in a dorm."

"No, I—I don't mind at all. I just didn't expect—"

One of the panel members stood, and the others followed suit, letting her know she was being dismissed. "You'll hear from us soon."

Emily headed back to Bonnie's place in a daze. She made her way to the tall building that offered a cozy refuge, feeling like she was in some sort of warped dream. None of it seemed real.

As soon as Bonnie saw Emily, she pulled her in for a hug. "You look like you've just seen a monster," she said. "Want to talk about it?"

"To be honest, I'm so confused," Emily explained how she'd been surprised the grant would cover all her expenses, but she still felt uneasy about everything. And worse yet, she wasn't eager to go to any art galleries. What was wrong with her?

"I can certainly understand," Bonnie said. "We'll pray about it. In the meantime, you still have a couple more meetings with faculty, so why don't you try to clear your mind until it's all over? Then we can discuss the pros and cons, if you'd like, and try to work through your concerns."

Emily was thankful for such a wonderful host. She knew that her life could possibly change in a huge way, and it was comforting to know she'd have someone she could talk to for the next couple of years.

Over the course of her meetings, people talked to her about the details of the program. They always started out stiff and formal, but when she got to meet some of the other students in the program, they all offered her a warm welcome.

Finally, when she walked out of the last meeting on the day before she was due to head back to West Virginia, she took a long look at the throng of people scurrying by. One man looked familiar from a distance, but when he drew closer, she realized she'd superimposed Noah's image over his face. That was when it hit her hard.

Chapter 16

This had been her dream for many years, but things had changed. She'd spent some time with her aunt and uncle, living the simple farm life that brought her a sense of peace. And she'd met Noah, a wonderful man who could be anywhere he wanted to be. He'd chosen Huntington, West Virginia, because he loved helping people and animals who truly needed his skills. And he loved her.

Now all Emily wanted was to be back in West Virginia with the people she loved, working beside Noah in his clinic and allowing their relationship to grow. Somewhere along the way her dream had changed, and that was why she felt so uneasy about being in New York. A year ago the hope of admission to NYU's graduate program and the possibility of a full grant would have made her over-the-moon happy. However, she now felt led in another direction.

In fact, the graduate art program at Marshall University in Huntington was starting to appeal to her. She'd met some of the faculty when they brought animals to the clinic, and they all seemed to be the type of people she wanted to surround herself with. Good, caring people who took pride in their campus. They didn't offer a master's in art history, but there was enough history included in their general art graduate studies that she could still accomplish her goal. That is, if her desire to pursue it ever returned. Now she was thinking she might want to stick around in the clinic awhile longer.

By the time she got back to Bonnie's apartment, she felt light on her feet. Bonnie's eyebrows shot up as soon as they made eye contact.

"You look mighty happy about something." She gestured toward the tone-on-tone ivory and white sofa. "Let's talk."

Emily felt like she might burst with joy as she explained how she felt. "All this time I thought the only thing that could possibly make me happy was this. And now that things have changed, I feel free."

Bonnie's smile faded as she leaned forward, propped her elbows on her knees, and looked Emily in the eye. "Can you be happy working in a vet clinic, going to a smaller school, and living the simple life?"

There was no doubt in Emily's mind. "Absolutely."

"Then do it. I'm sure if you change your mind in the future, NYU will still be there." She paused for a moment before continuing. "From what I've heard, Noah's quite a guy."

"Yes." Emily looked down then met Bonnie's gaze. "He's one of the nicest men I've ever met."

"And?" Bonnie tilted her head to one side and offered a teasing grin.

Emily's cheeks flamed. "He and I finally admitted our feelings for each other. I'm falling in love with him, and I'd like to see how things can be between us."

Bonnie leaned back and belted out a hearty laugh. "That's obvious. Now why don't you go on back to West Virginia and let him know how you feel?"

"I have to admit it scares me."

"Don't live in fear, Emily. I know you've had some tough times, but you can't let that hold you back from what you really want. Noah's a good guy. I suspect he has some fears as well. Sherry told me that you and Noah are perfect for each other."

"What if she's mistaken?"

Bonnie shrugged. "Then at least you'll know. Life's too short to hold back on matters of the heart. You need to trust God with your feelings and pray for His guidance. I bet He brought Noah into your life for a purpose. In fact I'm sure He did. From my perspective, it all looks like God's work—from your decision to stay with Sherry and Mel while you figured things out to coming here and realizing it's not what you really want."

"It's just that Noah's such a wonderful man. He never gave up on his other assistant, even though her boyfriend talked her into letting him into the clinic after hours. I think his kindness and gentle understanding make this even more difficult, since he's like that with everyone."

"Listen to me, Emily," Bonnie said with uncharacteristic firmness. "He's a kind man who loves the Lord. He takes care of animals and people in need. Don't you think he's also capable of having a loving relationship with a woman?"

Emily chewed her bottom lip and thought about all that Bonnie had said. It certainly made sense. Finally she stood up. "I need to go pack now. I guess I should call my faculty advisor and let her know I've decided to decline their offer—at least for now."

"Why don't you sleep on it tonight and call in the morning? I don't want you to have any regrets."

The next morning, Emily awoke feeling better than she'd felt in months. As soon as she had a cup of coffee, she called NYU and turned down the offer. Now all she had to do was go back to West Virginia and talk to Noah. Hopefully he hadn't started looking for someone to replace her. She knew Aunt Sherry and Uncle Mel wouldn't mind her sticking around a little bit longer until she had everything in place.

Bonnie went down to hail her a cab and gave her a hug before she got in. "I'll call Sherry and give her your flight number."

"Thanks for everything," Emily said. "I don't know what I would have done without you and Todd."

"You would have done just fine, but I'm glad I got to share this experience with you." She leaned over after Emily got into the cab. "E-mail me and let me know how it goes."

All the way back, Emily mentally rehearsed how she'd ask Noah if she could keep her job. She'd explain that she loved West Virginia and discovered how much she enjoyed working with animals. Hopefully he hadn't changed his mind and decided he was better off without her.

Her plane landed ten minutes ahead of schedule, so she took her time walking to the baggage claim area. When she rounded the corner, she had to blink to make sure she wasn't seeing things. What was Noah doing here?

"Hi there," he said as he walked toward her with a purpose. "How was the big city?"

Emily's lips quivered as she tried to act nonchalant. This wasn't the time to have that talk with him. "Good. Where are my aunt and uncle?"

He tilted his head and made a hurt puppy face. "You don't want to see me?"

"Oh no, it's not that. I just thought—they are okay, aren't they?"

"Yes, they're fine. I just volunteered to pick you up. You don't mind, do you?"

She grinned at him. "I'm glad you're here."

"I was worried there for a moment." He gestured toward the conveyor belt that had started moving. "Let's get your stuff and get out of here. We need to talk."

Emily thought her bag would never arrive. She was eager to leave the airport and find out what Noah wanted to talk about. What if he wanted her to leave sooner than they'd originally planned? What if he'd found the perfect person who wanted to start right away? All those thoughts filled her mind, until she thought she might pop with worry.

He tossed her bag into the back of the truck and opened her door for her before running around to his side. The second he got in, she knew she couldn't hold back anymore.

"Noah, I realize this makes me sound like a flake who can't make up her mind, but I really don't want to move to New York and go to NYU and work in a museum, and I love animals, and—"

He laughed. "Whoa, Emily, slow down. Let's start from the beginning. What happened?"

She closed her eyes and took a deep breath. *Lord, please help me get this out without scaring Noah.* When she opened her eyes and turned to face him, she saw the grin on his lips.

"What's so funny?" she asked.

Noah reached for her hand. "You. I know what happened in New York.

Sherry's cousin called her and said you've decided not to take their offer."

Emily nodded. "It's a really good offer. Very generous. But it's not what I really want."

As they pulled up to a red light, he turned to her. "What do you really want, Emily?"

She swallowed hard. "My job?"

The light turned green, so he accelerated and focused his attention on the road. "Okay, you have that. I'll never find anyone else who can do the kind of work you do with such a heart for animals."

"Thank you."

He cut a quick glance back at her. "Is there anything else you want?"

Her breath caught in her throat. "Like what do you mean?"

Noah shrugged. "I don't know. You seem awfully nervous about something, so I thought there might be more."

Emily didn't dare tell him what else she wanted because if he knew it was him, surely that would scare him away. But she didn't want to lie either.

He patted her hand. "You don't have to tell me now. We can talk when we get to Mel and Sherry's place."

Kingston didn't waste any time running out to the truck to greet them. The instant Aunt Sherry opened the screen door, he darted out and stood waiting by the truck.

"Hey, boy," she said as she got out of the truck and patted his head. He leaned into her side and let out a deep sigh of joy.

Aunt Sherry and Uncle Mel stood on the porch and waited. Noah brought Emily's bag inside and set it down.

He turned to Emily. "Why don't you go on in and change into some jeans? I'd like to go for a walk if you're up to it."

"Sure," Emily replied. "It'll be good to stretch my legs after being on the plane. Be right back."

Uncle Mel carried the bag to Emily's room then went back out to chat with Noah. Aunt Sherry followed Emily inside.

"We have a special dinner for your homecoming," her aunt said.

Emily laughed. "All your dinners are special." She patted her midsection. "And delicious."

"I'm just tickled pink you're back." She hugged Emily and gently pushed her into the room. "Now change out of your traveling clothes and go for that walk with Noah. You don't want to keep him waiting too much longer."

Emily gave her aunt a curious look, but Aunt Sherry just grinned and pointed to the room. "Okay, I'll hurry."

When Emily finished changing, she took off outside to find Noah sitting by himself on the porch steps. He stood and reached for her hand.

"Let's go down there," he said, pointing toward a clump of trees on the opposite side of the house from the barn. "I'd like a little privacy."

"Okay." Emily didn't understand his need for privacy, but she trusted him. "Looks like y'all got some more rain while I was gone."

"Yeah, we did, and I didn't get much sleep because of it. Some of the farmers can't handle much more rain after the last flood. It was an exhausting experience that'll take time to recover from."

"Was everyone okay?" She looked at him.

He stopped, turned her around to face him, and shook his head. "Not really."

"Did you have to move the livestock again?"

"No, not that. No one got flooded this time, but that wasn't what you asked."

Emily tilted her head. "Huh?"

"You asked if everyone was okay, and I said not really. I wasn't okay."

Fear gripped Emily. "Jillian?"

He shook his head. "No, not Jillian."

She was puzzled. "What's wrong?"

Noah held on to both of her hands and took a step back, never breaking their gaze. "I think I've been hit hard by love."

"What?" Her voice cracked.

He looked down at the ground before looking back into her eyes. "Emily, I've told you I'm in love with you. But I didn't realize how much until you started talking about going to NYU. I don't want to lose you. And I don't mean as an employee."

"Why didn't you say something?"

"I wasn't sure about things."

He shook his head. "I knew you weren't, which was why I didn't want to push too hard. I didn't want to stand between you and your dreams."

"I appreciate that," she said. She couldn't stop herself from smiling. "You're such a kind, selfless man."

"You think so?"

"Yeah, I know so."

"When Sherry told me you were coming back to stay, I was beside myself." Noah pulled her close until she could feel his heart beating. "I wanted to talk you out of going, but I held back. I didn't want to scare you."

"Oh, I'm scared," she said. "Very, very scared."

He groaned. "I was afraid of that."

"But only because I love you, too."

Noah suddenly froze. "You said that before, but I wasn't sure you meant it." He tilted her head. "Are you sure?"

"Uh-huh. Very much. In fact, the whole time I was in New York, all I could think about was how miserable I'd be without you."

"Emily, I am now the happiest man in West Virginia. No, make that the whole United States."

She laughed. "Let's see how things go, now that we've admitted our feelings. This is all new to me."

After he walked Emily back to her aunt and uncle's house, Noah had to leave. One of the farmers had called his cell phone and said he had a cow in labor, and it looked like she might need some help.

"I'll see you first thing in the morning," Noah said as he turned and ran toward his truck. "I hope this really happened and it's not a dream."

Emily smiled and waved as Noah drove away. She had the same fear as Noah, that it might be a dream.

❧

Noah wanted to shout his feelings at the top of his lungs, but he needed to contain his emotions—at least until he finished delivering the calf. He arrived at the farm in the nick of time.

"I think it's breech," the farmer said.

Noah got down to business and managed to save the calf with the farmer's help. When he stood up and shook the man's hand, he got a big grin and slap on the back.

"So when's the big day?"

Noah turned his head slightly and narrowed his eyes. "What big day?"

"I hear you and Mel's niece are sweet on each other. I figured you were about to get hitched."

"Where did you hear that?" Noah asked, unable to keep the grin from sliding over his lips.

"Little birdie told me."

"I'll have to have a talk with that little birdie. Getting hitched sounds pretty good to me, but in the meantime, try to keep it to yourself. I haven't asked her yet."

"You sly dog. Just make sure you send me an invite."

❧

Emily got to the office early the next morning and turned on the computer. Everything she'd taken for granted before seemed fresh and new to her now. She loved everything about this place—from the curve of the counter to the bell on the door. With Kingston by her side, she felt like she could conquer the world.

To her delight, Noah arrived fifteen minutes later. "Hey, I thought you might be here. Got a minute?"

"Sure," she said. "What's up?"

Noah crooked his finger and motioned for her to go outside with him. He locked the door and led her toward the back, through the cluster of trees, and to a clearing, where he stopped and turned her to face him.

"It's come to my attention that people are talking about us," he began.

She opened her mouth, but he gently put his finger over her lips. He didn't look unhappy, so she tried to erase the fear that welled in her chest.

"I'm not saying I mind them talking, but I do think they need something concrete to talk about." He pulled something out of his pocket and got down on one knee. "I know we just admitted our feelings for each other yesterday, but I'm a man who knows what he wants, and I go after it."

Emily giggled. This was such a strange experience for her that she had no idea what to do. So she just stood there and stared at him.

He kissed the back of her hand then studied it for a moment before he opened the box. "Will you marry me, Emily?"

Her knees grew weak when she saw the beautiful pear-shaped diamond ring. When she tried to answer, her mouth was so dry nothing would come out. So she nodded.

"I sure hope it fits. Your aunt said she thought this was your size." He pulled the ring from the box and slipped it on her finger.

"My aunt?" Her voice came out in a sudden squeak. "She knew about this?"

He rubbed his neck. "Um—yeah. I sort of needed to talk to her so I could get you a ring you'd like. I'm not very good at picking out jewelry."

Emily splayed her hand and looked at the dazzling ring. It was perfect—exactly what she would have picked for herself.

"Well, do you like it?"

She threw her arms around his neck and squeezed him as tight as she could. "I love it!"

Noah had to peel her arms away to give her a kiss. Afterward he looked into her eyes and stroked her cheek. "If you always act like this when I give you jewelry, we better go out and buy the biggest jewelry box we can find, because I'm gonna do it a bunch."

Emily laughed. "It's not the ring, silly. It's you."

"Well in that case, come here, Emily, and let me kiss you again."

Epilogue

H old still, Kingston." Jillian grabbed the Great Dane by the collar as Uncle Mel fastened the wedding rings to the attached pillow. Mr. Zimmerman had decided to go ahead with his plans to move to Florida, and Emily happily agreed to keep Kingston.

As soon as Mel had the rings secured, Jillian straightened up and turned to Emily. "Ready?"

Emily turned to Uncle Mel, who winked. "Ready as I'll ever be."

Jillian gave the signal to the church organist, who turned and started playing. Emily's heart lurched, so she lowered her head and said a prayer of thanks. She opened her eyes in time to watch her maid of honor, Jillian, and Noah's best man, Dwayne, guide Kingston toward his position as the ring bearer.

As Emily's heart stilled and her nerves steadied, Uncle Mel gave her hand a squeeze. "We're up next," he whispered. "You're a beautiful bride, Emily. Noah's a blessed man."

Emily felt her cheeks flame—not with embarrassment but with joy. "I'm the one who's blessed."

Her uncle laughed and nodded. "Let's agree that you're both blessed and get this show on the road. You don't want to keep your groom waiting."

All heads turned the instant the music tempo quickened, and Emily felt a flood of emotion as her entire life changed. For the first time ever, she had no doubt what she wanted—and that was to be the wife of a man whose faith in the Lord was as strong as hers.

After they said their vows, Noah lowered his head to kiss Emily. Suddenly she felt something nudging between her and her new husband. When she looked down, she saw Kingston straining against the leash, with Jillian on the other end wearing an apologetic grin. He was attached to his family, and he obviously didn't want to be left out. Everyone laughed as Emily and Noah included Kingston in a hug. They finally turned to walk up the aisle as a family—husband, wife, and family dog.

SPECIAL MISSION

Dedication

*I'd like to dedicate this book to my editors,
JoAnne Simmons and Rachel Overton, for all their time and
attention to the details that helped make this book as good as it can be.*

Chapter 1

Kimberly Shaw stared up at the bridal party, imagining herself getting ready to walk toward her own adoring groom, David. The wedding singer's voice echoed through the small chapel as the groom and his men stood in a line, waiting. Her heart hammered. This would be her in less than a year—at least that's what she hoped.

After the singer finished her song, the chapel grew quiet for a few seconds. The organist positioned herself on the bench and opened her music book. A soft murmur started at the back of the church, but Kim figured people were just getting impatient. The wedding was running behind by— she took a quick look at her watch—about fifteen minutes.

She glanced back up toward Brian's guys. His smile had faded, and David leaned over to whisper something. Then suddenly Brian's mother scurried up the aisle and spoke to the pastor.

The murmur behind Kim grew louder. She squirmed in her pew. Something was happening; she just wished she knew what it was.

"Where's the bride?" Kim asked. "This isn't good."

"Oh I'm sure it's nothing serious. I bet Leila couldn't get into her dress," Kim's best friend, Carrie, whispered. "Did you see her putting away two desserts last night at the rehearsal dinner?"

"Shh." Kim couldn't help but smile. "Yeah, I noticed. I don't know how she could eat the night before her wedding."

"Maybe she was nervous-eating. I do that with brownies." Carrie smoothed the front of her skirt.

Kim was about to comment, but the pastor returned to the front of the church. He whispered something to Brian, who hesitated, nodded, and tightened his jaw. The frown on his face deepened as he huddled with David and the rest of the guys, who all groaned then turned and headed for the side door.

"What is going on?" Carrie said. "You don't think we're taking this outside, do you? I hope not. These heels are hard enough to walk in on hard floors. There's no way I'll be able to walk in grass."

Kim nodded toward the pastor, who held up his hands to quiet everyone. "Folks, there's been a change of plans. There will be no wedding today."

Loud gasps resonated through the sanctuary.

"This is weird," Carrie said.

"C'mon." Kim scooted out of the pew and into the aisle, where a smattering of guests had already begun to congregate. "Let's go find out what happened."

"But—"

Kim didn't wait to hear what Carrie was about to say. After figuring out she'd have to deal with a crowded narthex, she turned and half walked, half ran up the front and out the side door. David held his cell phone up to his ear and paced. Brian leaned against a concrete wall by the fellowship hall, a stunned look in his eyes. Kim hesitated for a moment before heading toward David. He glanced at her and shook his head, the straight line of his mouth letting her know that something awful had just happened.

She turned toward Brian whose gaze locked with hers. Dread flowed through her, but someone needed to be with Brian, and all his friends stood several feet from him—as if they were afraid of him.

He'd always been there for her, no matter what. The least she could do was find out what happened and comfort him if needed.

Kim slowly moved toward him and forced a sympathetic smile. He remained fixed to one spot.

"What happened?" she asked as she reached for his hand.

"She changed her mind."

They stared at each other a couple of seconds while Kim's mind wrapped around what he'd just said. "I'm so sorry, Brian. I don't get it."

Brian shook his head. "Yeah, I don't either."

"Can I. . ." Her voice trailed off as she tried to think of something to offer, but nothing came to mind. "Is there anything I can do?" She squeezed his hand. He didn't budge from his position.

"Not really. I'll be okay after the shock wears off."

"I'm sure," Kim said. "Have you talked to Leila?"

"Nah. She didn't have the decency to tell me. I knew she was late, but that's pretty normal for her. Her mom called my mom."

Kim wanted to shake Leila until her teeth fell out for doing such a rotten thing to such a sweetheart of a guy. "Would you like for me to try to talk to her?" If she'd been better friends with Leila, she would have talked to her without asking.

"Wouldn't do any good," he said. "Once Leila sets her mind on something, it's a done deal." He finally shifted, pulled away from her, shoved his hands in his pockets, and moved a few inches from where he stood then let out a sardonic chuckle. "In fact she's the one who finagled the proposal."

"Yeah, I remember David telling me about that."

Brian pulled his hands out of his pockets and lifted them. "I was perfectly happy with the way things were going, but after you and David—well, you know, after she saw your ring and all. . ."

Kim held out her left hand and gazed at the sparkling diamond David had given her. After he proposed, she thought things would be wonderful—that they'd get married a few months or even a year later, and then they'd live happily ever after. She had no idea that what started out as his part-time career with the National Guard would take precedence over their relationship. Shortly after they got engaged, he let the law practice he'd inherited from his father slide in favor of his passion for the National Guard. The patriotism she'd seen when they first met had become a source of contention between them.

"Sorry," Brian said. "David told me you're getting frustrated about having to wait."

"I'm just glad he's stalling now," she replied. "Before we get married."

"Just don't rush things," Brian said. "Look where it got me."

Except Brian wasn't the one who'd rushed the wedding. Leila's fantasy of the romantic wedding and honeymoon had been the topic of her conversations with all their friends for the past couple of months. David had even accused Kim of being like Leila when she tried to press for a date.

"Did David tell you he's thinking about volunteering to go overseas? For some kind of top secret special mission. Only a few select people from his unit will be involved."

Brian's forehead crinkled as he gave her a look of concern. "Kim, he's already been accepted." He gestured toward David who was still on his cell phone. "In fact, he's talking to his commanding officer right now. Before we got to the church, he said he needed to contact him before the day was over, so I told him to go ahead and call."

Kim felt as if someone had pulled the turf from beneath her. She opened her mouth, but she had no idea what to say.

Brian stepped forward and gently draped an arm over her shoulder. "Trust me, Kim. It's better for him to go ahead and get this out of his system. When he comes back, he'll be ready to settle down."

She frowned and nodded. "Yeah, I guess you're right. Do you know when he's going?"

Movement captured her attention, so she looked up to see David striding toward them, a quick grin followed by a look of compassion for Brian. "Sorry, buddy, tough break."

Brian slowly removed his arm from Kim's shoulder and gently nudged her toward David. "Like I told Kim—it's better Leila does this now than decide she's not ready later."

"Maybe she just has cold feet." David offered a sympathetic grin. "I bet she comes around, and you'll be off on your honeymoon in a day or two."

"We'll see." Brian stepped away from them and waved. "I'd better go talk to some folks and thank them for coming to the party that didn't happen."

Kim and David watched Brian until he disappeared into the crowd, and then David casually placed his hand in the small of Kim's back. "I wouldn't wanna be Brian now." He gave her a squeeze. "But he seems to be handling it well."

She pulled away and studied David's profile—handsome in every way, from his deep-set eyes to his strong chin. "What choice does he have?"

"Huh?"

"You said he was handling it well. What else would a guy in his place do?" Kim paused and gave him a moment to think before adding, "What would you do if I stood you up at the altar?"

He gave her a mock look of shock. "That's not something I'll ever have to worry about, is it?"

Kim shook her head. "No, of course not."

David turned her to face him and placed a hand on each of her shoulders. "That's my girl."

"Now there's something I'd like to know, David."

"What's that?" He dropped his hands to his sides and lifted one eyebrow with one of his heart-melting gazes. She had to look away to say what she needed to say.

"When were you planning to tell me about being accepted for this overseas mission?" She frowned. "I thought you were just in the discussion stage with your commanding officer."

David closed his eyes and swallowed hard. Kim folded her arms and tilted her head as she watched him try to figure out how to explain. Why didn't he just come out with it?

"I was going to tell you today." His voice was barely audible.

"Okay." She cleared her throat. "Now that I know, let's talk about it."

He gave her an apologetic look and shrugged. "What's there to talk about? I'm going over to the Middle East on a special mission."

"How long will you be gone?"

"I don't know—a couple of months, maybe a little longer?" He forced a smile, cupped her chin, and tilted her face up to his. "Not too long though."

"What about our wedding? Will we be able to get married sometime this year?" She wasn't able to keep the sarcasm from her voice.

Suddenly his smile faded. "I was hoping to, but now I'm not sure."

"So what am I supposed to do? Send out invitations telling people that we're getting married sometime, like after you get back from your special mission, and they're invited, but we're not sure when. . . ." Her voice trailed off as she started shaking.

"I'm sorry, Kim."

"If you're sorry, why did you request this assignment?" Her voice cracked, but at this point she didn't care how she sounded. David had made a monumental decision without consulting her first. Was this how it would always be?

"It's important to me. I want to be part of this mission."

"More than you want to be with me?"

"Don't be like that, Kim. You've always known how I felt about our country and my responsibility. They need me."

"I love our country, too, David, but it's not just that." She pondered the right way to put her feelings to prevent sounding selfish. "One of the things I love about you is your patriotism and commitment to protect our country. But when you asked me to marry you, I thought you wanted me to be your partner. You should have discussed it with me before you volunteered to go." Kim fought hard to control the way she sounded, but the words sounded shrill. She cleared her throat.

He narrowed his eyes, but his voice was soft. "And what would you have wanted me to do?"

"I—" She cut herself off before she said anything she might later regret. "I don't know."

David leaned toward her and reached for her hands. "Kimberly, you know how I feel about you."

"I do?"

"You should." He paused, gently ran his hand up her arm, and smiled down at her. "I love you very much. I never would have asked you to marry me if I didn't."

"But—" She stopped when he put his fingers to her lips to shush her.

"All the love in the world can't negate the fact that our country needs me. I want to do everything in my power to make this world a better place for us." He managed a half smile as he gestured across the lawn. "And for everyone here."

No way could she refute any of that, or she'd come across sounding selfish. "I guess you're right."

"I know I'm right. Now let's go see how the jilted groom is doing. We don't want to leave him alone too long, or he might think no one cares."

Kim could relate to the jilted feeling, but she still didn't say anything. As strong as she was, she knew that once she got started talking about all the reasons she was upset and hurt, she might not be able to stop. David took her by the hand and led her to Brian, who stood in the middle of a group of guys, all of them silent and looking very uncomfortable.

Kim's parents had just spoken to Brian, and they approached her as David joined Brian. "This is terrible," her mother whispered. "But at least this happened now rather than later."

With a sigh, Kim nodded. "I'm shocked, but he seems to be doing okay."

Her dad squirmed, so her mother gave her a quick hug. "I don't think your dad wants to stick around, so I'll talk to you later. We'll pray for Brian."

"I'm sure he'll appreciate it," Kim said. She strode toward David and the group that now surrounded Brian.

"Hey, buddy," David said. "Things will look better tomorrow."

One of the other men coughed, and a couple of them walked away. Kim felt even worse for Brian now.

"Do you want us to hang around?" David continued. "I don't want to leave you alone if you need us."

"Um. . ." Brian glanced around Kim then looked David in the eye. "Nah, I don't think so. I'll be fine."

"C'mon, buddy, we can do something to get your mind off things," David urged.

Kim wanted to smack him, but she just tugged him away instead. "He's not in the mood, David." She offered Brian a sympathetic look.

Brian smiled back at her then turned to David. "You're a fortunate man to have someone like Kim. You'd better hang on to her."

David possessively wrapped his arms around Kim and squeezed. "She's not going anywhere." Then he let go and pretend-punched Brian. "Hey, thanks a lot for spilling the beans about my overseas tour."

"David. . ." Kim glared at him.

Brian shot David a serious look. "I assumed you told her before you mentioned it to the rest of us. After all, she *is* your fiancée."

"Oh well, no harm done." David loosened his tie and undid the top button of his shirt. "I think I'm gonna head home and get out of this monkey suit. Wanna do something later?"

"I think I'll pass," Brian replied as he stepped back and turned. "Why don't you spend some time with Kim before you have to leave?"

Kim dropped her hands into her coat pocket. It was a cool, early spring afternoon, but as the sun headed closer to the horizon, the temperature was heading closer to freezing. She shivered.

"Cold?" David asked.

She nodded. "Yeah."

"C'mon, I'll take you home. We can go out later if you want to. I think we have more talking to do."

※

Brian watched his best friend escort the sweetest girl in Charleston, West Virginia, toward the parking lot. David had no idea how blessed he was to have the love of a woman who'd never even think to do what Leila did.

Once upon a time, Brian had been in love with Kimberly Shaw. They'd been friends for as long as he could remember—since sometime in early elementary school. She was athletic, so they played on the same county-run soccer team. By the time they reached middle school, she'd moved on to the girl's volleyball team at school, while he went out for football. Kim remained his friend, but things had changed. Boys liked her, and she trusted Brian enough to confide her deepest thoughts and feelings. Somewhere along the way, he'd fallen in love with her, and it hit him hard when one of his buddies gave her his class ring in high school. Brian wished he'd made his move before it was too late, but he didn't want to risk losing what he had with Kim.

He managed to stand on the sidelines of her life until his friend dumped her right before their big senior event at school. When Kim called crying, he offered to be her date, and she'd accepted. Too bad he'd wimped out on letting her know then how he felt—but he wasn't willing to risk scaring her away. Instead he encouraged her to try new things and not let any guy get the best of her. He figured if they were meant to be together, it would happen one of these days. Surely God would see to that, right? He prayed every night for some opening into the romantic side of Kim's heart.

When he met David during a National Guard weekend, he'd been happy to meet someone else from his hometown. David had grown up on the other side of Charleston, so he'd gone to a different school. Brian invited him to church, and David agreed without a moment's hesitation.

Kim didn't seem all that interested in David at first. However, when David set his mind to pursuing her, she didn't stand a chance. That was two years ago, and now they were engaged.

Brian wanted to kick himself in the backside. What a chump he'd been. Meeting Leila had given him a little ray of sunshine. She was beauty-pageant pretty. Leila was a talented musician and singer, who loved doing solos in church. She laughed at his jokes and made him feel as if he were the only other person in the room. She still didn't match up to Kim, yet he was able to convince himself that he was in love with her. And since he couldn't have Kim, he knew he could grow old with Leila and never want to be with anyone else. She'd talked him into not reenlisting with the Guard because she didn't like him going away so often. He was willing to do whatever it took to make a marriage work.

God, why did this have to happen? Now what?

The second Kim closed the door behind her, she leaned against it and tilted her head upward. *Lord, what do You want me to do? I'm angry at David, and I don't know if I'll ever understand why it's so important to leave—especially now that we're supposed to be planning our life together.*

Guilt flooded her as she straightened and plodded toward her bedroom to change into her jeans. David said he'd be back in a couple of hours, so she had time to straighten up a bit and get herself mentally and emotionally ready for their talk. However, as the minutes ticked away, she felt even worse than when he'd dropped her off.

When the doorbell rang, Kimberly steeled herself and flung open the door. David handed her a grocery store bouquet.

"I'll put these in some water, and we can go."

Once she finished arranging the flowers, she turned to David, who quirked an eyebrow and grinned. "You okay?"

Kim shrugged. "I guess."

He touched her arm and broadened his smile. "I won't be gone long. You know how quickly the months fly by."

"That's not the point, David, and you know it." She had to speak her mind. "I'm not as upset about you leaving as I am the fact that you never discussed it with me."

"Do I have to discuss everything with you?"

"Not everything," she replied. "Just the important stuff. The stuff that impacts *us*."

"Kim, I love you, and I thought I knew you well enough to trust that you'd understand." He pulled her into his arms and rested his chin on her head as her mind swirled. When he drew back and looked into her eyes, she saw that familiar spark. "I'm just glad you're nothing like Leila. You're a good woman who'll be there for me, no matter what."

Chapter 2

Kimberly's heart ached as she thought about the meaning of "no matter what." If it involved David's making decisions without consulting her, she wasn't so sure she could live up to his expectations.

David shook his head. "Being a military wife can be rough, but it has its rewards, too."

She stood there for a moment as her thoughts scrambled in her head. "I'm sure." Her voice caught in her throat.

"Why don't you get to know some other military wives and girlfriends and hang out with them?" he said. "It'll make the time go by faster."

"I might do that."

"You do still want to marry me, don't you, Kimberly?" He twirled a lock of her hair then tucked it behind her ear.

Kim swallowed hard as she frowned up at him. "Yes, of course I do, but I wonder. . . ." In spite of trying to settle her shaky nerves, she couldn't keep the accusatory tone from her voice. "I just wonder if you want the military more than you want to marry me."

"Don't tell me what I really want," he said softly, "because I know. I want you."

"But you want the military even more."

David blinked and half smiled. "The military is a bigger calling for me, yes." He gently rested his hands on her shoulders and looked down at her until she allowed herself to meet his gaze. "But that doesn't negate my feelings for you in the least, Kimberly. You know how I feel about you. That hasn't changed one iota." He hesitated before adding, "My acceptance of this mission wasn't done without quite a bit of prayer. I feel that this is what God wants me to do."

How could she respond to that? They stood in silence for several minutes before Kim finally shook her head. "I don't want to change anything right now. If you've been called to this mission, then go. I'll wait for you." She cast her glance downward and pulled her bottom lip between her teeth to keep her chin from quivering.

He tilted her face toward his. "Are you sure?"

Sort of. She nodded.

"I'll talk to Brian and get him to look after you."

Kim bristled. "I don't need anyone to look after me. I'm perfectly capable of taking care of myself."

David leaned back and laughed. "Now there's the girl I fell in love with. Independent and strong."

"But I don't mind looking after him. After all, he just got jilted."

"Yes," David agreed. "That's an excellent idea. Do you want me to talk to him first?"

"I don't think that'll be necessary," Kim said. "Remember, I've known him practically all my life. And he introduced us."

"True. Maybe you can return the favor and find someone to help get his mind off Leila."

"It's not that easy," she said. "But I'm a good listener, so if he needs to talk, I'll just be there for him."

"Maybe some nice Christian girl will come into the salon, and you can talk him up."

Kim couldn't help but laugh. "Yeah, I'll hold her captive with a can of hair spray and some scissors."

"Attagirl." David chucked her under the chin. "Then you can give her a gorgeous haircut that he won't be able to resist. Whatever works to bring him back to life."

As difficult as it had been to hear that David was leaving, after he'd boarded the bus, Kim wasn't as devastated as she thought she'd be. When she turned around, she saw Brian standing by her car, watching. . .waiting. He grinned and motioned for her to join him.

"What are you doing here?" Kim shielded her eyes from the sun.

"David told me when he was leaving. I asked if it was okay for me to be here for you, and he thought that was a great idea."

They stood and watched as the bus took off down the street. After it was out of sight, Brian patted her on the shoulder. "I sure hope everything turns out like you want it to, Kim. You certainly deserve the best."

"Thanks." She smiled up at him. "I just wish he'd talked to me about it earlier."

"He really should have. I told him that when he first decided to request this assignment."

Her head snapped around. "You did? Why didn't *you* tell me then?"

"I wanted to, but David reminded me that it wasn't my place. He said he wanted to tell you, and I agreed that would be best." Brian shifted his weight and turned to face her. "But if I'd known then what I know now, I would have given him an ultimatum that if he didn't tell you right away, I would have."

"That's what hurts."

He gave her a brotherly hug. "Need some company for the day?"

"Not really. I have a pile of laundry and some hairstyle books I wanted to read."

"Let me know if you need me." After she unlocked her car, he held the door. "The least you can let me do is pick you up for church on Sunday—for old times' sake. I'm sure David wouldn't mind."

David's words about looking after Brian rang through her head. "Of course he wouldn't. He knows we're like brother and sister. Sounds good." She got in her car and took off, only casting one quick glance in the rearview mirror to see Brian standing there, still watching.

Carrie called shortly after she got home. "I got it!"

"Huh?" Kim knew whatever it was had to be good by the sound of Carrie's squeal of excitement. "What did you get?"

"You know, that job in Chicago."

Kim racked her brain, trying to remember something about Carrie applying for a job in Chicago, but nothing came to her. "I'm sorry, Carrie. I don't know where my mind has been, but I don't have a clue what you're talking about."

"That's probably because I didn't tell you where it was. All I said was that I was being considered for a promotion."

"Oh yeah. You got it?" Kim had assumed it was in Charleston. "So you have to move to Chicago?"

"Just temporarily," Carrie replied. "I'll train there and eventually come back here to manage the West Virginia district."

That was a relief. "At least you'll be back. When do you leave?"

"Tomorrow."

❧

Brian recovered from the public jilting much more quickly than he thought he would. What bothered him more than the wedding falling through was the humiliation of everyone staring at him when he found out Leila wasn't showing up. If it hadn't been for Kim, he would have been too embarrassed to show his face in church—at least for a while.

He'd taken his time getting ready. Kim had wanted to go to the early service, and he suspected it was for him, since they wouldn't see all the usual people.

The instant she opened the door, he gave her a once-over. "Hey, you look pretty good for a lonely woman."

She flicked her scarf at him. "Stop it, Brian. You don't have to go there with me."

"I'm serious. I half expected to see red-rimmed eyes and that drab brown dress you used to wear when you didn't feel good."

Kim pointed to her eyes. "If you look behind the concealer, you'll see the red. As for the dress, I sent it to Goodwill last year when David told me it was the ugliest thing he'd ever seen and I looked absolutely hideous in it."

A burst of anger rose in Brian's chest. "He told you that?" Kim couldn't look hideous if she tried.

She bobbed her head. "It's not like you don't agree. In fact, everyone I know hated that dress."

"The dress wasn't attractive, but you were still pretty."

"Oh you." She pulled out her keys and lightly pushed him toward the door. "Let's drop the fake stuff. We've known each other too long to be dishing out anything that's not real."

He knew how she hated compliments. She'd always been that way—even when their senior class voted her Cutest Girl. In fact, she'd reminded him that puppies were cute, so she could win the award for looking like a dog.

For the next three weeks, Kim and Brian went to church together, but that was it. The only other thing she knew he did was work—totally not like Brian, who loved nothing more than to be right in the middle of the social action.

Finally she couldn't stand it anymore, and she remembered David urging her to help keep Brian's mind off Leila, so on Tuesday she went to the back room at the Snappy Scissors and called him during her lunch break.

"Hey, Kim. Something wrong?"

"No. . .well, maybe. What's up with you? Where do you hide all week?"

He didn't answer right away, but Kim could hear him breathing.

"So you're giving me the silent treatment? You acted perfectly fine on Sunday."

"I've been working." His voice sounded off. She'd known Brian long enough to realize something was up—and he wasn't going to talk without some not-so-gentle prodding from her.

"What're you doing after work tonight?"

"I'm behind on paperwork," he replied. "Look, Kim, I'm really busy right now."

"No, you look, Brian. I've had one man keep secrets then take off for the other side of the world. I'm not letting one of my best friends do this to me. Either tell me what's going on, or I'm coming over tonight whether you like it or not."

After a brief pause, he said, "Okay, but not tonight. Why don't you and I meet somewhere for lunch tomorrow?"

"That's fine. How about we meet at the Blossom Deli at eleven thirty tomorrow?"

"Great. I'll treat you to a Reuben."

"Be still my heart," she said with a swoon. "You certainly know the way to get my mind off my sorrows."

"Yeah, yeah," he said, his tone lightening up a touch. "You say that to all the guys."

"Right," she replied. "I want to warn you, though. I need to vent."

"You and me both." He chuckled. "Just make sure you don't stand me up. My fragile ego can't handle that again."

Kim heard between the lines, and she knew there was seriousness behind his playful tone. "You've always been able to trust me, Brian. When have I ever let you down?"

"Never. You're not that kind of girl. See you tomorrow. I need to get back to these invoices, or I might not be able to pay for lunch tomorrow."

"It's my turn to treat anyway," Kim said, "so don't worry about it."

After they hung up, she stayed in the break room, got her salad out of the fridge, and sat down at the table in the corner. Tuesdays were typically slow, so only three stylists were scheduled, and they staggered their lunch breaks. She was relieved to be alone with her thoughts.

⚜

All afternoon Brian struggled to keep his thoughts on business. Kimberly Shaw's image kept popping into his head.

"Knock, knock."

Brian glanced up to see Jack Morrow smiling at him from the door. "Just wanted to tell you what a good job you did on the quarterly financials. Patterson was impressed."

"For a CEO of the largest tool distributor in the world, it doesn't take much to impress him, does it?"

"C'mon, Brian. You're the best comptroller we've ever had. Everyone thinks so."

Brian took his hand off the computer mouse and settled back in his chair. "Whaddya need, Jack?"

"Who says I need anything?" The district manager took a couple of steps into Brian's office and closed the door behind him. "Mind if I come in?"

Brian laughed. "Of course not." He gestured to the chair across from his desk. "Have a seat and tell me what's on your mind."

Jack glanced around the office, obviously stalling for time. Finally he looked Brian in the eye. "Anything I can do?"

"Do about what? What are you talking about?" Brian asked.

"You know. Leila. I'm a good listener."

"I appreciate that, but I'm fine." Brian smiled. "She actually did me a favor."

"Then what's been on your mind the past few weeks?"

"Why?"

"I don't know. . . ." Jack glanced down at his hands as he steepled his fingers and studied them before looking Brian in the eye. "You've done a great job here, but you haven't been your old self since the wedding. I'm concerned."

"I'm just fine. Leila and I would have made things work, but I don't think we were all that great of a match."

Jack stood up and flashed a sympathetic smile. "Good. I just wanted you to know that you can talk to me."

"Thanks, Jack. I appreciate it."

"See ya."

After Jack left, Brian closed his eyes. *Lord, give me the strength to get past all this. I appreciate the concern of my friends, but it's time to move on.*

The rest of the afternoon went by in a blur as he finished another report and started a new one. Brian was thankful to have such a mentally consuming job. Although his coworkers probably assumed he was immersing himself in his work because of Leila, he knew he was trying to get past thoughts of what could have been between him and Kimberly.

❧

The second Kim spotted Brian rounding the corner toward Blossom's, her pulse quickened, and some old feelings flooded her, bringing her back to much younger days when she'd fantasized about Brian telling her he cared more about her than he was letting on. The one time she thought they might get romantic, he'd gotten all flustered and challenged her to a race, which she knew he did to change the mood. That was probably for the best.

"You look great, Kimberly." Brian hugged her and gave her a kiss on the cheek before turning toward the door of the deli.

Kim fought hard to keep her nerves intact. She chattered incessantly about work and everything else she could think of. When there was a lull between them, she told herself the only reason she felt this way was that David was gone. Brian was like a brother to her—nothing else. And that was all it could ever be.

"Have you thought about going back to the singles group?" Brian asked.

She held up her hand and pointed to the diamond. "No, how about you?"

"Yeah, but it seems weird. Wanna go sometime?" He cleared his throat and quickly added, "Just until David comes back. I just thought maybe it would be fun to see some old friends."

Kim smiled. She was glad Brian let her know what he needed from her. "Of course I'll go with you, Brian. You should get back in circulation. You're too good of a catch to be roaming around without a good woman." She almost choked on those words.

A strange expression flickered across his face, but he quickly recovered. He laughed. "Now that's a new one."

"It's true," she insisted. "I can't imagine why any girl would ever let you go. You're sweet, smart, and fun—not to mention a great-looking guy who loves Jesus."

Color crept up his cheeks as he shook his head and made a face. "Apparently, that's not enough for some women."

"I think Leila will look back at what she did and regret it, but you'll be taken by then, I'm sure."

Brian shifted in his seat before reaching across the table for her hand. "Thank you, Kim. Now let's discuss the singles group. Wanna start tonight?"

If it weren't for David encouraging her to do whatever it took to get Brian's mind off Leila, she wouldn't have considered it. She slowly nodded. "Okay."

"Why don't I pick you up at six?"

"Want me to fix supper?"

"Maybe next week. Tonight's my treat. It's my turn, remember?"

She smiled and nodded. "You're on," she said as she wrapped what was left of her sandwich. "I need to get back to work."

Kim's schedule was booked the rest of the afternoon, so she didn't have time to ponder her situation. When closing time came, she hung up her apron and got her station ready for the next day. As she wiped down the counter and prepared her combs and brushes, the owner of the salon kept up a constant stream of chatter.

"I'm whipped," Jasmine said. "I can't wait to go home, take a shower, and curl up in front of the TV. What're you doing tonight?"

"Singles group at church," Kim replied.

Jasmine stopped midsweep. "Singles group? Do I sense trouble in paradise? What's up with you and David?"

"Nothing. I'm going with Brian so he doesn't have to face everyone alone."

"Oh," Jasmine said, nodding her understanding. "That poor boy getting stood up like that—and in front of all his family and friends. I bet he's a wreck."

"No, actually, he's handling it quite well."

Jasmine tilted her head and regarded Kim for a moment. "Ya know, if it weren't for David being in the picture, I think you and Brian would make a cute couple."

Kim let out a nervous laugh. "I don't think so. We're more like brother and sister. We've known each other since I can remember."

"And you're very close. Good friends for life, right?"

"That's right," Kim agreed.

"Well, I think it's important for married couples to be friends. The chemistry between them will come and go, but friendship lasts forever."

She should know, Kim thought, *Jasmine's been married almost thirty years.*

"Were you and Wayne friends before you got married?"

Jasmine grinned. "Yep. His family lived right next door to mine growing up."

"I never knew that. Why didn't you tell me?"

"You never asked." Jasmine reached for the dustpan and finished sweeping. "But that's a moot point, right? You're just keeping Brian company until he meets someone else."

"That's right." Kim pulled her bottom lip between her teeth as she thought about Brian meeting someone new.

"Okay, looks like I'm all done here," Jasmine said as she brushed her hands together. "I hope Wayne has dinner ready for me when I get home, 'cuz I'm too tired to cook."

"See you tomorrow."

Kim finished her work then headed home to get ready for the singles group. She barely had time to shower and change into some khakis and a sweater when the doorbell rang.

"Hey," she said as she flung open the door.

"Hey, yourself," Brian replied. "I'm starving. Ready to go?"

After dinner at the same diner they'd been frequenting since childhood, they rode to the church in silence. Brian was the only person Kim was this comfortable not talking with, and she knew he felt the same way.

As the Bible study progressed, Kim enjoyed the camaraderie among old friends and a few new people she'd just met. After she and David got engaged, they had joined a couples group. The time flew, so when they said their closing prayer, she was sad.

"We need a show of hands to see who all's going bowling Friday night," the group leader said.

Brian nudged her. "Wanna go?"

"I don't know if that's such a good idea with David being gone."

"Come on. David doesn't expect you to sit home every night while he's gone. At least you'll be with a group."

She hesitated. "It just seems strange."

"Strange?" Brian asked with a teasing tone. "This is me, Brian, you're talking to."

"Yeah, I know, but . . ."

"Okay, if you're that uncomfortable about it, I understand. But I think it'll be good for me to go." Brian lifted his hand, and the leader nodded his acknowledgment.

Kim really enjoyed bowling, and it had been awhile. "Okay, I might as well join you," she said as she followed suit and raised her hand.

"Thanks for doing this, Kim."

"What's a friend for?"

The smile that spread over Brian's face warmed her all over. She wondered if he realized she was doing this as much for herself as for him.

Chapter 3

On Friday night, Brian melted at the thought of hanging out with Kim. They must have bowled together at least a dozen times in their lives, but it never felt like this—almost like a date. He had to force himself to remember David. They drove to the bowling alley together.

Each time she stepped up to the line and got into position, he couldn't take his eyes off her. Everything about Kimberly Shaw put his senses into high gear.

She glanced over her shoulder and grinned. "What are you staring at, Brian?"

"You."

"I don't want you watching me when I do this."

He blinked then forced a laugh. "Why? Need some lessons?"

"From you?" she said as she wriggled her eyebrows. "Not in this lifetime. However, if you need help from me, I'll be there."

Suddenly he felt as though someone had pulled the plug on his life raft. She'd pretty much summed up what was between them. He needed way more help than she did.

Kim continued standing at the line. "We don't have all day," Matthew Hayes said. "C'mon, Kim, just roll it."

"I'm just getting into position—trying to find my groove. You want me to knock down some pins, don't you?" she asked as she shifted from side to side.

"Yeah, but it needs to happen sometime tonight."

She cut another sarcastic glance over at Matthew then turned back around to face the pins. "Brian," she said softly, "I need you."

Brian looked down at the floor to keep from showing the impact her simple comment had on him. When he heard Kim's soft voice calling his name, he almost thought he was hearing things.

"Brian, the lady needs you," Matthew said. "Go help her so we can get through this game."

"Uh. . .sure." Brian hopped up and joined Kim.

"I sort of forgot which foot to step out on." Kim glanced at him apologetically. "Sorry. It's been a long time."

If Brian could have captured that moment and held it in his pocket, he would have. "Remember, you like to walk down in four steps. Since you're left-handed, you'll start out on your left foot so you wind up on the right foot. As you approach, you swing back to get momentum. Then when you take your fourth step, you swing the ball forward and release." He gave her shoulders a squeeze and quickly let go.

Kim closed her eyes, mouthed what he'd just said, then opened her eyes and nodded. "Okay, I think I've got it. Thanks." She took a step but stopped.

"Ki–im," Matthew said, "just roll the ball."

"Want me to talk you through it again?" Brian asked softly.

"If you don't mind." She didn't look up, but Brian felt connected to Kim—almost as though they were a couple. And he liked it—way too much.

"Okay, pull back and slowly go, left. . .right. . .left. . .right and release."

&

Kim held her breath as she watched her ball slowly roll toward the pins. She'd let go a little too far to the left, but as the ball made its way closer to the pins, it started to veer toward the center. She did a little shuffle with her feet and scooted to the right.

"Looks like a good one, Kim!" Matthew hollered.

The ball came in between the front pin and the one just to the left and behind it. A couple of pins fell, and the remaining ones wobbled, until every last one of them fell. The ball clunked into the back, and there wasn't a single pin standing!

Kim jumped up and down, clapping. Brian came toward her with his arms open wide. She didn't hesitate a second before rushing toward him and giving him a huge hug. He lifted her off the floor then gently set her back down. When she glanced up into his eyes, she saw something different.

And her insides did a flippy thing—just like what had happened the first time she thought she might be in love with him. Her heart hammered as she put more distance between them. The feeling surprised her.

"If I didn't know the two of you were just buddies, I'd be worried for David," Brenda called out from a couple of lanes away.

Kim quickly glanced away as her cheeks flamed. When she recovered and opened her mouth to thank Brian for his coaching, her voice got stuck in her throat, and nothing came out. He grinned and winked, so she nodded and smiled right back at him, thankful he couldn't read her mind.

"Good job, Kim!" Matthew said as he cast a look of annoyance toward Brenda. Then he turned back and smiled at Kim. "Just don't take so long next time, okay?"

"She just bowled a strike," Brian said in her defense. "She doesn't even have to roll a second ball."

Kim looked back and forth between Brian and Matthew, who'd lifted his eyebrows. Brian slowly nodded.

"True," Matthew said. "You're up now, Brian."

"Need any help?" Kim asked Brian as he selected his ball from the return.

She had to work hard at controlling the shakiness in her voice, but she needed to act as natural as possible. "I'm pretty good at this, ya know."

"Yeah, got any pointers?" Brian asked.

"Just roll the ball and keep it out of the gutter. If everything works out right, you'll knock 'em all down, and you won't have to roll a second ball."

Brian chuckled. "Excellent advice from a pro. I'll see if I can manage that."

Kim really wanted him to make a strike. The last time she'd bowled had been with David, who loved the fact that his score was more than double hers. That was almost a year ago, but she remembered how he'd actually laughed when her ball rolled into the gutter.

Brian's ball hit the front pin head-on, and the two back corner pins were still standing. He turned around to face her with a lopsided grin. "I guess I just don't have your touch."

"I guess not," she said.

After his ball returned, he rolled it down and managed to knock over one of the remaining pins. He sat down next to Kim and patted her on the back. "Looks like you might carry the team tonight, Miss Kim."

"Okay, you two," Matthew said as he stood to take his turn, "let me show you how it's done."

He left three pins standing. "Want me to give you a few tips?" Kim asked.

Matthew rolled his eyes. "Brian, my friend, I think you've created a monster." Then he gestured for Kim to join him. "Sure. Come on up and tell me how to pick these up."

Kim stood next to him and studied the pins before she gestured. "What you want to do is aim for the spot between those two on the right. Then if you hit them at the right angle, one of them will swing over to the left and knock the other one down."

She noticed Matthew and Brian exchanging an amused glance, but it was all in fun. As Matthew took his approach toward the foul line, he swung and released the ball. It rode the edge for about ten feet then swung over and smacked the two pins on the right at exactly the angle needed to knock the other pin down. He made a spare!

Once again, Kim jumped up and shoved her fist into the air. "See? I told you! All you have to do is listen to me."

"Yeah," Matthew said as he headed for his seat. "I gotta give you credit. You knew exactly what I needed to do." He pointed to Brian. "Now you need to give him a little more coaching, and we just might win this game."

At the end of the night, Brian actually had the highest score on the team, Matthew came in second, Matthew's girlfriend, Ashley, was third, and Kim came up last with a score that barely broke one hundred. "I don't know how that happened," she told Brian as they left the bowling alley and walked toward his car. "I got off to such a good start."

"It was just a bad night," Brian said. "We should probably come back and practice before we bowl with everyone else."

"Yeah. I feel pretty uncoordinated after tonight," she said. "But it was fun."

Brian held the door until she got in, and then he ran around to his side to join her. "I had fun, too."

Kim's heart lightened. "I'm glad you're doing so well after what Leila did. I'm still in shock about it."

"Yes, but it turned out okay. She called me yesterday."

"She did? What did she say?"

Brian put the key into the ignition before turning to face Kim. "She said she knew the night before the wedding, but she thought it was just nerves at first."

Kim remembered Leila stuffing herself with food. "That's no excuse."

"I know, but don't be too hard on her, Kim. Leila's never been sure of herself."

Kim wanted to tell Brian that everyone had moments of not being confident or sure, but that was still no excuse to do what Leila had done. However, he was obviously too much of a gentleman to say anything bad about his ex.

"So what now?" Kim asked.

Brian shrugged. "Who knows?"

"Do you think she'll change her mind and decide she wants to marry you?"

"No, that's not gonna happen," he replied. "After being stood up at the altar and realizing I was okay with it, I knew it wasn't meant to be."

Kim felt an immediate sense of relief. "You're an amazing guy, Brian."

He winked at her. "I wonder if David realizes how fortunate he is to have a woman like you."

She shrugged. "I'm the fortunate one." Her stomach churned, and she couldn't look Brian in the eye.

Brian pulled up to Kim's house and waited until she walked up the sidewalk, opened the door, and waved. On her way back to the bedroom, she dropped her handbag and jacket on the back of the sofa. After changing into her pajamas, she booted up her computer and pounded out an e-mail to David, letting him know what all was going on at home. Maybe sharing her experiences with him through e-mail would help her feel better. She was disappointed that he hadn't answered her last e-mail, but he'd told her it wasn't always easy getting on the Internet from where he was.

※

Of all times for this to happen, Brian couldn't figure out why he couldn't get his feelings in check for Kim. She'd been his best friend since forever ago. In the past when this happened, he'd been able to refocus and get things back to how they should be.

Lord, I want to do Your will. Please give me the strength to get through whatever feelings I have for Kimberly. I want to be there for her since David's gone, so staying away from her isn't an option.

He opened his eyes and swallowed hard before bowing his head again. *I guess it is an option if that's the direction You want me to go. Just make it obvious, because I've never been good at reading between the lines.*

Brian thought about all the little nuances of his relationship with Kim. When they were little, they played sports together and exchanged baseball cards. In middle school they vacillated between being best friends and arguing over small, insignificant things, like whether to ride bikes or hang out and listen to music. As he looked back, he knew he'd picked arguments when he wasn't sure how to handle his attraction to her. Throughout high school they went to each other for advice about relationships—always regarding other people, because they never discussed their feelings for each other. And since they'd been such good friends, he'd never wanted to make her uncomfortable by trying to change their relationship.

After trying to read but not being able to focus on the words, Brian powered up his computer and checked his e-mail. No word from David yet, but that didn't surprise him. David had said his Internet access would be sporadic.

Finally, after answering all his e-mail and clicking on a few links from friends, Brian felt sleepy enough to go to bed. He said one last prayer for guidance before closing his eyes and falling asleep.

❧

"You look more chipper today," Jasmine said the second Kim walked through the door on Monday morning. "How was bowling?"

"I lost, but I had a great time."

Jasmine grinned. "That's what really matters." She turned and picked up a magazine from the counter and handed it to Kim. "I brought you a bridal magazine."

"Thanks." Kim took it, flipped through the pages for a few seconds, and slipped it into her tote. "I'll look at it later."

Kim went to her station and got ready for her first client before turning back to the other hairdresser. "Ya know, Brian is such a good guy. I can't imagine why Leila would do what she did."

"Like I said before, I can't imagine why you and Brian aren't together," Jasmine retorted.

Kim froze in place for a second before she cleared her throat. "That would be a disaster. We've been friends forever, and we know way too much about each other to make it work."

"Why?" Jasmine turned and faced her. "It seems to me that knowing a lot about someone and still caring about him is a good thing."

Kim lifted a shoulder, paused, then let it drop. "It really doesn't matter now anyway. I'm engaged to David."

Jasmine contorted her mouth and nodded. "True. I just hope y'all don't turn into one of those perpetually engaged couples who can't set the date."

"Oh, that won't happen. As soon as he gets back from. . .well, from wherever he is in the Middle East, we'll pick the day."

"I hope so for your sake," Jasmine said as her attention was diverted to the person who'd just walked in the door. "Your client's here."

The rest of the day was busy, which was exactly what Kim needed. As soon as the shop closed, she quickly cleaned her station and went home. She pulled the bridal magazine out of her bag and started looking at the pictures. But nothing about it interested her, so she tossed it on the end table and went to check her e-mail. When she spotted David's name in the incoming mail, she grinned.

> *To: KShaw*
> *From: DJenner*
> *Subject: Re: Missing you*
>
> *Hey there, hon! Sorry so much time lapses between my e-mails, but our Internet connection is very sketchy. Seems like it's down as much as it's up. I'm glad you have Brian there to keep you company (and busy) while I'm out of the country. I hope we can complete our mission soon, but it's not looking good at the moment. The insurgent activity is at an all-time high, and it's very dangerous here. Wish I could tell you more, but this mission has to remain top secret to protect everyone involved.*
>
> *Tell Brian thanks for watching after my favorite girl. Sounds like you had a great time at the bowling alley. Mostly I'm glad you're not sitting home being lonely. It makes my job easier if I don't have to worry about you. And I'm sure you've been good at helping keep Brian's mind off being left at the altar. My mission is here, and yours is with Brian.*
>
> *Can't wait to read your next e-mail. While you're back in the States having fun, have a little extra fun for me.*
>
> *Love you, babe!*
> *David*

Kim read David's message over several times before she finally clicked out of it and sank back in her chair. It was wonderful to hear from him. So what was up with the hollow feeling?

She instinctively reached for the phone to call Brian, but she quickly pulled back. Yeah, he'd understand and sympathize, but she needed to stop leaning on him so much.

The sudden ringing of the phone startled her. When she picked it up and heard Brian's voice, she laughed.

"What's so funny?" he asked.

"I was just thinking about calling you. What's up?"

"When I got home, there was a message on the phone from Matthew about the whitewater rafting trip on the New River on Saturday, and I wondered if you wanted to go."

Kim started to say no, but she thought about David's e-mail and how he'd encouraged her to help keep Brian's mind off Leila. Besides, it would be fun, and it would give her something else to write David about. It was harmless, and they'd be so active she wouldn't have time to think about how Brian was starting to make her feel. "Sure, I'd like that."

"You don't sound all that enthusiastic."

"Sorry. I just got home and read an e-mail from David."

She heard a quick intake of air on the other end of the line before Brian cleared his throat. "So what's he up to?"

"I wish I knew. He just said something about how dangerous it was there—"

Brian interrupted. "Enough to worry you, right?"

"Yeah. He also said to thank you for watching out for me."

Brian chuckled. "You watching out for me is more like it."

"Right. So if I go rafting, what all do I need to bring?"

"Food," he replied. "Lots of it."

"With you along, that goes without saying. Anything else?"

"Nah, I think we're good."

❧

Matthew assigned people to rafts then gestured toward the park employee who took the cue to give explicit instructions on safety. "We haven't lost anyone before, and we don't want to start now. Keep your eye on your buddy and don't take off your life jacket, no matter how good of a swimmer you are."

Matthew nodded toward the water. "Let's go have us some fun!"

Groups of four positioned themselves in the rafts. Brian held Kim's hand as she got in, and then he followed. Minutes later their raft had been taken over by the swiftly moving water.

"Take it easy, Brian," Kim said as they bounced along the rapids. "I don't want to lose my breakfast."

Brian laughed. "You think I can do anything about this?"

"Stop leaning. I don't want to get dumped into this crazy river."

"But you look so cute wet." He grinned and made a gesture around his head. "I especially like it when your hair is all tangled and plastered." The other two people, Shawn and Ashley, laughed.

"I'm serious. Stop trying to tip the raft."

The very thought of anything happening to Kim made him shudder. "I won't lean anymore. But if you do fall overboard, I'll go in after you."

She scowled then broke into a grin. "Yeah, and we'll both drown." She paused then gave him one of her warning looks.

Brian felt like he already was drowning. And rafting on the New River had nothing to do with it.

Shawn and Ashley had a loud conversation going with the people in the raft just ahead of them. Kim glared at Brian and whispered, "Just stop trying to tip the raft, Brian. I mean it. If you don't cut it out, I'll tell everyone about the bodysurfing incident."

"You wouldn't."

"Don't test me."

※

Kim had more fun on Saturday than she could remember having in a long time. Brian brought her home and helped her carry her bag and cooler inside then left to get cleaned up. As soon as she was alone, she showered and slipped into a jogging suit before sitting down in front of her computer. To her disappointment, there were no e-mails from David. She started a new letter to tell him about her day.

To: DJenner
From: KShaw
Subject: River fun

Dear David,
I just got back from having more fun than I can remember.

No, that didn't come across right. Kim thought for a moment before deleting it.

Dear David,
I just got back from a whitewater rafting trip on the New River. We had a lot of fun, but it would have been more fun with you there.
Matthew arranged the groups and made sure we knew the rules about the buddy system and life jackets. I hope he has kids someday, because he'd make a wonderful father. Matthew put us on the same raft with a new couple, Shawn and Ashley. The river was normal, but Brian made sure we had plenty of excitement. Every chance he got, he tried to tip the raft, until I told him to knock it off, or I'd tell everyone about the time he wiped out bodysurfing. Remember that? I'll never forget our church trip to the coast when you and I finally got together.

Anyway, after a few hair-raising experiences with Brian trying to tip the raft, we finally made it to the end, where our food was waiting. After we ate, Brian took the rest of the food home with him. I don't think he'll starve anytime soon.

Everyone says to tell you hi. Please stay safe. I want you to come home soon.

Miss you!

Love,
Kimberly

She sat back and read the letter again before clicking SEND. Then she grabbed the bridal magazine Jasmine had given her and headed straight for bed. Brian had asked her to go to the early service the next morning, and she said she'd meet him there.

Brian dabbed more lotion on the spot he'd missed with the sunscreen before the rafting trip. He compared himself to David, who never burned but only got darker in the sun. Brian couldn't help the fact that he was blond.

He slipped into his polo shirt, combed his hair, and took one last look in the mirror. He couldn't do anything about the red splotch on the side of his face but wait for the sunburn to go away. Kim had teased him and offered some concealer. He'd quipped back that he'd have to rub it all over his face for it to do any good, so no thanks. Then he changed the subject and talked about church.

Kim agreed to go to the early service, in spite of the fact that she preferred sleeping an extra hour on Sundays. She'd given Brian a hard time about his antics during the rafting trip, but she came through for him in the end. And she'd packed enough food to feed everyone on their raft and still have leftovers, which she'd sent home with him.

He pulled into the parking lot and picked his Bible up off the seat then walked around the church toward the front steps. When he glanced up, his mouth instantly went dry. On the top step, standing next to Kim by the double doors, was Leila.

153

Chapter 4

Kim saw the look of shock on Brian's face, and she instantly wanted to comfort him. However, she felt stymied by the fact that Leila was right there beside her.

"Hey, Kim," Brian said before turning to face his former fiancée. "Leila, you look nice. How are you today?"

Leila cleared her throat and shifted from one foot to the other. "I'm fine, Brian. Maybe we can talk later?"

Brian shrugged. "Sure, whatever." He looked back at Kim. "Are we still sitting together, or have you made other plans?"

"We're still sitting together." Kim turned to Leila, who'd just stopped to ask if she'd seen Brian. "It was nice talking to you, Leila. Maybe we can get together sometime?" She had to force softness in her voice, because there was no point in showing her animosity—especially not on the church steps.

Leila glanced down as she took a small step back. "Maybe."

"Have a good day," Kim said before turning and linking arms with Brian. "C'mon, let's go sit down."

After they sat and picked up their hymnals, Brian elbowed Kim. "Well? Are you gonna fill me in on the powwow?"

"There's nothing to say other than the fact that she wanted to know if I'd seen you."

Brian tilted his head and quirked a brow. "What did you tell her?"

Kim studied him for a moment before answering. "Why are you so concerned?"

"I just wondered, that's all. Don't forget, she and I were engaged to be married, and if things had gone as planned, I'd be sitting here with her."

"Well, too bad you're not," Kim quipped. "You're stuck with me instead."

"Yeah, too bad, huh?" he said with a lopsided grin. "I think I came out the winner here."

Kim's heart warmed. "Thanks, Brian. That was sweet."

"Don't get used to it."

"Oh trust me, I know better than that."

The pastor approached the pulpit, so they focused their attention on the service. After the last hymn was sung, the pastor announced that the nursery was shorthanded, and they were in dire need of people to volunteer to watch the children during adult Bible study between the early and late services.

Brian lifted an eyebrow and tilted his head. "Wanna go watch some kids with me?"

She angled her head forward and looked at him from beneath hooded eyes. "You're kidding, right?"

"No, I'm not kidding. They need help, and we're able to do it."

"You know I've never been around children that much."

"They're just little people," he said.

"Yeah," she agreed. "With high-pitched voices and constant motion."

"Oh come on, Kimberly. It'll be fun." He gave her a challenging glare. "Or are you scared? Maybe you're right. Some people can't handle the pint-size set."

Not one to back down to a challenge, she rolled her eyes. "Oh all right. I'll do it."

Brian's mouth spread in a wide grin. "I thought you might." He patted her hand. "You'll do fine. Just watch me and do what I do."

"All righty," she said as they headed toward the church nursery. Secretly Kim hoped others would be waiting to help out in the nursery and her services wouldn't be needed. However, just the opposite was the case. The sound of children's voices with their harried parents standing nearby, hoping to be relieved so they could attend Bible class, let her know she was a welcome sight.

"I'm so glad y'all are here," Carmen said from the split door. "Please come in and wash your hands. I need to change this one's diaper, and then we can decide who does what."

After she put a clean diaper on the child she was holding, Carmen turned toward Kim. "Any questions before I leave?"

"You're leaving?" Kim asked, her throat tight from panic.

Carmen smiled and let out a little chuckle. "I'm in charge of several age groups, so I'll be making the rounds while you're here. If you need me, I won't be far." She pointed to the door. "Just leave the top half of the door open and stick your head out. You'll probably see me rushing around."

"Okay," Brian said as he assessed the situation. "We'll be fine."

Kim immediately found herself surrounded by toddlers, all of them wanting her attention. To her surprise, Brian seemed completely at ease, making her wonder if something might be wrong with her.

"How do you do it?" she asked. "I've known you for—like—ever, and I had no idea you were a kid person."

"I have a baby brother, remember?" he reminded her. "And I used to have to entertain the younger cousins at family reunions."

Kim did remember him mentioning the family reunion thing. However, it hadn't really made an impact on her until now. Brian turned toward a little boy who tugged at his pant leg. Then as he leaned over, the child extended his arms to be picked up.

Carmen was by the door, watching. "Y'all will do just fine."

"Want me to read a story?" Brian asked Carmen.

"Sure, most of them really like to be read to," she replied. "Pick any book that looks good."

Brian nodded toward Kim. "Wanna pick me out a book? Make sure it's one with lots of colorful pictures."

She quickly chose one off the shelf then carried it over to where Brian had sat down, the little boy still in his arms. The other children took their places on the multicolored mat in front of Brian.

"Want Miss Kimberly to hold you while I read this story?" Brian asked the child still in his arms.

The little boy snuggled closer to Brian, making Kim feel terrible. "I don't think he likes me," she whispered.

"Oh sure he does." Brian whispered something in the child's ear, and the little boy reached for Kim.

She took him as she gave Brian a questioning look. "What did you say?"

"It's our secret, right, buddy?"

The child offered a shy grin and nodded. Kim found a comfortable position on the mat, and a little girl climbed up beside the boy. She felt an unfamiliar emotional tug.

Brian warmed her heart as he read the book and showed the colorful pictures on each page. The children scooted even closer so they could see. When he finished the story, a couple of them hugged him. The sight of this still-in-shape, former high school football player and soldier being so gentle with all these toddlers touched Kim. It also made her realize there were some things she didn't know about him—mysterious things that attracted her in a way she never dreamed.

With each passing minute, Kim felt her emotions swirling in a whirlwind toward Brian, who captivated her not only with his love of sharing his faith but with his ability to relate to the children. She'd been thinking her feelings for Brian were displaced affection for David. But that wasn't the case anymore. As he patiently answered the children's questions, her heart felt like it would explode with love for him.

After Brian finished the last story, he tilted his head and gave her a questioning look. "Are you okay, Kim? You look like you don't feel well."

She licked her dry lips and nodded. "I'm fine."

The rest of the hour seemed to crawl, but eventually the adult Bible studies let out, and parents who'd been to the first service came by to pick up their children. One of them entered the room and informed Kim and Brian that they could leave because she and her husband were taking over.

"Are you sure?" Brian asked. "We can stick around awhile if you need us."

Kim wanted to kick him, but she faked a smile instead.

The woman shook her head. "No, that's okay. I know how exhausting it can be, and now it's my turn."

Carmen stopped by as she made the rounds between nursery rooms. "Thanks, you two. I don't know what we would have done without you."

After they were out of hearing distance, Brian laughed. "That wasn't so bad, now was it?"

"Bad?" Kim thought for a moment before shaking her head. "Not really bad but maybe a little scary at first."

"They're just little people."

"Little people who can reduce adults to bumbling idiots."

"Oh come on, Kim. Admit it. You had fun."

She bobbed her head a little then smiled back at Brian. "It was okay. But you owe me."

"I owe you?" He tilted his head and looked at her. "For what?"

"For volunteering me to do something without giving me a chance to think about it or say anything."

"Oh okay, I see how it is," he teased. "So what do I owe you?"

"I'll think of something good."

"How about I buy you lunch?"

She glanced at her watch. She needed to get away from Brian and try to sort out her thoughts. "Nah, that's okay. I need to get back and see if David responded to my e-mail."

Brian squinted his eyes and shook his head. "You have to eat. Let's go have some lunch, and then I'll take you home."

Kim felt her muscles tighten. She couldn't explain her need to put some distance between herself and Brian to recover from whatever was happening between them. He obviously wasn't going to let her get away with that.

"Okay, lunch," she finally agreed. "But my car is here." She'd have to work hard to keep an emotional distance—at least until she understood what was happening.

"Fine. I'll follow you home, and we'll go from there."

Fifteen minutes later, Kim's car was in her driveway, and she was about to get into Brian's car. He held the door for her then went around to the driver's side. Before Brian put the key into the ignition, he turned to Kim. "What're you in the mood for?"

"A huge stack of pancakes," she replied without looking at him. "Dripping with blueberry syrup."

"I know just the place." He drove straight to her favorite pancake restaurant where they served breakfast all day. "How's this?"

"Perfect." She hopped out of the car and met him around front, still avoiding his gaze. "Watching little kids really does something to the appetite."

"Wasn't Mackenzie cute?" he asked.

"They're all cute." Kim chuckled. "But you're right. I love that little curl on Mackenzie's forehead."

After the server took their orders, Brian studied her for a few uncomfortable seconds. Kim tried looking away, but when she turned back to him, he was still staring at her.

"What?" she asked.

"I was just thinking about how cute your kids will be. Have you and David talked about a family?"

She wanted to crawl under the table. How would she get through a conversation like this without breaking down and saying what she'd been thinking? "Not really," she replied softly. "We haven't even discussed the wedding, and that has to come first."

"Do you think you might want kids?"

"I haven't really thought about it," Kim said. "But I probably will. . . eventually."

Brian frowned. "You really need to bring all that out in the open before you settle on a wedding date. What if David doesn't want kids?"

Kim thought for a moment. "I'm pretty sure he does."

"You need to be totally sure. If one of you wants children and the other doesn't, that's setting your marriage up for disaster from the get-go."

Kim played with her spoon for a moment as she thought about it. He was right, and she was dying to know if Brian wanted children. When she looked back up at him, he was still watching her. "Yeah, I guess we should discuss that when he comes back. How about you? I guess you probably want a house full of children."

Brian pulled back and made a face. "Not a houseful. Maybe two or three."

"You're so good with them, I thought you might want more."

"I'm good with a few at a time. I didn't mind this morning because I knew it was only for an hour or so, but if I had that many all the time, I don't know what I'd do."

"If your wife wanted a bunch of babies, you'd deal with it," Kim said.

Brian shook his head. "I'm not willing to just deal with it. I want the person I marry to be right for me in all the important areas. Not only does she have to love the Lord like I do, but she has to have similar values and expectations for a marriage and family."

Her heart thudded. She already knew that she and Brian had the same Christian values, and this conversation about children made her think about them. She had to find something that would get her mind back on the friendship track with him. "This isn't exactly a perfect world we live in, Brian. You can't place your order like that and expect to get it."

"True," he agreed, "but there are some things I feel are important to discuss. If my wife and I agree to have two children, and the second time she gets pregnant we have twins, I'll know that the Lord wanted us to have three children."

Kim had only eaten half her pancakes, but as Brian continued staring at her, she lost her appetite. "Can you take me home now? I really want to check my e-mail."

Brian paid the bill and they left. Kim appreciated how he didn't ask any more questions.

"It was fun," Kim said as she got out of the car at the curb.

"Wanna go to the singles Bible study next week?"

"I'm not sure." Kim held the door and thought about it for a second. "Call me tomorrow night and we can talk about it."

As soon as she closed the door, he waved and took off. She went inside, kicked off her shoes, and booted up her computer.

Lord, please let there be an e-mail from David.

After clicking on her incoming e-mail, her heart grew heavy. Nothing from David. It wasn't as if he hadn't warned her, but she was still disappointed.

She was tempted to shut down her e-mail, find a good book, and read the rest of the day, but then she remembered how David said he enjoyed hearing from her daily—even if he got several days' worth of mail in one sitting. So she sat down and pounded out a letter letting him know about how Brian had hoodwinked her into working in the church nursery between services. She tried to keep it light and funny, but she kept thinking about what Brian said about children. So she added a few sentences at the end:

> *We've never discussed how many children we want after we get married. After hanging around with a bunch of active toddlers, I thought maybe it's something we should talk about. Would you like to have a couple of kids someday?*

Kim sat and stared at her e-mail before she clicked SEND. This might not have been the best time or way to bring it up, but Brian's comments would play in her mind until she had some idea of what David wanted.

❧

Brian felt bad about making Kim squirm, but as a friend he felt it was his duty. He wanted to make sure she knew what she was getting into with David. The fact that David was so focused on the military concerned Brian—not so much that he wanted to serve his country but the fact that he made all his career decisions without consulting Kim.

Right.

To be totally honest, Brian knew his intensifying feelings for Kim made his motives not all that honorable. He still loved her as a friend, but it was so much more than that now. So much more romantic. Even after years of seeing her at her worst as well as her best, he loved everything about Kimberly Shaw, and it irked him that he hadn't acted on it before it was too late.

Time dragged by, but bedtime finally came. He fell asleep with Kimberly on his mind, and the first thing that popped into his mind when he woke up was their conversation at the pancake restaurant.

Brian reached for the phone but quickly yanked his hand back. He had to resist the urge to call her—especially this early in the morning. She worked long hours at the shop, and she might still be asleep since it was only seven o'clock. The Snappy Scissors didn't open until ten.

After drinking a cup of coffee and eating a piece of toast, he was on his way to the shower when the phone rang. It was Kimberly.

"Brian." Her shaky voice was barely audible.

He instantly went on alert. "What happened, Kim? What's wrong?"

"It–it's David. He. . ." She sniffled.

"I'll be right over. Just let me throw on some clothes."

Chapter 5

The doorbell rang fifteen minutes later. Kim opened the door then gestured toward her computer. "His e-mail is still on the screen."

He started toward the computer, but suddenly he stopped. "I'd rather hear whatever it is from you."

Silence fell between them for a few seconds, but Brian didn't push. He patiently waited until she was ready to talk.

Finally she faced him. "David doesn't want kids."

Brian frowned. "Are you sure?"

She nodded and pointed to the computer. "I wrote and told him about working in the church nursery and then I asked if he wanted to have children someday. He said he's never wanted to bring babies into this already over-populated world."

"Maybe that's something the two of you should talk about in person instead of through e-mail."

Kim thought about it for a moment then shook her head. "What's interesting is that we don't really discuss all that much when we're together. We actually have more back and forth conversation in our e-mails than we do in person."

Brian held her gaze with a look of concern etched on his forehead. He patted her hand before pinching the bridge of his nose between his index finger and thumb.

"I know you're probably thinking it's my fault as much as it is his," Kim said, "and you're right."

When Brian didn't respond, she touched his arm but pulled away as soon as she felt the powerful pull she'd tried to resist. He repositioned himself to face her—and moved a few inches away as he looked her squarely in the eye. "Kim, you know how serious marriage is. After my experience, I've had quite a bit of time to think about it. If you don't talk—I mean really open up with heart-to-heart dialogue—how do you know that you love each other enough to be husband and wife?"

She'd been asking herself that same question since David had been gone—especially after she realized her feelings for Brian had shifted. She wanted to discuss it, but now didn't seem like the right time.

"Kim, is there something else?"

She gave herself a mental shake, squared her shoulders, and bravely looked him in the eye. "It's weird. When David was here, everything seemed

161

so good. Although we didn't have a lot of two-way conversation about the important stuff, he always talked to me about what he wanted, and it sounded really good. I loved the fact that he studied his Bible before making the commitment to Christ. With him, it was intentional and extremely well thought out."

Brian nodded. "Yes, I understand, and that's one of the reasons he and I are such good friends. When I was in the Guard, we had that to talk about. And we have sports in common. That's all we need to be good friends, but that's still not enough for a marriage."

"I know." She shook her head and fidgeted with the edge of her sleeve. Brian touched her cheek, and she turned to face him. "When he told me he was falling in love with me, I was caught up in the excitement of being half of a couple."

"There had to be more to it than that."

"Oh yeah, there's more. When he kissed me the first time, I got all tingly and silly. You know how it is." She flopped onto the sofa.

Brian snickered and sat down in the chair across from her. "Yeah, I know."

"It seemed that something exciting always happened when David was around. Between the kisses and his patriotism, I guess I just got caught up in my romance-novel-style hero."

"I can see how that would happen," Brian said softly. "Do you regret being engaged?"

She closed her eyes. "Well, maybe. . .sometimes."

"You can't live your life like this, Kim. If you're not sure you want to marry David, it's not fair to either of you to stay engaged."

"I think I missed an opportunity to put our engagement on hold."

Brian lifted his eyebrows in surprise. "Opportunity?"

"I sort of had an opening before he left." Kim thought back and tried to remember precisely how it went, but she couldn't. "We talked about it. It seemed like he was thinking of me and my feelings, and I'm pretty sure he would have understood if I'd said we needed to wait."

"That's only right."

"I know." Kim swallowed hard then faced Brian again. "Oh Brian, what should I do?"

He stood, placed his hands on his hips, shook his head, and offered a sympathetic grin. "With God, there are no shades of gray. I can't tell you what to do about something so serious." He pointed to the computer. "Why don't you write him back and let him know that the two of you have some things to discuss when he gets back?"

"I will."

"In the meantime, you need to think about why you're engaged in the first place. If you love him and think you can work through these issues, stay with him. However, if you don't think he'll take your feelings into consideration about some of life's most important events, like having children, you're setting yourself up for trouble."

Kim stood up and took Brian's hands in hers. "You are the best friend a girl could possibly have. Thanks. There's never been a time when you haven't been there for me."

"Yeah, I know." He suddenly sounded grumpy.

"Okay, what's wrong with you?" she asked. "I've been so wrapped up in my own feelings, I didn't even notice you were sad about something. . .until now. Is it Leila?"

Brian lifted a hand to wave off her concern. "No, it's not Leila. I'm fine."

"C'mon, Brian, I want to be here for you just like you are for me."

His eyes narrowed as he faced her head-on. "I didn't come here to talk about me, Kim. This was about you."

"But—"

"If you're okay now, I really need to get to work." He glanced at his watch and issued a mock salute. "We can talk later."

Kim blinked as he took off without another word. She had no idea what had just happened, but whatever it was didn't seem good.

She turned around and looked at the computer. The multicolored squiggly lines on the screensaver danced across the front of her monitor. She started to sit down and pound out another e-mail to David, but she decided to get ready for the day first to give herself time to think about what to say.

After she showered, dressed, and put on her makeup, she sat down at the computer. Even though Brian thought she needed to wait until David returned, she needed to get some things out now.

To: DJenner
From: KShaw
Subject: We need to talk

Dear David,
I had no idea you didn't want children. I guess I just assumed you did because it seems like a natural progression after a couple gets married to want to start a family. I have to admit I hadn't thought about it until Brian and I worked in the church nursery.

There are probably other things we need to discuss before we plan our wedding. I wish you were here so we could talk now. Have you heard anything about when you'll be coming home? I miss you.

Love,
Kimberly

She sat back and studied her note before she clicked SEND. Her letter wasn't flowery or gushy, but she didn't have much more to say, feeling the way she did at the moment. The clock on the computer let her know it was time to go to work. At least she had a full appointment book, so she wouldn't have time to think about what she'd just done.

※

Brian's first goal when he entered his office building was to avoid Jack. He didn't feel like explaining anything to the only coworker who seemed in tune to his life.

He slipped past the receptionist and made it to his office, thinking he was home free. But as soon as he unlocked his office door and entered, he heard the footsteps coming toward him. A quick glance up let him know he hadn't been successful.

"Hey, Brian. Don't forget we need six copies of that report—" Jack squinted his eyes, twisted his mouth, and studied Brian. "What's going on?"

"Nothing," Brian replied as he went around behind his desk. "I just had to run an errand this morning, so I'm a few minutes late. I need to print the report, and I should be good to go."

Jack hung back with his arms folded. "Are you sure you don't wanna talk about something?"

"Positive." Brian smiled. "Let me get everything together, and I'll be in the conference room in a few. We can go over it before the meeting."

"Fine."

Brian shuffled through a few papers while his computer powered up. As the report printed and collated, he prayed that he'd be able to focus on work and not his thoughts of yanking David by the collar for upsetting the nicest girl in the free world.

※

Over the next several days with no response from David, Kim started getting worried. She called Brian, but he told her she should give her fiancé more time. Her mother reminded her that David wasn't always able to get online, so she shouldn't get all up in arms about a few days going by.

Then another week passed and still no word, and she got worried. So she called David's mother.

"Hi there, Kimberly. I wondered if you'd ever bother calling me with David gone."

"I've been super busy with work and church. Sorry I haven't called sooner."

"Oh, I know how it is. I was young once." She exhaled loud enough to echo in the phone. "David seems to be doing quite well overseas."

"That's what I was calling about. I haven't heard from him in more than a week, and I was starting to get worried."

"You haven't heard anything? Oh my. I hope everything is okay between the two of you."

Kim paused. "Has he e-mailed you?"

"Why yes, I heard from him last night. He told me he requested to stay an extra month so they could complete this mission." Before Kim could utter a word, Mrs. Jenner added, "You do realize how important my son is, don't you? I believe the security of our country rests in his hands."

"I know he's very important," Kim said as she tried to compose herself. David's mother obviously thought her son was single-handedly fighting for freedom. "Since I didn't get an e-mail from him, I thought maybe I'd missed his call because I've been sort of busy lately. I'm glad he's okay."

"Oh, he's fine. I'm sure he's even busier than you are, so don't worry about him."

"Well. . ." Kim racked her brain to find the right way to word what she wanted to say. Mrs. Jenner's condescending tone came across strong as ever. Kim found herself at a loss for words, because no matter what she said, Mrs. Jenner would cut her down to her knees. "Um. . .you're right. I just wanted to know if you'd heard from him."

"Okay, dear. Just don't forget how important this mission is. You're doing the right thing in staying busy. If he really needs to talk to you, though, he's not one to give up, even if you don't answer your phone."

When Kim hung up, she felt worse than before she'd called David's mother. David had once confided that his mother had gone to church on special occasions, but she never discussed a relationship with Christ. Church for her was more of an obligation rather than true, heartfelt worship. Until now, Kim thought that David might have misread his mother, but she didn't feel an ounce of Christian love or compassion from the woman. She sent another e-mail to David, asking him at least to let her know he was okay.

Kim continued her struggle with the combination of not hearing from David and the fact that Brian had started avoiding her. What was up with that? She'd called and left a message several days ago, and he hadn't bothered to return the call. That wasn't like him at all. Maybe he sensed that something about her feelings toward him had changed. To top it off, he hadn't asked her to go with him to the weekly singles Bible study since last time they went together. She worried that she might have scared him off.

"What's got you all in a snit?" Jasmine asked as they prepped their stations for the day.

"Nothing."

Jasmine paused, pulled back her chin, and lifted a severely tweezed eyebrow. "Don't try to pull that on me, girl. We've worked side by side long enough for me to know when you're out of sorts."

Kim laughed. "Yeah, I guess I'm out of sorts. . .a little. I haven't heard from David in a long time, and Brian's been avoiding me."

"I don't know David all that well," Jasmine said as she resumed arranging her combs. "But I know Brian well enough to advise you to call him."

Kim shrugged. "He's never home anymore."

"Then call him at work. You know he'll be there."

"I'll think about it."

Jasmine shook her head. "Y'all have been friends for a long time, Kimberly. This is silly."

Kim nodded her agreement. Jasmine was right. Finally she grabbed her cell phone, went to the back room, and called Brian's direct line at work. His voice sounded weary as he answered on the first ring.

"I wondered if you were still alive," she said.

He cleared his throat. "Yeah, I'm alive. What do you need?"

In all the time Kim had known Brian, the only time she'd heard him so abrupt was when he broke his arm in the middle of football season and was mad that he'd been benched for the rest of the year. "Why don't you and I go out for pizza tonight?"

"I don't know, Kim. It might not be such a good idea for us to hang out so much."

So she was right. He was worried by the way she was acting. Kim resolved to get everything out in the open. "David told us to keep each other company while he was gone. He knows you and I have been friends for—like—ever. Where's the harm? I really need to talk, Brian."

Brian paused for a moment. "I guess you're right. You've always been there for me, so I'll be there for you."

"You don't have to make it sound like such a chore. If you don't want to talk to me, don't do it."

"Well, I'm not really in the mood to go out tonight. How about—"

"Then we'll just order in. You can come to my place. I really need to talk to you."

He cleared his throat. "What time do you want me there?"

His question came so quickly, Kim knew she'd played on his guilt and won. Suddenly she felt bad.

"Look Brian, I didn't mean to pull a guilt trip. It's just that David hasn't even bothered to e-mail me. I called his mother, and—"

"Say no more. I've met her."

"Why don't you come over around seven? I'll order the pizza after you get to my place."

"I'll be there," he said. "I'll bring the drinks. Cola or root beer?"

"Let's get crazy and have root beer."

Brian chuckled. "Sounds good. See ya tonight."

After Kim got off the phone, she put the phone in her pocket, rocked back on her heels, and thought about the differences between Brian and David. Brian had been brought up in a Christian home. David had come to Christ as an adult. When he made his commitment to the Lord, he turned his back on anyone who'd cause him to stumble, including his former girl-friend Alexis. Kim later learned that Mrs. Jenner and David's old flame had been very close, which explained the older woman's coolness toward Kim in the very beginning. David told Kim not to worry about that, but she couldn't help feeling bad about it.

She glanced up when Jasmine appeared at the door. "Your next appointment is here."

Kim took a step toward her. "Sorry about that."

"No worries. She just arrived." Jasmine paused and glanced over her shoulder. "You okay? I can get her started at the sink if you need a few more minutes."

"Nah, that's okay. I'm fine."

The afternoon was slow, giving Kim a chance to think even more about what was going on with David. By the time she left for the day, dozens of scenarios had run through her head.

When she got home, she showered to get rid of the chemical smells from the salon. Brian arrived shortly afterward, and she immediately placed the call to have the pizza delivered.

"Let me check my e-mail and see if David responded yet," Kim said.

Brian held her gaze for a moment before he nodded. "I'll put this root beer in the fridge while you do that."

Kim didn't expect a response this soon since she hadn't heard from him in so long. The instant she saw David's e-mail, her pulse quickened.

Chapter 6

Brian took his time in the kitchen to give Kim some space. When he figured she had enough, he joined her.

"Any news?" he asked, trying to keep his voice steady.

Her shoulders rose as she inhaled, but she didn't say anything. This concerned him.

"What happened?" Brian urged.

Kim glanced down at the floor. "David heard from his mother, and he thinks I need to make more of an effort to get close to her."

Brian pulled a chair over from the dining table and sat down beside Kim. He took a moment to find the right words before speaking.

"What does he think you should do?"

She didn't meet his eyes for a few seconds. Then she turned to face him. "I have no idea."

Brian shrugged. "What does David have to say about it?"

"He's annoyed by her comments. I can't say I blame him, considering the life-and-death situations he faces on his job." Kim snorted. "I can't believe his mother is worrying him like this."

"Yeah, it does seem like she's got some issues that have nothing to do with you."

Kim smiled at him, warming him from the inside out. "Thank you, Brian. You're the most amazing man. Leila made a humongous mistake."

Brian allowed himself to get lost in a shared look between them, in spite of his internal alarms sounding off louder than ever. If only he'd acted when he still had a chance with her—before he introduced his two best friends— he might not be having this conversation.

As Kim turned back to finish reading her e-mail, he sank back in the chair and reflected. When they were kids, he was afraid of rejection, so he kept his feelings to himself, half hoping she'd give him a sign that she wanted more than friendship and half hoping his infatuation would fade. Now that they were adults, he saw the flaws in his earlier thinking.

A couple of times, he'd started to make his move, but the timing was never right. He wanted something special—a mood or setting they'd always remember. However, the couple of times he thought he'd arranged everything just right, someone else was always there.

When he'd brought David to church, it wasn't his intention to fix him up with Kim. However, David spotted something special in Kim, and he didn't waste any time.

Shortly after David and Kim met, Brian tried to see if she wanted more than friendship, asking her out and being there all the time. He actually caught her looking at him in a way that made him feel he had a chance. Then two sentences stopped him cold. She'd grabbed his hand and squeezed it before she said, "Thank you so much for introducing me to David. I think he's the one."

He'd stumbled and stuttered as he asked questions. "Are you sure? I mean, this is serious, Kimberly."

She nodded. "I'm positive. Last night he told me he loved me."

Brian was dumbfounded. Now that he looked back on that afternoon, he wished he'd said something—at least let her know how he felt. But now it was too late. Making moves on another man's fiancée wasn't the honorable thing to do. If nothing else, Brian Estep was an honorable man.

Kim clicked off the screen with the e-mail and stood up, jolting him from his thoughts. "The pizza should be here any minute. Let's go get our drinks while we wait." Some of the light he'd seen in her eyes earlier had dimmed.

He followed her into the kitchen. "Nothing from David?" he asked.

She shook her head. "Nothing important. Oh good, you got my favorite kind." Kim pulled the two-liter bottle from the refrigerator. "Last time I had root beer was when I asked David to pick some up on his way here. Of course, there was no way he could know my favorite kind, and I didn't want to hurt his feelings. . . ."

The more she talked, the more agitated Brian became. He knew what Kim liked because he'd actually listened to her all these years.

"I think you and David need to sit down and really get to know each other."

He saw Kim's jaw tighten. She gave him a look of annoyance. "We talk—just not about the same things you and I talk about. I know what he likes."

"Then why doesn't he know what your favorite root beer is?"

She snickered. "You're kidding, right? That's just root beer. Not important."

"Does he know that you like pink but you prefer peach?" Brian knew he was being ridiculous, but suddenly he didn't care.

"C'mon, Brian. This conversation is getting silly."

"No, it's not silly. I just think it's time you and David sat down and had a heart-to-heart. I bet you know what his favorite color is."

She nodded. "He likes blue. Royal blue."

"His favorite drink?"

Without a second's hesitation, she blurted, "Dr Pepper."

"Okay, that's what I'm talking about. You know things about him because he does all the talking." Brian started pacing as thoughts raced through his head. "I've tried hard not to do this, but Kim..." His voice trailed off as he met her gaze. Before he melted and said anything he might later regret, he lifted his hands and let them drop to his sides, making a loud slapping sound on his thighs. "Never mind. I need to butt out."

Kim quickly closed the distance between them and gripped his upper arms as she positioned him to look at her. At first he saw a tenderness in her expression, but she released her hold on him and glanced away, then turned back with a whole different look. "Brian, what you're doing is very sweet, and I appreciate it. You've been the best friend I've ever had, and I know you're looking out for me. But I'm a grown woman now, and I know how to take care of myself."

He had to use every ounce of self-restraint to keep from reminding her how upset she'd been earlier. Finally when he was able to get a grip on his thoughts, he took a step back. "Yes, you're right, Kim. You are a grown woman. And I was right when I said I needed to butt out. Let's get our drinks now and go wait for the pizza." He started for the living room then stopped and turned to face her. "What kind did you order? Mushroom and olive for you or Canadian bacon for me?"

She rolled her eyes and grinned. "Half mushroom and olive, and half Canadian bacon."

That pretty much said it all. Kim was thoughtful to a fault, and it would be very easy for someone to take advantage of her. David was a great guy, but he wasn't right for Kim.

Kim was relieved when the pizza arrived. It broke up their conversation, and she was able to steer it in a different direction without too much effort. She was getting weary of discussing David and his e-mailed reactions—especially since she had no idea what was really going on with him.

Brian hung around for another hour after they finished eating. Since they both had to work the next day, he gave her a hug and went home.

Kim stood at the door and waved as he backed out of her driveway. Once he was out of sight, she closed her front door and leaned against it.

Lord, I don't know why I get so confused when I'm around Brian. Maybe it's just because I'm lonely with David on the other side of the world. Or perhaps I'm worried that his mother will affect our relationship. Kim opened her eyes and pondered what to pray for before closing them again to continue. *Please give me some peace and protect David. Help me to keep my thoughts and feelings to myself so I won't worry Brian and scare him away from being my friend.*

Kim went to bed and woke up still feeling unsettled. After she started the coffee, she resisted the temptation to reread David's e-mail. There would be plenty of time for that after work, and she didn't need to torture herself by trying to read between the lines. She wished Carrie was nearby to talk to.

Later that morning, Jasmine grinned at her as she walked through the door of the salon. Kim forced a smile back, but Jasmine could see through her. "What's wrong, Kim? Did something happen between you and Brian last night?"

"No, we just had dinner and talked." There was no point in letting on how confused she was about her feelings for Brian.

"I'm tellin' ya, girl, you need to take another look at Brian."

"And I'm reminding you," Kim said through a smile as she held up her hand and tapped her ring finger, "not to forget that I'm engaged."

"Which means you're not married, and it's not too late to change your mind."

Kim let out a nervous laugh. "When I agreed to be David's wife, I made a promise to always love him. Besides, I think this ring set David back a pretty penny."

"Trust me when I say that's nothing compared to what you'll pay if you marry the wrong man," Jasmine said. "I'm not talking divorce, either. Did I ever tell you about my cousin who regretted marrying the wrong man?"

"You mean the one who died young of a broken heart?"

Jasmine nodded. "Yeah, I guess I did tell you. Marianne was like you—a Christian woman who wanted to do the right thing, even if it meant being miserable."

"If she was so miserable, why did she marry the wrong man?"

"She thought she was in love with Paul in the beginning, so she took his ring. About three months later, she started to change her mind, but she was convinced it was just cold feet."

"Well," Kim said, "there is that."

"Yeah, but if your feet keep getting colder and colder, and not even thoughts of your wedding day can warm them up, you need to reconsider—or at least postpone the wedding until you're sure."

Kim thought about what had happened to Brian. "Yes, I can see your point."

Jasmine smiled. "I thought you might. I'm not asking you to break your engagement. All I want you to do is think about how you feel now and magnify that by at least ten. It doesn't get better after the vows."

"Thanks, Jas. I'll put more thought into it."

At the end of the long day, Kim went home with Jasmine's advice lingering in her head. She hesitated for a moment before turning on her computer. After the troubling conversation with Mrs. Jenner and frustrating e-mails from David lately, she felt conflicted about checking her e-mail.

❧

Brian sat down at the computer with a slice of cold pizza he'd brought home from Kim's the night before and a glass of root beer. He was surprised to see David's name on his incoming mail list.

> To: BEstep
> From: DJenner
> Subject: Coming home
>
> Hey, Brian. I need you to help me out with something. We finished our mission early, so I'm coming home.
>
> Here's where I need you. I want to surprise Kim. Do you think you can arrange a small get-together for family and close friends? I'd really appreciate it, buddy.
>
> Let me know as soon as possible, okay? Once my leave is confirmed, I'll let you know the dates. Thanks.
>
> Always,
> David

A surprise, huh? Brian read and reread the e-mail several times before he typed a reply.

> To: DJenner
> From: BEstep
> Subject: Re: Coming home
>
> I've known Kim most of my life, and she's not big on surprises. Why don't you tell her you'll be here, and we can just have a nice party with a bunch of friends?
>
> Brian

By the time he finished checking the rest of his e-mail, he had David's response. He clicked on the subject and leaned back to read it.

> To: BEstep
> From: DJenner
> Subject: Re: Coming home
>
> What are you talking about, man? All women love surprises. Kim just doesn't want anyone making a fuss over her. This is important to me, so do me a favor and help me out with this.
>
> Always,
> David

Brian hesitated for a few seconds before he clicked the REPLY button and typed his message.

To: DJenner
From: BEstep
Subject: Re: Coming home

Sure, I'll do it. Let me know the details when you have them.

Brian

After he clicked SEND, Brian sat back and thought about Kim and all the possible reactions she might have to a surprise of this magnitude. Would she be happy? He hoped so.

Was he happy? Nope, not at all.

When Brian had first met David during a two-week National Guard duty, he'd been impressed with David's focus and authority among his peers. His integrity had come through as unbendable. He seemed like a great guy, and Brian was happy to introduce him to all his friends at church. What he hadn't counted on was David putting all of his energy into sweeping Kimberly off her feet.

Kim was reluctant to get involved with David at first. From the moment Brian had brought David to church, he realized how powerful David's dark, brooding good looks were with the women. The minute David walked into the room, many of the single females became tongue-tied, or they made it obvious that they'd love to get to know him better. However, David instantly set his sights on Kim—perhaps because she proved to be the biggest challenge.

It took David several months of actively pursuing Kim before her guard came down. However, once he had that ring on her finger, Brian noticed the change in his friend. Kim seemed to have taken a backseat to David's passion for the military. When Brian confronted David, he got a lecture. He even tried to talk to Kim, but she reminded him that relationships required give-and-take—and she couldn't stand in the way of David's desire to do what he thought was right for his country.

Brian rose and carried his plate and glass to the kitchen. He needed to stop worrying so much about Kim and David's relationship. They were adults, and if either of them didn't like something, they were perfectly capable of changing it.

So what if his own feelings for Kim had changed? It was a moot point since she wasn't available.

He needed to find something else to get his mind off Kim. But first he'd have to honor his commitment to David on the party thing—even though David wouldn't listen to him about Kim hating surprises.

❧

Kim checked her e-mail and spotted a message from David. This time, however, her pulse didn't quicken.

To: KShaw
From: DJenner
Subject: Checking in

Dear Kim,
How are you, sweetheart? I hope everything is going well back home.
We've gotten everything here under control—at least for now. After we tie up a few loose ends, I'm sure something else will pop up. I wish I could share some of my experiences with you. Maybe someday. . .
I've been thinking about getting you and my mother together so the two of you can get to know each other better. Due to the circumstances, it's been difficult. However, there's no doubt in my mind that my two favorite women will be the best of friends. I feel blessed to have both of you loving me and waiting so patiently while I help protect our country.
Tell Brian thank you for being such a gentleman and watching out for you. I owe him big-time. And I appreciate how much you've been able to help get him through the days following what he calls "the wedding that didn't happen."
I love you and miss you very much.

Your future husband,
David

Kim chewed on her bottom lip as she thought about David's e-mail. He said all the right things, but something about the tone of the message bothered her. She could be wrong, but it looked like he was leaving something out. Because she had harbored romantic thoughts of Brian, it bothered her a little to read his words of love.

The temptation to call Brian nearly overwhelmed her, but she resisted. There was no news—good or bad—in this e-mail, so what was the point? Brian was a busy man who'd shoved enough of his own life aside to cater to her moods. He'd always been there for her, and she knew he wasn't likely to stop anytime soon.

Too bad she couldn't be more like him. Brian not only lived his faith, but he accepted what Leila did without anger. Kim didn't think she could do that. The fact that her love for David had faded was proof.

❧

The next twenty-four hours were rough for Kim. She refrained from calling Brian every time her mood changed, and that was one of the most difficult things she'd ever done. It also showed her how much she'd come to rely on him.

She had just come home from work when her phone rang. It was Brian. "Don't make any plans for three weeks from tomorrow," he said.

"Why?" she asked. "What's going on?"

"I'm, uh. . .having a little get-together for some close friends."

Kim picked up a pen and tapped it against the desk. Brian had an odd tone to his voice. "Are you okay, Brian?"

"Yes, I'm fine."

"So what's this all about? Your birthday isn't for a couple more months. Did you get a promotion?"

"Don't ask questions, Kimberly." He cleared his throat. "Just pencil me in on your calendar, okay?"

Chapter 7

Kim laughed. "Okay, consider it done, but only because it's you. Anyone else would have some explaining to do."

"So how was work today?" he asked.

"Are you changing the subject?"

"Yes, and don't ask any more questions."

Again, she laughed. "Okay, okay, I won't. Work was fine. We've been busy—mostly with cuts. People aren't getting as many perms as they used to, and most of my customers are coloring their own hair."

"You never really did like working with chemicals, so that's a good thing, right?"

Kim knew he was avoiding something, so she played along. "Yes, it's a very good thing. I prefer cuts over everything else."

Silence fell between them for a couple of seconds. Normally, that would have been fine, but Brian cleared his throat, and her insides constricted.

"You and I need to talk soon," he said.

She forced a laugh. "You make it sound so serious. Why can't we talk now?"

"Maybe because it's too serious to discuss over the phone."

"C'mon, Brian, this is me. We've been through a lot together."

"Yes," he agreed as his voice lowered. "And that's what makes this so difficult. Mind if I stop by tomorrow night?"

"Sure, that's fine. Want to come for dinner?"

"No, I'll eat something before I come. I just want to talk."

After Kim hung up, an overwhelming sense of dread washed over her. She didn't want to keep worrying Brian with doubts about her relationship with David.

All night and the next day, Kim pondered what could be so serious that Brian couldn't bring it up on the phone. She felt Jasmine watching her until the last customer left. Jasmine finally laid down her scissors, turned to face Kim, folded her arms, and tapped her foot. "Okay, what gives?"

Kim avoided her friend's glare. "I don't know what you're talking about."

"You've been acting weird all day. Did David e-mail you with bad news or something?"

With a quick roll of the eyes, Kim shook her head. "No. In fact he wants his mother and me to get together soon."

"Oh, that should be fun," Jasmine said with a wicked laugh. "Not."

"I'm sure we'll get along over time. It can't be easy for her to deal with her son getting involved with someone she barely knows."

"True," Jasmine agreed. "So why have you been so—I don't know—pensive all day?"

"I don't know how you can say that, Jazzy. We've had a steady stream of clients from the moment we opened."

"True, but you're still not acting like yourself."

Kim lifted her arms and splayed her fingers. "I can't always be Miss Suzie Sunshine."

Jasmine cackled. "You've got a point. Having your fiancé and best girl-friend leaving so close together must be hard."

"Yes," Kim agreed. "Very."

"Just remember that you can talk to me about anything. I've probably been through almost everything."

"Thanks, Jazzy."

Kim finished cleaning up and headed home, stopping off for a burger on the way. She didn't want to mess with cooking and cleaning, as eager as she was to find out what Brian wanted to talk about.

Time seemed to drag before he finally arrived. She flung open the door seconds after he rang the doorbell. Seeing him significantly brightened her mood.

"Whoa," he said as he lowered his hand. "You must have been standing right there."

"I was waiting for you," she admitted. "So come in and tell me what's going on."

Instead of heading for the living room, he turned toward the kitchen. She followed.

"Want something to drink?"

Brian shook his head and pointed to the kitchen chair. "Just sit down, okay?"

She silently obeyed. He was obviously in no mood for argument or ceremony.

As soon as she sat, he paced a couple of times. Suddenly he stopped, placed his hands on the back of the chair, and leaned forward. "Kim, I don't think it's right for you and me to. . .well, you know. . . ." His voice trailed off, but he continued staring at her.

"No, Brian, I have no idea what you're talking about." She frowned, and he remained silent. "What *are* you talking about?"

Brian pulled his lips between his teeth and looked down. When he lifted his head, he offered a half grin. "Kimberly, you're an engaged woman."

His closeness nearly took her breath away. "So? We've been friends forever."

"Well..." He took a step back and shook his head. "Things have changed."

"Changed? How?"

"I don't know. They've just changed."

"Have you met someone new?" *That must be it.* Disappointment shrouded her as she forced a grin. "You have a new girlfriend, and she doesn't understand about me. Want me to talk to her?"

"No, I don't have a new girlfriend. I haven't been anywhere to meet a girl."

"What's the problem, Brian?"

He lifted his hands. "I'm just not feelin' this whole friendship thing with you anymore."

Kim suddenly went numb. "Okay," she said, her voice barely above a whisper. "That's fine."

Brian's stone-cold face softened, and he let out a snort. "It's not fine. I have to admit, I have feelings for someone, Kim."

Kim felt like her eyes would bug out of her head, and she had to steady herself. "So there is someone else—someone besides Leila?"

Brian hung his head. "Yes, I'm in love with someone else." When he looked back at her, a sad expression had clouded his eyes.

"Who?"

He pursed his lips and shook his head. "Can't tell you."

"That's insane, Brian. You can tell me anything."

"Nope," he replied. "Not this."

He'd rocked Kim's world way more than she ever thought he could. "Maybe it's just displaced feelings from Leila," she offered. "I'm sure that had a huge impact on you."

"Nope. It's the real thing. In fact, deep down, I think I was relieved when Leila didn't show up."

"That's crazy. Why did you get engaged to Leila?"

"The girl I love is off-limits."

Kim lifted her eyebrows. "Is she married or something?"

"Not married."

"Then she's involved with someone else?"

"Yeah, very involved."

"Like I said earlier, that's insane."

Brian chuckled and shrugged. "Probably, but it's the truth."

"Why have you never told me about...this girl you think you love?"

"There's no way you'll ever understand this, Kim."

"Then why did you tell me?"

"I thought you needed to know. From me."

"You're not going to get away with this, Brian," she said, forcing a smile. "This is me, remember?"

"Let's just drop it, okay?"

"That's impossible."

"Try, okay?"

She closed her eyes for a moment then opened them to find Brian staring at her. "You make me nervous just standing there."

He sat and fidgeted before looking her in the eye. "Now I'm doubting myself for telling you."

"You can tell me anything." She traced her finger along the edge of the table, trying to hide the jealousy that had bubbled inside her chest. "Why are you afraid to confide in me about this girl?"

"It's really complicated."

"And I'm pretty smart, ya know," she said. "Maybe I can help you figure out how to deal with things."

"There's nothing to figure out." He studied his hands before looking back at her. "So how are things going with David?"

"I told him we need to talk."

"That's good," Brian said. "At least it's a start," he said without an ounce of conviction in his voice. "I think it's best if I stay out of your relationship with David."

"Okay."

Brian had never acted this strange before, but it was obvious he wasn't going to fill her in on what the real problem was. Or who the girl was. Everything in her life suddenly seemed so off-kilter.

"So what now?"

"I bow out of your life—at least for a while."

Kim wanted to touch Brian, but she didn't dare. Instead she stood and pushed her chair under the table.

Brian took the hint and got up. "I'd better head on home now." He turned and walked to the door but stopped and turned back to face her. "Kim, there is that little get-together in three weeks. I, uh. . ."

"That's okay, Brian. I understand if you don't want me there."

"No!" He spoke so quickly it startled her. "I do want you there. You *have* to be there."

"But I thought—"

"There will be a lot of people, so it's different. You have to come." His gaze met hers. "Please?"

"Okay," she said, nodding her head.

"It's important." He frowned, adding to her confusion.

Kim held up her hands. "Okay, I'll be there. I just don't understand."

"You will," he said as he reached for the doorknob. "I'll see you around."

She stood at the door until he got in his car and pulled away. When she closed and locked it, she felt as though she'd just shut the door on the best

APPALACHIAN WEDDINGS

friend she'd ever had in her life. How could such a solid friendship change so quickly and without her having a clue what had just happened?

⁂

The next day, Brian stayed in his office with the door closed until Jack e-mailed him and asked where the report was. Brian shot him an e-mail right back letting him know it wasn't due for another couple of days. This elicited a return note, requesting an impromptu meeting ASAP. Brian wasn't in the mood for this, but he agreed to meet in the conference room in ten minutes.

This gave him time to say a prayer, grab the paperwork he had ready, and swing by the break room for a soft drink. Jack was sitting at the head of the table, waiting for him when he walked into the conference room.

"So what gives, Brian?"

Brian grabbed a coaster and carefully placed his soda on it then spread the paperwork out in front of Jack. He was about to sit down when Jack started laughing.

"What's so funny?" Brian asked.

"I didn't want to see all this." Jack gestured over the papers. "I just wanted to find out if you're okay. You haven't been yourself lately."

Brian raked his fingers through his close-cropped hair. "I've just been swamped with all the reports and—"

"Don't give me that, Brian. You can handle your job with your eyes closed. Something else is going on."

"Everything's fine."

"Okay, let me guess." Jack leaned forward. "Girl trouble?"

"C'mon, Jack, you know what happened. A guy can't get over being jilted this fast."

Jack tilted his head and folded his arms. "I don't think this is about Leila. It's Kimberly, isn't it?"

If Brian hadn't already confided in Jack when they first started working together, he would've been angry for the man sticking his nose where it didn't belong. He'd regretted it ever since.

"C'mon, man, that was a long time ago. David's coming home soon, and he wants me to have a party to surprise Kim."

Jack made a face. "David wants you to have a surprise party for him? That sounds rather presumptuous to me."

"Nah, it's not like that. He just wants to see some old friends, and while we're at it we'll surprise Kim. That's all."

"Take some advice from a man with a few years on you, Brian. If you love Kimberly, and it looks like you still do, even though you refuse to admit it, don't stand back and let her go without a fight."

"David's one of my closest friends," Brian argued. "Don't forget I introduced them."

180

"That's beside the point. This is serious business. Your entire future is at stake."

"Thanks, Jack, but I'm fine."

"Kim's future is at stake."

Brian nodded. "David is a good man, even if he doesn't know how to show it. If anything, I should probably talk to him about improving communication with his future wife."

Jack leaned toward Brian. "Have you told her how you feel?"

"Discussion closed." Brian glared at his coworker, willing him to stop pressing.

Jack stood, walked over to Brian, and placed a hand on his shoulder. "Man, I wish I could make things better for ya, buddy."

"I'm fine."

"Think about what I said. Have a talk with David. Let him know how you feel about Kim."

"Good-bye, Jack."

Jack snorted. "Okay, fine. Do what you need to do."

"Thanks." Brian smiled. "I appreciate your concern."

"Anytime," Jack said. "Today's meeting should be a barrel of fun." He rolled his eyes upward.

"I'm sure."

After Jack left the conference room, Brian stared down at the papers he'd brought. Until Leila stood him up at the altar, Brian was able to keep his feelings for Kim in check and his life mapped out in a very logical manner. However, that one act—or non-act—turned everything upside down.

Kim couldn't put her finger on it, but she knew something was going on—some sort of secret. Everyone around her seemed to be in on it. Last time she visited her parents, they kept exchanging surreptitious glances. David's mother called and asked if she'd like to go shopping for a new outfit. Even Jazzy kept looking at her, snickering, and shaking her head, like she knew something but wasn't telling. Normally, she would have called Brian and asked him to help her figure things out, but after their talk, she knew she couldn't count on him to be straightforward.

Everything was just too bizarre.

Each day that passed brought even more strange events. She accepted David's mother's shopping invitation, and the woman insisted they go the following weekend. That never would have happened before, because every time Mrs. Jenner made an offer in the past, it was hollow and nothing ever came of it. Jazzy grew silent and only smiled when Kim commented about David or Brian.

Then she called Carrie, who tried to get off the phone. But Kim wouldn't have it.

"Okay, what gives? Everyone's acting like I have a disease."

Carrie laughed. "I think everyone's just really busy."

"The people I want to see don't have time for me. But David's mother actually wants me to go shopping. I can understand everyone else being busy, but Mrs. Jenner hates me."

"Oh I'm sure she doesn't hate you," Carrie said. "I bet David finally convinced her that you're a nice girl and that she really should get to know you."

"Oh right." Kim couldn't keep the sarcasm out of her voice.

"Guess what!" Carrie said.

"I can't imagine. What?"

"I'm coming home the day after tomorrow."

"Then let's get together this weekend."

Carrie cleared her throat. "Sorry, I can't."

"So what are you so busy doing?"

"I, uh. . . I have to clean my house."

"I've known you a long time, and you've never put a clean house before having fun."

Carrie laughed. "Okay, I'll level with you. Something is going on, but I can't talk about it now."

So Kim's hunch was right. "When can you talk about it?"

"Um. . .not for a while."

"Just answer me, Carrie. When?"

"How about a week from Monday?"

"Now that's just weird." Kim let out a sigh of frustration. "Looks like the only choices I have are to keep agonizing over this or coming over there and beating it out of you."

"Right. As if you'd ever resort to violence."

"Okay, so I'm not into using physical tactics. Just answer one question. If you don't tell me, will I ever find out what's going on?"

Without a second's hesitation, Carrie blurted, "Yes."

"When?"

"You said one question," Carrie said, "and I'm holding you to it. I have to go now. My boss needs to talk to me."

Next on Kim's list was Mrs. Jenner. She dreaded spending a day of shopping with the woman, but since they would soon be related, she might as well start now. She opened her phone, scrolled through her list until she found Mrs. Jenner's number, and punched SEND.

Chapter 8

"Hello, dear," Mrs. Jenner said in a saccharine-sweet voice. "Why don't you plan for a full day of shopping. I want to make sure you get the perfect—" She suddenly stopped talking, as if she were afraid of saying the wrong thing.

"Perfect what?" Kim's radar was sounding an alarm louder than ever.

"Oh, never mind," the woman said with a giggle in her voice. This was so out of character for her.

"Okay, so what time did you want me to pick you up?"

"Are you sure you don't mind driving?" Mrs. Jenner asked.

"I love to drive."

"Then be here at nine thirty. The stores open at ten, and I want to get as much shopping in as possible."

Kim hated to shop, but if it would help her relationship with David's mom, she would sacrifice. "That's fine."

"And don't make plans for later in the day. I suspect we'll be out until dark, at least."

Kim held back a groan. "See you Saturday morning at nine thirty."

"That's right, Kimberly." Mrs. Jenner's stern tone had returned. "And don't be late. Punctuality is important to me. I'm sure David must have told you."

"Yes, I know that. I'll be on time."

After they hung up, Kim felt like she'd been through a wringer. She leaned against the storage room door and closed her eyes for a prayer. *Lord, give me the strength to endure shopping with Mrs. Jenner, and help me keep my thoughts to myself.*

"Hey, girl, are you okay?"

Kim jumped back to the present at the sound of Jasmine's voice. "Uh, yeah. Sorry. I just got off the phone with David's mom."

"I hope she appreciates the fact that you're taking one of your busiest days off work to spend time with her."

"Who knows what she appreciates?" *Sorry, Lord.*

Jasmine offered a sympathetic grin. "You'll be fine. If you want, I can call midafternoon and see how you're doing. There's always an emergency around here that can cut your time short."

"Thanks, Jazzy, but I need to do this. . .for David. He really wants me to spend some time with his mother, and I think I owe it to him."

With a smile, Jasmine nodded. "You're a very sweet girl, Kimberly. I hope

David's mother will learn to appreciate you." She started to turn away but stopped. "Another thing. I've been wondering about Brian. I haven't seen him around lately. Is he doing better?"

"Yes." Kim heard the clipped sound of her response. She offered Jasmine an apologetic look. "At least I think he is."

"Okay, I get it. You don't want to talk about Brian."

Kim opened her mouth to explain, but she quickly snapped it shut. She was sick of talking about her feelings.

Early Saturday morning, Kim got out of bed and examined the outfit she'd chosen for her shopping trip. It was a pink and black color-block dress with matching black flats and a pearl necklace—very safe and not something she'd normally choose. She'd bought the dress to go to one of her mother's events at church, and the pearls took on a completely different look when she wore them with jeans.

Dread filled her at the thought of wearing something she wasn't crazy about while pretending to enjoy shopping with a woman who didn't even like her. She trudged into the kitchen and got the coffee ready as she thought about what would make this day more tolerable.

For one thing, she could ditch the dress and wear pants with a fun top. The ballet flats would work, and the pearl necklace would add enough sophistication to keep Mrs. Jenner from thinking she didn't care. Now she felt a little better about things.

However, that feeling was short-lived when Mrs. Jenner answered her knock. A quick once-over glance was a strong hint that the woman didn't approve.

"You're wearing *that*?"

Now she was certain Mrs. Jenner hated her. Kim forced her best smile and nodded. "Since we're making a day of it, I wanted to be comfortable."

"Comfort is all in the mind."

Kim noticed that Mrs. Jenner wore a black knee-length skirt, a ruffled white blouse, and a pink cardigan with tonal beading stitched into a floral design. "You look very nice," Kim said.

Mrs. Jenner's lips barely widened into a half grin. "In spite of what you must think, I'm comfortable, but since you've decided to be so casual, I might as well change."

"Oh no, don't feel you have to—"

"Sit down, Kimberly. I'll change into some slacks. It won't take long." She nodded toward the coffee table in front of the sofa. "While you're waiting, you might as well look through the photo album of David's life. I'm sure it'll give you some insight."

Kim did as she was told. As she flipped through the pages of the album, she saw a sweet little baby boy transform into the handsome man he was today. She knew he'd always been athletic, so she wasn't surprised to see him suited up in various team uniforms. However, when she got to the second to last page, she paused and stared.

There he was, wearing a tuxedo, standing beside a tall, dark-haired woman with dramatic eyes and a very curvy figure shown off by a glittery dress that looked as if it had been painted on her. Based on David's description of his former girlfriend, Kim knew this was Alexis.

Kim stared at the picture as a myriad of feelings flooded her. She was intrigued, amazed, and almost dumbfounded by the woman's exotic beauty. But not an ounce of jealousy surfaced.

"Looking at the snapshot of David and Alexis?"

Kim glanced up at her future mother-in-law, who hovered by the doorway. The only change she'd made was from her black skirt to some black slacks.

"Yes. He looks quite handsome in a tux."

Mrs. Jenner smiled as she crossed the room and sat in the chair adjacent to the sofa. "He certainly does. And get a load of Alexis. That is one beautiful woman. I don't know what. . ." Her voice trailed off as she shook her head and flipped her hand. "I guess you don't want to hear about the woman David almost married, do you?"

"I'm okay with it." Kim closed the photo album and squared her shoulders. Even to her, the fact that she wasn't jealous seemed really strange.

"Well, I suppose you have no reason to be bothered, since you're the one who caught the prize."

The way Mrs. Jenner had worded that, Kim felt as though she'd been in direct competition for David. But she hadn't. David and Alexis had broken up almost a year before Kim had even met him.

Kim stood and gestured toward the door. "Ready to go?"

Mrs. Jenner allowed a lingering, wistful glance at the closed photo album before closing her eyes and nodding. "As ready as I'll ever be."

"I thought we'd start at the mall," Kim said. "That is, if it's okay with you."

The woman shrugged. "That's fine. The mall's not a place I generally frequent, but I shouldn't expect a hairdresser to shop in the finer stores."

Kim's insides clenched. Until now, she could pretend that the only problem with her relationship with Mrs. Jenner was that they didn't know each other very well. Now she'd been verbally assaulted, but since she didn't know what to say, she didn't say anything.

After helping Mrs. Jenner into the car, Kim got in and drove toward the mall. Each time her future mother-in-law asked a question, she felt as if she were being interrogated in court. When Kim couldn't take it anymore, she maneuvered the car into an empty parking lot beside an office building.

"What are you doing?" Mrs. Jenner asked.

Kim stopped, put the car in PARK, then turned to face her fiancé's mother. "I know you don't like me, but don't forget, David and I are engaged to be married."

"Whatever do you mean, dear? Why wouldn't I like you? Is there something you're not telling me?"

"I know that Alexis is an attorney, just like David. I've known for a long time you wish he was still with her, but he's not."

"My son is a grown man. It's not my place to tell him what woman he should date."

"You seem to have a problem with me, and after that comment about my being a hairdresser—"

"It was simply an acknowledgment of what you do for a living."

That wasn't all it was, but Kim didn't want to continue with this confrontation. "Okay, fine. But I want you to know that I'm a very good hairdresser, and I have a large clientele who count on me to make them look good."

"I'm sure you do a very nice job with. . .hair."

Kim caught a glimpse of Mrs. Jenner in time to see the curled lip. She pursed her lips and said a silent prayer for the courage to make it through the day and the ability to keep from snapping. She bit back the words flitting through her mind as she drove the rest of the way to the mall.

The first couple of stores didn't have anything Mrs. Jenner liked, but the mall was big, and they hadn't covered even half of it by noon. Kim was getting hungry, but she wasn't about to be the first to bring up the subject of food after a comment Mrs. Jenner had made shortly after they'd met. She actually asked Kim if all she ever thought about was her next meal.

"Let's see what they have here, and then perhaps we can stop for a bite," Mrs. Jenner said as they approached one of the large department stores.

Kim nodded and followed the older woman toward the misses department. This wasn't a store Kim was familiar with. It catered to an older, more moneyed crowd. She gulped as she glanced at one of the price tags—way out of her price range.

As they approached one of the most hideous ensembles Kim had ever seen, Mrs. Jenner pointed to it and turned to Kim. "That looks like you. Let's find it in your size so you can try it on."

"I. . .uh. . ." Kim studied the bright purple sweater that topped a blouse that actually clashed with itself with orange and purple circles on an ecru background. She didn't want to insult Mrs. Jenner, but she'd never waste her hard-earned money on something like this.

"It's not my taste," Mrs. Jenner said, "but I know you like the. . .shall we say, *bolder prints?*"

Suddenly an idea struck Kim. "Why don't we find something that's not me? I think it's time to step outside the box."

She held her breath as David's mother pondered the point. Finally the woman nodded and smiled. "Yes, I think that's an excellent idea." She placed her hands on her hips and scanned the racks then gestured toward the door. "I'm getting hungry. Let's go grab something to eat, and we can talk about your makeover."

Kim didn't want a makeover, but who was she to argue? She dutifully followed Mrs. Jenner out the door and to the food court.

"I'm not used to eating like this," Mrs. Jenner said. "But I suppose when you shop at a mall, you're expected to eat. . .mall food."

The afternoon wasn't much better than the morning. Mrs. Jenner shot down everything Kim liked. Finally they agreed on a simple black knit dress with three-quarter sleeves for Kim. And to Kim's surprise, it was on a clearance rack. The only thing Mrs. Jenner purchased for herself was a silk scarf to go with something she already had.

All the way home, Kim listened to Mrs. Jenner talk about how they'd unearthed a treasure from the piles of rubbish. "I haven't done this kind of shopping in years—not since the early days of my marriage."

Kim pulled up in front of Mrs. Jenner's house and stopped. "Thank you for helping me pick out this dress."

Mrs. Jenner placed her hand on Kim's arm and offered a condescending smile. "We could have saved hours if we'd gone to one of my favorite stores downtown. Oh well, I suppose it'll make my son happy that we spent the day together." She got out and closed the door without so much as a good-bye.

"Yes, I'm sure it will," Kim muttered to herself as she pulled away from the curb.

When she got home, Kim hung the dress in her closet then changed into her jeans and sneakers. She was exhausted.

✄

Kim barely made it to church on time the next day, so she slipped into the back pew. Most of the time she liked to sit closer to the front so she wouldn't be distracted by all the people.

As the congregation stood for worship songs, Kim found herself looking around for Brian. She didn't see him, but there were quite a few tall people between her and the front. She spotted Carrie in the second row from the front.

The pastor's sermon held her attention, but immediately after church, her mind flitted back to Brian. They normally went to the fellowship hall to hang out, but Kim wasn't in the mood to face Brian or Carrie today. Instead she darted out the back door toward the parking lot. The sound of someone calling her name caught her attention, so she turned around.

When Brian didn't see Kim in church, he decided to forgo the usual coffee in the fellowship hall and just go on home. He spotted Kim practically running toward her car. She was obviously in a hurry, but he wanted to talk to her.

"Hey, Brian. I didn't see you in church. Did you want me for something?"

"Uh, not really." He shrugged and shoved his hands in his pockets.

Kim made a face. "If you hadn't lectured me about how you weren't 'feeling our friendship anymore,' I'd ask you if you wanted to have lunch with me."

"About that. . ."

She folded her arms, tilted her head, and glared at him with a smirk. "Well?"

Brian lowered his head and stared at the pavement beneath him. When he looked back up at her, she was still in the same position, still staring, waiting. "Forget everything I said. It was stupid."

Kim tilted her head back and laughed. "Why is everyone acting so crazy? I feel like I've been abducted by aliens and dropped off at a planet of confusion."

Brian chuckled in spite of all the turmoil boiling inside him. "Let's have lunch together, okay?"

"Fine with me," she said. "Why don't we grab some deli food and head over to Magic Island? I haven't been there in a while."

Brian couldn't think of a more romantic place, but he didn't want to complicate things again. "Sounds good. Let me follow you home; and we can take my car."

All the way to Kim's house, Brian gave himself a mental lecture. He challenged himself to keep the conversation light and away from his feelings for Kim. Once they got there, she asked if he wanted to come inside while she changed.

"No, that's okay. I'll wait in the car."

"I'll hurry."

Brian shoved a CD in the car stereo and settled back to wait. When her front door opened, he glanced at her, and his heart thudded. Suddenly this didn't seem like such a good idea.

Chapter 9

Kim felt strange getting into Brian's car this time—especially after their last talk. He was still acting peculiar, too.

"So do you want the usual from the deli?" he asked.

She thought about it for a moment then shook her head. "No, why don't we shake it up a bit today? Blossom's isn't open, so we'll need to go to the grocery store deli. How about chicken and potato salad?"

"And maybe some baked beans," he added.

"You don't like baked beans," she reminded him.

He grinned. "I know, but you do."

"Okay, let's get some baked beans." Kim folded her arms and turned to stare out the front window. Normally she was fine with silence between them, but even a few seconds of quiet felt wrong. "So how's work?"

He shrugged. "Same. How's the hair business?"

"Good." Kim couldn't stand it any longer. "Okay, Brian, this is crazy. You and I have never been like this before."

"Like what?" He stopped for a light and cut a glance her way.

"You know, like a couple of dorky teenagers who don't know what to say to each other."

Brian tilted his head back and laughed. "Now that's a good one. We might not be teenagers, but we have every right to be as dorky as we want."

Kim grinned back at him. "Okay, now that's better. Do me a favor, okay?"

"I'm not making any promises until you tell me what it is."

"Let's try to get back to the way we were."

He hesitated before nodding. "Good idea."

"I'm starving, so let's get a family-size order of chicken."

He chuckled. "That's the Kimberly I know."

They were in and out of the grocery store in fifteen minutes, on their way to the Magic Island Park. As Kim spread the blanket on the grass, Brian dug through the sports equipment box in his trunk and pulled out a Frisbee and a foam football.

Kim had a wonderful time relaxing after lunch. Brian gave her just enough time for lunch to settle before he jumped to his feet and extended her a hand. "Ready to toss the Frisbee?"

"Sure," she replied as she stood. "I can't believe how gorgeous it is today."

Brian's expression grew pensive. "Yes, it is gorgeous, isn't it?"

The best thing about throwing the Frisbee with Brian at that moment was the distance between them. Kim sensed that at times he was uncomfortable. She had to do something to relax him.

She'd just missed the Frisbee to the sound of Brian's laughter when a solution hit her. He'd fixed her up with David, so she could return the favor and introduce him to some new people. Even if he didn't fall in love with one of them, it would get his mind off the off-limits woman—whoever she was. There had to be some nice Christian girls who'd love to date Brian.

They played for more than an hour before Kim held up her hands. "I need to get back home."

Brian checked his watch. "It's still early."

"Tell that to the mountains of laundry piling up beside my washing machine."

He snorted and tucked the Frisbee under his arm. "You win."

As they rounded up the trash and carried it to the bins nearby, Kim chattered about how much fun she'd had. Brian didn't speak until they got back to the blanket, where all they had to do was stuff the food into the basket and carry it to the car.

"You are still planning to come to my party, right?"

"Of course I'll be there." Kim felt terrible that she'd forgotten about it. "Can I bring anything?"

Brian's eyes twinkled at first then dimmed as he slowly shook his head. "No, I have everything covered."

"I don't mind bringing a bag of chips or some dip or something."

"It's not that kind of party," he said. "It's a little. . .well, nicer."

"What do you mean?" Kim stopped in her tracks and stared at Brian.

"I don't mean anything other than the fact that I've decided to have a party where people dress up and we actually eat decent food."

Kim laughed. "Like what? Caviar?"

"Maybe."

"That's so not you, Brian."

"What? Are you saying I don't have class?" He gave her a mock hurt look.

"Oh you have class, but as long as I've known you, you've been a chip and dip kind of guy."

He unlocked his trunk and dumped the sports equipment into the box. "And look where that's gotten me. I'd say it's time for a change."

All the way to Kim's house, she tried to talk him into having a more casual party. "Your friends don't care if you're not fancy, Brian. Don't stop being yourself." She narrowed her eyes as she remembered his comment about his complicated feelings for the girl. "Are you trying to impress someone?"

"No," he snapped. He stared straight ahead, not even casting a glance her way when he came to a stop and put his car in PARK. "You can't change my mind."

Kim grunted. "So you're saying I have to dress up?"

"Yes."

"That's just plain silly."

Brian's lips twitched, but he didn't smile.

"What's going on, Brian?"

"I already told you. I'm having a dress-up party. We're adults now. It's time we acted like it."

Kim couldn't help but howl with laughter. "Who are you? Where did you put Brian?"

He turned to face Kim. "Do me a favor, Kim, and stop asking questions. Just come to my get-together in something nice. You'll understand later."

The seriousness of his expression let her know it was time to quit arguing. He wasn't playing games. This whole dress-up party thing was for real—and it was important to him. But why?

"Will your boss be there?" she asked.

"Uh-uh-uh. No questions, remember?" He wiggled his index finger in the air. "Now go on inside. I have stuff to do to get ready for work tomorrow."

Kim nodded and opened the door before something dawned on her. "Wait a minute. I was the one who had stuff to do. You wanted to stay later."

"You reminded me of laundry."

She laughed. "Okay, Brian. I'll leave you alone about this party thing. If you need help with it, just let me know."

"What would you know about a fancy party?" he teased.

"About as much as you." She winked and grinned as she shut the car door.

Once she got to her front porch and unlocked the door, she turned and waved. Then she went inside. Yes, it was definitely time to introduce Brian to some new people. Since he was ready to move on and she couldn't have him, perhaps she could find someone to make him happy. That thought made her stomach hurt, but she was so confused she couldn't think of another solution.

First she called Carrie and told her the plan. "Good idea," Carrie said. "But who do you know that Brian doesn't?"

Kim tapped her pencil on the table and thought. "I have a few customers he might hit it off with."

"Are they Christians?" Carrie asked.

"One is for sure, but the other two I'll have to ask."

"So, smarty-pants, how do you plan to execute this scheme?"

"That's why I called you," Kim replied. "I figured you could help me out with this."

"What makes you think I'd want to be involved in something so underhanded?"

Kim pretended to gasp. "Underhanded? *Moi?* No, I'd never resort to underhandedness. All I want to do is help Brian like he helped me."

Carrie chuckled. "Since you put it that way, I'll look around and see if I can think of someone good, too."

"Perfect. Brian will probably be okay with one or two introductions, but we can't force too many on him too quickly."

"I agree," Carrie said.

"We'll each make a list and get together later—that is, when you have time—to put them in order of how we think they'd get along."

"No problem, I understand. I'd like to hang out with you and plan Brian's future, but let's wait until after this little party of his."

Kim chuckled. "I don't know if it can wait. Oh, speaking of the party, do you have any idea what's going on with him? He told me I have to dress up."

"Yeah, I know," Carrie agreed. "It's weird, isn't it?"

"Even worse, he told me he's not serving chips and dip. It's. . ." Kim cleared her throat and deepened her voice in a hoity-toity tone. "It's a party where people dress up and eat fancy food."

Carrie giggled. "Did he actually say that?"

"Yes. Something is definitely going on."

"I'm sure."

"You don't know something I don't know, do you?" Kim asked. "I mean, has anyone from church mentioned anything about this party. . .besides Brian?"

"Um. . ." Carrie coughed. "Look, Kim, I really need to run."

"Wait—"

"See ya." *Click!*

Kim held out the phone and stared at it before placing it in the cradle. One minute Carrie was with her, and the next minute she was back to acting just as strange as Brian.

Kim worked on involving Jasmine in her plan to find someone suitable for Brian. At first Jasmine balked.

"I don't think this is such a good idea, Kim," Jasmine said. "If you take a step back, you might see that he holds every woman up to you, and there's no way anyone can withstand that."

"Don't be silly," Kim said. "He's just lonely and floundering after what Leila did."

"Well, if you want my opinion—even if you don't want my opinion— Leila did him a huge favor. He wasn't in love with her."

"Oh I'm sure he loved her," Kim argued as she thought about his confession. "But you're right. She did him a favor." She didn't mention how he'd found someone else to love—the complicated relationship with the woman he wouldn't even discuss with her.

"There's a difference between loving someone and being in love." Jasmine nodded toward the door. "We can resume this discussion after work."

Not only did they resume their discussion after work, but they talked about it every morning and afternoon, until finally Jasmine relented. "Okay, if you're going to be that stubborn about it, I'll keep an eye open for a nice girl for Brian. Just remember it was your idea."

Kim smiled. "I'll take credit for it when he finally meets the woman of his dreams."

Jasmine shook her head. "That's the problem, Kim. He already has."

Chapter 10

Y ou what?" Brian couldn't keep his voice down. Had Kimberly lost her mind?

"Calm down, Brian."

"How can I calm down with you trying to play matchmaker?"

He heard her quick intake of breath over the phone line, letting him know she was startled by his reaction. "I'm not being a matchmaker. I just want you to meet this girl. She's very nice."

Brian forced himself to lower his tone. "I'm sure she's a very nice girl. Probably the nicest in all of Charleston."

"Just do me a favor and meet her. I'm not asking you to marry her."

"No, but that's probably next on your list of things to do."

"Look, all we'll do is get together for pizza or something—"

"What—you, this girl, and me?"

"I was thinking the singles group from church."

Brian snickered then dropped his voice to a growl. "So you want to involve everyone we know? That's not gonna happen."

"How about lunch sometime? That way you'll have a set amount of time and a good excuse to leave."

"Just the three of us?"

"Yep. You, Michelle, and me."

"Fine. We'll get together for lunch." He figured he might as well give in, or she'd bug him until he did.

"How about Thursday, eleven thirty, at Blossom's?"

Brian laughed. "You little schemer. You had this whole thing set up, with every last detail already planned, didn't you?"

"Well. . ." Kim cleared her throat. "You'll really like her, Brian."

"So you said. Okay, but if this is as big of a disaster as I think it might be, you have to promise never to do this kind of thing again."

Silence fell between them.

"Kim, did you hear what I just said?"

"I'm thinking."

"Promise you won't try to fix me up after I meet Michelle."

"Oh Brian, I can't make that kind of promise."

"That's what I thought." He decided to change the subject. "So have you thought about what to wear to my party?"

"Your fancy-schmancy, hoity-toity party where everyone has to dress up and eat pretentious food?"

"That's the one."

"I bought a black dress I didn't need when David's mother and I went shopping, so I'll probably wear that, just to get my money's worth."

"Excellent," Brian said.

"I don't know why you sound so down about it when you're the one who came up with this harebrained idea to be something you're not."

"I know," he said. "It was probably a huge mistake."

"So now you're going for drama? Brian, you're such a goofball. Anyway, we'll see you on Thursday at Blossom's. Why don't you wear that light blue dress shirt instead of a stark white one?"

"Okay, I'll wear whatever you want me to," Brian agreed. "I've already learned there's no point in arguing with you."

"Smart boy."

After they got off the phone, Brian hung his head and closed his eyes. *Lord, get me through lunch on Thursday and the party for David, and keep me from making a fool of myself either time.*

"Hey, are you okay?"

Brian opened his eyes just as Jack sat down in the chair across from his desk. "You have great timing."

Jack made a face. "Seems like there's never a good time for you anymore. What's going on now?"

"Kim's trying to fix me up with some girl."

"And you're complaining?" Jack leaned back in the chair, folded his arms, and crossed his legs. "Kim knows you well enough to know what you like." He tilted his head and squinted. "Maybe that's what you need."

"Nah, I don't think so. Getting fixed up is not my thing."

"According to the experts, it's the best way to meet people. They've been prescreened by your friends."

"I don't need Kimberly Shaw prescreening my dates."

Jack chuckled softly but stopped when Brian glared at him. After a couple of seconds, Jack stood. "If I were you, I wouldn't turn down any opportunity to meet people. You never know what might come of it." He took a couple of steps toward the door, turned to face Brian, and shook his head. "On second thought, maybe you're better off not meeting people."

"Why do you say that?" Brian asked.

"You might find someone you like, and then you'd have to risk meeting the real Ms. Right."

Brian lifted his hands and looked up at the ceiling. "It's a conspiracy, I tell ya."

"Yeah, a conspiracy to get our friend back to the living."

"Okay," Brian said as he escorted Jack to the door. "Point taken. Now I gotta get back to work."

Michelle shifted in her seat. "Are you sure he agreed to do this?"

"Positive," Kim said, trying to sound more sure of the situation than she really was. When she'd first planned the meeting, it seemed like the right thing to do, but now she wasn't so sure. Deep down she was conflicted over her own feelings for Brian.

"What if he doesn't like me?"

Kim turned to face her client of two years. "What's not to like, Michelle? You're very sweet, you're pretty, you're smart, and you love the Lord."

Michelle tilted her head and glanced down at the table before looking back up with a shy smile. "Thank you for saying such nice things, but you know as well as I do that there's more to people liking each other than all that."

"Maybe so, but it's a good start." Kim spotted Brian as he walked in the door, so she lifted her hand and waved. "Over here, Brian!"

Michelle cast a glance over her shoulder then turned back to face Kim. "He's cute," she whispered.

"Told you." Kim smiled at Michelle as she waved him over. "Brian, I'd like for you to meet one of my favorite clients, Michelle."

Brian extended his hand and tipped his head forward. "Nice to meet you, Michelle. Kim has said some very nice things about you."

"Aren't you gonna sit down?" Kim asked, pointing to the chair.

Brian grinned at Michelle then turned to Kim with a teasing glance. "I need to talk to one of my buddies I haven't seen in a while. Do you mind ordering for me?"

"Of course not." Kim said. "Want the usual?"

As soon as he left the table, Kim turned back to Michelle. "Well, what do you think now?"

"He's very nice." Michelle rested her elbow on the table then propped her chin on her hand.

"But?" Kim sensed her friend's reservation.

"I saw the way he looked at you." Michelle frowned. "Are you sure there's nothing going on between the two of you?"

"Oh come on, Michelle. You know I'm engaged. Besides, Brian and I have been very good friends for so long, we're like brother and sister."

"I know, but—"

"Anything but friendship with Brian would be flat-out creepy."

One of Michelle's friends walked up to the table. After Kim met her, Michelle and the other woman chatted, giving Kim a chance to think. She decided that she needed to look at Brian less and focus on everyone else more.

Shortly after Michelle's friend left, a server came to take their order. By the time Brian came back, their drinks had arrived.

Brian turned his attention to Michelle. "Are you from West Virginia?"

She nodded. "Yes, originally from Huntington."

"So what brought you to our lovely town of Charleston?"

"My job."

Kim piped up to help out. "She manages a fashion store."

Brian lifted his eyebrows and nodded his approval. "Managing a store is hard work. Do you like your job?"

"I love it," Michelle replied. "I've always enjoyed fashion."

An unexpected pang of jealousy shot through Kim as she watched Brian give Michelle a once-over glance. "Yes, I can tell you're very good with fashion."

They chatted throughout lunch until finally Kim couldn't handle the situation anymore, so she stood up. "Well, gotta get back to work. I have an appointment in about fifteen minutes. It's been fun."

Brian lifted his hand in a wave. "See ya." Then he turned to Michelle. "Can you stick around and talk for a few more minutes?"

Michelle's face lit up. "Sure!"

"You two have fun." Kim paused with a forced grin then turned and left.

All the way back to the shop, she gave herself a mental lecture. What was going on with her? Not only had she and Brian been friends forever, she had a fiancé, and she'd been the one to introduce Brian to Michelle. Why did she have such an unsettling sensation in her stomach? The better question was why did she have to have these feeling for Brian and complicate things?

The second she shoved open the door to the shop, Jasmine's eyebrows shot up. "Whoa, what happened to you? Did one of them not show up? Don't tell me Brian chickened out." She contorted her mouth before continuing. "Did Michelle change her mind?"

"No, they were both there," Kim replied without stopping on her way to the storage room.

She heard footsteps and wished she'd been better at hiding her feelings. Talking to Jazzy right now was the last thing she needed.

Fortunately the bottles of color were on the far shelf, so she had her back to the entrance. But she could still hear her coworker.

"So what happened that has you all in a snit?" Jazzy asked.

"I'm not in a snit. I just had to rush to get back before my appointment arrived." She perused the color for a moment. "Have you seen the dark golden blond?"

"To your right, where it always is."

"Oh okay, thanks." Kim pulled the bottle off the shelf and loaded her arms with the rest of what she needed.

"You don't wanna talk about it yet, huh?"

Kim turned to face Jasmine. "There's not much to say. Michelle and I got there first, and then Brian showed up. We talked over lunch, and I had to go." She swallowed hard. "They're still at Blossom's."

Jasmine turned her head slightly without taking her eyes off Kim. "And this bothers you, doesn't it? I was afraid of that."

She shrugged. "Why should it bother me?"

"You are in such denial, girl. Trust me when I tell you what's obvious to other people. You're conflicted between Brian and David."

Kim hung her head and let her shoulders sag. "I don't know why I feel the way I do."

Jasmine closed the distance between them. Kim leaned into her as she felt her caring friend's arms envelop her. "David's been gone for a while, and Brian's always here, that's why."

"So I need to keep praying for David's overseas tour to end, and everything will be fine, right?" Kim looked into Jasmine's eyes, hoping to see agreement. But she didn't.

"Who knows? Sometimes it's not that easy dealing with matters of the heart."

"Have you ever felt torn like this?"

Jasmine nodded. "Yes, several times."

"What did you do?"

"When I was a teenager and in my early twenties, I played the field. But when I got older and realized that wasn't good for anyone, I spent some time alone to figure out what I really wanted."

Kim snickered. "I've spent way too much time alone, and I think that's part of my problem."

"Just remember what I keep saying—that you're not married yet. After David returns, you can see how things go with him. The Lord will work this out in His own way. Try praying about it and leave the rest up to Him."

With a nod, Kim headed for the door. "You're right. I need to stop trying to figure everything out by myself."

The timer at Jasmine's station dinged. "I need to finish up with my client. We can talk later."

Shortly after that, Kim's client arrived, and both hairdressers were busy for the remainder of the day. Jasmine's husband came to pick her up because her car was at the shop.

"Hi, Wayne. Jasmine's in the back. She'll be right out."

"Hey, Kimberly," Wayne said as he plopped down in his wife's chair. "You're lookin' good."

"Thanks," Kim said. "So how's everything at the auto shop?"

"Going great! Business is better than ever now that people are hanging on to their cars longer." When his wife came back, Kim noticed the spark between them.

"I'll finish up here," Kim offered.

"Don't forget what I said."

"Trust me," Kim replied. "I'll be thinking about it all night."

After Jasmine and Wayne left, Kim swept the shop, put everything away, and headed home. As soon as she walked in, she sat down at the computer to check her e-mail. It had been awhile since she'd heard from David, and she was surprised there was an e-mail from him.

To: KShaw
From: DJenner
Subject: Thanks!

Kimberly, sweetheart, Mom told me you spent the day with her. I'm so happy my favorite girls got to spend some time together. Remember I said you'd love her after you got to know her? I'm sure that over time you'll become the best of friends.

I'm counting the days until I come home. So far the mission has been successful.

Tell Brian I want to challenge him to a game of golf when I get back—that is, after my knee heals. I'll tell you all about it later. But don't worry. It's nothing permanent.

I love you, Kimberly. I know you're probably eager to start with wedding plans. As soon as I know something, we can talk about it.

Until next time.

Love,
David

Kimberly sat back and read the e-mail a couple more times. She wished David had been more concrete about when he was coming home, but not even an ounce of disappointment had broken through the shell of numbness that surrounded her. He'd mentioned his knee needing to heal, so she wondered about that.

Michelle was a very pretty woman, and she was nice enough, but Brian couldn't see himself falling for her. After Kim left, he tried to force himself to focus on Michelle, but his mind kept wandering to the picnic with Kim at Magic Island.

After he left the office, he stopped off at the store and picked up a few frozen dinners. He knew he should eat healthier, but he wasn't motivated to cook full single meals. Besides, he had a big lunch, and he wasn't even hungry yet.

After unloading the groceries and putting them away, he checked his e-mail. He'd been expecting to hear back from David, who was obviously too busy to reply to his question about the details of the big homecoming.

David's e-mail popped up. Finally. It was about time.

To: BEstep
From: DJenner
Subject: Our surprise

Hey, Brian! How's it going, buddy? Mom sent me a note letting me know she helped Kim pick out a pretty dress for my homecoming. I'm sure she'll be gorgeous as usual.

I just wanted to confirm my arrival. I'll be at my mom's place at 1800 hours on Friday night. She didn't think it would be a good idea to go to my apartment until after the party, in case Kimberly drove by. Mom said Kim's been moping around. What can I expect? I suppose my absence has been rough on her.

Saturday morning I'll swing by your place and help you with the finishing touches. I want this to be the best surprise ever for Kim.

You don't have to reply to this. I just wanted to confirm. See you soon.

David

Brian's jaw tightened. So David's big homecoming was actually going to happen. A shroud of disappointment fell over him. Then his phone rang.

Chapter 11

Brian glanced at his caller ID and saw Kim's name and number. He stared at it for a second before answering.

"So did you make plans with Michelle?" she asked, her voice light and lilting—and very unnatural sounding.

"Um. . .no."

"Huh? I thought you two hit it off."

"She's a very nice girl."

"But?"

Brian cleared his throat. "She's really not my type, Kim."

"What exactly is your type?" Kim sounded annoyed, but that was too bad. He was annoyed, too.

"I'm not sure."

"Then I'll keep trying."

"Look, Kim, I appreciate what you're doing, but if and when I decide it's time to jump back into the dating pool, I can find my own women."

"That would be fine, Brian, but there's just one problem."

So now she was going to tell him what was wrong with him. "And that is?"

"If you want to meet someone new, you have to go places where the nice girls are."

Yeah, that was true. "Maybe someone new will show up at church."

"Maybe so, maybe not. What if I just happen to meet some really cute, single, Christian girl at the salon? Wouldn't you rather I introduce you to her than leave you to wander around trying to figure it all out?"

"Figure what out?" Brian asked. He couldn't keep the grumpiness out of his voice.

"How to meet girls. Isn't that what we were talking about?"

"That's what *you* were talking about, Kim. I'm just the innocent bystander in this situation."

She laughed, which irked the daylights out of him. Brian found himself getting annoyed much more frequently these days.

"Innocent bystander, huh?"

"That's what I said." He felt his jaw tighten. "So why don't we forget about fixing my love life for a while and talk about something else?"

"Okay. Did you think of anything I can do to help you with this get-together Saturday night?"

"Nothing. Everything's all set."

"You have all the drinks and food? How about music and games?"

Brian could tell she was hurt, so he quickly came up with something. "Why don't you bring one of your group games?"

"Okay!" she said. "See? I knew there was something you'd forgotten."

"Thanks, Kimberly. Now I really need to run."

"Oh, one more thing I almost forgot to tell you. I finally heard from David."

Brian tensed. "Anything I need to know about?"

"Not really. He just said he wants to challenge you to a game of golf."

"Sounds like fun." But it didn't really.

"Are you okay?"

"Yeah," he replied. "I've just had a really long day."

"I guess I'd better let you go then. See you Saturday night?"

"Yep. See ya then."

⁂

Kim was tired of being in limbo. She was ready to get on with her life. And her moods were getting worse every day. She stormed into the salon the next morning. "I don't get why David bothered getting engaged if he planned to go on special missions."

Jasmine had a quick answer for that. "I think he just wanted to stick that ring on your finger to let all the guys know you're off-limits."

"All the guys, huh?" Kim snorted. "It's not like I have a bunch of them standing in line."

"That's your own fault. Why don't you e-mail David and tell him you're not going to wait around forever?"

Kim tilted her head forward and gave Jasmine a hooded look. "The man is over in the Middle East fighting for peace, while I'm here in the cushy United States, complaining like a brat. How can I do something like that to him?"

Jasmine rolled her eyes. "You're not acting like a brat. He should have waited to propose. What he did to you was very unfair."

"He didn't do anything to me," Kim retorted. "I didn't have to accept."

"Then tell me this. When he asked you to marry him, did he first tell you he was planning to request to be assigned to this. . .special mission?"

"No."

"Would you have agreed to take his ring if you'd known?"

Kim paused and lowered her gaze. "I'm not sure."

"There ya go. He withheld information, so I think you have good reason to break off the engagement—or at least postpone it."

Jazzy had a valid point. "Maybe so, but I don't know about doing it via e-mail."

"How else can you do it?"

Kim lifted a shoulder and let it drop. "That's the problem. The only way we communicate is through e-mail."

"Maybe something will come up." Jasmine quickly turned away.

"What do you mean?"

"I don't know. Perhaps you'll figure something out soon."

"Yeah," Kim said with a snort. "I'll just hop on a plane and have them fly me to the Middle East. Maybe I can stay at a luxury resort and make a vacation of it while I'm there."

Jasmine lifted an eyebrow and shook her head. "You don't have to resort to sarcasm, Kimberly. It's not becoming."

"Now you sound like my mother."

"Speaking of your mother, have you talked to her lately about all this?"

"No." Her mother loved both David and Brian, and Kim didn't want to discuss her confusion until she had things sorted out in her own mind. But it would be nice to see her parents.

"Your mother is a wise woman. Perhaps she'll have some insight that might help."

"Maybe," Kim said. The bell on the door jingled from the sound of Jasmine's next client. A few minutes later, Kim's appointment showed up.

Between up-dos and blow-dries, Kim thought over what Jazzy had said. By the time the workday ended, she'd decided to stop off at her parents' house and see if her mother had time to talk.

Her parents had just sat down to dinner when she arrived. "There's plenty of food," her mother said. "Grab a plate and help yourself."

Kim soon joined her parents with a plate full of her mother's fabulous chicken ziti.

"This is good, Mom," Kim said.

Her mother smiled. "I'm glad you like it. Now what's on your mind?"

Kim cut her eyes over to her dad, who was busy shoveling food into his mouth, clearly oblivious to anything the women were saying. Some things never changed, and this time that was good.

She turned back to her mother. "I'm getting really frustrated about my engagement."

Her mother put down her fork, blotted her lips with her napkin, and leaned toward Kim. "I think that's normal. A lot of brides-to-be have sort of a. . .what do you call it? Buyer's remorse?"

Was that what she had? Maybe, but she didn't think so.

Kim shrugged. "I don't hear from him for days, and I find myself wondering if we really should get married, then I get an e-mail like. . ." She lifted her hands as her voice trailed off.

"Honey, I'm sure everything will be just fine between the two of you. This separation has been extremely stressful, not only on you but on David, too, I'm sure."

"Why do you think he proposed before he left, knowing he was about to go?" Kim asked.

Her mother pursed her lips as she thought about it, and then she smiled. "David loves you, and he knew he wanted to spend the rest of his life with you. I think he felt that this was the best way of letting you know his intentions."

Kim stood and carried her plate to the sink. "He could have just told me what was on his mind."

"True, but would it have been as powerful as a proposal?"

Her mother had a point. "Probably not."

"There ya go. David doesn't do anything halfway. You'll be glad about that later—after you've been married a few years and have children."

"Maybe." Kim shrugged and turned away.

"Sweetheart." Her mother placed her hand on Kim's shoulder and turned her around. "I wish I could do something to make everything better, but this is something I can't fix. If you love David and still want to marry him, you'll have to wait until he comes back. But if you're having real second thoughts, perhaps you need to rethink your engagement."

A lump formed in Kim's throat as she nodded. "Thanks, Mom. Right now all I need is a listening ear."

Kim helped her mother clean the kitchen while her dad went to make a business call to California. As they cleared the table, they talked about everything they'd been doing.

Then Kim brought up the get-together at Brian's on Saturday. She noticed that her mother almost dropped the plate she'd been holding.

"Are you okay, Mom?"

"Yes, I'm fine." Her mother put down the plate and cleared her throat as she turned to face Kim. "I can finish up here. Why don't you go on home and get some rest?"

"But—"

Her dad arrived in the kitchen. "Sorry to interrupt your girl talk, but I need to see your mother," he said to Kim. Then he looked at his wife. "Barb, do you have a few minutes? I need to talk to you about this trip we have planned."

"Trip?" Kim turned to face her parents. "Y'all are going on a trip?"

"We're thinking about it."

"When?" Kim asked.

Her mother looked at her father, who spoke. "That's what I wanted to discuss."

Kim wiped her hands on the dish towel. "Okay, I can take a hint. The two of you want to be alone. Call me tomorrow and tell me more about your trip."

"Okay, honey," her mother replied. "And stop trying to overthink your engagement. David will be home very soon, I'm sure, and you'll wonder why you worried so much."

"Thanks." Kim left her parents' house wondering what had just happened. For the first time in her life, they'd nearly pushed her out the door.

Everyone continued to act strange. Saturday morning Kim noticed that her schedule ended at noon. Her standing early afternoon appointment had canceled.

"This is odd," she said as she looked over the appointment book. "I'm generally busy all day on Saturday."

Jasmine continued combing her client's hair and didn't look up. "Sometimes it just works out that way. No big deal. Why don't you call it a day and go on home?"

"I can stick around here and help you," she said.

"No." Jasmine stopped what she was doing and looked Kim in the eye. "You have that thing at Brian's place tonight. Go home, take a long bubble bath, and pamper yourself a little. You'll have more fun if you're rested."

Kim chuckled. "It's just a little get-together. Brian has some harebrained notion that he needs to throw a sophisticated party with fancy food. He even wants his guests to dress up."

"All the more reason to do a little primping." She made a shooing gesture. "Now go on; get out of here."

"Okay, okay," Kim said as she swept the last of the hair into the dustpan. "Just promise to call me if you get a walk-in. I really don't mind coming back if you get swamped."

"I'll be just fine," Jasmine said with a self-satisfied smile.

On her way home, Kim's thoughts wandered back over the past several days, and she reflected on how secretive everyone was. And the tension was growing.

It wasn't her birthday, so no one was planning to surprise her. She couldn't think of any reason for people to keep a secret from her.

Kim thought about her parents and how they practically pushed her out the door. They were planning a trip. Without her. It shouldn't have bothered her, but with David out of the country, she felt left out of everyone's lives. No one understood that she needed to be part of something as much as ever.

Maybe her problem was that she was standing still watching the world move forward without her. And as long as David was overseas, she'd be this way. She didn't know what to make of her feelings for Brian. She'd always loved him, but as her romantic thoughts about him increased, she felt like she was sinking deeper into unknown territory—something that frightened her. If she acted on her feelings now, she not only risked hurting David, but she was afraid Brian would freak out.

And then her annoyance annoyed her. When David had proposed, she loved him—or at least she thought she did. But now as she looked back at the way he'd kept his plans to volunteer for the mission a secret, she wished she'd given him back his ring and told him they'd wait for his return to be officially engaged.

She could still do that, but it meant e-mailing him. Was that bad form? But then again, he'd proposed without letting her know his plans. What if he did that kind of thing after they said their vows? Could she go through life with someone like that?

By the time she pulled into the driveway, she'd made her decision. She was going to send David an e-mail and tell him she wanted to end— no, make that *suspend*—their engagement. They could discuss it when he returned.

She heard her phone ringing as she unlocked her door, but it stopped once she was inside. A glance at her caller ID let her know it was Brian.

He must have realized he couldn't pull this thing off without help, she thought with a chuckle. She put her purse down and punched in his number.

"Want me to come help you get ready for this shindig?" she asked.

"Nope. Everything's all set."

"Why did you call?"

Kim heard some whispering in the background. "Who's there?"

"Oh, just someone who stopped by for a little while. Hold on a sec." She heard Brian put his hand over the mouthpiece for a couple of seconds. "Why don't you plan to get here right at seven?"

"That's when it starts. Don't you want me to come help you greet people?"

Brian laughed. "I think I can handle it by myself."

Then it dawned on her. "You have someone else helping out, don't you?"

"You might say that."

"Oh, so there's a mystery woman, huh?" At least something made sense. She forced a smile. "Okay, I'll show up at seven."

"Oh, and Kim, why don't you wear that pearl necklace David gave you for Christmas?"

Kim let out a nervous laugh. "Why do you care what jewelry I wear? What's going on, Brian?"

"I just think it's really pretty on you. This is a dress-up party, remember?"

"Okay, whatever. I'll be there," she said, "wearing my pearl necklace if it makes you happy."

"See you at seven. And not a minute before. In fact it's okay if you're a couple of minutes late."

"Are you sure you still want me to come? I'm thinking you might want to be alone with. . .your new lady."

"There'll be a lot of people here." He snickered. "You'd better come—just not early, though."

Kim changed into a jogging suit and lay down on the couch to watch some TV and rest before getting ready. She'd hung her new black dress on the closet door. She didn't know what she'd been thinking when she let Mrs. Jenner talk her into buying it.

After alternately channel surfing and dozing, Kim finally got up and took the bubble bath Jazzy thought was so important. Then she carefully applied her makeup and got dressed. She looked at the clock on her dresser, and it was only six fifteen. If Brian hadn't told her not to get there early, she would have gone ahead. Now she had to wait.

Time dragged until Kim felt safe to leave and not arrive before seven. As she turned the corner and drove up Brian's street, everything seemed very still. There were a lot of familiar cars parked along the curb, but something seemed strange. Brian's front door was closed, the blinds were pulled, and there was only one window showing a light on in the house.

She felt a gripping sensation. Something was wrong. Kim pulled into his driveway, threw her car into PARK, turned it off, and hopped out.

Kim ran up the front steps of his small, red-brick house and banged on the door. She needed to be there for him. He'd be so—

"Hello, sweetheart," David said as he opened the door. "Surprised?"

Chapter 12

Kim suddenly froze to her spot on the porch, while David grinned back at her. A group of friends stood in the background, but she was in such a state of shock, all their faces were blurred.

"Hi, honey," David said as he reached for her hand. "Come on in and join the party."

This so wasn't how she wanted to see David when he first came back.

"Are you surprised?" Someone shouted from the other side of the room. "Isn't this exciting?"

"Hey, Kimberly! Looks like we really gotcha this time."

One voice rang out after another, but all Kim wanted to do was turn around and run. She felt oddly like she was in a bad fairy tale, with all the creepy characters staring at her as she walked through the forest of her nightmare.

David put his arm around her and pulled her close. "You're shaking, Kimberly. Are you cold?"

She opened her mouth, but she still couldn't talk. So she shook her head.

Brian suddenly appeared with a look of concern. "Find her a place to sit, David, and I'll get her something to drink." As he walked away, Kim overheard his voice as he softly told someone, "Maybe surprising Kim wasn't such a good idea."

No kidding.

Having a surprise welcome home party for David would have been awesome. After all, she would have known he was back, and it wouldn't have been such a shock. But this was frightening. Terrifying, in fact. Kim wasn't sure she'd ever get over the jolt of seeing David standing at Brian's door.

Brian arrived with a glass of something with ice in it. "Take a sip of this ginger ale, Kim."

David steadied her hand as she took her first sip. Some of the other people dispersed and talked among themselves, giving her a chance to recover. Finally Kim felt that she was of sound enough mind to question what had happened.

"How long have you been back?" she asked.

He grinned. "Since last night."

"Here?" Kim shot Brian a glare. "You've been staying with Brian?"

"No," David's mother said as she sneaked up from behind Brian. "He's been with me." Mrs. Jenner gave her a once-over. "That dress looks very nice on you. I was afraid you might not wear the one I picked out."

David's face showed joy. "Is this what you bought when the two of you spent the day together? I love it!"

Kim managed a half smile before looking at Brian as she touched her necklace. "I wore the pearls you asked me to."

David turned her around to face his mother. "These are the pearls I gave her for Christmas."

"They're lovely," Mrs. Jenner said. "Now you need a pearl bracelet to go with it."

"Oh, I don't wear—"

Mrs. Jenner interrupted Kim. "I might have one that matches your necklace."

"She doesn't wear bracelets," Brian said.

"What's wrong with bracelets?" David's mother glared at Brian before turning to Kim. "All girls wear bracelets." She turned to David and patted his arm. "David loves to shower his women with jewelry, don't you, son?"

Kim wondered how many women he'd showered with jewelry. He looked panicked.

"Working in a hair salon makes wearing bracelets difficult for Kimberly," Brian explained. "I'm sure she likes them, don't you?"

She saw his pleading expression, so she nodded. No doubt Brian had the best of intentions when he'd planned this party, and she didn't want to ruin it for him. With that in mind, she made a quick decision.

Kimberly forced the biggest smile she could manage. "I'm sorry I acted like a grump. I was just so surprised to see you, David."

"I knew you would be." His eyebrows lifted as he took her hand and looked into her eyes. "I hope you're as happy as I am."

She swallowed hard and nodded. "Yes, of course I am. Very happy."

Brian tapped Mrs. Jenner on the shoulder and gestured for her to follow him. "Let's leave the happy couple alone for a few minutes so they can catch up."

Once they were alone, David smiled at Kim and gently touched her cheek. "You're as beautiful as ever, Kimberly. I've really missed you."

She felt her heart soften a bit as her fiancé spoke to her with the sweetness she remembered, but she didn't feel that heart-stopping romantic love she so wanted to have. Instead she found herself wondering what Brian had been thinking. He knew she hated surprises. "Why didn't you tell me you were coming home?"

"I thought a surprise would be more fun."

"Maybe so, but I would have appreciated some warning."

"Why?" he asked. "Would you have done anything different?"

"Probably not, but I wouldn't have felt so lost when you opened the door."

"The look on your face was priceless." He held a lock of her hair between his fingers and twisted it before tucking it behind her ear. That simple, familiar gesture bugged her. "I hope someone got a picture."

Kim pulled her hair away from him and scooted a few inches away from David on the sofa. "They better not have. I don't want pictures of that moment."

David gave her a mock pained look. "It'll be fun to show our grandkids."

That reminded her of one of their earlier conversations, and she felt a tinge of anger. "We have to have kids to have grandkids, and you said you didn't want kids."

"I've been thinking about it, and I'm not sure yet," he said. "Do we have to discuss this now?"

"There are a lot of things we need to discuss."

Now David's frown was real. "Are you mad at me, Kimberly?"

Some of her anger dissipated, and she shook her head. "No, I'm not mad. But we do need to talk."

"Okay, so talk."

"Not here, David. Not now." She studied his face as he looked her over. "Are you home for good?"

"The first part of the mission is over." He pointed to his leg. "We're not sure if we'll have to go back, but if we do, my part in the plan depends on how quickly I heal."

"What happened to your knee?"

He rubbed it. "That's a long story. I'll tell you about it later. I just hope it's better soon so I can be ready if needed."

"So you're still not sure if you're going back?"

David stroked her hair from her face. "Kimberly, hon, you know there are no guarantees in life." As she started to look down, he cupped her chin and tilted her face toward his. "Let's make the most of the time we have now."

Slowly she nodded. He was right. There were no guarantees. And *now* was all they had.

❧

Brian gripped the tray of drinks as he stood at the door watching David and Kimberly. He sensed the tension between them, and he had to use every ounce of self-restraint to hold back and not see if he could help.

"Don't they look happy?" Kim's mother said as she came up and took a cup from the tray. She stared at him until he looked her in the eye.

"Uh. . .yes, very happy."

Mrs. Shaw blew out a breath of exasperation as she took the tray from him and put it on the breakfast bar. "You know good and well I was just trying to get your attention, Brian."

He blinked and cocked his head. "What do you mean?"

"My daughter looks absolutely miserable."

Brian licked his lips as he turned back to see what Kim's mother was talking about. David was still talking, and Kim was looking at him, but the chemistry between them seemed off.

"Something's been bothering her lately," Mrs. Shaw continued. "Has she spoken to you about what's on her mind?"

"No, not really," Brian replied. "But I think she's still a little ticked about David not telling her he was planning to volunteer for this special mission in the Middle East."

"Well, I can certainly understand that. I just hope they have a chance to work through some of these issues before they tie the knot."

"Yes, me, too."

Mrs. Shaw lovingly placed her hand on Brian's shoulder and gave him a gentle squeeze. "I know you do. You and Kimberly have been close for so long, you're almost like brother and sister."

He forced a smile. "That's right. Like brother and sister." *Not so much anymore.*

The time seemed to drag for Brian. He thought the party would never end. Finally all of his guests had thanked him, welcomed David back, and left him alone with what appeared to be a slightly unhappy couple.

"I don't know how to thank you, man," David said as he half-hugged Brian and shook his hand. "It was a bigger success than I ever dreamed."

"Yeah," Brian grunted and cut a glance toward Kim. She cast her eyes downward.

"So is everyone meeting at church tomorrow?" David looked back and forth between Brian and Kim. "I thought we could make plans then."

"Sure, that's fine," Brian said when he realized Kim wasn't helping out.

When she looked at him, he glared at her. She rolled her eyes and smirked.

David reached for Kim's hand. "C'mon, Kimberly, let me walk you to your car." On their way to the door, he looked over his shoulder. "Thanks again, buddy. I owe you big-time."

"No problem."

Brian stood on the porch and waited until they took the last step off his porch before he went inside and closed the door. He left the light on for a few more minutes until he heard Kim's car back out of the driveway. David had parked his car around the corner in the opposite direction from where Kimberly had come.

As he picked up the last of the plates and cups, he felt like kicking himself for contributing to Kim's misery. He didn't know what he'd been thinking when he agreed to spring this surprise on her. Kim hated surprises. Even back in high school when one of her best friends had arranged for a bunch of people to suddenly appear at a little birthday dinner, she'd gotten mad.

❧

So it was all a setup. Kim lifted her new dress over her head then carefully hung it on the padded hanger. No wonder everyone had been acting so strange lately. They all knew David was coming home. Jazzy, people from church, David's mom, and even her parents had been there. And to think Brian had been the ringleader. She'd have to let him know what she really thought—but not in front of David. She had a special message for him.

Too bad she wasn't sure what it was yet.

❧

Kimberly awoke Sunday morning to the sound of rain pelting her bedroom window. She got up and pulled back the curtain to see how bad the storm was. A bolt of lightning flickered across the sky, followed a few seconds later by a boom of thunder.

Ugh. The weather matched her mood.

After seeing David, there was no doubt she couldn't marry him. The romantic, forever-and-ever kind of love just wasn't there. And what was up with Brian? He should have known better. He'd been with her once before when she was the surprise guest of honor, and she let him know how much she hated it. Maybe he assumed that since David was officially the focus of the get-together, she'd be okay with it.

Kim was sick of thinking about everything. She went about her morning routine of coffee, toast, and a shower. Now, what to wear?

She didn't want to ruin a good pair of shoes in the sloppy mess of the church parking lot, which ruled out half her wardrobe. Finally after staring at the lineup of clothes, she settled on a gray skirt, a burgundy blouse, and a black sweater. That way she could wear her boots and have a somewhat pulled-together look.

David arrived at her door at precisely the time they'd agreed upon. He held the umbrella as he walked her to the car, held the door, and made sure she was safely inside. He was doing all the right things, but she was still irked.

"You look very pretty this morning," David said. "I thought maybe we could go out after church—just the two of us—and grab a bite to eat."

Of course he never consulted her. She stared straight ahead without a comment.

After a few moments of silence, David touched her arm. "You okay, sweetie?"

She edged away from his touch. "I'm fine."

He blew out an exasperated sigh. "All right, what gives? Why are you acting so testy?"

Kim really didn't want to discuss it now—not before church. But he'd cornered her, and she didn't see that she had a choice. "Why do you always act like I should be happy with all of your decisions?"

"What?" His perplexed expression made her cringe, but she needed to be honest.

"You thought we could go out for a bite to eat after church, but you never asked me what I wanted."

"Well?" he said slowly as he drew his eyebrows together. "Do you want to go out for lunch after church?"

Her shoulders sagged. "Maybe. . .I guess so."

"Something else is going on, I can tell."

Kim squeezed her eyes shut and asked God for help. When she looked at David, she saw his clenched jaw and pulsing temples. He was annoyed, which bothered her even more.

"I'm not happy about the fact that everyone kept your homecoming a secret," she blurted.

"But that was supposed to be a nice surprise."

"A bouquet of flowers is a nice surprise. The musical trio you had at dinner the night we got engaged was a nice surprise. But something as significant as you coming back after not seeing you so long. . ." Her voice trailed off as she tried to think of how to word her thoughts. "It made me feel off-kilter."

He laughed. "Your expression was pretty funny."

Kim shot him a scowl. "It wasn't funny to me. It was humiliating."

David lifted a hand and let it slap back down on the steering wheel. "Okay, I won't do that again. No more surprises—at least not any that will make you feel so—what did you call it? Off-kilter?"

She nodded. Kim knew she should be satisfied, but she still wasn't. And she wouldn't be until she had *that talk* with David. She had to be kind and sensitive, and the timing had to be just right.

They arrived at church a few minutes early, so they were able to get a good seat near their friends. The first thing Kim did was look for Brian. Once she spotted him, she relaxed. Even if she couldn't have him, she liked knowing he was in sight.

David slipped his arm over Kim's shoulder as the pastor began his sermon. And there it stayed until time to sing the next praise song. Kim felt like she was going through the motions of worship, and that made her feel even worse.

After church was over, they went down the hall to the multipurpose room, where David chatted with a few old friends who hadn't been able to make it to his homecoming party. Kim smiled and nodded as everyone told her how happy she must be.

Brian occasionally glanced in her direction and offered a reassuring smile. She felt like he was the only person in the room who really knew her. And after last night, she wasn't even sure about that.

"Would you like something to drink?" David asked. "Coffee?"

Kim started to say, "no thank you," but when she saw that Brian had gone over to the beverage table, she nodded. "Let me get it, okay? Why don't you stay here and talk to everyone? What would you like?"

David tilted his head and narrowed his eyes. "Are you sure? I don't mind going with you."

"No, I'll do it."

As soon as David told her what he wanted, she took off toward the drinks, leaving him in the midst of a small group. Brian turned as she approached him.

"Feeling better?" he asked before taking a sip of his drink.

"I guess." Kim busied herself pouring coffee and dumping in the right amount of cream and sugar before turning to face Brian. "Why did you do it?"

Brian cast an apologetic glance her way and shook his head. "I'm really sorry. I should have known better."

"Yes, you should have."

"Forgive me, okay?"

"Fine." She held Brian's gaze for several seconds.

"You better give David the coffee you just fixed, or it'll get cold."

Without another word, Kim picked up the Styrofoam cups and carried them over to where David now stood talking to one man. When she got close enough to listen, she heard him talking about the military.

"Thanks, hon," he said as he gave her a quick glance and took his coffee. Then he turned to the man Kim had only seen once but couldn't remember his name. "I promised my lady some lunch, so we'd better go."

"Great talking to you, David. See you next week?"

"I'll be here," David replied.

As they got to the door closest to the parking lot, Kim saw that the rain had let up, but the pavement was covered with puddles.

"Want me to go get the car and pick you up?" he asked.

"No, that's okay," she replied. "I don't mind walking."

Brian joined them, and they walked out together. Just as she stepped off the sidewalk onto the road, her foot found a slick spot and she started to fall.

Chapter 13

Suddenly she felt David's hand beneath her elbow and Brian's arm around her waist. David quickly moved his hand and pulled her to his side, giving Brian a playful glare.

"I'm back now, buddy. I can take care of my own girl."

Brian's arm lingered at Kim's waist for a couple of seconds before he pulled back. His expression suddenly turned hard.

David hugged Kim to his side. "You okay, hon?"

"Yeah," she said as she continued watching Brian with interest. "I'm fine."

Brian's stern scowl remained as he lifted a hand in a wave. "Gotta run. Glad you're home, David. See you around."

"Let's get you off this slippery parking lot and into the car." David kept his arm around Kim all the way to the car, making it difficult to stay steady without leaning into him.

As soon as Kim was settled in the passenger seat, she lowered her head and silently prayed. *Lord, please be with me and help me handle David's feelings with care.* She kept her eyes closed for a few seconds to reflect on what she needed to do.

"Hey, I thought you were okay. You're not hurting anywhere, are you?" David asked as he clicked his seat belt. Funny, she hadn't heard him get into the car. Her thoughts were still on Brian.

"No, I told you I'm fine. That step down was slick."

"Someone needs to do something about this parking lot. It's treacherous."

And so was the emotional slope she was on, Kim thought.

"What are you in the mood for?" David grinned at her as though they didn't have a care in the world.

She shrugged. "Anything's fine."

"As I recall, you like Chinese food." He turned the key in the ignition. "I'm in the mood for some moo goo gai pan."

Kim really wasn't in the mood for Chinese food, but if he wanted it, she wasn't about to deny him. "That would be fine." Brian would have known she'd rather have something more traditional after church.

No matter what David talked about, Brian was in the back of Kim's mind. She wondered where he'd run off to or if he was as mad as he looked. Did he have plans for lunch?

"Hey, hon, did you hear what I just said?"

"Uh. . .you want moo goo gai pan?"

David chuckled. "That was at least five minutes ago. I've talked about several things since then."

She turned to him with a sheepish look. "Sorry."

"You're still overwhelmed by the surprise, aren't you, hon?"

"Yes, I must be." All she really wanted now was to go home and think.

"I'm sure a good meal will fix you right up. I was hoping to go for a walk in the park later, but there's no telling what the weather will do."

Kim looked at him, gave him a closed-mouth smile, and nodded. "Nothing much has changed around here."

After they were seated at the restaurant, David leaned toward her, elbows on the table, his gaze fixed on her. "You've always intrigued me, Kimberly."

"Intrigued you?" She lifted an eyebrow.

"Sometimes when I look at you, I can't help but wonder what you're thinking. It's like you have some deep, dark secrets." He paused and reached for her hands across the table. "And I have to admit, that's part of the attraction."

"It is?"

"I like the mystery of the relationship," he admitted. "With some women, I always know what they're thinking. But with you, I'm never sure."

"So you like it when I don't tell you what's on my mind?"

He twisted his mouth and frowned. "That doesn't sound right, does it?"

Kim laughed, in spite of her inner turmoil. "No, it really doesn't."

"Mind if I start over?"

"Go right ahead." She made a sweeping gesture with one hand and tried to pull back the other hand, but he held tight.

He traced the backs of her fingers while she waited to hear what he meant. Finally he looked into her eyes. "To be honest, I'm not sure what I mean, except you're different from most women."

"Are you trying to tell me something, David?"

After a brief hesitation, he covered her hand with both of his. "Yes, I am. Kimberly Shaw, I'm the most fortunate man alive to have you here waiting for me."

"Thank you." Her stomach ached. This was going to be much more difficult than anything she'd ever done.

"As soon as we're able to, we'll have the biggest and most elaborate wedding of the century."

The very thought of an elaborate wedding made her stomach hurt. In fact, she couldn't even get through the bridal magazine Jazzy had given her. "David, I—"

He lifted one hand and gestured. "I'll hire a skywriter to announce to the world that you and I are finally husband and wife. When we come out of the church, I'll have someone release dozens of birds."

She frowned and shook her head. "I don't think so, David."

"You don't want birds? How about butterflies? I went to a wedding a few

216

years ago, back before I met you, where each of the guests had little cardboard boxes of butterflies. I'll call my buddy and ask him where they found them. We'll release hundreds of butterflies to announce our love for each other."

"David!" She caught herself as the sharpness of her own voice came through.

He tilted his head and looked at her with a pained expression. "You like butterflies, don't you?"

"Yes, of course I do. But that's not what I want."

"Then what do you want, Kimberly?"

"I..." Now that she'd been cornered, Kim didn't know what to say or do. She and David had so much to talk about, she didn't know where to begin. And this wasn't the place to do it.

"Would you like something more traditional? Or more of a no-frills wedding?"

She shrugged. "You caught me off guard with this, David. We need to discuss it, but not right now."

He let go of her hands and leaned back in his chair. "You're right. We don't need to be discussing the nitty-gritty details of the wedding until we know when it's gonna be."

Kim's thoughts collided with her emotions. One thing was for certain though. She couldn't marry David.

"What are you thinking, hon?"

She shook her head. "Not much of anything at the moment."

"Still dumbstruck, huh?"

With a nod, she replied, "Yes, I guess you can say that."

David dug into his moo goo gai pan, while she picked at her chicken fried rice and egg roll. Not only was she not in the mood for Chinese food, but she'd lost her appetite, period.

After David cleaned his plate, he started to stand but hesitated. "Ready?"

She nodded and stood, and he led the way to the exit. He paid at the register on the way out, so Kim stood by the door and waited. The one time she'd tried to treat David, his ego had been bruised, so she didn't even bother anymore.

After they got in the car and started toward her house, Kim cleared her throat. "David, you and I really need to talk."

"I know, hon. It's been way too long."

She didn't expect this to be easy, but it appeared to be even more difficult than she thought. "I have to do a few things around the house this afternoon, but can you come back later?"

He glanced at his watch. "I promised Mom I'd help her with some things, but I don't think it'll take all day."

"Call me when you're done, okay?"

He pulled up in front of her house. She opened the car door before he had a chance to get out. "Kim—"

"I'm perfectly capable of walking to my front door." She gave him a look that she hoped would keep him right where he was. It worked.

Shortly after Kim got home, Brian called. "Will you be home for a while?"

"Yes, but I have to do some laundry."

"Put a load in your washing machine, and I'll be there in fifteen minutes."

Kim started to tell him to wait, but then she remembered that David would probably be over later. "Okay, but I really don't have long."

"I don't need much time," he replied.

Brian arrived five minutes early. Kim had known him long enough to know he'd be early, especially when she heard the sound of urgency in his voice.

"What's so important that can't wait, Brian?" She gestured toward the sofa. "Have a seat?"

"Yeah, but not in there. Let's sit at the table."

Kim shrugged. "Suit yourself." She led the way to the kitchen, where they took seats adjacent to each other. "So what's on your mind, Brian?"

He closed his eyes, lowered his head, and folded his hands in front of him. When he glanced up at Kim, she saw the pain in his eyes. "I can't deal with this whole charade anymore, Kim. I care about you, and I don't like seeing you hurting."

Kim gulped. As much as she wanted to tell Brian everything she'd been thinking, she didn't want to do that until she talked to David. "I care about you, too, Brian, but we've been like brother and sister for so long, I'm not sure you can see things clearly."

"It's different for me," he admitted. "Sure, I used to tease you and treat you like you were a sister. But my feelings—well, I don't know. I'm not sure about them anymore. . . ." His voice trailed off as he looked at her.

"You're not sure?" she whispered.

He blinked and nodded. "I'm not sure when it happened, but I care about you more than—well, more than I should."

"Oh, Brian." Kim's heart fluttered with his words. She shook her head. "I don't know what to say." She wanted to throw her arms around him and profess her undying love.

He leaned forward and narrowed his eyes. "Look me in the eye and tell me how you feel about David."

She blinked. Could it get any harder? "I–I'm engaged to him."

"Do you love him enough to want to spend the rest of your life as his wife?"

Kim lowered her gaze to keep from stumbling. Now that he'd cornered her, she had no choice because she couldn't lie. "No."

Brian flopped back in the chair. "That's what I thought. You don't know how to tell him, do you?"

She gathered her thoughts for a few seconds before looking him in the eye again. "Brian, this is so difficult. How does a person tell someone she can't marry him?"

"So you'd rather follow through with this marriage than do what you feel is right in your heart?"

"No," Kim replied. "But I need to be very careful how I handle things."

Brian's jaw tightened. Kim could see his frustration, and she felt it, too.

"Kimberly," Brian whispered. "I—I really care about you."

"I care about you, too."

"Did you hear me?" he asked.

"Yes, of course I did."

"I don't want to lose you, Kim."

Kim let out a nervous laugh. "You never lost me, Brian. We've always been friends, and that'll never change." Her urge to pull him close nearly won out, so she pushed her chair back to put a few more inches between them.

"You know what I mean." He slowly stood up beside his chair. "I understand what you're going through. Just remember that until the wedding vows are said, it's not too late to change your mind. I like David. He's a good man. Just not the right man for you."

"That's not what you said before," she reminded him.

"I didn't realize it then." Brian shook his head.

"This whole thing feels so—I don't know—strange."

"Look what he's done to you, Kim. He always makes decisions without consulting you. Is that what you want for the rest of your life?"

"No." She held his gaze as they fell silent for a moment.

"Kim." He tilted his head forward and gave her one of his serious looks. "People don't change just because they're married. If anything, it'll get worse."

"Brian. . ." Kim buried her face in her hands. She heard his footsteps as he walked to the door.

"I'll see you around, Kimberly Shaw. You're a wonderful woman. I'm just not sure you trust yourself to go with what you know is right."

Neither of them said good-bye before he walked out the door. Kim didn't even try to stand up right away after he'd gone.

The sound of the washing machine cycle ending prompted Kim to get up. As she moved the clothes to the dryer and refilled the washing machine, Brian's words reverberated through her mind. *Until the wedding vows are said, it's not too late to change your mind.*

She'd already made her decision. But now that she was aware of the spark between her and Brian, she felt like a traitor.

All afternoon as she did laundry and tidied up her house, she thought about David, Brian, and her feelings for both of them. She deeply cared for both men but in different ways. David was strong, smart, and very much a gentleman. Brian was goofy, fun, and someone she could always be herself around—at least until recently. She couldn't think of anything really bad about either guy. In fact they were both as close to perfect as a human could get, even though they were different.

She'd never forget when Brian first brought David around. He'd prepared her by saying how courageous and patriotic David was. That he was a Christian made him seem even better. He'd come to Christ later in life, but the fact remained that his faith was as strong as anyone's.

She allowed her memories of Brian to take over her conscious thoughts. Over the years, Kim had felt little crushes on Brian. Once when they were in high school, jealous pangs shot through her heart as she listened to him go on and on about how cute one of Kim's friends was. Brian dated the girl a couple of times, and when he quit seeing her, Kim was secretly happy. She told Brian he could do better, so he went in search of someone else. Brian was so charming, he never had to wait long for another girl to latch on to him.

Kim was different. She had dates and even crushes every now and then, but she was never all that enamored of the guys. David was the first man she ever told she loved in a romantic way. She always saw herself only falling for the one man she'd spend the rest of her life with. Brian was the fickle one. For as long as they'd been friends, Brian had fallen in and out of love more times than Kim could count. She knew he'd had romantic thoughts of her at times, but only when she was involved with someone else.

The more she thought about Brian, the more convinced Kim was that he wanted her when she was off-limits in the romance department. But even so, she couldn't marry someone she wasn't sure about.

She made a mental list of things to discuss with David. After she finished all her housework and laundry, he still hadn't called. Finally she picked up the phone and punched in his cell phone number.

"Hey, hon, I was about to call you. I'm just finishing up something for Mom. I'll be right over."

"Okay, good." She let out a nervous breath. "About how much longer do you think you'll be?"

"Half an hour here, and then I thought I'd stop off for a pizza on my way over. Do you have soft drinks?"

She started to say she wasn't in the mood for pizza, but she paused and decided to let it go. "I have tea, lemonade, and a couple cans of soft drinks."

"Okay, good. Any of those will be fine. See you soon, hon."

After she hung up, she went to her room to change into something a little nicer. If it had been Brian, she would have stayed as is.

Stop comparing them! Kim was frustrated with herself for continuing to do that. David and Brian were both wonderful men who loved the Lord.

She settled on a soft, flowing, purple floral skirt, a fitted T-shirt that matched some of the flowers, and some ballet flats. David always liked seeing her in a skirt.

An hour passed, and he still hadn't arrived. Kim went to the kitchen and poured herself some lemonade, which she carried out to the living room. She was about to sit down and do a little channel surfing when the doorbell finally rang.

As soon as Kim opened the door, she noticed his wide grin. "I just heard from my commanding officer," he said.

David had arrived empty-handed. "Did you get pizza?" she asked.

He slapped his forehead. "Sorry, I forgot. I was about to call and place my order when I got the call. We can just have one delivered."

After he ordered the pizza, David turned to Kim. "Looks like I might have an opportunity to head back for the next portion of our mission."

"But I thought—"

Chapter 14

Kim stopped herself before she began an argument. No matter what she did, David was going to continue making decisions without consulting her first. It was clear that he still didn't see her as an equal partner in their relationship, and she felt more justified than ever in her decision.

David reached out and stroked her cheek. "You were saying?"

She reached up and removed his hand. "David, that's what I wanted to talk to you about. I don't think this whole engagement thing is working out."

A flash of pain shot across his face. "What are you talking about, Kimberly? I love you." He folded his arms. "Do you not still love me?"

"I don't know, David. I thought I did." She backed away. "I don't understand why you volunteered to leave again without discussing it with me first. The whole time you were gone, I struggled on so many levels. Doesn't it matter to you what I think—and how I feel?"

"Why didn't you say something before?"

Kim shook her head. "I wanted to." She closed her eyes to gather her thoughts before looking him in the eye.

He narrowed his gaze. "And why didn't you?"

"I felt—I don't know—unpatriotic?"

"Unpatriotic?"

"Yeah. You were doing your duty to protect our country, and I was frustrated because you didn't discuss it with me first. I'm not sure you would have even listened to me anyway."

"C'mon, Kim, you know I can't talk about my mission. It's top secret."

"We're obviously on two different wavelengths. It's not your mission I wanted to discuss. I wanted you to talk about the *decision* with me and at least listen to how I feel about it."

David snorted. "How you feel?"

"Yes."

"Okay, tell me now. How do you feel?"

Now he was starting to irritate her. "That's not the point, David."

"Oh?" He lifted an eyebrow as he regarded her. "So what *is* the point?"

She raised her hands at her sides then let them drop. "The point is I don't feel that I have any say in anything regarding us. You are deciding to volunteer for these missions without talking to me. You choose where we eat when we go out. You even decided you wanted pizza tonight, and without even asking what I thought, you told me you were bringing it." She gulped back the urge to cry. "And then you forgot. But that's not really the point."

"Why do you get so upset over all this insignificant stuff?" His voice had reached a higher pitch, which made Kim feel even worse.

"It's not insignificant to me."

"I didn't realize that. So tell me what else is bothering you."

"I don't know, David, but that's not all that's important right now. I thought that once a couple was engaged, they got together and discussed kids and houses and furniture and china patterns." She paused for a couple of seconds before adding, "And jobs."

"Oh Kim, honey," he said as he reached for her and pulled her to his chest. "I never wanted to make you feel that I don't pay enough attention to you."

Don't cry, don't cry. She bit down on her lip to redirect the pain and keep a tear from falling.

David stroked her back a few times then held her at arm's length. "What if I promise to be more attentive? Would that make you happy?"

"It would have before." Kim hung her head then slowly raised it and looked him in the eye. "David, I don't think we should stay engaged."

"Shh." He reached over and gently touched her lips. "I know I've hurt you. I love you. I'll try to do better."

"But—" Kim's chest ached. "It's not that—"

"Being a fiancé doesn't come naturally to me," he admitted. "Someone should teach a class on how an engaged man should act." He grinned and tweaked her chin. "Why don't we talk about everything tonight and get it all out? That's the best way we can settle any problems before they get out of hand."

She opened her mouth, but nothing came out. Breaking her engagement with an insensitive man would have been much easier. This surprise show of tenderness had caught her off guard.

The pizza arrived a few minutes later. David paid for it while Kim went to the kitchen to get their drinks. They sat down at the kitchen table.

David took her hand closest to him. "I'll say the blessing—unless you'd rather do it."

She shook her head. "No, that's okay. You can do it."

As they ate, David explained as much as he was able to about his mission—when he'd leave again and when he expected to be back home. He asked if she wanted him to call his commanding officer to see if it was too late to back out. "I've told you already how much I love you, Kimberly. I don't want to risk losing the best thing that's ever happened to me."

Her heart felt like it would pound right out of her chest. "You don't need to do that. There's a much bigger world out there besides what's going on with me."

David leaned forward on his elbow. "I just want to make sure you know how important you are to me. I want you to be happy. I'll do anything to please you, Kimberly, because I love you so much."

His willingness to do whatever it took to make her happy stunned her. She should have been over-the-moon thrilled. How could she break the engagement after what he'd just said?

After he left, Kim twirled the engagement ring on her finger, something she found herself doing when she was deep in thought about anything related to David. It still bothered her that she had to tell him things any intelligent man should have known.

🌿

When Brian's cell phone rang, he jumped. He glanced down and saw David's number, so he flipped it open and answered.

"Hey, Brian. Man, I had a close call tonight."

"Oh yeah? What happened?" Brian put down his book and repositioned himself in the chair.

"Kim let me have it."

"What did she let you have?"

"You know," David said, chuckling. "She read me the riot act about what a lousy fiancé I've been."

"Why don't you start from the beginning and explain?"

David cleared his throat before giving Brian a play-by-play account of his conversation with Kim. "Who knew she was so sensitive? I never saw that in her before."

"She's not any more sensitive than anyone else would be in her situation." Brian had to work hard not to blast David for his lack of understanding.

"I don't know, man. She obviously doesn't get how the military works."

Brian bristled. "Have you thought about explaining it to her?" Anger bubbled in Brian's chest, but he used every ounce of self-restraint to tamp it down. He needed to keep his head straight for Kim.

"Yeah, maybe I should."

"I think so." Brian dug deep to find the right words to say—for Kimberly. "I know you're the one putting your life on the line for our country, but you need to remember that it's not easy on Kim not knowing where you are or when you're coming home."

"Point taken."

Finally he couldn't take it anymore. He had to know. "Did the two of you work things out?"

David chuckled. "Yes, of course we did. You don't think I'm a fool, do you?"

"No, I never thought that."

"The last thing I need to do is have Kim mad at me when I take off again," David continued. "I love her, and I want to marry her as soon as I return."

Whoa. "Back up, David. You're leaving again?"

"Yes, that's the next thing I wanted to tell you. I'm being deployed in two weeks. You did such a nice job of looking after Kimberly, I wanted to thank you and ask you to do it again. Maybe you can remind her how much I love her when she's unhappy."

"I don't need someone to tell me to look after Kim. First of all, she's perfectly capable of taking care of herself. And second—"

"Okay, okay, I hear ya. I just don't want some other guy coming in and sweeping her off her feet."

"Kim is trustworthy." Even if he couldn't have her, he'd defend her honor to the end.

"I know she is, Brian." David let a couple of seconds pass before he continued. "In the meantime, I think we all need to get together as much as possible before I leave. It'll give me some memories to reflect on when I'm in the trenches."

"Just say when," Brian said as he continued to hold back his temper. "I'll be there." *For Kim.*

Brian couldn't help the fact that he resented David more as each day passed.

Kim got to work five minutes early the next morning, but Jasmine had already arrived. The shop was open and ready for customers.

"Enjoying having David home?" Jasmine asked.

Kimberly nodded and looked away. "Of course."

Jasmine regarded Kim with suspicion. "Really, Kimberly?"

"Yes." Kim heard the frustration in her own voice.

"Oh sweetie, what's wrong?"

This was one time Kim wished she'd waited a few minutes and come in late. Oh well. She figured she might as well fess up or she'd have to pretend all day.

"David told me he's going back on another mission."

"You're kidding." Jasmine shook her head and made a hen-like clucking sound. "What is that boy thinking?"

"He's a dutiful military man."

Jasmine cast a you've-got-to-be-kidding look her way. "There's dutiful, and there's obsessed. I'd say he's about to cross that line if he hasn't already. Did he discuss it with you first?"

"Well, sort of."

"Sort of?" Jasmine asked.

"Not exactly. He was asked if he wanted to put in for the assignment, and he accepted. But when I told him how I felt—"

"You told him?"

Kim nodded. "Yes, and he was surprised by my reaction."

"Good for you, Kimberly! I'm proud of you." Jasmine beamed. "So what did he say when you told him your feelings?"

"He said it probably wasn't too late to talk to his commanding officer. But I could tell he really wanted to go."

"Don't tell me you said it was okay."

Kim's shoulders sagged. "Jazzy, what could I do when he reminded me that he's in the military to protect our country? It makes me feel like such a slacker for whining about my feelings."

"No, you are not a slacker, Kimberly Shaw. You're just a woman who wants her man around so you can get on with your life."

"But he has this really important job, and I knew how much his military career meant to him when I first agreed to be his wife."

"That doesn't mean you have to let this continue." Jasmine widened her stance and planted her hands on her hips. "Have you discussed this with Brian?"

Kim shuddered as she remembered her conversation with Brian and the unspoken words that still lingered in her thoughts. "No, but I'm sure he probably already knows."

"Don't make a mistake with your life just because you thought you knew what you wanted before you had all the facts."

"I'll try not to," Kim said, just to end the conversation. She had to change the subject. "Have you seen the latest flatiron? That thing's amazing. It can straighten a whole head of ringlets in minutes."

Jasmine offered an understanding smile. "There are a lot of things we need to straighten out, Kimberly. Too bad the latest and greatest flatiron can't fix everything."

Kim laughed. "You got that right."

"Oh, your first appointment canceled. There was a message on voice mail when I got in."

Relieved, Kim went to the storage room and pulled out what she needed for her next appointment. After she got everything organized at her station, she went to the break room with her cell phone and called Brian.

"You're not gonna believe what happened," she said as soon as he answered his phone.

"David called me." Brian sounded angry. "He said you weren't happy about it."

"That's putting it mildly. But we talked it out, and I think he understands how I feel now."

"But it doesn't change anything, does it, Kim?"

She thought for a moment before replying, "No, I guess it doesn't. He's still going, but I told him I was okay with it."

"Are you, Kim?" Brian asked with a sarcastic tone. "Do you know what you want?"

"I have no idea how to answer that. Please don't make this harder than it already is."

He audibly exhaled. "So why did you call me?"

"I just wanted to make sure you knew he was leaving again."

"Does this mean I have to have another party when he comes back?" Sarcasm was evident in his voice.

"Only if you tell me first."

"Trust me, I will," he said. "I learned my lesson."

"David mentioned something about everyone getting together before he leaves. Got any ideas?"

"Why should I have ideas for David? If he wants to get together, he can organize it himself."

"I'm sorry, Brian. It's just that—"

"Don't worry about it," he said, interrupting her. "What do you think about bowling and pizza one night?" His monotone let her know he'd put his emotions on the back burner for her. Again.

The line grew silent for a second. "Brian?"

"Yes, Kim?"

"Thank you."

He laughed. "Why are you thanking me?"

"For being there," she said softly. "For being my friend."

❧

After they hung up, Brian stared at the phone. Even though he felt a kick in the gut every time he saw her with David, she'd always brought light into his life by being there when he really needed her, even when he didn't deserve it. He couldn't let her down, no matter how he felt about her.

In the afternoon meeting, Jack gave him a thumbs-up for his presentation. At least something was going his way.

That night David called. Brian told him the same thing he'd said to Kim about things the group would enjoy.

"Sounds good," David agreed. "How about bowling this Friday night?"

"Fine. I'll e-mail everyone."

"Thanks, buddy. See you then."

After he got off the phone, Brian sat back and thought about hanging out with Kim and David. He knew it wouldn't be easy, but he wasn't about to disappoint Kim.

She called him on Tuesday just to chat. When he said he was too busy to talk and cut their conversation short, she sounded hurt but said she understood.

On Wednesday Brian felt bad, so he called her and asked if she was okay.

She was slow to respond, but after he prodded her with a couple of teasing comments, she chuckled. The sound of her laughter warmed him from the inside out. He'd settle for any kind of relationship he could have with Kim—just to be in her life.

"I've contacted everyone about getting together Friday night," he said. "Too bad about the circumstances though."

After they got off the phone, Brian prayed. *Lord, give me the strength to handle the inevitable with Kimberly. You know what is right for both of us, so if I can't be the love of her life, help me to be a better friend.* He opened his eyes for a few seconds before shutting them again. *And I pray that these romantic feelings I have for her will subside.*

Thursday and Friday seemed to crawl by, but finally Friday night arrived. After work he went home and changed into some bowling clothes. Everyone was supposed to meet at Graziano's for pizza then head over to the bowling alley.

Brian was the first to arrive, so he secured a couple of tables next to each other. People from their singles group trickled in—some in pairs and others alone. The last to arrive were David and Kimberly. All heads turned when they entered.

As people tossed jokes and comments about David taking off again, Brian sat and tried hard not to stare at Kim. However, he did allow himself a glance every now and then, and he could tell she wasn't happy—even behind that plastic smile frozen on her face.

When the pizzas arrived, Brian forced himself to eat. But when he looked in Kim's direction again, he saw that she'd barely nibbled the one piece on her plate. David, on the other hand, was reaching for his third slice, talking with Jonathan on the other side of him and acting as if he didn't have a care in the world.

Brian was about to speak to Kim, but David leaned over in her direction and pointed to something behind Brian. *Must be nice to have someone to whisper to—especially if that person was Kim.* He worked at averting his gaze, but David stood up and tapped his fork on the side of his glass.

David lifted his hand, cleared his throat, and looked directly at Brian. "Now that everyone's here, we can finish dinner and head on over to the bowling alley."

Brian glanced over his shoulder and saw a very tall, very blond, very made-up woman smiling back at David. He'd never seen her before in his life.

Chapter 15

Kim glanced up to see what David was gesturing toward. An unfamiliar woman stood at the door, looking dazed, but when she noticed David, she smiled and took a step toward their group.

"Do you know her?" she whispered to David.

"Yes, this is Mercedes, my commanding officer's niece. I figured that since she was visiting and didn't have anything to do, she might want to join us." He patted the chair next to him. "Have a seat, Mercedes."

As soon as Mercedes sat, the murmur of the group came to a grinding halt, and the silence grew very uncomfortable. Kim's next reaction was to look at Brian, who hung his head.

"Brian," David said loud enough for everyone at both tables to hear. "This is Mercedes." He turned to the woman. "Mercedes, this is the guy I told you about."

Kim was surprised that Mercedes' already-wide smile got even bigger as she stood, leaned across the table, and extended her hand. Brian stood and shook hands then waited for Mercedes to sit back down.

"Nice to meet you," he muttered through an awkward smile.

David leaned toward Kim and whispered, "I thought they might like each other. Looks like I was right."

Suddenly an odd sensation coursed through Kim. Although she knew David had invited a guest, she had no idea he wanted to fix Brian up. She wanted to shake David until his teeth fell out for making her look involved in his scheme. From the look on Brian's face, she knew he wasn't any happier about it than she was.

"Let's go, folks," David said as he stood. "I'm feeling a few strikes coming on."

As they left the restaurant, Kim fell back from the group, and Brian made his way to Kim's side. "Why didn't you warn me?" he asked without looking her in the eye.

"I had no idea. I'm really sorry, Brian."

"Yeah, I bet." His tone left no doubt that he didn't believe her. With all these people around, she couldn't grovel and beg for his forgiveness.

"Hey, hon!" David called out. "You coming?"

Kim gave Brian an apologetic look then ran to catch up with David. "I don't think this was such a good idea."

He gave her a what's-your-problem look. "They'll be fine after they get to know each other."

"Did you see his face?" Kim shook her head. "He's mad."

"Better mad than sad. I don't like my buddy being lonely. He needs a pretty girl to talk to." David put his arm around Kim and gave her a squeeze. "I think he might even be jealous that I have you."

Kim's breath caught in her chest. "I don't think he's jealous of you."

"Maybe not, but I still think it'll do him some good to get out and date a little."

Kim glanced over her shoulder in time to see Mercedes and Brian talking as they walked toward the row of cars at the edge of the parking lot. Brian looked up at her, so she snapped her attention back to David.

"See?" David said. "They're hitting it off just fine. Now we won't have to worry about him."

Kim thought for a moment. "I guess you're probably right." An overwhelming sadness filled her, but she tried not to let on. She knew Mercedes wasn't Brian's type, so she didn't feel jealous. It just bugged her that he was angry, thinking she knew about David's plan.

All the way to the bowling alley, David talked about how Mercedes and Brian would be a great match because she was so pretty and fun to be around. Kim half listened as she thought about all the reasons Brian and Mercedes *wouldn't* be a good match. Brian was an outdoorsy kind of guy, and she looked like a high-maintenance girl. Brian had moods, but all this girl did was smile. Brian liked—

The sudden realization smacked Kim so hard, she nearly fell over. Kim now had no doubt that she couldn't marry David. She couldn't discuss it now, but she wouldn't wait much longer.

"What's wrong, hon?" He gently jostled her.

Kim had to come up with something quickly. "Do you know where she is spiritually?" she asked David. "Is she a Christian?"

David shrugged. "I would assume so. Her uncle and parents go to church."

"That doesn't make her a Christian." She thought for a moment as she realized what he'd just said. "You know her parents?"

He nodded. "Her dad retired shortly after I met her uncle. I went to his retirement party."

Kim sat back and pondered her next question before asking. "Does she like sports?"

"Why are you asking me? We'll be at the bowling alley soon, and you can talk to her. I think it would be nice for you to get to know each other—especially since she and Brian seem to be hitting it off."

Once they got inside the bowling alley and she took one good look at Brian's face, she wanted to talk to him. He looked absolutely miserable, while Mercedes stood there jabbering away.

David arranged for the four of them—Brian, Mercedes, Kim, and himself—to be on a lane together. He nudged Kim and whispered, "That way we can keep an eye on them and make sure everything goes well."

"We can't force them," Kim argued.

"No, but we can toss out some conversation starters."

Throughout the first game, Kim watched David try his hardest to engage Brian, but all he got was a sulky demeanor and a few grunts every now and then.

Most of the group agreed that they were having too much fun to stop after the first game, so they decided to bowl another one. Brian didn't say anything, but he didn't leave.

"I need a little break," David said as he motioned for Kim to follow him. "We'll be right back, folks," he told the others. "I need to talk with my fiancée for a minute."

"I don't get it," David said as soon as they were out of hearing distance. "He's not even trying. That's not like Brian."

It was very much like Brian. Over the years that Kim had known him, she'd learned to sense when to back off, and that time had come more than an hour ago.

"Let's just back off for now, okay?" she asked. "Don't try so hard. Brian has a mind of his own."

David lifted his eyebrows and shook his head. "I give up. I can't make Brian happy."

"No, you really can't," Kim agreed. She leaned over and nodded her head toward the lanes. "Let's go back with the others."

After David quit trying so hard with Brian and Mercedes, Kim felt a sense of relief. Brian relaxed a little, too.

Mercedes wasn't as interested in bowling as she was in David's stories about military life. "I've always enjoyed listening to my uncle and dad talk about the military." She tilted her head and grinned at David. "Did you always know you wanted to be in the National Guard?"

"No," he replied. "When I was younger, I thought I'd go into the army, but when I met Colonel Anderson, my thinking went in a whole new direction." He snickered. "Then there was my dad urging me to follow him into his law practice."

"Are you talking about Colonel Harley Anderson?"

"That's the man," David said with a grin and a quick nod. "How did you know?"

Her eyes lit up. "He and my dad used to play golf together."

"Oh yeah," David said with a chuckle, "I heard about that. Your dad was a decent golfer back in his day—at least according to your uncle."

Mercedes tossed her blond hair over her shoulder and laughed. "Better not tell him that. He thinks he's still all that on the golf course."

"Maybe I should challenge him to a game one of these days."

Kim sat back and watched as Mercedes continued giving all her attention to David. "That would be great. Ever since he retired, he's been moping around and acting like there's nothing left to live for—that is, except when he can find someone to play golf with."

"Everyone needs something to motivate them," Kim said.

David let his glance graze her before turning to face Mercedes again. "Kim's right. If golf is what gets your dad out of the house, I need to give him a call before I leave."

Kim cast a glance toward Brian, who gave her an odd look. Kim felt uneasy as she watched the chemistry between David and Mercedes.

Mercedes bounced around in her chair. "I can't wait to tell Dad about you."

Kim felt as though she and Brian were invisible. This whole outing had turned into a David and Mercedes event.

What made it so weird was that she really didn't even care about David turning his back on her to talk to Mercedes. What bothered her was how it made Brian feel. As the evening wore on, Brian got grouchier and more agitated.

Finally, after he bowled his last frame, Brian stood and faced David. "It's been fun, folks, but I need to run." He lifted his eyebrows as he turned toward Mercedes. "I'll take you back to your car now."

David snapped his fingers. "Oh, that's right. I forgot some of us carpooled over here. Too bad."

Brian stood nearby waiting. Kim felt an emotional tug, but she wasn't sure what to do.

"Would you like for us to take you to your car, Mercedes?" David asked.

"Oh," she said, "I wouldn't want to impose."

"We don't mind, do we, Kim?" David asked.

Before Kim had a chance to say a word, Brian stepped up. "I want to take her. The two of you need more time together, since you'll be going back to the Middle East soon." Brian glared at David, almost in a dare.

Kim held her breath as she realized that Brian was coming to her rescue. She felt pulled toward her childhood friend, but David reached for her hand and held it between his. "You're right, Brian. Besides, I think it would be great for you and Mercedes to spend a little more time together." He glanced at Kim and winked before looking back at Brian. "Get to know each other better."

Once they turned in their bowling shoes and everyone else was out of hearing distance, Kim touched David on the arm. "David, we need to talk. Now."

He stopped tying his shoes as he looked up at her. "Sure, hon. Wanna talk here or go somewhere quiet?"

"Somewhere quiet would be nice."

"I know just the place."

There he goes again, she thought. "Why don't we just go to my house?" she said.

"I was thinking—"

"We'll go to my house."

He lifted an eyebrow as he regarded her with interest. "Well, okay then. Your house it is."

As soon as they got to her place, David closed the door and stood facing her. "I assume you want to set the date."

"David, I—uh. . ."

"Hey, hon, I understand. I feel awful about keeping you on hold like I have. Would it help to get it all nailed down tonight?" He took a step toward her and started to put his arms around her.

"No," she said as she backed away. "That's not what I want."

He put his hands in his pockets. "You don't want me to hold you?"

"I don't want to set the date," she replied. "And I don't want to marry you."

Kim worked the ring off her finger and tried to hand it to David. He shook his head.

"I don't think you need to react so strongly," he said. "She was flirting with me, not the other way around."

"What are you talking about?"

"Mercedes." He rubbed the back of his neck and chuckled. "I had no idea you were jealous of Mercedes and me."

"I am not jealous of you and Mercedes!"

"Then what's your problem?" he asked, glancing down at the ring. "What's this all about?"

"I already told you. I don't want to marry you."

"But why? I thought you loved me."

"I did," she said then corrected herself. "At least I thought I did. But after you left, I had some time to myself to think about things—to think about us."

"Is there someone else in your life?"

Kim didn't want to let on how she felt about Brian. But she didn't see any way around it, since he'd find out soon anyway. Lies were never good.

"David, I feel really bad about this, but after you left, Brian did what you asked him to do and made sure I wasn't lonely."

"Did he introduce you to someone else?" David said.

"Why would he do that?"

With a shrug, David replied, "He's been your best friend for a long time, and he doesn't want you to be lonely. Don't think I haven't noticed the way he glares at me."

"No," Kim said slowly. "He didn't introduce me to someone else." She closed her eyes for a few seconds then looked directly at David. "This is hard for me to tell you, but I think it's only fair to be the one to say it. I'm in love with Brian."

David's eyes popped wide open in complete shock. "You're what?"

"I know. Brian and I have been such good friends for so long, it almost seemed wrong."

"So my best buddy has been making the moves on my girl when I turn my back. I never saw this one coming."

"No. That's not true. He never made any moves on me."

David's handsome face suddenly turned to a scowl. "You do realize that he's on the rebound after what Leila did. I can't believe you haven't figured that out."

She didn't feel like arguing about Brian's feelings or defending herself or Brian. Instead she went on the offense. "It doesn't matter. Even if Brian doesn't feel like I feel, I can't marry you."

"This is a huge mistake, Kimberly. You and I are great together."

"I don't think so. I would have become frustrated, and you would have eventually gotten bored with me."

"That never would have happened." He actually smiled for a split second. "I'm a good provider, and you're a sweet Christian woman who would make a wonderful wife."

"How do you know that's what I want?"

"I thought you did."

"I want more, David. I want to know that the man I'm married to considers me an equal partner in big decisions. I want to be consulted before my husband decides to volunteer for dangerous military assignments."

"You should have told me this before I left. Why didn't you say something?"

"I never had the opportunity."

David stared down at the floor as they grew silent. When he looked back into her eyes, she saw that he'd resigned himself to accepting her decision without further argument.

"Are you okay?" she asked.

"Yes, I'm fine. I just have a little self-examination to do."

"David, I think you're a great guy. I have no doubt you'll make some woman a wonderful husband. But not me."

"Okay. I guess I need to leave now."

She stood at the door and waited until he got in his car and drove away. Then she closed the door and leaned against it with her eyes closed.

Lord, I pray that Your will be done in David's and my lives.

"She what?" When Brian saw David's number on his caller ID the next day, he assumed it was to find out how things went with Mercedes, not this.

"You heard me, buddy," David said. "I just got the kiss-off because she's in love with you."

Chapter 16

Brian was so astounded he didn't know what to say. All he managed was a grunt.

"So what did you do when I was away, man? I asked you to watch after her, not betray me."

Suddenly fury rose inside Brian. "Trust me, David, I didn't betray you."

"Then what did you say to make her break off our engagement?"

"We don't need to discuss this over the phone. If you want to talk about it, let's do it face-to-face."

"Fine," David snapped. "Name the place and time, and I'll be there."

This suddenly felt like a duel. "How about the church after I get off work?"

David snickered. "So now you wanna hide behind your piety?"

Brian tamped back the anger that felt as though it might blow through the top of his head. "No, I just want to make sure we don't forget our faith." And it didn't hurt that the pastor would be nearby if they needed him.

"That's okay with me. It doesn't matter where we meet, because I know I've been faithful to the woman I love, even though my best buddy was working his way into her heart."

"We'll discuss that this afternoon," Brian said in the calmest voice he could manage.

After he hung up, Brian bowed his head and prayed for mercy for his anger, terrible thoughts about David, and asked for guidance in how to talk to him. This was by far one of the most difficult things he'd ever had to do.

Jack waved as he passed Brian's open door. He'd barely gotten a couple of steps away before he backed up.

"Whoa, why the wild look?"

Brian relaxed his face and rubbed his neck. "It's complicated."

"Wanna talk about it?"

Brian thought about it then shook his head. "I don't think so. I need to finish balancing this"—he held up a stack of pages—"and it looks like it might take me the rest of the day. I can't stay late tonight."

"Got a date?" Jack asked.

"Not exactly. We can talk some other time, okay?"

Jack held up both hands. "Fine, I can tell when I'm being dismissed. Just don't let whatever it is get to you so bad. They're not worth it."

"Who's not worth it?"

Jack smirked and shook his head. "C'mon, Brian. You know what I'm sayin'."

"Thanks for the advice," Brian said with a forced smile. "Would you mind closing the door on your way out?"

After he was alone, Brian called the pastor and asked if he could stick around a few minutes late. Then he managed to shut everything out while he finished his work. Kim called, but Brian told her he was too busy to talk.

She sounded hurt, but this was one day he couldn't stay even five minutes late, and he didn't need to talk to Kim just yet. Since David was the first to tell him about the breakup, he thought it would be best to hear his side first. Kim would understand later.

At five thirty Brian took off toward the parking lot, practically running so no one would stop him. He was relieved when he got to his car without so much as a good-bye from anyone.

All the way to the church, Brian prayed to keep his mind focused on the mission of working through things and clarifying his intentions. He didn't need to express everything he thought with David. Pastor Jeremy Rawlings motioned him into his office as he walked through the side door.

"What's going on?" Pastor Rawlings asked.

Brian gave him a quick rundown of the phone call. He tried to keep his tone neutral.

"You're not worried, are you?"

"Just a little—for Kimberly's sake, anyway."

Pastor Rawlings offered a sympathetic nod. "I can certainly understand why. I'll stick around until I hear from you."

"Thanks, Pastor."

The sound of a car pulling into the driveway caught their attention. "Why don't you go on into the adult Bible classroom, and I'll let him know where he can find you."

"Great idea," Brian said as he turned and headed off in the direction of the classroom wing.

Three minutes later, David's shadow darkened the doorway. "We have some serious issues to discuss, buddy."

"Come on in." Brian patted the table. "Why don't we sit across the table from each other so we can really talk?" He'd set up folding chairs and put a couple of Bibles on the table in case they needed them.

As soon as they were situated, Brian leaned back and looked David in the eye. "Why don't you start at the beginning and tell me what happened?"

David folded his arms and narrowed his eyes before shaking his head. "First, you tell me what's been going on between you and Kimberly."

"Nothing that hasn't been going on for the past fifteen years," Brian replied.

"Something had to happen for her to suddenly think she's in love with you."

Brian's mind spun with all sorts of possibilities, but he worked hard to maintain his composure. "Did she actually come right out and say that?"

"Yes."

That sure did complicate things. Brian wondered why Kimberly told David before cluing him in—that is, if she really did.

"And you don't think you assumed this, based on something else she said?"

"Look, buddy, I don't assume things. I know what I heard. She flat-out said, 'I'm in love with Brian.' "

If he'd heard this news at any other time from anyone else, Brian would have jumped out of the chair, kicked up his heels, and shouted his joy from the mountaintops. However, joy wasn't what he felt at the moment. He wanted to comfort his friend and at the same time process this new information. But he couldn't do either.

"Want me to talk to her?" Brian asked.

David let out a sinister snicker. "Yeah, so you can laugh at me behind my back? No thanks." He pounded the table hard enough to send an echo through the room. "I can't believe I've been such a big sucker, believing in my girl and my best friend. I trusted both of you."

Pastor Rawlings appeared at the door. "You two okay?"

Brian nodded. "We're fine."

David stood. "Looks like we're done here. I have nothing else to discuss."

"Would you like to give me a chance to tell you my side of this?" Brian asked.

"So you admit there is something going on?"

"No," Brian replied. "Don't put words in my mouth."

"Then tell me your side."

"Before you left, you asked me to watch after Kimberly. I found out from her that you told her to look after me, since I'd just been jilted at the altar."

"Looks like the two of you did your jobs, then," David said with a sneer. "Both of you are a couple of two-timers, and that's all there is to it. Neither of you can be trusted." He glanced over at Pastor Rawlings. "And you call yourselves Christians."

"We didn't need you to tell us to be friends," Brian said as he stood to face David. He wasn't going to let David steamroll him, but more than that, he wasn't about to let David get away with what he was saying about Kimberly. "She and I have always been there for each other, and you know that. Kim is one of the most committed Christians I've ever met." He tilted his head forward and glared at David. "And loyal to a fault."

"Not from where I stand."

"What would you have wanted her to do then, David? Should she have just stayed engaged to you, even though she didn't want to be your wife?"

"Well—no, but I would have thought—"

"I think you know as well as I do that neither Kimberly nor I would have done anything behind your back."

"Right," David said with a sarcastic snicker.

Brian was glad the pastor was still there, he was so angry. "Do you realize what you've done to Kimberly?"

David narrowed his eyes. "What I've done to her? Hey, buddy, you're getting this whole thing all twisted."

"No, you're the one who's twisting things. You started out making her feel like she was the most important person in your life and that made her very happy. She fell in love with the David who treated her with kindness and respect. Then after the engagement, I watched as you slowly pushed her out of your inner circle."

"That's ridiculous. I don't even know what you're talking about. Inner circle?"

Brian had to pause to keep his temper in check. "After you got engaged, Kimberly never knew where she stood with you. When you came to her and announced that you'd volunteered for this special mission, she was hurt that you didn't consult her first, but she accepted it. The whole time you were over there, she worried about you. For all she knew, you could have been blown to bits by a suicide bomber."

David rolled his eyes. "Aren't you being rather melodramatic now, buddy?"

"When you came home, she had to fall in line with everything you wanted—from the party to the places you went."

"Did she tell you all this?" David asked.

"I already told you, I figured it out on my own. Kimberly and I have known each other long enough we can almost read each other's thoughts."

As Brian talked, he noticed a gradual change in David's demeanor—from combative to remorseful. Brian figured he'd said enough.

David glanced over at the door, so Brian looked up. The pastor was no longer there.

After a long, uncomfortable minute, David turned back to Brian. "Look, man, this was a shock. I had no idea Kimberly wasn't still madly in love with me."

"Same here," Brian said as he held up his hands. "All I knew was that she was hurting."

"Give me some time to think through this, okay?" David pursed his lips and waited.

"Sure, that's reasonable." Brian was relieved.

"I'll talk to you again before I take off for my next assignment."

"That'll be good."

After David left, Brian bowed his head and gave thanks that only words had been exchanged. When he looked up again, Pastor Rawlings was back.

"Wanna talk?" the pastor asked.

Brian didn't want to talk, but he felt that he owed the pastor an explanation. "It's complex."

"I bet it's nothing I haven't heard before."

"Maybe so, but this is the first time anything like this has happened to me."

"Let's go to my office where we can be more comfortable."

Brian followed Pastor Rawlings out the door, down the hall, and into the wood-paneled office. As soon as the pastor sat in the overstuffed chair, Brian positioned himself on the sofa on the other side of the table.

"So, what's up?" Pastor Rawlings said. "Obviously woman trouble."

Brian nodded. "In the worst kind of way. It's a long story."

The pastor nodded. "Jennifer is staying with her sister for a few days, helping with the new baby, so I have all the time you need."

Brian started slowly from the beginning, about how he and Kimberly had met and become fast friends in elementary school. He talked about how he'd had a huge crush on her off and on since their early teen years, but he never felt he stood a chance, so he settled into remaining her buddy and confidant.

"Did you ever open up to her and see how she felt?" the pastor asked.

"I started to a couple of times, but I always chickened out."

The pastor laughed. "Some men struggle with communication. Perhaps we should take lessons from women who love to talk."

"I kept hoping she'd say something—you know, give me some kind of hint that she might consider me more than just a good guy friend."

Pastor Rawlings leaned forward and listened with all his attention as Brian spilled everything that had been on his heart for the past fifteen years. Finally Brian shook his head.

The pastor leaned back and rubbed his chin. "Seems I recall you're the one who brought David to church and introduced him to Kimberly."

Brian snickered. "Yup, that was me, chump of the year. I thought they'd hit it off, but I had no idea what David had up his sleeve. I didn't even have a chance to tell him how I felt about her."

"Why didn't you say something before you introduced them?"

"I didn't think it was an issue." Brian shrugged. "Then I had to go away for the National Guard a few weeks during the summer. He'd changed units, so we went at different times, and when I came back, they were tight."

"Yeah," the pastor said as he nodded in understanding, "I can see how that would pose a problem."

"My timing has been off with Kimberly since I met her. The one other time I thought I stood a chance with her, I waited a couple of weeks to say anything. That was back in high school. Some new guy came along, and next thing I knew, she was swooning over him—just like the rest of the girls. I listened to her go on and on about how great he was, and next thing I knew, they were together."

The pastor laughed. "How long did that last?"

"About half our junior year. Then one thing after another happened. . . ." Brian held out his hands. "And now this."

"This is different for you, huh?"

"Very different," Brian agreed as he reflected on how he'd almost shared his feelings with Kim. "I just don't understand why she told David how she felt about me before she said something to me."

"Well, she was engaged to David," the pastor said. "I agree it would have been better to break it off with him without telling him she loved you, and then come and let you know how she felt. I'm sure it was just an honest error in judgment."

"I always thought Kimberly was one to speak her mind," Brian said. "Back when we were kids, she was able to keep other people's secrets, but she's never been good at hiding her own." He held out his hands. "She was always transparent."

"That's actually a good trait for a person to have."

Brian nodded. "She has a lot of good traits."

"I'm sure she thought she was doing the right thing by keeping her thoughts to herself. So now we need to figure out how to lighten things up with David and get you and Kimberly on the same track."

"Without upsetting anyone," Brian added.

Pastor Rawlings shook his head. "I don't think it's possible not to upset anyone, but that's okay." He offered a sympathetic smile. "We're human. We get upset."

"I'm sure you're right." Brian started to stand but sat back down when the pastor bowed his head.

"Dear Father, in Your holy wisdom, please lead Brian, David, and Kimberly closer to You as they make life-affecting decisions. I pray for peace as well as healing of hearts that are surely broken. Give me the wisdom to offer advice when needed and the knowledge to know when to be quiet and let Your will show itself in a way only You can do. In Jesus' name, amen."

Brian whispered, "Amen," before opening his eyes.

Pastor Rawlings stood first, so Brian followed. Without another word, they shook hands, and Brian left the church.

The pastor's prayer played through Brian's head all the way home. He needed to rely more on prayer and less on his own will.

Kim paced then flopped down on the couch where she couldn't sit very long without starting all over again. She'd been trying to call Brian, both at home and on his cell phone, for the past hour. She knew he'd already left work, because she'd tried there after not reaching him the first couple of times she called.

When her phone rang, she jumped. She paused long enough to look on the caller ID and saw that it was Brian. Her heart pounded, and her mouth suddenly felt dry.

As soon as she answered, Brian spoke. "What is going on, Kimberly?"

She swallowed hard, but the lump stayed at the base of her throat. "I had a talk with David."

"Yes, I know."

"I told him I couldn't marry him." Her hand shook, so she cradled the phone between her shoulder and ear.

"What else did you tell him?" He sounded strange.

"Do you already know?"

"Yes," he replied softly. "He said you told him you were in love with me. Why did you do that?"

Kim's knees felt weak, so she stepped across the room and sat down on a kitchen chair. "Because—well. . ." It was hard to tell her best friend something that would change their relationship for good. She sighed. "Because it's true."

"Why am I always the last to know stuff like this?" Brian asked.

"Are you mad?"

"Mad? No. Why should I be mad?"

"So what did David say after that?"

Brian snorted. "He was furious. But I think he's fine now, after we met face-to-face at the church."

"So that's where you've been. I've been trying to get ahold of you since you left work."

"I turned off my phone." A brief pause fell between them before he spoke again. "You and I need to have a heart-to-heart talk, Kimberly Shaw. This is a serious matter that needs to be resolved before David leaves for the next mission."

"It's over between David and me, Brian," Kim said. "You and I can deal with our own issues after he's gone."

"That brings up another point."

"What's that?"

"Do we have issues?"

Kim sucked in a breath and blurted, "I think we do."

"Then let's talk about them."

"Not on the phone," she said. "Why don't you come over here, and we can discuss them in person."

"I'll be there in ten minutes."

After they hung up, Kim ran to her room and changed into something a little more flattering than the jeans and T-shirt she'd put on after work. Then she brushed her hair until it gleamed.

The instant the doorbell rang, Kim flung it open. He reached for her, pulled her into his arms, and lowered his face to hers for the most heart-stopping kiss she'd ever experienced.

Chapter 17

Brian hadn't planned the kiss. It just happened.

When he opened his eyes as he took a step back, he saw that Kim was just as stunned as he was. Without a word, he followed her into her house and all the way to the kitchen.

She turned to face him. "I figure we're better off in here because the lighting is better."

"Uh-huh." Nothing more intelligent than a simple grunt entered Brian's mind. He needed some time to recover from the kiss.

"I'm really sorry I messed things up between you and David," she said. "I know you were best friends and all, but. . ." She lifted her hands and let them fall back to her sides. "I knew I couldn't stay engaged to him, and I felt like I needed to explain why I was giving him his ring back. It just came out, and by the time I realized what I'd done, it was too late."

Brian took a step closer to Kim and placed his hands on her shoulders. "I understand. You didn't do anything wrong."

"But—"

He gently touched her lips with his finger. "Shh."

Kim nodded and blinked then smiled. "So what are we gonna do now?"

His heart flipped a little, causing him to pause before speaking. "I guess we need to see how you and I are as a couple."

She lifted her eyebrows. "A couple?"

He nodded. "Yes. That is, if you want to."

"A couple," she repeated. "You and me." A giggle came out of her beautiful, bow-shaped lips. "That sounds so—I don't know. . ."

"Wonderful?"

Her cheeks reddened, and she nodded. "Well, yeah."

"So what now?"

Kim shrugged. "I guess we should start dating or something."

"Ya think?" His tone came out teasing, and she looked stricken, so he added, "I agree."

Brian felt a sense of peace as she smiled at him. Then he remembered David. "We need to be very careful about how we handle this."

Sadness washed over her face. "I know. I never meant to hurt him."

"David's a strong guy, so he'll be fine. But you're right. We need to be very careful with how we show our new relationship to the public." He gently stroked her cheek with the back of his hand. "We have to be respectful."

Kim wanted to kiss Brian again, but she agreed that they needed to take their relationship slowly, even in private. After being engaged to the wrong man, she didn't want to make the same mistake twice. The chemistry was certainly there, and she liked everything about Brian. However, she needed to be sure that the excitement from changing their relationship didn't fade into a dull regret.

"I have to get to the office early tomorrow morning, so I need to run," Brian said as he edged toward the door. "Let's plan to see each other Friday night. Maybe we can rent a movie and watch it at my place or yours."

She nodded. They didn't need to flaunt their relationship to the world—especially since David was still in town.

The rest of the week seemed to drag. By the time Friday night rolled around, Kim was so happy she felt like she could jump out of her own skin.

They'd decided to watch the movie at Brian's house. When Kim arrived, she was greeted by a smiling man and the aroma of homemade chili.

"I feel like a princess," she said. "This kind of thing only happens in fairy tales."

Brian leaned down and dropped a quick kiss on her lips. Her knees instantly felt rubbery, but she managed to make it to the nearest chair.

"Want to eat first or start the movie?" Brian asked.

"Let's eat while we watch the movie," she replied. That way they would have something to do besides kiss.

Brian grinned. "Good idea. Help me set up some TV trays."

They were halfway through the movie when the phone rang. Brian frowned, but he put the movie on pause. "I'll get off the phone as fast as I can."

Kim noticed that Brian paused after looking at the caller ID. When he picked up the phone and answered, his voice cracked. She sat and watched him as he listened before saying, "Uh-huh, that's great." He got quiet again then added, "I'm sure she'll be perfectly fine with that. Would you like for me to talk to her first?"

After Brian hung up, he turned to Kim with a wide smile. "That was David. You'll never guess what he just told me."

"What did he say?"

"He called Mercedes, and they're now dating. After you broke up with him, he ran into her at Blossom's. They started talking, and before he knew what hit him, she asked if she could go to his place and fix dinner."

Kim tilted her head. "He called to tell you that?"

Brian planted his fists on his hips, and the smile never left his face. "He called to ask if you'd be okay with him bringing Mercedes to church on Sunday."

"Wow." As Kim thought back to the night they were all together, she wasn't surprised. "David and Mercedes did seem to have quite a bit in common." She snickered. "He didn't waste any time, though, did he? Well, I'm glad he's not sitting at home seething."

"I think this changes things for us, too, Kimberly." Brian sat down next to Kim and placed his arm around her. "Would you like to go to church with me on Sunday—I mean as my—um, girlfriend?"

She laughed and nodded. "I thought you'd never ask."

"You will be okay seeing David with Mercedes, right?" Brian looked her in the eye.

"Of course, but I have to admit it'll seem a little weird."

"I know what you mean." Brian turned back to the TV. "Let's finish watching this movie. I have to go to the office in the morning, so I can't stay up too late."

❧

Since Brian had to leave straight from church on Sunday to help a friend move, Kim agreed to meet him in the pew. They figured that would also feel less awkward if they ran into David and Mercedes on their way in. Kim arrived early to save a spot. She kept turning around to watch for Brian, who slipped in with five minutes to spare.

"Before you ask," he whispered, "I saw David and Mercedes in the parking lot. She didn't look happy about something."

"I wonder what," Kim said.

"Couldn't tell, but don't worry about it."

The music started, so they turned their attention to worship God. After church was over, Brian took Kim's hand and led her to the fellowship hall for Bible study. David and Mercedes stood outside the door of the big room, deep in discussion. Brian cleared his throat as they walked by.

David glanced up and did a double take. Kim felt awkward as she smiled at David first then Mercedes, who broke into a very wide grin.

"Hey, Kim!" Mercedes said a little too loudly. "I want to talk to you. Is there someplace we can get away for a few minutes?"

Kim glanced at Brian, who nodded. "Bible study doesn't start for another fifteen minutes. I'll save you a seat."

Mercedes looked at David, who nodded and said, "Why don't you go outside and talk to get away from all the ears?"

Kim bristled. David still liked to be in control and tell people what to do. She turned to Mercedes. "Where would you like to go?"

Mercedes pointed to the exit door. "Let's go outside. I don't want to start anything with David's friends."

As soon as they were out the door, Mercedes stopped and turned to Kim. "Thank you so much for being understanding about David and me. He was worried you'd be upset."

"Why would I be upset?" Kim asked.

"After he dropped you off that night we went bowling, I called him, and we talked for hours." Mercedes let out a dreamy sigh. "I was crazy about him, but he's loyal to a fault." She paused. "I want to assure you that nothing happened between us."

Kim folded her arms and chuckled. "Oh, I believe you."

"I know he wanted Brian and me to hit it off, but he's just not my type. I hope he's not too heartbroken."

Obviously David hadn't told Mercedes all the details. "I think Brian is just fine. In fact he would probably be the first to give you his blessing to be with David."

"Oh good." Mercedes cast a nervous glance over her shoulder. "Now I have a really important question to ask. I'm way overdressed for this church. It's been a long time since I've stepped foot in a place of worship, so I feel totally dorky and out of the loop. I didn't know it was okay to wear pants in front of God. Is there any way you and I can—well, you know—get together, so you can fill me in on all the latest God stuff? I'm thinking about moving here permanently, and I really want to fit in."

Kim had to bite the insides of her cheeks to keep from laughing. She nodded, and when the urge to laugh subsided, she said, "I'd love to talk about the gospel sometime."

"Since you're a hairdresser, maybe I can book an appointment and we can talk then." Mercedes patted her hair. "I've been doing it myself for the past year because—well, finances have been rather tight lately."

Kim rummaged around in her handbag and pulled out a card. "Give me a call and we can set up an appointment. Your first visit is free." She was so relieved not to have to worry about David being mad at Brian, she would have given Mercedes more if she'd asked.

Mercedes nearly fell off her stilettos. "You'll do that?"

With a grin, Kim nodded. "Just call me early next week and we'll find a time you can come in."

"You're a very sweet person, Kimberly. I think we just might wind up being best friends."

Kim had her doubts, but she wasn't about to tell Mercedes that. "Let's go back inside, okay? I think you'll enjoy the Bible study."

"I hope so. To be honest, it kind of scares me. Will someone call on me and, like, expect me to know stuff?"

"No," Kim replied. "It's actually the opposite. So many people want to talk, you have to really be on your toes to get a word in."

Mercedes visibly relaxed as they walked inside to join David and Brian, who'd saved them seats between them. Kim shared her workbook with

Mercedes, who appeared to take everything in.

After the Bible study was over, Mercedes invited everyone to her place for brunch. Brian immediately said he had plans to help his friend move. Kim didn't want to hurt her feelings, and she didn't want to make things any more awkward than they already were.

"That sounds nice," Kim replied. "What can I bring?"

Mercedes touched her manicured finger to her chin. "How about juice? I have orange juice, but David said he prefers apple or grape."

That was the first Kim had ever heard this about David, making her think she might not have known as much about him as she thought. "Okay, I'll bring both. How many people are coming?"

Mercedes shrugged. "I'm not sure. David invited a few people, but we don't have a count. Good thing I bought a bunch of muffins and bagels."

"Hey, Kim, I gotta go," Brian said.

Mercedes handed Kim a card. "Here's my uncle's address. It's really easy to find."

"See you in a little while," Kim replied.

Brian walked Kim to her car and held the door while she got in. Then he leaned over and whispered, "Mind if I stop by your place after I'm done?"

"That'll be great!"

"How long do you think you'll be at your new best friend's brunch?" Brian quirked a smile that Kim tried to ignore.

"Not long."

He pushed back from her car. "I didn't think so. I'll have my cell phone on me, so call if you need me, okay?"

"I can't believe this is happening. It feels sort of strange."

"One of the things I love about you, Kim, is your ability to look past yourself and see someone else who needs to hear the gospel."

Kim left the church parking lot and stopped off at the grocery store. With four bottles of juice, she took off for Mercedes' uncle's house. All the way there, she did some mental role-playing about how to talk to David. The problem was she didn't have any idea how he'd act toward her.

The second she pulled into the parking space in front of the address, she spotted David coming toward her. "Kim! I'd like to have a word with you before you go inside."

"Okay." She pulled the bags from the passenger seat and got out.

He cleared his throat as he studied her face. When he spoke, his voice cracked. "Kim, I want you to know that I've thought about us."

She braced herself for anything. "David, I—"

"Give me a chance to tell you what's on my mind. I can't say I blame you now that I've thought it all over. At this point in my life, I'm not good husband material, so I think this is for the best. When I met you, I got all caught up in the way you lived your life. I'd never met any other woman so committed to her faith. You're a good woman, Kimberly Shaw, and Brian is a fortunate man."

She glanced down to hide her embarrassment before looking back at him. "Thank you, David."

"You did the right thing."

"I appreciate your understanding."

He took one of the bags from her and pointed toward the house. "Ready to face a roomful of people?"

"Ready as I'll ever be," she replied. "Let's go in."

Several people seemed confused, but David pulled a couple of the guys aside and explained what happened. Mercedes appeared oblivious to everyone and everything but David, whom she openly adored. Kim found herself feeling bad for Mercedes until she got everyone's attention for an announcement.

After all eyes were on Mercedes, she grinned at David then turned to everyone else. "I've been thinking about going back to college for the longest time. When I told David, he encouraged me to go for it, even after I said I was too old."

"You're never too old to follow your dreams," David said.

"I have two years left to get my nursing degree, and I'm going for it!" She pumped her fist into the air, eliciting a round of applause from everyone in the room.

Kim saw the sparks between David and Mercedes, and that gave her a very good feeling. When she had a chance to turn her back without being conspicuous, she shut her eyes and softly said, "Thank You, Lord."

As soon as she was able to get away without being rude, Kim went home. Brian was in her driveway waiting for her. She ran straight to him.

He wrapped his arms around her waist, and she placed her hands on his face. "I think we should have thought about getting together a long time ago," he said. "Life would have been much simpler."

"Maybe," she said, "but we might never have appreciated what we have."

"True," he agreed. "The Lord's timing is much better than ours." He leaned down and dropped a quick kiss on her lips. "Wanna tell me how things went at the brunch?"

"Later," she said. "But right now I want another kiss."

※

As soon as Jack's furniture was in place, he handed Brian a soft drink. "So tell me, when are you gonna propose to Kim?"

Brian chuckled. "What makes you think I'm going to propose?"

Jack chuckled. "You're a smart man. You're not about to let her get away again."

"You're right. I thought I'd do it soon."

"Good idea."

Brian finished his drink and tossed the can into the recycling bin. "Enjoy your new house, Jack."

※

First thing Monday morning, Kim walked into the Snappy Scissors feeling all giddy. Jasmine glanced at her and turned away then snapped back around. "I see you had a good weekend."

"Yeah, it was great."

Jasmine gave her a told-you-so smile. "See? Brian was the man for you all along."

"I should have listened to you," Kim admitted. "But oh well. At least we're together now."

"Don't let him get away," Jasmine said. "If he makes any sounds about making this relationship permanent, you'd better jump."

Kim laughed. "You don't mince words, do you, Jazzy?"

"Why should I?" Jasmine picked up the towel hanging on the back of the chair and shook it out. "I'm old enough to know what I want and go after it."

"Me, too," Kim said.

The day was busy, which was good, because it flew by. Kim had just picked up her handbag from the back room when her cell phone rang. It was Brian.

"Hey, wanna go for a drive and grab some dinner in a little while?" he asked.

She closed her eyes and allowed the contentment to fill her soul. "Sure, sounds good."

"I'll pick you up in half an hour, if that's okay with you."

"Okeydoke. I'll be ready."

※

This was it. The big moment of reckoning. His nerves were on edge as he headed straight for Kim's place. She was standing at the door waiting for him.

"You look beautiful," he said as he gave her a hug.

"Thanks." She pulled back and winked. "So do you."

"Hungry?"

"Always."

Brian laughed. "Then let's go." They passed the jewelry store on the way to the restaurant. If everything went as planned, they'd be there before the night was over.

Kim ordered first, and then Brian told the server what he wanted. Kim kept tilting her head and giving him an odd look.

"Why do you keep doing that?" he asked.

"You're acting strange."

Brian opened his mouth then shut it. He grinned.

"Okay, what gives?"

He glanced down at the table then looked back into her eyes. He'd hoped to do this in a more romantic setting, but anywhere he was with Kim was romantic, so he figured he might as well let her know what was on his mind.

"I love you, Kim."

"I love you, too, Brian."

"I was wondering. . . ." He paused and made a face.

Her eyebrows shot up, and she leaned forward with her hands on the table. "Out with it, Brian. What were you wondering?"

He reached for her hands and held both of them. "How do you feel about spending the rest of your life with me?"

Kim closed her eyes, and when she opened them, he saw the tears. "Absolutely, yes!"

Epilogue

Six months later, Kim and Brian said their wedding vows. When it was time to walk out of the church as husband and wife, Kim glanced over her shoulder at Mercedes. "Be ready," she mouthed.

Mercedes gave her a thumbs-up. "I'll be front and center."

Brian gave her a confused look. "What was that all about?"

"I'll tell you all about it later."

After they got outside and people closed in on them, Carrie found her way to Kim's side. "I'll be standing over to your right. Just look at me, and I'll let you know where she is."

"Huh?" Brian tilted his head and gave Carrie a questioning glance.

Carrie laughed. "I figured if she catches the bouquet, it'll at least get him thinking." She gently pushed Kim and Brian toward the waiting limo. "Better get going so we can start the party."

Brian snorted as people continued to wave and blow bubbles when they passed. "Promise you won't tell, and I'll let you two in on a little secret."

"You've been keeping a secret from me?" Kim teased as Carrie helped her fold the bridal dress train into the car.

"Just this one."

"C'mon, Brian," Carrie urged. "Spill it so we can get this show on the road."

Brian winked at Kim then announced, "David's been looking at rings."

"Good!" Kim wriggled her eyebrows. "All the more reason she has to catch the bouquet. She's next!"

"Better her than me," Carrie said. "I'll run interference and make sure she gets it."

After she turned and walked away, Brian pulled Kim toward him and dropped a kiss on her nose. "I love you, Mrs. Estep."

PORTRAIT OF LOVE

Dedication

Thanks to Jennifer Fleahman with the Wheeling, West Virginia, Chamber of Commerce, and Margaret Prager at Suzanne's Bridal Shop for helping me with some of the facts about the city.

Chapter 1

More than twenty elementary-aged children swarmed Mandy Pruitt the instant she snapped the last picture. She laughed as she handed out the candy she'd promised. A group of moms had gotten together and brought their homeschooled children for their fall "class" photo.

The smallest of the children, a boy with floppy red hair and big green eyes, touched the camera. "Can we see the picture, Miss Mandy?"

She placed one hand on his shoulder and gestured for the other children to come around behind her with the other. "If you're very still, I'll show you what I have here. It'll look a little different after it's developed."

Mandy enjoyed her job of being a children's photographer at the Small World Portrait Studio on Market Street in Wheeling, West Virginia. A year ago, jobs were scarce, so she'd resorted to walking up and down Market Street, handing out copies of her résumé to anyone who'd take one. The former photographer had just walked out the day before, and the manager was stuck snapping pictures of unruly children.

As soon as she'd walked into the studio, one of the children in the Sunday school class she taught at church recognized her. "Miss Mandy!"

"Hey, Bailey!"

"What are you doing here?" Bailey had glanced around behind her. "Are you getting your picture took?"

"No," she'd told him. "I'm not getting my picture *taken*. I'm here to apply for a job."

When the manager saw her instant rapport with the pint-sized set, he hired her on the spot. "All we have to do is a background check, and you've got yourself a job photographing kids," he told her. "I'll put a rush on it, and you'll hear back from me in the next couple of days."

"Um. . ." Her mindless scattering of résumés had landed her a job she had no idea how to do. "I'm not exactly an experienced photographer." She'd been thinking more along the lines of receptionist since her degree in business didn't seem to matter.

He'd snickered. "That's fine. We train our photographers."

"Are you sure?"

The manager rocked back on his heels and studied her with a narrowed gaze. "Do you want a job or not?"

"Oh yes, of course I do."

"Good." The man smiled. "As soon as we have the required background check in, I'll call and you can start right away. I'll teach you how to use the equipment. Shouldn't take more than a day or two."

The squirminess of the children now surrounding her jolted her back to the moment. "Miss Mandy, can I have another piece of candy? Tyler took mine."

Mandy leveled the tallest boy with a stern gaze. "Tyler, keep your hands to yourself." She reached into the bag and pulled out another piece of candy for the girl. "Here ya go, Mackenzie. Why don't you save it for later?"

Mackenzie nodded and turned toward the waiting room mothers. "Mommy, looky what Miss Mandy gave us."

After the children left, Mandy went to the front desk and checked the appointment book. She didn't have another sitting for a couple of hours, but she was the only person in the studio, and she couldn't leave since they took walk-ins.

Tony Mancini stood directly across the street from the studio and watched the pretty woman with the short blond hair and expressive eyes work her magic. He'd been told what a dynamo Mandy Pruitt was. If this was Mandy, her reputation didn't do her justice. She was a magician as far as he could tell. As the children filed out of the studio, they all waved and hollered their good-byes, while she smiled and waved back. After they were gone, she didn't drop the smile, but he saw her shoulders lift and fall in what appeared to be a deep sigh. The woman obviously enjoyed her job.

Tony didn't want to manage a studio, but he'd been warned when he first left and joined the army after college. His mother's brother Edward had always wanted his own son, Ricco, and nephew, Tony, to take over the company, but at that time it wasn't what Tony had wanted. Things had changed. His father had passed away, and Tony had gotten out of the army. Now he'd have to do his time and prove his commitment to the family, starting at the store level.

Movement in the studio captured his attention once again. Mandy had the phone at her ear while she jotted something down. He watched as her expression changed. Tony decided it was time to quit standing on the sidewalk staring and go on inside. He squared his shoulders, set his jaw, and headed for the entrance.

Mandy glanced up as he entered. "May I help you?"

Tony stopped at the counter and nodded. "Yes, I'm Tony Mancini, and I'll be working with you." He pulled out his company ID and showed it to her.

She frowned. "I just found out you were coming. Sorry I didn't have more time to prepare." Her voice cracked, and she stopped talking. "Ever

256

since Parker left, it's just been me and a couple of part-timers. I wish someone had told me before today I was getting help."

"I'm not just here to help out," he said before she buried herself any further. She obviously didn't know he was related to the owners. He resented having to take this job, but he didn't want to take it out on her. "I'm the new manager."

She blinked as the surprise registered on her face. She didn't look any happier than he felt. "Did you come from another Small World studio?"

He shook his head. "No, I just finished a few weeks of crash training at the home office, and they sent me here."

"Oh." She looked down and her shoulders sagged.

"But I have photography experience. I was a photographer back in college, and I did a little stringing for newspapers on the side, but it was mostly journalistic work."

She didn't even try to smile when she looked back up at him. "Like car wrecks and stuff?"

He couldn't help but grin, in spite of the tension. "Yeah, something like that."

"Then you should do just fine."

At least she had a sense of humor.

⁂

The one thing that annoyed her most about the Small World company was how they never let the store personnel know their next move. As annoyed as she was, she didn't want to risk her job, so she forced a smile.

"Oh, by the way, my name is Mandy Pruitt, and I've been here about a year."

His instant smile was warm, and she wanted to like him. "Nice to meet you, Mandy Pruitt." He extended his hand.

She wiped her palm on the side of her slacks before taking Tony's. His handshake was firm and quick.

"Mind if I take a look around?" he asked.

"C'mon, let me give you a tour of the place." She turned and walked toward the back, hoping he'd follow. The soft sound of footsteps behind her let her know he wasn't far behind. Suddenly she heard a thumping sound, so she spun around in time to see him catch himself after nearly tripping over a stuffed animal. "Sorry," she said as she bent over to pick it up. "Kids leave things—"

He held up his hands. "Don't worry about it."

Their gazes locked, and her voice stuck in her throat. She quickly glanced away.

"Nice," he said, breaking the silence. "It looks just like the studio in the home office."

"It is." When she met his gaze again, she saw a flash of something—concern, maybe?

Tony opened his mouth to say something, when the phone rang. He nodded to the chirping receiver in her hand. "Don't let me keep you from your work."

Mandy pushed the TALK button and lifted the phone to her ear as Tony added some distance between them. "Small World, this is Mandy. How may I help you?"

"I'm stranded, and I don't know what to do. Mom said to call you."

It sounded like her sister. "Christina?"

"Yeah, Joe told me he didn't want anything to do with me anymore, and I couldn't get an acting job, so here I am stuck in LA, no job, no boyfriend, and I can't pay my rent."

Christina had the worst timing possible. "Do you have a way to come to West Virginia?"

"No, I'm flat broke." She sniffled. "I really wanna come home. I should have listened to you and Dad about how hard it was to make a living in Hollywood."

Mandy only paused for a second before making a decision. "I'll order you a ticket, and you can pick it up at the airport."

"Thanks, Mandy. I promise I'll pay you back."

"Shh, don't worry about that now, hon. I know you'd do the same for me. I'll call you after I book your flight."

"Can you do it now? I don't have a place to stay tonight. I–I've been evicted."

"Um. . ." Mandy glanced up at Tony, who'd once again backed away. "Sure." After Mandy hung up, she gave Tony an apologetic look. "I have a family situation."

"Better handle it then. I'm not going anywhere."

She made a beeline for the front desk to book Christina's flight. She felt Tony's presence as he joined her.

Mandy was embarrassed. "I don't do this kind of thing often, but my sister is stranded in California, and I have to buy her a ticket home."

Tony grinned. "The two of you must be close. Have you always gotten along?"

"If you don't count the childish squabbles we used to have in the backseat on long family car trips, yes. We're very close."

"Good. I'll just look around some more while you take care of this." Still smiling, he turned and left.

As Mandy went to the airline website, she thought about how nice Tony seemed to be—or was at least trying to be. If she'd met him anywhere but work, she would have wanted to find out more about him—like whether or not he was a Christian, and if so, was he single. But as a coworker, the single part didn't matter because she had no intention of having an office romance.

It only took her a couple of minutes to book Christina's flight and make a brief phone call to let her know. As soon as Mandy finished her family business, she joined Tony.

"So what do you think?" she asked.

"Looks like you've done an excellent job of keeping this place running. I heard you haven't had a manager in more than a month."

Mandy wasn't about to tell him she was applying for the manager position. Last time she'd brought it up to Ricco, the corporate regional manager, she'd been advised to wait until it was posted companywide.

"Are you always here with your part-timers?" he continued.

She shook her head. "Not always, but they're both very good and reliable. I can leave either of them alone, but during the busy times, I try to schedule two people." She paused and made a face. "I'm here as much as I can be, though."

"That must be challenging." He rubbed his chin as he turned and scoped everything out. "Now that I'm here, I hope you're able to relax and maybe take some time off."

"I'm relaxed."

He nodded toward the white knuckles of her hands folded in front of her. "Oh yeah?"

"I'm fine," she said as she dropped her hands to her side, her voice tight and squeaky. She cleared her throat. "I'm a very organized person."

He studied her for several seconds before nodding. "That's nice."

The way he looked at her was unsettling. "I, uh. . . I need to go back to the front desk. Let me know if you need anything."

"I'll be up there in a few minutes. Ricco said to give him a call after we met."

Once Mandy was alone, she tried to force her nerves to calm down, but they were still jangled. She never liked surprises like this.

The second line on the phone at the desk was lit up, meaning Tony was still on with Ricco. She was tempted to call Ricco's assistant to ask what was going on, but she refrained. Too many people knowing her insecurities would only make things worse.

Since the next appointment wasn't due for another hour, she busied herself filing cards and organizing the desk. School was in session, and it was too close to lunchtime to expect preschooler walk-ins.

The sound of Tony's voice startled her. "Got a minute for a quick chat?"

"Now?"

He nodded. "Yeah."

Her heart pounded. Here it was, the reason he suddenly appeared without warning. She swallowed hard and nodded. "Here or in the office?"

"Here is fine."

She took the liberty of studying his face as he gathered his thoughts. Thick eyebrows hooded his deep-set dark eyes. His jawline was strong, and his temples pulsed when he wasn't talking.

"So what did you want to discuss?"

He lifted the top sheet from the notepad and pulled out a slip of paper she recognized. The one she'd jotted her to-do list on. And that included—oh no. Her heart sank.

"I see that you were going to apply for the manager's position," he said softly.

Mandy's mouth went dry. She nodded. There was no point in denying she wanted the title and pay to go with what she'd been doing since Parker had left. If she'd known someone else was coming, she wouldn't have left it by the phone in the office.

"I wasn't trying to snoop," he said. "It was right there in front of me."

"That's okay." What else could she have said?

"Sorry."

The straight line of his lips and his sympathetic gaze made her stomach churn. She hated people feeling sorry for her.

"There's something I think you should know about me," he said.

"Really?" Her own sarcasm surprised her. "Sorry, I didn't mean it to sound so. . ."

He smiled sympathetically. "That's okay. This is very awkward, and I understand, but there's a reason I was brought here. You see, I'm—well, Edward is my uncle."

"Edward?" she asked as realization dawned on her. "As in Edward Rossi, founder and president of Small World?"

"Yep, that's the one."

She couldn't think of anything to say.

"I didn't really want this job," he went on, "and I don't expect to be here long, so I'll make sure to put in a good word when they move me back to Atlanta."

"Thanks." She didn't dare say anything else or she'd risk sounding surly.

As conflicting thoughts continued to collide in her head, Tony jotted down a few things on his pad. She wanted to grab his pencil and break it in two then snatch the notepad and read what he was writing about her.

He stopped writing and looked directly at her. "If it's any consolation, I've heard you're one of the best photographers in the district."

※

Tony knew he shouldn't continue standing there staring at her while she processed what he'd just said. She needed time alone.

"I have a few things to do, so I'll be in the office. If you need me, just holler."

"I'll be fine."

He offered a smile. "I'm sure you will." After he took a few steps toward the office, he stopped, turned, and waited for her to look up. "Mandy, I'm sure someday you'll make an excellent manager. I'm sorry you had to find out this way."

Her lips quivered for a split second before she nodded. She opened her mouth to say something, but all that came out was a squeak.

"If you need some time off, let me know, okay?"

Her face looked stricken. "Why would I need time off?"

"I'm just saying. . . ."

"I don't."

She took a step back and slammed into the corner of the wall. Tony instinctively reached for her as she rubbed her shoulder.

"I'm fine," she said softly before glancing at his hand resting on her arm.

He quickly pulled his hand back and shoved it into his pocket. "That's fine. I just wanted to let you know it's okay if you need time to think about things."

There wasn't even the hint of a smile on her pretty face as she stood there staring at him with those wide, long-lash-framed hazel eyes.

Tony didn't want to torture her, so he added, "After I get acclimated to the place, I'll need to start interviewing for another full-time photographer. Since you'll be training the person, I'd like for you to participate."

She didn't say a word, so he took off for the office. This had been much more difficult than he'd anticipated.

He closed the door behind him and hesitated as he looked around the room. Mandy had all but made the space her own.

A trio of butterfly prints adorned one wall, while a collage of portraits, probably from this very studio, hung on the adjacent wall. A small dish of pastel mints rested on the corner of the desk—behind the vase of spring flowers.

His first inclination was to remove some of the feminine touches, but he paused and closed his eyes. *Lord, guide me in how to handle this situation. Mandy is obviously distressed, and rightfully so. I don't want to upset her, but I want to do well with the job I've been hired to do. Oh, and while You're at it, help me work on my attitude about being where I don't want to be.*

Chapter 2

Christina's flight was two hours late. Mandy had thought to check the flight before leaving to pick her up, but she left early to avoid talking to Tony more than necessary—at least until she had time to process his being there. Why did he have to be so nice and so...good-looking? When Mandy arrived at the terminal, she spotted Christina standing between two tall, very attractive men. The only surprise was that Christina was already there—not the fact that she was flanked by guys.

Mandy popped her trunk, and the guys loaded it. "Thanks for everything," Christina said. "I hope your mother gets better soon."

"Thanks, Chrissy, I'm sure she'll be fine," one of the men said.

The other guy looked like he was about to hug her, but when she leaned away from him, he pulled back. "Try to look at the bright side of things. Call me if you need more advice."

"Thanks, guys."

"Nice talking to you, Chrissy."

As soon as Mandy got in the car and snapped her seat belt, she turned to her sister. "Chrissy? I thought you hated people calling you that."

Christina shrugged. "A lot has changed since I left."

Mandy gave her a once-over before starting the car and pulling away from the curb. "You'll have to tell me all about it after I get off work tonight. I'll take you to Mom and Dad's, but I have to run back to the studio."

"Can't you take some time off?" Christina sounded hurt. "Mom says you haven't taken a vacation since you started that job."

"There's been a new development at work, and I'm not sure what's going on," Mandy explained. "I have a new boss."

Christina groaned. "Is this person a jerk or something?"

"I can't tell yet, but so far he seems okay."

"Did he get the job you were talking about applying for?"

Mandy nodded. "Yeah, and not only that, his uncle is head of the company."

"Sorry, sis. That's always the way it is though."

"Okay, what gives?" Mandy asked. "I've never seen you so negative. What happened in LA?"

Christina lifted her hands and dropped them in her lap. "So many things I don't even know where to begin. That place is insane."

"Did you expect anything else?"

"I knew it would be different from here, but I figured once I got to know the right people, things would fall into place."

That's how it has always been for Christina, Mandy thought. Between her sweet disposition and drop-dead gorgeous looks, most people loved her. She was smart, too, but no one ever bothered to take the time to find that out.

"You weren't there long though," Mandy said softly. "Maybe you just didn't give it enough time." She cut her glance over to Christina who smoothed the side of her skirt.

"I was there long enough to realize that's not what I really want. There's so much more to being an actor than acting."

Mandy chuckled. "It's like that with everything."

"I'm sure it is, but I like it here better, where you can take people at face value and not some image they've created for the public."

"Wanna talk about Joe?" Mandy patted her sister's hand. "I understand if you don't."

"I guess I might as well tell you now," Christina said. "Joe was such a sweet guy at first. He even went to church with me, but then he got offered this really big part. Suddenly I had to take a backseat to his career, and church wasn't important to him anymore. I just never saw it coming."

"Is that why you left LA and came home—just because some guy dumped you?" The instant the words left Mandy's mouth, she regretted the harshness. "That didn't come out right."

"Nah, that's okay. I know what you're saying. It's not the whole reason, but after all the stuff I went through, it was the final straw."

They'd reached their parents' house. Mandy turned off the car and turned to face her sister. "I have to get back to the studio, and I'm working late tonight, so why don't you relax with Mom and Dad, and we'll get together tomorrow after I get off?"

"Sounds good."

As soon as they had all of Christina's bags in the foyer, Mandy left. All the way back to work, she thought about the parallel between her and Christina's lives. Both had high expectations, and now they faced disappointment due to naïveté.

Mandy found a parking spot close to the studio entrance. She took a few deep breaths before getting out of her car and heading back to work. Fortunately, her appointment hadn't arrived yet, so she had time to get the studio ready before the children came in. She headed to the back with props in one basket and candy in another.

"Are you always this organized?"

She glanced up to see Tony leaning against the studio door frame, one long leg crossed over the other, arms folded, eyes twinkling, and his lips twitching into a grin. So far, with the exception of the fact that he had the job she wanted, there was nothing about this man *not* to like.

"Makes it a lot easier to handle squirmy kids."

"No wonder you're one of the company favorites."

She lifted one eyebrow and looked at him. The fact that he was trying too hard to be nice bugged her. He glanced at her in amusement.

"Maybe you'll want to give me some pointers before I start working with the children."

Mandy paused, hand in midair. "Haven't you worked with children before?"

He shrugged. "Just a few times—but I always had their parents' help. I'd like to be able to do it on my own like you do."

Mandy shook her head. *This was so unfair.*

Then she remembered the sermon from a few weeks ago about how life wasn't fair. She swallowed hard and tried to focus on how much more Jesus had to face than she ever would.

"Will you be able to work with me, Mandy?"

She knew he'd closed some of the distance between them, but she didn't look up. "Yes, of course."

"I believe in open communication, so if there's anything you want to discuss, don't wait until it's too late."

"Too late?" She snapped her gaze to his.

"I don't want you to worry about anything. If you need to discuss something, I want you to let me know right away, instead of assuming things." His empathetic—or was it sympathetic?—expression made her stomach churn. "And now that I'm here, you don't have to take on so much responsibility."

She bristled. "Okay."

Mandy wished Tony would leave her alone to do her work. With him standing there watching, concentration was difficult.

"Just wanted to make sure." The phone rang. "I'll get that."

After he left, she quickened her pace. She adjusted the last light when Tony appeared at the door.

"Your sister needs to talk to you." He held the cordless phone toward her. "I'll finish up here."

"No need. I'm done." Mandy took the phone and walked toward the hallway leading to the offices and storage area. "I won't be long."

Christina got right to the point. "Mom wants to know if you can come for dinner."

"I don't know."

"She's making chicken fried steak and mashed potatoes and gravy."

Mandy laughed in spite of her frustration. "She sure knows how to lure me in."

"It was my idea," Christina said. "I wanted to make sure you came."

"That's very sweet, but my job—"

"I miss you, Mandy. Please come, do this for me. It'll be like old times."

Old times, where the family sat around the table, Mom at one end and Dad at the other. All the attention focused on Christina and whatever she'd been up to lately. Okay, so she was being childish.

"Let me see what I can do. One of the part-timers is scheduled to come in, so I might be able to get away."

"Call and let us know, okay?"

"Sure," Mandy said. "I gotta run. My appointment will be here any minute."

She clicked the button to disconnect and brought the phone to the office to place it back on the cradle. Tony still hadn't changed anything in the room. Even her mints remained untouched.

"Everything okay?" Tony hovered in the doorway, watching her.

She nodded. "My sister wants me to come to my parents' house for dinner. I told her I'd have to get back with her, since it's one of our late nights."

"You should go."

"Bella is scheduled to come in at four thirty, and she's pretty good with the kids."

Tony pursed his lips for a moment before speaking. "I'm perfectly capable of handling clients."

"I didn't say—"

"You and I need to sit down and come to some terms, Mandy. Yes, I understand if you have hard feelings toward me, but we'll be working together—at least until Uncle Ed thinks I'm ready for the home office. If I hadn't taken time out to join the army, I'd be where I want to be right now, but until then—"

"I don't have hard feelings." At least she didn't want to.

A sympathetic grin flashed over his lips. "Good. But we still need to talk. Maybe we can squeeze in some time between appointments."

The electronic buzzer sounded, alerting them that her appointment had arrived. "Sounds good." She took off toward the front and greeted the family. "What a pretty dress, Audrey!"

"My mommy got it for me." The little girl gestured toward her sister. "Anna got a new dress, too."

"Both of you look so nice. Come on into the studio, and we'll get started."

The girls had been to the Small World Portrait Studio before, so they knew the ropes. Mandy waved at their mother, who waved back as she sat down with a magazine. Mandy noticed Tony's eagle eyes, watching, waiting. Her hands shook until she was out of his vision.

"If we're good, do we get candy?" Anna asked.

Mandy tilted her head and nodded. "Absolutely."

Anna giggled and poked Audrey in the side. "Don't make baby faces when she takes our picture. I want candy."

If Tony hadn't made another appearance, Mandy would have commented, but he managed to render her incapable of her normal silly retorts that resulted in giggles from the kids. Instead, she lifted the multicolored toucan from the basket of props. "Say hi to Mr. Toucan."

She snapped the shot at the precise moment both girls grinned. Her next prop was a soft, brown teddy bear.

"Can I hold him?" Audrey asked as she stuck her thumb in her mouth.

Anna yanked on Audrey's hand. "Don't act like a baby, or we won't get any candy."

Fifteen minutes later, Mandy had enough shots for the girls' mother to choose from. As soon as Mandy was done, Tony lifted the basket of candy and motioned for the girls. Mandy started to tell him to hand them each one piece, but before she had a chance to say a word, they rushed toward him and knocked the basket out of his hand, sending candy flying in every direction.

Anna squealed with delight, and Audrey gathered as much as her tiny hands would hold. Anna pointed to Mandy, who gave them the sternest look she could manage. "Put it back in the basket, Audrey. Miss Mandy only lets us have one."

Audrey pouted but did as her sister told her. "I want two pieces."

Mandy sighed. "Okay, just for being such good girls and helping me pick up all this candy, you may each have two." A couple of minutes later, all the candy was back in the basket and each child had a lollipop with a safety stick. "Give me a few minutes to organize them, and you can see what we have," Mandy said to their mother.

Anna and Audrey sat down at the play center in the corner of the waiting area, while their mother continued to read her magazine. Tony joined Mandy as she organized the pictures on the computer screen.

"You're a gifted photographer," he said softly. "I only have one concern that I didn't think about until after the, um, candy incident."

She paused and turned to face him. "A concern?"

"Was it okay with your manager to bribe kids with candy? What if their parents don't approve?"

"When I suggested giving the kids little rewards, Parker said it would be okay, so we always ask the parents when we book the appointments and note it in their files. Most parents don't mind candy, but if they do, we have other thank-you rewards like stickers or age-appropriate trinkets. A little positive reinforcement can go a long way."

Tony studied her then nodded. "Sounds like you have everything under control." He shook his head and laughed. "You were good back there. I had no idea what to do."

I have control over everything but my career. "When people pay to get photos of their children, they expect us to do it right. There's such a small window of opportunity."

He lifted his eyebrows. "True."

"Do you have children?" The instant those words left her mouth, she regretted saying them. Tony's personal life wasn't any of her business. But now that she'd brought it up, she wanted to know.

It didn't seem to bother him. "Not yet." After a brief pause, he added, "I'd like to someday, though—when the right person comes along."

"Sorry, it's none of my business." She cast her glance downward.

"That's okay, Mandy. We'll be working closely, and I don't mind if you ask personal questions."

He obviously hadn't read the same manual as Parker, the former manager, who felt that work should be all business and personal lives should remain at home. That had taken some getting used to, but she'd adapted and appreciated it after he quit. Not knowing much about the man had been a blessing when she didn't feel anything but the combination of annoyance that he'd left without warning and relief that he was gone.

After she had all the pictures arranged and the girls' mother had chosen those she wanted made into prints, Tony encouraged Mandy to call her sister back and accept the dinner invitation. "After I get back to Atlanta, you better believe I won't turn down a good meal," he said with a smile.

Maybe she should stay at the studio and send Tony to her parents' house instead. The thought flickered through her mind so quickly she caught herself smiling.

"I'm glad I made you smile," he said. "Now go on and have fun with your family. We'll be fine here."

She nodded then looked pointedly at her watch. "It's not time yet."

"Committed to your job." He paused and looked at her. "Every manager's dream."

She didn't want to be the manager's dream; she wanted to be the manager. All kinds of sarcastic thoughts darted around in her mind, but she knew enough to keep them to herself.

Christina answered the phone when Mandy called to accept the dinner invitation. "I am so excited! It'll be like old times."

"Yeah. Old times."

She'd barely hung up the phone when Tony walked up. "Everything okay?" The look on his face was one of concern.

"Sure." She smoothed the sides of her pants. "Thanks for giving me some time off this evening."

"It's not exactly time off," he reminded her. "You've already worked more than forty hours this week. I don't want you getting burned out."

"I don't think my work is suffering."

"That's not what I'm saying." His instant seriousness disarmed her.

Mandy had to clear her throat. "I've always been committed to my job," she said softly. "I don't mind working long hours." She left out the fact that she didn't have anything or anyone to go home to.

He chewed on his bottom lip for a few seconds. "That's going to change. From now on, you'll only work forty hours. If my uncle or cousin saw you were still working long hours, they would be upset with both of us."

"I understand."

He looked at her then nodded.

She would have preferred his job—not fewer hours. "I have work to do." She turned around and walked away, leaving him standing there alone. It took the rest of the time in the studio to calm down, and when it was time to leave, she stuck her head in his office. "I'm going now."

He narrowed his eyes and nodded without saying a word. That was just fine with Mandy.

When she got to her parents' house, she was annoyed even more that their mother was treating Christina like a child. Occasionally Mandy caught Christina studying her as if seeing her for the first time.

"What?" Mandy finally asked.

Christina tilted her head and pouted. "You're mad at me, aren't you?"

"No." Mandy realized she was taking her frustrations out on her sister. "It's just that work, well—"

"You work entirely too many hours. You need to get out and have some fun." Their mother looked at Christina. "Perhaps the two of you can find something interesting to do."

"Sounds good to me," Christina said.

"Now that we have a new manager, I'll have more time. He's trying to cut back on overtime."

"You have a new man in your office?" Their mother leaned forward and grinned. "Is he single?"

"Mo—om," Mandy groaned. "He's my boss. That's it."

"You never know," Mom said. "Lots of women meet their future husbands at the office."

Maybe so, but Mandy would be willing to bet those future husbands didn't steal the jobs those women wanted. "Let's just drop this, okay?"

After dinner, Mandy automatically started clearing the table. Christina was about to go into the living room, until she locked gazes with Mandy. She pursed her lips then lifted some dishes and followed Mandy into the kitchen.

"You don't have to do that," their mother said. "You just got home."

Mandy held her breath, waiting for Christina to put everything down. To her surprise, Christina shook her head. "I don't want Mandy stuck with the cleanup. It'll go faster if I help." She made a shooing gesture. "Why don't you go hang out with Dad while Mandy and I load the dishwasher?"

After their mother left, Christina turned to Mandy. "Now I get why you always acted the way you did."

Mandy had been about to stick the flatware in the tray. She stopped and looked at Christina. "What are you talking about?"

Christina frowned. "I always thought you were jealous of me."

Chapter 3

Y ou're kidding, right?" Mandy glared at Christina then rolled her eyes. "I don't think so."

Christina persisted. "Mom and Dad don't expect as much from me as they do you."

"Why would that make me jealous?"

"That's what I want to know," Christina said. "I always wished I could be as smart as you."

"So while you thought I was jealous of you, you were actually jealous of me?"

Christina made a face. "Something like that. Weird, huh?"

Mandy shrugged. "I dunno. Sibling relationships can be complicated, I suppose."

"I want you to know how much I appreciate you."

That simple comment caused a lump to form in Mandy's throat. She swallowed hard. "Thank you."

"I mean it. When we were little, you always made sure people were nice to me. Then when I started high school, you and your friends were so helpful."

"We didn't exactly travel in the same circles," Mandy reminded her. "Your friends were a lot cooler than mine."

"But yours were smarter, and look at them now."

Mandy cast a comical glance at Christina. "Uh-huh, right. Ya know, there were times I would have traded smart for pretty."

"You're just as pretty, but you never noticed." Christina shrugged. "But that's not the point. I had the best of both worlds—my circle of friends and yours."

Mandy bobbed her head. "True."

Christina gave Mandy a playful shove. "You don't have to be so agreeable."

Mandy smiled and picked up a towel. "If we don't agree, you know who'll win." She winked and pointed her thumb to her chest. "*Moi.*"

Silence fell between them as they finished doing the dishes. Mandy was about to say good-bye when Christina's eyes lit up.

"Hey, I have an idea! Why don't you spend the night?"

"I have to work tomorrow," Mandy said. "Maybe some other time, and I'll bring my stuff."

"Small World doesn't even open until ten. You can go home in the morning to get ready for work. Mom always keeps extra toothbrushes."

"I don't know."

Christina tilted her head and gave Mandy one of her irresistible puppy-dog looks. "Please?"

Mandy laughed. "You still have it, baby sister. Okay, I'll stay."

Christina didn't bother trying to hide her joy. She pumped her fist, grinning. "I knew you couldn't say no. Let's watch one of our old movies. I'll get Mom to make popcorn, and we can have a party."

Mandy tilted her head forward. "I think we're perfectly capable of making our own popcorn. Let's show Mom how grown up you can be."

"Sorry. It's so easy to fall back into old habits around Mom and Dad."

"Especially since they still want to baby you." Mandy was proud of Christina for acknowledging the truth. "Are you planning to stick around and get a job here in Wheeling?"

"Looks like I don't have a choice," Christina admitted. "I obviously don't have what it takes to be an actress. I thought all I'd have to do was go into an audition, say a few lines, and walk around the stage. It's a lot harder than it looks." She crinkled her nose. "Plus they want actors to do all kinds of other stuff that's totally not fun, like talk shows and interviews and stuff."

"I understand."

Christina leaned against the kitchen counter and looked down at the floor, shaking her head. "I have no idea what I want to do now though. All I ever wanted was to be an actress."

Mandy gave her sister a sympathetic pat on the shoulder. "I know, sweetie, but things don't always turn out like we expect. I'm going through my own disappointment now, and it's not fun. I always thought I'd be in a high-level management position that commanded respect, but instead I'm working for the boss's nephew." She got in her sister's line of view. "We'll get through this. Let's go find a movie."

❧

Tony arrived at the studio an hour before they opened. He expected Mandy to be there, or at least follow soon after. She was such a dedicated employee, he started to worry when he looked at the clock fifteen minutes before opening time and she still hadn't arrived.

As he worked on getting the front ready for customers, he thought about how good Mandy was with the children. He even caught himself thinking what a good mother she'd be someday, and then he quickly forced those inappropriate thoughts from his mind.

Every few minutes, he opened the front door to look down the street but still no Mandy. He checked the phone messages, and there was nothing from her. Just as he was about to look up her number, he saw her approach the door.

Her short blond hair glistened as she walked in and glided across the floor. He loved the flicker of acknowledgment in her hazel eyes when she glanced in his direction. Tony couldn't ignore the fact that he was immensely attracted to Mandy Pruitt.

"Sorry I'm late," she said. "I stayed at my parents' house, so I had to go home and get ready for work this morning."

"You're not late."

"I like to get here early to prepare."

"Everything's all done." He glanced at his watch and nodded toward the back. "Why don't you go put your stuff in the office, and I'll open?"

As soon as she walked to the back, Tony relaxed his shoulders. *Lord, please don't let me step over the line with Mandy.*

An awkward silence fell between them. At ten thirty, the phone rang.

"Mandy," Christina said, "Mom says Dad wants me to get a job right away, but I have no idea where to start looking."

"Why don't you call some of your old friends and see if they know of any job openings?" Mandy rested the phone on her shoulder while she slipped the envelope from the last client into the file slot.

"They all work in boring office jobs. I want something fun."

"Then why don't you try some of the shops in town? You like fashion."

"I don't know," Christina said.

"You'll even get a discount."

"I'll think about it."

A shadow at the doorway drew Mandy's attention. She glanced up to see Tony leaning against the door frame, watching her. "I gotta go. I'll call you later." She pressed the END button on the phone and looked him directly in the eye. "Did you need something?"

"What time is your first appointment?"

"Eleven. Why?"

"Just checking. What do you normally do between appointments?"

Why was he grilling her? She bristled at the very thought of having someone standing over her, expecting the worst, since every minute of time she'd spent at the studio was focused on work—at least it was until her sister came back to town.

"I do follow-up and make calls," she replied. "Did you have something else you wanted me to do?"

He shook his head as he pulled away from where he'd been leaning. "You're doing everything right. In fact the folks in the home office are impressed by how well this location has done without a manager."

Then why did they send Tony? She kept her thoughts to herself. "I follow the guidelines from my training."

"That's another thing," he said. "We're in the process of overhauling the training program. Apparently some of the managers think it has some antiquated concepts."

Mandy thought for a moment. "I think it can use some updating, but the basic concepts are good." She shrugged. "At least they work for me."

Tony glanced at his watch. "I need to let you go get ready for your appointment. We can discuss this later. If you have some suggestions, I'm sure Edward and Ricco would appreciate input from a *successful* employee."

As Mandy prepared the studio for her next appointment, she thought about Tony's comments. If she'd been such a successful employee, as he'd put it, why had they brought him here? She slammed the basket of props on the tiny table next to the camera, sending a few skittering over the edge and across the floor, then instantly regretted it. Not getting to even apply for the promotion didn't justify bad behavior—and she certainly didn't need to let Tony see her acting out.

"Drop something?" When she glanced up, she saw Tony standing six feet away, holding one of the stuffed animals from the basket.

Lord, please work on my attitude and spirit. You know what I need and what I should have. I need to trust You more with my future.

He gestured over his shoulder. "Your appointment's here."

She took a deep breath and slowly let it out. She needed to maintain a positive attitude for her clients—especially since these were some of the most difficult preschoolers she'd ever worked with.

It took several attempts to get the children to calm down, but Mandy finally managed to capture some cute poses. Their mother was frantic as she crossed the studio floor and took the hands of her three- and four-year-old. "I'm so sorry they can't sit still. I do everything the doctor says, including not let them have sugar, but they won't stop wiggling."

Mandy sympathized with the young mother. "Maybe they'll grow up to become athletes."

The woman looked at both of her children then offered a grateful look to Mandy. "That would be nice."

She heard Tony's footsteps as he entered the studio. "You have a visitor," he said. "It's your sister."

"Thanks, I'll be there in a few minutes."

"I can take over," he offered. Mandy looked him in the eye, and they both smiled. "Maybe not." Still grinning, he headed for the door.

After he left, the children's mother ushered her kids toward the front. "I'll take them for a little walk while you get the computer proofs ready."

"Thanks. Come back in half an hour, and I'll have them done."

After they left, Mandy straightened up for the next session before going to see what Christina wanted. When she arrived in the lobby, she was surprised to see Christina and Tony engrossed in a conversation about her parents. "You wouldn't believe how good our mother's cooking is. Maybe you can come for dinner sometime."

Mandy cringed. She needed to get her sister out of there—and fast!

Tony offered Mandy an amused look and winked. "I just might. That is, if Mandy doesn't mind."

Christina looked at Mandy, clasped her hands, and put them beneath her chin. "Can you go have coffee with me?"

"I don't normally take a break," Mandy said. "What's up?"

"It's okay if you need to take a break," Tony offered. "I can show the proofs."

"No," Mandy said. "I'd like to do that."

Tony winked at Mandy then turned to Christina. "After a little fiasco with a basket of candy and a couple of starving kids, she doesn't trust me here alone."

"That's not—"

She stopped when she noticed the smirk on Tony's face.

"Why don't I go to that cute little boutique on the corner, and I'll come back for you later?" Christina said.

"Can you give me about an hour?"

"Um. . .sure."

After Christina left, Mandy quickly organized the proofs on the computer screen. The children and their mother arrived shortly afterward.

"I like all of them," the young mother said. "You're the only photographer who's been able to make them look like normal kids rather than little monsters."

"Monster!" As soon as he hollered the word, the four-year-old lifted his hands with bent fingers to look like claws and started chasing his little sister around the waiting area.

The mother rolled her eyes. "Why don't we just go with the first three? I'd like the economy package."

Mandy smiled. "Sounds great."

Tony cleared his throat, but Mandy forced herself to ignore him. She knew he was trying to get her to upsell the customer—something the company put high on their list of priorities.

Once the mom and her children left, Mandy finished the order then turned to Tony. "I never try to upsell her because they come in every three months and get the economy package. She can barely afford that."

"You don't even try?" he asked.

"I did once, and I thought she might break down and cry when she had to tell me they couldn't afford what she really wanted."

Tony pursed his lips. By the time he finally nodded his agreement, she was ready to argue. "You did the right thing. There is a line we shouldn't cross at the risk of losing good customers." He gestured toward the door. "Your sister's back. Why don't you go for coffee?"

Christina stood by the door twirling her bright yellow handbag. Mandy blinked. She'd had a tan one earlier.

"C'mon, I can't take too long."

"Don't look now, but that guy from the electronics store across the street is staring at us," Christina said.

Mandy groaned. "That's Brent. He gets these crushes on people, and it's my turn."

Christina giggled. "He's cute in a geeky sort of way."

"Yeah, he's not bad-looking, and he's pretty nice, but he can be annoying."

As they got farther away from the studio and the electronics store, Mandy pointed to the bag. "New purse?"

"Yes, isn't it cute?" Christina held it up for Mandy to get a better look. "I saw it in the store window, and I had to have it." She held it up for Mandy to touch. "Feel it."

Mandy gently slid her hand over the soft, pebbled leather. "Very nice. Feels like real leather."

"Lambskin."

"I thought you were broke."

"Dad gave me some money."

"He did?" Mandy asked. An odd feeling swept over her—a blend of shock and sibling rivalry. "To go shopping? Does he know what you're doing with the money?"

Christina slowly shook her head. "Please don't say anything."

"How about reimbursing me for the plane ticket? You said you were going to."

"Um. . .I'll do that after I get all settled." Christina gave Mandy a sheepish look. "Dad said it was to get me through until I found a job."

"I don't think he intended for you to go on a shopping spree." As they approached the coffee shop, Mandy dug her wallet out of her modest bag. "I'll treat this time. Just please don't keep spending his money on things you don't absolutely have to have."

The instant they sat down, Christina's eyes lit up. "Why didn't you tell me your new boss was so cute?"

"He's my *boss*. I don't think of him that way."

Christina rolled her eyes. "C'mon, we're sisters. You're not blind."

"I really don't want to talk about my boss."

"That's just silly," Christina said. "If he were my boss—"

"He's not your boss, so don't worry about it," Mandy interrupted.

For the next fifteen minutes, Christina talked about how she'd called all her old friends, and they didn't have time to talk because they were so busy. "I can't believe no one has time for me anymore."

"Work has a way of doing that to people," Mandy said. "Did you ask anyone if they knew of a job?"

"No. I don't think any of their jobs sound like fun."

"While you were shopping, did you ask if they had openings?"

Christina frowned. "Not yet. Why are you grilling me so hard?"

"Because I think Mom and Dad are right. It's time for you to get a job."

"Okay, okay." Christina held up her hands. "I didn't expect you to be so grouchy."

Mandy glanced at her watch. "I need to get back to the studio now. While you're here, why don't you walk around and see if you can fill out at least one application for work? There are so many businesses, one of them is bound to be hiring."

Still frowning, Christina nodded. "All right. I'll try, but there aren't that many jobs out there."

"Just ask. That's all I'm saying. If you keep trying, you'll eventually get a job."

When they got back to Small World, Tony glanced up. "Did you two have fun?"

"A blast," Mandy said sarcastically.

Tony blinked in confusion before turning to Christina. "It was nice meeting you."

"Same here," she said. "Um, Mandy, I don't have anything to wear to church, and Mom said she wants me to go with you."

"How about all those clothes in your overstuffed suitcases?"

Christina flicked her hand from the wrist. "Those are LA clothes. Mom says they're not appropriate for church here."

Since Christina was a good four inches taller and at least two sizes smaller, Mandy couldn't very well offer to lend her one of her dresses. "Why don't you use some of Dad's money to get a new outfit? I'm sure he wouldn't mind."

Christina glanced down at her shoes—which probably cost more than Mandy's entire outfit—before looking back. "I used it all on the purse—and these shoes."

Rather than cause a scene in front of her boss, she pulled some money from her own bag and thrust it at her sister. "You can pay me back when you get a job."

"Thanks." Christina looked at the wad of money then frowned. "I'll have to find something on sale." She paused then broke into a grin. "It'll be fun—sort of like an Easter egg hunt."

Mandy was embarrassed that this happened in front of Tony, but it was too late. After Christina left, she turned to Tony.

"Sorry about that. My sister is very sweet, but being the baby, Mom, Dad, and I gave in to her a lot."

He chuckled. "I understand. I have a baby sister, too."

"We have three sessions scheduled for this afternoon, so I'll get the studio ready."

"Before you do that, Mandy, I have a question."

She stopped and turned to face him. "Okay."

He rubbed his chin and studied the floor. "Your sister mentioned going to church with you." He looked up and directly into her eyes. "I've been looking for a church home. Where do you go?"

Chapter 4

Mandy was caught off guard. It never dawned on her that Tony might be a Christian.

"It's okay if you don't want to tell me," he said. "I understand if you don't want me to go to your church."

She felt terrible. "No, I'm okay with it." She reached for a slip of paper and jotted down the church address. "We have Sunday services at nine and eleven, with Bible classes in between."

He took the paper and looked at it for a few seconds then met her gaze. "Thanks, Mandy. I'll be there on Sunday morning, probably first service."

"That's when I go," she said. "I've always been sort of an early bird."

"Me, too."

As soon as Mandy got to the camera area, she felt like kicking herself. What did he care if she was an early bird? He wasn't her friend; he was her boss.

※

Tony loved that Mandy was a Christian. Even though Small World was founded and owned by Christians, they didn't limit themselves in who they hired, as long as the applicant's references and backgrounds checked out. Their philosophy was to be a shining example from management on down, knowing Christ would do all the work to win hearts.

※

Mandy had had back-to-back appointments until late afternoon, when Tony joined her at the camera. "Bella just called in sick," he said.

"She was supposed to close tonight."

"I know. She also had an appointment scheduled right when you were supposed to leave."

Inwardly groaning, Mandy thought about how exhausted she was. But she didn't want to let on to Tony, so she squared her shoulders. "That's fine. I don't mind closing."

He shook his head. "Let's split the responsibility. If you don't mind taking her client while I go grab a quick bite at the deli, I'll close."

"But—"

"You're not in this alone anymore, Mandy," he said firmly.

Mandy's gaze locked with Tony's. His kindness filled her with warmth. She quickly looked away. "Okay, that's fine."

Tony waited around until her appointment arrived, then he left with a wave. "I'll get my food and bring it back here," he said.

"You don't have to—" His expression stopped her, midsentence. "Okay."

Once again, he held her gaze a couple of seconds longer than necessary, causing her insides to feel as though they were plummeting to the floor. She looked away to regain her focus.

As difficult as it was to admit, he'd been kind and fair from the moment they first met—even though he did seem a bit grouchy at first. If he'd been a dictatorial jerk, it would have been easier to justify being angry at the company.

The buzzer on the door sounded, alerting her to the next client appointment. After she assured the parents everything would be okay and letting them know they could even watch from the door, she began positioning the children for their photos. Her notes stated that they weren't allowed candy, so she pulled out some of the more colorful props to get their attention. It took her forty-five minutes to get a half-dozen good shots.

After she finished, she ushered the children back to their waiting parents. "Give me a half hour to put this together, and you can choose the package you like," she said.

The father looked pleased. "Last time we had studio portraits done, we had to wait weeks for the proofs."

His wife laughed. "I forgot to tell my husband this is all high-tech now."

Mandy grinned. "You'll have the finished package in just a few days."

"That's wonderful," the children's father said. He slapped one of the company brochures on his palm. "And from what I've seen of your prices, we can come here often as the kids grow up."

She heard a rustling sound from the office down the hall, letting her know that Tony had slipped back into the studio sometime while she was photographing the children. After the family left, he joined her.

"Why don't you head on out now, Mandy? I'll stick around until closing."

"Are you okay with walk-ins?" The instant those words left her mouth, she remembered she wasn't in charge. He was the manager, not her, and if he wasn't okay, he'd have to deal with the consequences.

He didn't seem fazed. "I'm fine. Remember, they put me through the crash course. I'm sure I'm not as good as you, but I don't think anyone is." He grinned and winked. "At least now I know what to do if some kid gets out of control and sends candy flying. Your family is waiting."

Mandy smiled. "If things get crazy, call, okay?" She grabbed her purse and made a beeline for the door, where she stopped, turned, and faced Tony, who stood behind the counter, head down, focused on some of the reply cards from their last mailing.

When he glanced up, the look of consternation on his face touched her heart. "Need something?" he asked.

"No, I'm fine. I just wanted to. . ." She licked her lips and smiled. "I wanted to thank you for being so understanding." Then she ran out the door before he had a chance to say a word.

She was at her parents' house in just a few minutes, and her mother pointed to the table. "Set a place for yourself, dear."

Dinnertime conversation centered on Christina's lack of a job, which was typical, but now it suited Mandy just fine. However, right before dessert, her father put down his fork and leaned toward Mandy. "Have you discussed that promotion with the company executives?" he asked.

Mandy had been perfectly content not being in the limelight, but with such a direct question, she had to answer. "No, but that's a moot point now. They put a family member in charge."

"They might not have known you were interested," he said. "Did you ever tell anyone?"

"Well, yes, but I was told to apply as soon as they posted the position." She squirmed in her chair. "They never posted it."

"Mandy, hon, I know you like to play by the rules, but sometimes the rules don't apply."

Christina had been quiet, but now she nodded her agreement. "Yeah, you really do need to let people know you're not a doormat. Show them what you're made of. Maybe if you dressed a little nicer—"

"Christina," their father said with a warning tone, "you're not exactly the voice of authority on gainful employment."

"But—"

Their dad cut Christina off. "I think your sister knows better than you do."

"It would definitely help if she had clothes that didn't make her invisible," Christina said.

"Stay out. . . ," Mandy said before glancing down at her plate. This was exactly what she dreaded.

"Okay," Christina said, holding up her hands. "But at least you can step up the wardrobe a bit."

Their mother grinned. "I think Mandy looks professional."

"Professional—yes," Christina agreed. "But boring. What's wrong with adding a splash of color here and there, or carrying a great handbag to let people know she's important?"

Mandy shook her head. "I don't need a handbag that costs more than most people's mortgage to feel important."

Christina shrugged. "Maybe not, but you definitely need something." She smiled at Mandy. "Next time you go shopping, take me with you and I'll get you out of your rut."

"I think you need to let your supervisor know that you'd like to move up with the company," their dad said, ignoring Christina. "It's his job to relay that information and make sure you have all the tools you need."

Mandy nodded to close the conversation. "Okay, I'll do that."

After she finished helping clear the table, Mandy gave her mother a hug. "Thanks for the food. I really need to go home now."

Her mother followed her to the door and gave her a pleading look. "Please, Mandy? Help your sister—for the family. Christina will be much happier in the long run if she has a good job with her own paycheck."

Mandy couldn't argue. "Okay. Just give me a day or two to think about what I can do."

Before her mother had a chance to say anything else, Mandy took off. All the way to her apartment, she thought about how to help her sister.

Even though Mandy and Christina had the same basic features and people could tell they were sisters, there was a huge difference between them. Christina's blond hair was brighter, and she wore it long, to the middle of her back, while Mandy kept hers cut short to keep it out of her face. They had the same shape of eyes, but Christina framed her blue eyes with black eyeliner and mascara, while Mandy barely swiped her eyelashes with a stroke or two of brown mascara to complement her hazel eyes.

Once she reached her apartment, she locked the door, kicked off her shoes, and flopped onto the sofa. Then she turned on the lamp and picked up the book she'd been reading. As her eyelids drooped, she allowed herself to fall asleep right where she was. The next morning, she awoke with a crick in her neck and her rumpled top twisted around her torso.

With three hours to get ready, Mandy decided to take a long shower and spend a little more time on her makeup. Christina had given her one of the free makeup bags last time she'd been to the cosmetics counter, so she had a trial tube of black mascara and some shiny, tinted lip gloss. The image that stared back from the mirror was in stark contrast to her usual plain look.

Mandy was tempted to wash it all off and start over. She reached for her washrag then stopped. No, she'd keep her clown face on for the day. The children wouldn't care, and the only other people who'd see her were their parents and Tony. The parents were always so frazzled, so she didn't worry about them. Tony, on the other hand. . .

Okay, the last thing she needed to worry about was Tony. Even if he thought she looked ridiculous, so what? She wasn't trying to impress him.

Next, she went to her closet and inspected the contents. Three pairs of black pants, a brown pair, and a couple of khakis were on the left side. She had three skirts—a black pencil skirt, a muted floral tulip skirt, and a brown A-line. Her tops were equally boring, with mostly neutral colors and basic styling. Even the way she organized her closet was boring, with groupings of sleeveless, short-sleeved, and long-sleeved lined up in order of light to dark—white, tan, brown, and black being the predominant colors. On a whim, she'd bought a red cardigan, but the tags still hung from the sleeve, and it was shoved all the way to the end of the rack.

She reached for her typical black slacks and white top. Then, after only a slight hesitation, she grabbed the red cardigan and yanked off the tags. It was time to step outside her narrow box and take chances.

Mandy got in her car and drove to the studio. As she came to a traffic light, she glanced in the mirror over her visor and shook her head. She felt silly about fretting over her makeup and wardrobe.

Shop lights along the street were still dim when she arrived, since most of the businesses hadn't opened yet. A few groups of seniors sat at the tables outside the coffee shop down the street, chatting and enjoying each other's company. Mandy scurried past them, head down, hoping none of the familiar ones would notice her. She was glad when no one called out to her.

She slipped inside the studio and went through her normal routine of putting her purse in the office and setting up for their first customers. The sound of shuffling papers in the manager's office alerted her that Tony was in, but she didn't want to face him yet.

Five minutes before opening time, Tony appeared on the other side of the counter from where she stood. He stared at her for several seconds before she looked up.

His eyebrows shot up. "You look very nice, Mandy."

"Thank you." Her voice squeaked, so she cleared her throat.

"Is something special going on today that I need to know about?"

"No."

"Red is a good color for you," he continued.

Mandy didn't know what else to say, so she repeated her thanks and changed the subject. "We have several appointments today, and both studios are booked after Bella gets here."

"Oh, Bella called in. She's still sick, and I have to leave for a meeting at the regional office." He offered a smile. "But I called and left a message for Steve to come in."

Mandy nodded. "Good. Thanks."

"We need to hire someone else. I don't know how you've held up as well as you have, but this isn't a good situation."

The phone rang. It was Steve calling to say he couldn't come in because he was studying for finals.

Mandy looked over the schedule and figured out a way to handle all the clients. She only had to call one and reschedule, and they agreed without any problem.

After her first appointment left, Tony handed her a slip of paper with the message, *Your mom called, and she'd like you to call ASAP.*

Mandy took it and went to the smaller of the two offices. Her mother answered after the first ring.

"I'm sending Christina over to see you."

"That's fine but not now. This isn't a good time," Mandy said. "Today's schedule is crazy. I have to work late and handle an extra load."

"You really need to help us out on this. Your father is upset that she's not out looking for a job, and I told him I'd have you talk to her during your lunch break. She listens to you."

Mandy felt the weight of the world on her shoulders as her mother explained what she wanted her to do. Finally, she agreed and hung up.

Tony appeared at the doorway right when she was leaving. His expression turned to one of concern. "You okay?"

"I'm fine. My sister is having a hard time finding a job, and my mom wants me to talk to her during lunch."

He grinned. "I think it's good that you and your sister are close like that. Why don't you take an extra hour for lunch, since I'll be here and you'll have to handle everything by yourself tonight?"

"Thanks."

Mandy had one more photo shoot before lunchtime. When she finished, she went out to the front in time to see her sister standing at the counter, with Tony grinning.

Chapter 5

Mandy turned to Tony. "You did say I could take extra time, right?"

"Absolutely. In fact, if you need even more time, I'll be here until three."

Christina's eyes lit up. "Maybe we can get in a little shopping."

Mandy glanced back and forth between Christina and Tony. "No shopping, Christina. An extra hour is plenty."

Once they were out the door, Christina glanced toward the electronics store. "Where's that cute guy?"

"If you're talking about Brent, he's there somewhere, probably waiting on a customer."

"Maybe I'll go there later and let him wait on me."

"Christina. That's an electronics store."

"What are you saying?"

"You're not exactly a technical genius."

"I can buy electronics as well as the next person."

Based on Mandy's experience with her sister, there was no doubt she could buy *anything* as well as the next person. "I'm sure you can—if you have the money."

"Your boss is *so* cute!" Christina stopped and turned Mandy to face her. "Don't tell me you haven't noticed his cuteness."

Mandy shrugged but wouldn't meet her sister's eye. "He's okay, I guess."

"Okay?" Christina snickered. "Girl, you need some serious man-finding lessons."

"I'm not looking for a man."

"Oh, come on. Don't give me that. You used to tell me that you wanted a traditional marriage, with kids, a house, and"—Christina waved her arms—"the whole kit and caboodle."

"One of these days, yeah."

"One of these days is here, Mandy. Open your eyes. You'll be thirty in a couple of years, and the man of your dreams just might be standing in front of you every day."

"Tony's my boss. He doesn't count."

"Sure he counts." Christina grunted. "He's cute and nice. He's probably a Christian, since he asked about churches."

"Yeah, well. . ."

"Don't let a good one get away without at least exploring the possibilities."

Mandy shook her head. "I can't risk losing my job."

"You won't lose your job. He values you too much."

"I don't know about that. He seems annoyed."

"That's because he wanted his family to give him a better job."

Had he actually told her that? She thought of the chatty men at the airport. Mandy let the comment slide. "How am I supposed to, um. . .as you put it, explore possibilities without making a fool of myself?"

"Just keep your eyes open for opportunities to let him know you're interested."

Easy for Christina—guy magnet from way back—to say. "Nah, I'm not interested."

Ignoring her, Christina started making plans. "First, we need to get you some decent clothes."

"What's wrong with my clothes?"

Christina tilted her head and gave her a you're-kidding look. "I've already told you. Bo–ring."

"I'm wearing a red cardigan." Mandy lifted her head slightly as she pulled the sweater together in front.

"*And* black mascara *and* shiny lipstick." Christina nudged her and smiled. "Yes, I noticed."

During lunch, Mandy managed to turn the conversation back to Christina's job hunt. "Did you revamp your résumé to fill in some of those gaps I mentioned?"

Christina nodded. "Yes, and I included the volunteer work you reminded me of. Who would've thought to do that?"

"That's work, and it shows that you didn't just sit around all that time," Mandy said. "And it shows that you care about others."

"True." Christina tapped her finger on her chin. "I'm just not sure where to start."

"How about the places where you love to shop?" Mandy said.

"I'm not so sure about mixing business with pleasure."

Mandy couldn't help but laugh. "There's nothing wrong with selling what you love."

Christina's eyes lit up, and a wide smile broadened her face. "I'll start with that electronics store!"

"You might want to—"

"It's perfect, Mandy! I'll walk up to that cute, geeky guy and ask if he's the manager."

"But he's—"

Christina held up her hand. "Don't tell me anything about him. I don't want to lie."

Mandy settled back in her chair. She might as well accept Christina's scheme, so she smiled back. "Okay, so start there, but don't limit yourself."

"Oh, trust me, I won't." A smile played on Christina's lips. "Ideas are popping into my head all over the place. This job search thing might be fun."

"Whatever you're up to, remember that your main goal is to find employment." Mandy paused and gave her sister a serious look. "Not a man."

"Well that's all fine and good, but if the Lord gives me an opportunity to meet a man, who am I to turn Him down?"

"Since you put it that way, you're right." Mandy opened her hand. "Mind if I take a look at your new résumé?"

Christina opened the envelope and pulled out a stark white sheet of paper with bulleted lists, just as Mandy had told her to do. "I still don't understand why I shouldn't use fragranced pink paper."

Mandy studied the new résumé and was impressed. "Very nice. You did everything I recommended."

"I'm not stupid," Christina said. "I might be better than you with fashion, but you have it all over me in the business department."

"If you keep this up"—Mandy thumped the paper—"you'll be a business whiz, too."

Christina's eyes crinkled as she grinned. "Thanks, sis."

Mandy knew the Lord was working in their lives, but she wasn't sure what He was doing. She watched Christina put the résumé back in the folder. As flighty as her sister seemed, there actually was some depth to her. The biggest problem was that no one ever expected much from her. Or maybe that was a good thing.

Tony heard the buzzer on the door, so he hopped out of his chair and left the manager's office. It was Brent, the guy he'd met the day before when he stopped by the electronics store across the street for a new phone charger.

"Hey! How's the new job?" Brent asked.

"It's going great." Tony leaned against the counter. "What can I help you with?"

Brent pointed toward the street. "Who was that hot-looking girl I saw Mandy leave with?"

"Her sister, Christina," Tony replied. "I thought you were interested in Mandy."

"I was, but now that I've seen her sister, I think I'm in love."

"With Christina?"

Brent snickered. "Yeah. Think you can arrange for us to meet?"

Tony barely knew Brent, and he was fairly certain that Christina was a Christian. He didn't want to participate in anything that might backfire. "Why don't you talk to Mandy?"

"That would be weird. I've been trying to get a date with her for months, so she might not understand."

"Yeah, that could be awkward." Tony fought the urge to ask Brent why he'd changed his mind, since Mandy was just as pretty and obviously an amazing woman. He spotted the sisters slowing down in front of the electronics store. Mandy said something then waved as Christina entered the store. "Don't look now, but I think you have a customer."

"That's okay. Matt's there."

"So is Christina," Tony said. "And Mandy's on her way here."

Brent shuffled around in time to face Mandy as she entered the studio. "Hi there, gorgeous!"

Mandy's face reddened. "Uh, hi, Brent."

"Gotta run," he said. "Can't keep the customers waiting."

After he left, Tony pondered how much to tell Mandy. He figured it wouldn't hurt to lay it all on the line. "Brent came here to ask about Christina. He wants to meet her."

Mandy smiled. "Christina thinks he's cute, so this should be interesting."

"Not to be nosy, but what do you know about Brent? Do you think he's a decent guy?"

"I think so—just a little unpolished and slightly annoying, maybe, but he's sweet and harmless."

"Good. I wouldn't want Christina to get herself in a bad position with someone."

Mandy tilted her head and gave him an odd look he couldn't decipher. "Why would you be so concerned about my sister?"

Tony couldn't answer that—even to himself. He was the manager of Small World, not a bodyguard. He couldn't let on how he felt about Mandy so quickly, or she'd think he was taking advantage of his position.

"I just like to see men respect women, that's all," he said.

She narrowed her gaze to study him, and then she nodded. "Okay, sounds honorable. I need to set up for the next appointment." With that, she disappeared around the wall separating the lobby from the back, leaving him alone, pondering what was happening.

From the moment he first laid eyes on Mandy Pruitt, he couldn't help but notice the combination of beauty, grace, professionalism—and skepticism toward him, which he found intriguing. Some of the resentment for having to take a job at studio level subsided as he got to know Mandy. The reaction to Christina's presence by Brent and a couple of other men who worked in surrounding stores had amazed him. They were all in awe of Christina, overlooking the sister Tony found more attractive.

Tony shook himself. He needed a swift kick to the backside for even thinking thoughts like that. Mandy was his employee, and he had no business thinking of her in such an unprofessional way.

· He had to leave soon, so he made sure Mandy had what she needed. She barely glanced at him when she nodded.

"You know I'll be fine."

"Sorry if I insulted you."

"You didn't."

Except his heart wouldn't slow down when she met his gaze. He looked away. "Good. I'll have my cell phone on vibrate, so if you need me—"

"I doubt if I'll need you. Go on, or you'll be late."

Rather than argue anymore, he took off toward the parking lot. He'd barely gotten past the electronics store when he heard his name. He spun around to see Christina running to catch up.

"Did you meet Brent?" he asked.

She tossed her hair over one shoulder. "Yes. So how's everything going back at Small World?"

"Great. Your sister is a dynamo at running the place single-handedly."

"She has experience." Her tone instantly changed.

"Does she..." He caught himself before asking a personal question about Mandy.

Christina laughed. "Does she what?"

"Never mind." Tony slowed down, and Christina glanced at him before meeting his stride. "Are you upset about something?" he asked.

"No," she said quickly. "But I have to admit, my sister deserves to be the manager."

"We have other plans for her future."

"Other plans?" she said with sarcasm. "They better be good ones, or I'm sure another company will snatch her right up."

"I'll keep that in mind." He certainly didn't want to lose Mandy.

"Good." She laughed. "Fortunately for you, Mandy doesn't hold grudges like I do. She says I need to move on and not let other people get me down, but I can't help it, no matter how much I pray about it." When she stopped talking, he glanced over at her in time to see her chew on her bottom lip. She blinked before looking back at him then smiled. "You're a Christian, right?"

"Yes," he said. "I have been all my life."

"Us, too. Our parents said they couldn't always give us the things we wanted, but they fed us, made sure we had plenty of love, and took us to church every Sunday."

He wanted to ask more questions about Mandy, but this didn't seem like the right time. "Your family sounds quite a bit like mine," he said as they reached the parking lot. "I gotta run, but maybe we can resume this conversation at another time, okay?"

She nodded. "Don't tell my sister I blabbed so much. She hates when I can't keep my mouth shut."

That was a good thing to know for the future—in case he couldn't find out about Mandy on his own. He offered what he hoped was a reassuring grin. "Your secret's safe with me."

The rest of the afternoon and evening were busy beyond anything Mandy had ever experienced. She had one appointment after another—a couple of them even overlapping. Fortunately, she'd juggled a busy schedule long enough to not get rattled.

After her last client left, and she was closing out the register for the night, Brent walked in. "You sure have been slammed," he said. "I kept waiting for things to lighten up over here to talk to you."

She wished he'd waited until tomorrow, but she didn't want to be rude. "So what can I help you with, Brent?"

"Oh, nothing," he began as he glanced around the room before turning back to face her. "Okay, I might as well come clean. I met Christina today, and I'd like to get to know her better. I thought you might give me some helpful hints."

"Just be yourself, and you'll do fine."

"You sure that'll work? In case you haven't noticed, I'm not exactly the smoothest guy in town."

"There are other, more important things than being smooth," Mandy said. "If being yourself doesn't work, then it's not meant to be."

"Are you almost ready to leave?" he asked. "I'll walk you to your car."

"Sure, let me finish here and I can go."

As they walked out together, he asked some questions about her sister. Mandy explained that Christina was looking for a job.

"Yeah, she told me. We have a full staff, so I wasn't much help. However, Tony said he was hoping to add some people to Small World. Is there a nepotism policy with your company?"

"I doubt it, but I'm not so sure she'd want to work with me." They stopped when they got to her car.

"So will you put in a good word for me?" he asked.

"Even better than that, why don't you call her?" Mandy suggested. Brent was nice enough—just not someone Mandy would be interested in. Her sister, on the other hand, seemed smitten.

"If you're sure she won't mind."

Mandy dug in her purse for paper and a pen. She jotted down her parents' house line number and handed it to him. "My mom or sister will probably answer."

He took the paper, folded it, and stuck it in his pocket. "Thanks, Mandy. You sure are being understanding about things."

"What do you mean, Brent?"

"You know, after it didn't work out between you and me."

Chapter 6

B etween you and me?"
He nodded. "We were just starting to get to know each other, but
when Christina came into the picture, that was it for me."

Mandy had to squelch a giggle. Mandy had never been attracted to
Brent, so if he liked Christina, that was a good thing—and a relief.

Well, wasn't it? Protectiveness toward her sister overtook the relief.

"Why are you looking at me like that?" he asked.

"Ya know, Brent, I don't really know that much about you. Do you go to
church?"

He shuffled his feet and looked down at them before meeting her gaze.
"I used to, back when I was a kid, but I have to admit, I haven't been in a
while."

"My family is committed to our faith," Mandy said. "Christina might
not agree, but I think one of the reasons she came back to West Virginia was to
reconnect to family and get her Christian bearings again."

"Wow." Brent looked happier than she expected. "She's not only a looker,
she's a nice Christian girl! I hit the jackpot with this one."

The guy was clearly missing something. "How do you figure that?"

"Look at her," he said. "Maybe it's hard for you to see this since you're her
sister, but she's gorgeous. The problem with that, though, is the pretty girls
aren't always the ones you want meeting your family." He paused and gave her
a conspiratorial look. "Know what I mean?"

"I think so." She forced herself to suppress a groan at his assumptions.

"She's smart, too."

Mandy was surprised at that last comment. She agreed that Christina
was smart, but not only did she not often show it, most people couldn't get
past the pretty face.

"Just remember that my sister is still trying to find herself, but she's not
going to do anything to compromise her Christian faith."

Brent held up his hands and gave her a serious expression. "Oh, I wouldn't
ever ask her to do that. By the way, where does your family go to church?"

She told him the name and location. After they parted ways, she laughed.
Looked like their church was about to experience some sudden exponential
growth.

The next morning, Tony frowned at her as she approached the studio
door. "You weren't scheduled until noon," he said.

She was so used to opening every day, she forgot to check the schedule. "Oops." Stopping in her tracks, she tried to figure out what to do now.

Tony's frown turned to a sympathetic smile. "Look, I have some stuff to do. If you'd like to swap mornings, I'm fine with it."

"You don't mind?"

"Not at all. In fact having you here now makes my life a lot easier."

"What day do you want me to come late?"

He glanced over the schedule then looked up. "How about tomorrow? My sister and her kids are coming to town in the morning, so if you work later tomorrow, I'll be able to spend some time with them."

The fact that he was a family guy made him likable, but she tried to stifle the thought. But she had to admit, her first negative internal reaction to him was long gone by now.

"How many children does your sister have?"

"Two," he replied. "A girl and a boy—both in elementary school. Any ideas for activities they might like?"

She thought for a moment then remembered where some of her clients took their kids. "How about the Children's Museum?"

"Where is it?"

After giving him the address, she added, "It's small, but our customers seem to enjoy it."

"Thanks, Mandy. You really are special. I can't imagine this place without you."

"Thanks, Tony."

"You're good at everything—with kids, keeping this place running, your sister—everything."

"Not everything."

"Everything that matters." Tony reached out and lightly touched her arm then pulled back as though he thought he'd made a mistake. He put away what he'd been working on and walked toward the door as he cleared his throat. "I'll have my cell phone on, so if you need anything, just call."

Mandy swallowed hard and nodded. She bit back the automatic response that she'd been handling everything just fine without him.

"Oh Mandy, before I forget, I wanted to talk to you about some things that came up during the management conference call. We need to schedule a meeting—like when we're slow around here, or I can bring in a part-timer to handle the front desk. There's a lot of information that I think pertains to you."

She couldn't imagine what, since she'd been overlooked as manager. Unless... *Uh-oh.* "There is?"

He nodded. "Yes, and I think you'll like it." Tony pulled on his jacket. "We'll discuss all that later. If I'm going to get this stuff done and be back so you can leave early, I gotta run."

"That's okay. You don't have to—"

"One of the things we talked about was working too much. We want you to take some time off."

"Oh." Mandy lowered her head.

"See ya."

After he left, she rested her elbows on the counter and buried her face in her hands. Tony's take-charge personality left her feeling out of sorts.

The phone rang several times, one of the calls being her mother. "Have you thought about a place where Christina can work?"

"Mom, I know this is important to you and Dad, but give her some time, okay?"

"She listens to you," her mother said.

Mandy disagreed, but this wasn't the time or place to argue. "I'll keep my eyes open, but if you really want to help her, maybe you can advise her to call a temp agency to line her up with a temp-to-perm job."

After she hung up, Mandy finished organizing the files. She only had one photo session before Tony returned. He brought lunch.

"I thought that since we were slow, we could talk today. We can use the front office, and I'll leave the door open so we can see if anyone comes in."

Right when they sat down, a woman walked in with a pair of toddlers. Mandy jumped up and headed straight for the desk, with Tony right behind her. Tony offered to work the camera, but Mandy insisted she could handle it.

"What if I promise to keep my hands off the props?" he whispered.

"And candy?" she countered with a playful grin.

"That, too."

"Well. . ." She glanced around, pretending to ponder then directed her gaze at him. The second their eyes met, her insides lurched, and she wished she hadn't looked at Tony. "Um, sure, that's fine."

An hour later, when she was finished, she went to the front desk and pulled up the company order forms on the computer. A message popped up, alerting her that the page no longer existed. She marched straight to Tony's office.

Tony was on the phone. "Sure, I'll do that. . .yes, that's right." He glanced up and pointed to the chair across from him. When she didn't sit, he frowned but glanced away. He wrapped up his conversation in less than a minute then looked back at Mandy. "What's up?"

"I just tried to order some supplies, but the company order form is no longer there."

"That's one of the things I wanted to discuss," he said. "They weren't supposed to change that until next week, though. What all did you need to order? I'll take care of it."

She handed him her list. "Is *everything* changing around here?"

"Pretty much, yes."

Mandy's shoulders fell as her breath escaped her lungs. "Looks like I'll need to be totally retrained."

"Everyone will." As Tony looked down at the paper in front of him, she noticed the anxiety on his face. "The company is in the process of restructuring."

Tony felt awful that he couldn't share more with Mandy yet. Uncle Ed had made him privy to some company changes, but he wasn't at liberty to discuss any of them—not even the ones that involved Mandy's future with the company. They hadn't finished hammering out the details yet, which complicated everything for him at the store level. But he couldn't be too secretive with Mandy—not after all she'd done for the company. He'd have another talk with Uncle Ed and Ricco.

"I—uh, I guess I'll go back out to the front and get ready for my next photo session," she said as she shuffled backward out of the office.

The second she was gone, he picked up the phone and punched in the number of the regional manager. His cousin Ricco answered on the first ring.

"I need to talk to Mandy soon," Tony said. "She knows there are changes, and I can tell she's worried."

"Look Tony," Ricco said in his understanding but firm voice. "I know this is tough on you, but we don't have anything firm to tell her yet. Have you discussed the changes in the first rollout?"

"Not yet. We haven't had the opportunity to sit down and discuss it."

"As long as you're both doing your jobs, I don't see what the problem is. Go ahead and tell her about the first phase."

Ricco had been away from the trenches so long, he obviously didn't remember all the interruptions. Ricco had never wanted to work for Small World, but when Tony left for the army, Ricco's dad, who promised it would be temporary, pressured him into it. Last they had talked, right after Tony got out of the army, Ricco said he actually liked the job now—especially since they were making some of the changes he'd wanted since he started.

"Okay, I'll just have to get one of the part-timers to come in early."

"You have the budget to hire another full-timer," Ricco reminded him. "There are plenty of people out there looking for jobs. Why don't you hire one of them?"

Tony wanted Mandy's input during the hiring process, but he couldn't very well do that before telling her about the changes. "It takes time to find the right fit, Ricco."

"You're right. It does." He chuckled. "You really like Mandy, don't you?"

"Of course I do. And I'd like to discuss Mandy's options." Tony knew his persistence could get on Ricco's nerves, but he was willing to take his chances.

"She's worked so hard to keep this place running smoothly, and I'm sure she's frustrated."

"Are you saying she's got an attitude?" Ricco asked. "Because if that's the case, maybe we should rethink—"

"No, that's not what I'm saying. Mandy has been professional at all times. I just don't want to risk losing her."

"It won't be too much longer. Just tell her what you can now, and let her know we haven't forgotten about her." Ricco paused before adding, "If you want her input, let her know that, too. Maybe it'll appease her until you have something more concrete to share."

Tony doubted that. Mandy was a smart woman who'd see through any actions designed to hide the fact that she wouldn't get what she wanted.

When it was almost time for Mandy to go home, Tony took advantage of the few minutes of quiet. "I'll get Bella or Steve to come in so you and I can have a meeting."

"Will this be a regular thing now?" she asked. "Even when Parker was still the manager, we never had meetings."

Tony racked his brain as he tried to think of a way to explain without saying more than he should. "I'm not big on meetings either, but I do need to let you know some new corporate policies and decisions."

"Can't you just tell me now?"

"No, it's sort of complicated, and you'll probably have some questions." He paused before adding, "I don't want to get started and then be interrupted again."

She pursed her lips, tightened her jaw, and offered a clipped nod. "Okay." The resignation in her voice let him know she didn't completely trust him, but she knew who was in charge. That hurt.

After she was gone, Tony rubbed the back of his neck. Now all he cared about was making Mandy understand and gaining her trust.

※

For the first time since working at Small World, Mandy couldn't get out of there fast enough. Her job was about to change, but the only change she wanted was the promotion.

Mandy needed to talk to someone, but not her sister or parents. Her best friend, Dahlia, had moved to Chicago, so she decided to call her.

"Maybe you expect too much," Dahlia said. "You've always worked so hard but never tooted your own horn. If you don't let people know what you want, don't expect them to read your mind."

After they got off the phone, Mandy thought about expectations. Were hers unrealistic? She hadn't even dated since college because no one measured up to what she thought she wanted.

She had a tough time falling asleep, but when she finally did, she dreamed about Tony. The next morning, she got ready for work knowing he wouldn't be there because his sister was in town.

There were so many walk-ins that morning, the hours went by in a blur. She'd barely finished with her last family before lunch, when she glanced up and spotted Tony walking toward the studio. He sure looked handsome in his charcoal gray pinstriped suit. Flanked by a woman holding the hand of a little boy on one side and a little girl on the other, he would have made an excellent model for a dad on his way to have his family's pictures taken.

"Hey, Mandy, I'd like for you to meet my sister, Angela."

The attractive woman with the shoulder-length dark hair extended her hand. "I'm so happy to meet you, Mandy. Tony has said many nice things about you."

Tony nudged her. "Shh. Don't tell her my secrets."

"What secrets?" Angela said playfully before turning back to Mandy. "He said you were the best thing that ever happened to Small World Portrait Studio and that if you weren't here, his job would be miserable." She wiggled her eyebrows. "He also told me you were very family oriented—just like us." After smiling at Mandy, she turned to Tony. "And you're right. She's beautiful."

Tony lifted both hands and let them fall to his sides, clearly pretending to be annoyed. "Well, there ya go. Anything you want to know, just ask my sister."

"Thank you." Mandy laughed, in spite of the heat that had crept up her face. "It's nice to meet you, too, Angela. Are you here to have your children's pictures taken?"

Angela grinned and winked at her brother. "And she's an excellent salesperson, too." She turned back to Mandy. "Not today. I just wanted to meet you after all the nice things Tony said. He told me about the Children's Museum, so I thought we'd go there."

After Angela left, Tony went back to his office before coming out with a stack of papers. "Going somewhere important?" she asked.

Chapter 7

Tony nodded. "Chamber of commerce meeting. It won't be a long one though," he said. "I'll be back this afternoon."

He walked toward the door, turned around to face her, and paused. She had the feeling he wanted to say something, but he didn't. He just lifted a hand and waved before walking away.

Mandy barely had time to gather her thoughts before the next family arrived. She got the children in place, snapped their pictures, and arranged the computer proofs without any trouble.

"Mommy, look what the nice lady gave me!" the youngest of the three boys said.

The woman looked at the plastic dinosaur Mandy had pulled from her bag, and then she glanced up, grinned, and mouthed, "Thanks."

Mandy smiled then refocused her attention on the computer proofs. The children had been extremely good for her once she got their attention, but they were bundles of energy. She had a tremendous amount of respect for mothers—particularly those with more than one small child.

She worked as quickly as possible before the children's attention spans ran out. Finally she motioned for the mom to come take a look.

"I wanna see!" the middle boy said.

Mandy pulled a couple of step stools out from behind the counter. "How's this?"

The two older boys each took a stool, and the mother picked up the smallest child. Mandy handed the mother the mouse and encouraged her to let the boys help.

It didn't take long for them to agree on a package. "Thank you so much," the mother said. "My husband will appreciate the fact that I didn't spend a fortune, since we just had pictures taken six months ago."

She spotted Tony walking toward the door. It took all her concentration to keep her mind off his presence as he came in.

"We want you to come back." Mandy pulled out a coupon for the family's next visit. "Put this someplace safe and use it toward your next photo session."

"You're amazing with people," Tony observed. "I'd like to take you to the next chamber of commerce meeting with me."

Her sister called, so Tony went back to his office to give her some space. "Hi, what's up?"

"Mom and Dad are really after me to get a job."

"I agree with them," Mandy said.

"It's not that easy. I've e-mailed and sent my résumé to a few places."

"You have to put a lot of effort into a job hunt."

"If those people in Hollywood weren't so mean, I'd have an acting job."

"But you're not in Hollywood anymore. You're in Wheeling, West Virginia, where hardworking, decent people live."

"I can work hard," Christina said. "Someone just has to give me a chance."

"I'm getting off early tonight. Why don't you come to my apartment after dinner?"

"Mom said she'd fix dinner, and I can bring you some."

"When did she say that?"

"When she told me to call you and see if I could come over one night this week. Sorry."

Mandy chuckled. So she'd been set up, and she'd fallen right into the trap. But that was okay. This was for a good cause.

"Perfect. I'll call you when I leave here."

A half hour later, Tony came walking into the studio. "I just heard from Ricco. He's scheduling a meeting for you." He breezed past her on his way to the back before he stopped and added, "In Atlanta."

"When?"

"As soon as possible." Weird. He wouldn't look her in the eye.

"Do you know what it's all about?"

"I'm not at liberty to say." He edged away from her. "But I do know they want you there in two weeks."

"Two weeks?"

"Yeah, and he wants you to go over to the store in Pittsburgh to show the new photographer some tips on getting the children to cooperate."

"When?"

"This afternoon."

Before she had a chance to say another word, he'd left her alone with the cameras.

She rounded the corner, where she spotted him punching some numbers into the phone. He was clearly avoiding conversation with her, so she backed away.

Rather than press Tony for answers, she decided to wait until she met with Ricco in two weeks. She gathered her things, stopped at the desk, and stared at him until he looked up at her. She needed to brief him on the children he'd be photographing. "The little girl is diabetic, so their mother doesn't want either of them having sugar. She'll smile for the purple dinosaur, and her brother likes action figures."

"I can handle them," Tony said. He managed a slight smile and a glance in her direction. "Especially now that I know I won't have to handle the candy." He leaned back in his chair, still looking at her. "Seriously, Mandy, I appreciate your concern for this place, but I promise I won't mess things up too bad."

She pursed her lips and nodded. He was right. She did need to let go.

"You don't have to come back this afternoon," he added.

Mandy opened her mouth but decided it was pointless to say anything. On the way to the studio in Pittsburgh, all sorts of things flitted through Mandy's mind. Why the urgency of helping this new photographer? She'd heard he'd had his own studio for years.

Right when she pulled into a parking spot, her cell phone rang. It was Tony.

"Are you there yet?" he asked.

"I just got here, but I'm still in the parking lot."

"I wanted to warn you that Ricco is there. The new photographer has never worked with children before, and he threatened to quit. We needed someone, and he's got a tremendous amount of experience, as well as a name in the area, and Ricco wanted to give him a chance. I told Ricco to give you some time with him, and he agreed."

"I don't get why he needed a job if he was so good or why he was hired if he had no experience with kids."

"People couldn't afford his prices, and he waited too long to drop them, so his business folded. Don't bring this up to anyone, but I think he begged, and they were desperate for a photographer. At least his background checked out, so I think he's trainable."

A nervous chuckle escaped her lips. "That's good."

"I didn't want you to be surprised. As for the meeting at the home office—well, try to relax and let things happen as they're supposed to. Ricco's a good guy. He knows what a valuable employee you are."

"I'll try."

"I asked him to explain some stuff while you're in Pittsburgh, and he said he would."

"I appreciate that."

"I said a prayer for you."

"Thank you, Tony."

Mandy squeezed her eyes shut and prayed that she could remain calm, no matter what Ricco wanted to discuss. She opened her eyes and took several deep breaths. She wished she'd worn something a little nicer, but at least there was nothing offensive about black slacks and a white-collared blouse. Boring, as Christina would say, but not offensive.

She shoved the door open and walked into the reception area where she was greeted by Peggy, who'd helped her when she first started with the company. Peggy lifted a hand and waved. "Come on back, and I'll introduce you to James, the new photographer." She lowered her voice and added, "He's a little out of sorts today, so don't be too upset by anything he says. Want some coffee?"

"No thanks." Mandy smiled at Peggy then looked around at the photos covering the walls.

The hallway was wide but short, so they didn't have to go far. The studio was bigger than the one in Wheeling, but everything else was basically the same.

"Children these days are so bad! How can you expect me to get decent portraits of them?" He flailed his arms. "They need to listen."

Ricco sat on a stool across from the ranting man. He glanced up and waved as he spotted her.

"C'mon back, Mandy," he said as he gestured.

She gulped hard and did as he asked. She felt her cheeks flush.

"Mandy, this is James, one of the best photographers in Pennsylvania. He recently decided to shut down his studio, so we talked him into working for us."

Mandy extended her hand as she realized how Ricco was trying to flatter James while he was there. "Nice to meet you, James."

He reluctantly shook hands with her. "So you're the one everyone's raving about."

"I am?"

Ricco let out a nervous laugh. "Yes, you've developed quite a reputation for getting kids to cooperate."

"It's just a matter of getting down on their level and figuring out what they like."

Ricco got off his stool and took a couple of steps toward the front. "I'll leave the two of you to talk. Come see me when you're done, Mandy."

After Mandy got an earful of how terrible he thought the working conditions were, she gave James a few helpful hints. When his appointment arrived, she even showed him how to position the children and get them to smile. He resisted at first, but after a couple of awkward attempts, he succeeded in getting them to behave. Once he had the children under control, the session was great.

After the children went to the front to wait, James shook his head. "No wonder they like you so much, Mandy. Thanks. Maybe I'll give this a little more time before I make my decision about staying or leaving." He pointed toward the office area. "Ricco wants to talk to you now."

Mandy found her way back to the office where Ricco waited for her. "Have a seat." He glanced down at some paperwork on the desk, until she got settled. "Tony gave you a glowing report. Says you were doing a great job of running the studio single-handedly before he arrived."

Mandy smiled. "I did the best I could."

"We appreciate all your hard work. Unfortunately, while we've been in the process of reorganizing, we overlooked some important details."

"I understand." Her voice came out much weaker than she wanted, so she cleared her throat.

"The company is still in a state of change, but we have some thoughts about how to utilize your skills."

Mandy blinked. This sounded like a good thing. She leaned forward, hoping to hear that she was under consideration for a promotion—or at least something concrete.

"But unfortunately, we haven't ironed everything out yet." He offered an apologetic smile as he tapped the end of his pencil on the desk. "There are two reasons I wanted to bring you in. First, we needed you to spend some time with James. How did that go?"

"Okay, I think. His photography skills are obviously there, but I think his pride was getting in his way."

Ricco's eyebrows lifted as he nodded. "Good observation."

"Only time will tell, but he just needed some kid tips."

Ricco laughed. "Your specialty. This can't be easy for him after having his own studio for so long." He steepled his fingers. "Next I'd like for you to clear your schedule for the week after next, so you can spend some time at the home office in Atlanta." He typed something into the computer then glanced back at her. "Will that be a problem?"

She shook her head. "No, that's fine. I can go then."

"The other reason is that I'd like for you to help Tony interview prospective photographers to help you in the studio. Have you ever been involved in the hiring process before?"

Again Mandy shook her head. "No, Bella and Steve had already been hired when I started."

"They've both asked Tony if they can cut their hours, so we really need to find some people to replace them. Tony can fill you in until we have a chance to work on the interview manual." He typed some more then glanced up at Mandy. "How does that sound?"

"They never told me they wanted to cut their hours."

"They probably didn't want to leave you in the lurch. So how about it?"

She smiled. "It sounds fine."

"I wanted to make sure you had some of the basics before you screen potential applicants. Give me a minute to print some of the information so we can go over it. I was going to do this before you got here, but with James threatening to leave, that had to come first."

She forced a smile. "I can imagine." After a short pause, she added, "Do you really think he would have left?"

"No." Ricco gave her conspiratorial look. "But we don't want him to be miserable, so I thought seeing you in action might inspire him. I went over some of my ideas with Tony, and he thought you'd have the insight to know what we're looking for in photographers."

"I think I have a pretty good idea."

"Mainly they need to know how to deal with kids." He smiled. "Obviously."

Mandy grinned back. "True."

After the printer spit out several pages, he looked them over, stapled them, and handed them across the desk. "We have to follow some hiring policies," he explained. "I want to make sure you understand what we're allowed or not allowed to say, according to the law."

Mandy sat there and followed along as he went over the legal issues. Some of it she knew and other stuff made sense. When he got to the last paragraph, he looked up at her.

"Any questions?" he asked.

She shook her head. "No, not really."

"Are you comfortable interviewing prospective photographers?"

She pondered that question for a moment. Interviewing people who would be hired in at the same level as her made no sense, but she'd do it if that was what they wanted. Finally she squared her shoulders, looked him in the eye, and nodded. "I'm fine with that."

"Good." Ricco stood and smiled. "I'm glad you're on our team, Mandy. We're very impressed with your work. Tony is especially impressed."

"Thank you." She shook hands with him and got out of there as quickly as she could. Tony had said not to come back into the office, which was a relief. The emotional weight of the meeting had worn her out.

Mandy kicked off her shoes as soon as she got home. She picked up the TV remote and did some channel surfing, but there wasn't anything on TV that interested her. Finally she gave up and picked out a CD to listen to. The ringing phone jolted her.

"I tried calling you at work, but Tony said you weren't coming back in," Christina said.

"He told me I didn't need to after I left the regional office."

"Mind if I come over now? I really need to talk."

Mandy sighed. Even though she'd agreed for Christina to come, she really didn't feel like having company, but she couldn't very well turn down her sister. "Sure, that's fine."

"You don't have to sound so mad."

"I'm not mad," Mandy replied. "Just tired."

"Good thing you won't have to cook. Mom loaded up some food, and she's letting me use her car. I've got some great news. See ya in a few minutes."

She hung up before Mandy had a chance to say another word.

Mandy went through her apartment and straightened up a few things, put her work shoes in the closet, and shoved her feet into some clogs. By the time Christina knocked at her door, she was mentally ready for her sister.

"You're not gonna believe this, Mandy!"

"I'm sure I won't. What happened?"

"I got an e-mail back on a job I applied for online, and you'll never guess where I'm interviewing in a couple of days."

"Where?" Mandy tried to sound enthusiastic, but she was still too drained.

"I answered a blind ad for a management training job, and it's with Small World Portrait Studio!"

Chapter 8

A management training job at Small World?" Mandy's throat tightened. Christina couldn't contain her excitement. "I answered a bunch of ads at online job sites, and I heard back from Small World. Isn't that the coolest?"

Mandy chewed her lip for a moment before slowly shaking her head. "I don't think that's such a good idea—you and me working together." Her body had gone numb.

"Oh it's not a problem," Christina said. "I called the number they sent me and talked to someone who said it's okay with them to have more than one family member working there."

That wasn't the point, but Mandy didn't want to upset her sister, and she certainly wasn't about to dampen her enthusiasm for getting a job. "So who did you talk to?"

"Some lady named Peggy. She said she knows you."

Mandy nodded as she wondered why Peggy never mentioned talking to Christina. "She works in the Pittsburgh office."

"She's very nice, in spite of the fact that I called her when she was about to leave."

That explained it. Peggy talked to Christina after she left.

"What else did she say?"

Christina sat down and clasped her hands together as she looked up at the ceiling. "She put me on the phone with some guy named Ricco who told me they were looking for trainees—that they're putting together a management training program for people who are willing to relocate."

"Do you have an interview lined up yet?"

Christina made a face. "I have to take an aptitude test, and then they'll interview me. They want me to talk to a bunch of people."

"When and where are you supposed to take the test?"

"First thing tomorrow in Pittsburgh!" Christina leaned forward. "They'll have the results within a few minutes after I finish, and if I pass I'll get to interview at your studio!"

Mandy felt a groan coming on, but she stifled it. "Have you told Mom and Dad?"

"Of course, and they're thrilled, although Dad warned me that I need to act all professional, or I might mess things up for you." She tilted her head and pouted. "I can't believe he would say something so mean. I'd never do anything to hurt you, Mandy."

Guilt set in as Mandy realized she'd thought the same thing. She smiled and tried to dig deep for a positive angle as she reached for her sister's hands. "I know you wouldn't." *At least not intentionally.* "Just make sure you're honest on the test and give direct answers during the interview."

"Hey, I have an idea! Why don't we do a practice interview?"

Mandy's stomach rumbled. "Let's eat first."

She got plates and sat down at the table. Christina folded her hands. "I'll say the blessing."

Mandy bowed her head as her sister thanked God for the food and the possibility of being able to work together. When she opened her eyes, she felt a wave of remorse wash over her. At that moment, she realized how her control issues had affected her.

Christina tilted her head. "Are you okay?"

With her lips between her teeth, Mandy slowly nodded. She sucked in a deep breath and looked down as she let it out. "I want to apologize for being so bossy."

"Bossy?" Christina laughed. "Isn't that what big sisters are supposed to be?"

"Forgive me, okay?"

"Of course. So what kinds of questions are on this test?" Christina asked.

"I have no idea," Mandy replied. "When I was hired, after the background check all I had to do was get through the probationary period without messing anything up. But then I wasn't hired to be in management."

A look of shock popped onto Christina's face. "Don't tell me I'm training to be your boss."

Mandy felt sick to her stomach. "I don't know what you'll be training for—that is, if you get hired."

"I'm so sorry. If you don't want me to do this, just say so. I was so excited about being able to work with you, this never dawned on me."

"That's okay," Mandy said. "If I have another new boss, it might as well be you. At least I know you love me no matter what."

Christina offered a sympathetic smile. "I've got your back, Mandy. You've always been there for me, and I'd love to do whatever I can for you."

After they ate, Mandy grabbed the plates and set them in the sink. "Since you have to get up early, I'll take care of cleaning up."

"I don't mind helping." Christina had already picked up her handbag and taken a step toward the door.

"Thanks, but I'll be fine. Get some sleep and don't worry about the interview."

Christina's eyes widened. "We didn't practice interviewing."

"I don't think you need to practice. Just answer the questions honestly and be direct. I'm sure everyone will love you."

After her sister left, Mandy sat down with her Bible and flipped through to some passages that had always gotten her through difficult times in the past. She settled on Psalm 25. She'd always thought of herself as a committed Christian, but it was time she accepted that her true thoughts and actions didn't reflect it. She needed to work on trust in His Word.

Tony got to work early the next morning. When Ricco told him about Mandy's sister interviewing, he wondered how Mandy would feel, and it kept him up all night.

The sound of the door signaled Mandy's arrival. He stood, took a deep breath, and sent up a plea for divine guidance then walked out to greet Mandy. One look at her face let him know something was different.

He smiled. "Hi there. How was your meeting with Ricco?"

She bobbed her head. "It was good. He basically just went over interviewing techniques for new photographers."

"In the future, you'll be screening them before I talk to them."

"That's what he said."

"Mandy, I heard that your sister applied for a job here and she's coming later, after her interview with Ricco."

"Why didn't you say something?"

"I didn't find out until last night when Ricco called. He sounded excited about it."

"Good."

"Wanna talk about it?"

Her expression concerned him. "Not really."

This was going to be a very long day. "I saw that you have several appointments this morning, but you have some free time this afternoon."

She remained at the door and just stood there staring at him. She wasn't smiling, but her lips naturally turned up at the corners. Tony had no doubt she wasn't aware of how gorgeous she was.

"What time is Christina coming in?" she asked.

"Right after lunch. I thought you and I could interview her together since it'll be your first time, sort of a practice session for you."

"She told me this is for a management training position."

Tony nodded. "That's part of the company restructuring. They want full-timers to be well rounded, so they're bringing them in with more of an opportunity for advancement."

He wasn't sure what he should do. If she was upset, he wanted to comfort her, but this wasn't the time or place, and he couldn't overstep the bounds of company policy—even those he disagreed with. The changes had clearly thrown her off-kilter.

"So how many managers will we have in this office?" she asked, still not smiling.

"Just one. The person who will officially be in management training will learn photography, how to manage the books, and other company policies. After that, we're not sure. The ad says the person has to be willing to relocate."

Mandy chewed her bottom lip for a moment before she slowly nodded. "So I suppose you'll need me to help with the photography training."

"Yes."

"Okay then." She swung around and walked away, leaving him standing there feeling like a heel.

Mandy was confused by everything—all the changes that seemed to have taken place overnight. She hadn't seen any of this coming, which was her own fault. If she'd had more contact with the home office before Tony arrived, things might have been different. Instead she'd kept her nose to her tasks, making sure the studio ran smoothly—and she'd done an excellent job, according to what both Tony and Ricco had said.

She remembered her prayers from the night before. It was time to put all her trust in God and stop trying to take it all on herself.

She stayed busy all morning. Tony popped into the darkened studio and let her know he'd gotten lunch for both of them. "I'll be in my office," he said. "Come on back when you're done."

After she finished showing proofs to her last client of the morning, she joined Tony. "You didn't have to do this," she said. "I could have run out to the deli and picked up something quick."

"What's going on with you?" he asked, his voice barely above a whisper. "Are you upset about something?"

She shrugged as she tried not to show her anger. "Not really."

"You are. I can tell." He stared at her until she met his gaze. "Are you unhappy about your sister coming in for an interview?"

Mandy's body tensed. She wasn't ready to talk about her feelings just yet. "Not unhappy, but things aren't always as they seem."

"I know, Mandy. Please trust me. Some things are out of my control." He reached for her hand but quickly dropped his hand to his side.

There was that *trust* word. She saw the tightness in his face, letting her know he felt awful about what was happening—or not happening. Mandy shrugged. "I understand. I'll be okay." She needed more time to think about things before she said or did anything she might later regret.

He chuckled nervously as he gestured toward the food. "I got chicken, turkey, and tuna. Take your pick."

"Turkey would be good."

He handed her a wrapped sandwich. "I realize there are probably some family dynamics going on. I want you to know that we won't evaluate you based on your sister's performance, and the same goes for her."

Mandy slowly unwrapped her sandwich as she thought about what he'd said. "If my sister winds up being the manager here, will she be my supervisor?" She tried to keep the question matter-of-fact, but she wasn't sure she succeeded.

"No," he said. "In fact the only working relationship you'll have is that you'll be training her in photography. Once she's ready to move up, we'll know more about where you'll be."

She almost choked on her first bite. "Are you saying I might be moved?"

His face tightened. "Don't look too far ahead, Mandy. Once we get to that point, we'll deal with it."

The phone rang so Tony answered it. She only heard his side of the conversation, but she could tell it was about Christina. After he hung up, he lifted his eyebrows and folded his hands.

"Your sister is a very smart woman. She scored very well on the aptitude test."

"That's good."

"It is. Small World hired a company to help us screen potential employees based on a balance of basic aptitude and ability to think on their feet. And that's what I wanted to discuss with you. Have you had a chance to go over the interview questions?"

"Ricco and I went over them yesterday."

"Good," Tony said. "What we need to do is plan a strategy for the interview before Christina arrives. Since she's your sister, I'm sure it'll be a little different for you." He leaned forward and held her gaze. "But the outcome has nothing to do with your employment here."

Mandy didn't have anything to say, so she nodded. She listened to Tony as he explained how they were going to tag team the interview.

"You start with the basics then turn her over to me. I'll let you sit in on the entire interview, so you'll know what to do next time."

The buzzer on the door sounded, and they both turned toward the front. It was Mandy's next appointment.

"When you come out of the session, I'll take over and show the proofs while you talk to your sister."

⚜

Tony watched Mandy leave his office, her shoulders drooping a tad. He wished he'd stood up to Ricco and requested Christina's interview at another studio. But it was too late now. Mandy's feelings mattered more to him than anything at the moment.

Christina arrived as Mandy came out of the studio with the children. He nodded for the sisters to use his office, while he stepped behind the counter to work on the proofs.

After his part of the work was done and the parents had chosen the pictures they wanted, he knocked on the door then opened it. Christina tossed her long blond hair over her shoulder and grinned at him.

"This is so cool!" she said. "Who'd have thought I'd get to interview with my own sister for a job?"

"Yes, it's very cool," he said as he worked hard to keep from smiling.

Mandy looked comfortable behind the desk, her hands folded in front of her, the list of questions beside them. "I've gone over the company's expectations and discussed the first five questions."

He looked at Christina. "So what do you think so far? Is this something you think you'd like to pursue?"

She nodded with enthusiasm. "My sister loves her job, so I'm sure I'd like it, too!"

Tony glanced over at Mandy, who now looked amused. A surge of relief flooded him. "Excellent! Now let's get on with the rest of the interview."

After Christina left the office, Mandy hopped up out of the manager's chair. "I should have let you sit there," she said, "but I wasn't thinking clearly."

"You were fine." They held a gaze for several seconds. "Perfect, in fact." So perfect his heart pounded nearly out of control. If he didn't keep his feelings in check, he knew he could fall hard for Mandy.

"Now what?"

"We turn our interview notes over to Ricco and let him make the decision. Of course, we have to make separate evaluations, and we're not supposed to discuss it until after we fill out our separate forms."

"This is almost scientific, isn't it?" she asked.

"As much as an interview can be." He handed her another form. "Since no one is scheduled to come in, why don't we do this now?"

She took the paper and left him alone in the office. Fifteen minutes later, she returned and placed the sealed envelope with the form on his desk. "All done."

*

The phone rang, so Mandy left to answer it at the front desk. It was Christina.

"Well? How'd I do? Did I get the job?"

"You just left here."

"How long does it take to decide whether or not you want to hire me?"

"It's not that easy," Mandy explained. "Tony and I had to fill out forms from your interview, and then someone from the home office will look them over. You'll have to come back for another interview."

"That's silly," Christina said. "It's just a job."

"It won't be long," Mandy assured her. "Just remember that the interview works both ways. They're interviewing you to see if they think you'll be a good fit for the company, and you're interviewing them to see if it's a place you'd like to work."

"I already told you, if you work there, it must be good."

"If it's meant to be, it'll work out." After Mandy got off the phone, she leaned against the counter and closed her eyes to ask the Lord for clarity.

"Are you okay?"

Chapter 9

Tony's voice startled her. Mandy opened her eyes in time to see him standing about a foot away. She felt a catch in her throat.

He took a step back. "Oh, sorry. I thought you might not be feeling well. I didn't realize you were praying."

"That's okay." Now that he wasn't so close, she could look at him without the flutter. "My sister just called and wanted to know how long it'll be before she has an answer."

"I wish I knew." He shoved his hands into his pockets and grinned down at her. "They're being ultracautious. Apparently they made some hiring mistakes in other studios, and they want to make sure they do everything they can to avoid that in the future."

"Oh, I understand." Mandy paused before deciding to come right out with the question that had been gnawing at her since Tony had arrived. She was trusting the Lord, but she still wanted an answer. "Is there any reason why I'm not being considered for this management training position?"

Tony had been waiting for this. He had no doubt Mandy would make an excellent studio manager, but the position they'd made for her was even better.

"You know I can't discuss it."

"Is it because they don't think I can do it?"

"I didn't say that. You asked if there was a reason you weren't being considered for *this* management training position, and I answered you." He narrowed his eyes and tried to communicate without coming out and telling her anything.

She studied his face then pulled her bottom lip between her teeth. He'd seen her do this when she was deep in thought.

"There just might be something else," he said softly. "Something better."

Mandy gave him a quizzical look. "I can't imagine what that would be, but okay, I get it. You won't betray the confidence, and that's being a good company man."

Her comment hit him wrong. "Mandy, it's not that I'm just a good company man. I've already told you there are some things in the works that aren't clear yet. I don't even know the details."

"And I'll find out in Atlanta, right?"

He nodded. "That's one thing I *can* say. You'll learn everything—or most of it—during the Atlanta trip, including things I don't even know yet."

"Okay then."

With that she turned and walked away, leaving him standing there staring at the wall as she disappeared around it.

He walked back into his office, closed the door, and picked up the phone to call Ricco. "I want to tell Mandy something," he said as soon as Ricco came on the line.

"C'mon, Tony, you have to understand why we don't want to do this yet," Ricco reminded him. "Not all of the details have been worked through, and we want to offer her a full package—not something we're not sure we can deliver."

"At least let me tell her that. I want to give her something to look forward to."

Ricco hesitated then snorted. "Oh all right. Just make sure she knows we don't have it all worked out. I don't want her expecting something we can't deliver."

Tony thanked him and hung up. He leaned back in his chair and stared at the closed door. Ricco had a point. Once he told Mandy, she would have expectations. Tony didn't want to get her worked up, only to feel let down if things didn't turn out as he expected. He still felt like he should give her something to look forward to, so he jotted down some thoughts before getting up to see if she was available.

The door to the studio was propped open, and there were a couple of adults in the waiting area. He made small talk with them until their children ran out with Mandy right behind them. Not everyone would have the parents' complete confidence like Mandy did. She went behind the desk to organize the computer proofs.

He walked up behind her and whispered, "As soon as you're done, I have some news."

She leaned away, tilted her head back, and looked him in the eye. "News?"

"Yes, about your trip to Atlanta. I just talked to Ricco, and—"

"How much longer?" the children's mother asked. "We're overdue for nap time."

"Just a few more minutes," she replied.

Tony stepped toward his office. "I'll leave you alone while you finish up here."

⚜

Mandy thought the parents would never make up their minds. They started out wanting the economy package, but after they saw how many good shots there were, they moved up a couple of levels.

"Their grandparents will love these," the woman said. The toddler on her hip started kicking his feet and squealing, so she put him back in his stroller. "How much do I owe you?"

311

Mandy swiftly took the deposit, thanked the parents, and said good-bye to the children. Then she squared her shoulders and marched toward Tony's office. Funny how, until he arrived, she'd mentally made that her office.

She rapped on the door. "You had some news?"

He glanced up from his desk and pointed to the chair across the room. "Yes, have a seat."

The way he looked at her made her squirm. "Did I do something wrong?"

Tony steepled his fingers for a few seconds then smiled. "I spoke to Ricco and told him that you needed to know something. We can't continue keeping you in the dark—at least not where your future is concerned."

Mandy's stomach instantly let out a deep growl. She wrapped her arms around her midsection. "Sorry. I'm just nervous."

"Don't be." He leaned forward with his elbows propped on his desk. "The reason you weren't considered for the promotion to studio manager was that the company has something even better in mind for you."

Mandy sat up straighter. "You've already said that, but what?"

"You already know we're restructuring. They've always hired people with no photography experience if their background checks came up clean and we thought they'd be good, but they've had some consistency issues, which is why they're planning two separate tracks."

"I'm not following you."

Tony lifted an index finger. "One track will be to manage the studios." Then he lifted another finger. "The other is for photographers."

Mandy thought about it for a few seconds. "In the past, the managers were able to do photography."

"That won't change," Tony said. "However, they still need to go through training, and that's where you come in. We need someone who can teach others a system. Your methods obviously work."

"I'm still missing something."

Tony snickered as he leaned back in his chair. "They're looking at you to be a regional trainer."

Mandy opened her mouth, but she couldn't think of anything to say. The concept of regional trainer had never dawned on her.

"It will be a management position because the photographers will rely on your expertise and experience to get the quality we need."

"Interesting." It sounded good.

"Yes," Tony agreed. "I thought so, too. That's as much as they've nailed down. The details are still on the drawing board, though."

Mandy pondered the new information. "Will I be able to continue working with the kids?"

Tony shrugged. "I don't know yet. Like I said, it's all part of the restructuring, and the home office folks don't have everything figured out yet."

"So are you part of the restructuring?" she asked. "In the past, they promoted from within."

"That's another thing I'm not sure about."

Mandy lifted an eyebrow. "What do you mean?"

"As you know, I really didn't want to be a studio manager. I wanted the job I was offered before I decided to go into the army. They put my cousin Ricco in that position, and now I see that he's done better than I would have. Now they're trying to figure out what to do with me, since I've settled down and I'm ready to have a career with the family business."

"So what does all this mean?" Mandy asked.

He leaned forward again. "It means that we're in for some exciting times, and you're part of it."

The sound of someone entering the studio caught their attention. Mandy hopped up and left the office.

She took care of the walk-in customers then got the studio ready for the next scheduled appointment. Her head still spun from Tony's surprise. But before she got too dizzy, she sent up a prayer for the ability to accept the surprises as they came.

※

Tony hadn't expected to develop feelings for Mandy. He didn't want complications, but he knew how hard it was to find the right woman—a sweet, intelligent, Christian woman—who was strong enough to handle a roomful of children. The fact that she was beautiful was a bonus.

All the way to church on Sunday—Mandy's church—he thought about what he should do. Small World didn't have antinepotism policies, but they frowned on people dating their direct employees. And since he was the nephew of one of the company founders, he had to be above reproach.

He arrived about a minute before church began, so he quickly found a chair near the door. As the first worship songs played, he had a chance to glance around the sanctuary and get a feel for the church's personality.

It appeared to be mostly twenty- and thirty-somethings, with a few forty-somethings in the mix. People were dressed business casual, and they appeared focused on what they were there for. He sighed. It felt wonderfully similar to his church in Georgia. The sanctuary was big, and most of the chairs were filled, which made it difficult to see everyone who'd come to worship. He was pretty sure Mandy was there, but he couldn't find her.

After the music, everyone sat and opened their Bibles, and the pastor read from the Old Testament then the New Testament. They bowed their heads for the prayer before the sermon began. Pastor Chuck Waring, a gifted speaker, paced back and forth on the stage. The sermon was powerful—filled with examples of God's grace. Tony knew he'd be back; this church felt right.

He filed out of the sanctuary, shook the pastor's hand, introduced himself, and said Mandy had told him about it. "It's nice to have you here, Tony. I hope you decide to come back to worship with us."

"Oh I will," Tony replied. "In fact if you have time this week, I'd like to stop by and talk to you."

The pastor grinned as he pulled a card from his pocket and handed it to Tony. "Call my assistant and schedule an appointment. I look forward to getting to know you."

The crowd had thickened behind Tony, so he said good-bye and left. He found his car and headed to the condo he rented.

⚘

Mandy spotted Tony chatting with the pastor right after church. She was all the way in the front, and it was packed, which made it impossible to get to him. She'd have to ask what he thought on Monday since that would be the next time they were both scheduled to work.

Pastor Waring patted her shoulder as she slipped past. "Thank you for inviting Tony. He seems like a nice fellow."

Mandy smiled. "Yes, he's very nice."

A slight smile quirked the pastor's lips. "Anything I need to know about?"

She quickly shook her head. "No, we're just friends. Well, not just friends, but—well, we work together. He's my boss."

The pastor nodded, still looking amused. "I understand. Have a good week, Mandy."

She couldn't get out of there fast enough. Once she reached her car, she let her head fall forward and rested it on her steering wheel. Why had such an innocent comment from the pastor gotten her all worked up? The second she questioned herself, she knew what the answer was. She was falling for Tony.

In spite of the fact that he got the job she wanted, and he kept a secret from her for so long, she knew his principles were solid. He not only talked about going to church and actually showed up, he apparently lived his faith—at least from what she'd seen so far. It didn't hurt that he was handsome, too.

How would she be able to face him now? Would she be able to hide her feelings, now that she was aware of them?

She'd have to. This so wasn't the time to let down her guard. He'd told her she was about to get a new position—one with more responsibility and she hoped a raise. This was what she'd been wanting.

But it would be nice to have a guy in her life. Brent from the electronics store used to flirt with her, but she had never been interested. However, Tony was a different matter.

Over the next week and a half, Mandy managed to avoid being in close quarters with Tony. When he was in his office, she stayed in the studio or at the front desk. When they had to communicate, she kept her comments brief but polite.

314

A few times she noticed that he looked puzzled, but she didn't want to address that. Her job had to be first on her mind. Getting worked up over the boss wasn't good under any circumstances.

Tony hired a couple more part-timers to work at the counter—students who had no desire to be photographers or even have a career at Small World. They both admitted that they were short-timers, but at least they'd fill in the gap until some longer-term part-timers could be found. She appreciated the freedom to work in the studio without distractions.

Tony had hoped that hiring a couple of extra people would ease things up for Mandy. She'd been so stressed lately, he worried about her. The way she avoided his gaze led him to believe something else might be going on.

Maybe telling her about the new career track hadn't been such a good idea. The last thing he wanted to do was put additional pressure on her.

After his appointment with Pastor Chuck, he knew he'd found the perfect church home—one where he'd be spiritually fed, he could get involved in some community outreach, and he'd find friends of like mind. The pastor was open and friendly, letting him know he was approachable. It was an excellent fit.

When Pastor Chuck asked about his relationship with Mandy, Tony had quickly let him know they were coworkers and that was all. The pastor nodded and changed the subject. Tony appreciated the lack of pressure.

He heard the buzzer at the door and glanced up in time to see Mandy walk into the studio. She lifted her hand and waved but then quickly glanced away.

"When you have a moment, I'd like to see you," he said.

"Sure," she replied. "Let me put my things down, and I'll be right there." In less than a minute, she was at the door of his office. "What's up?"

"Since you're leaving for Atlanta in the middle of the workday tomorrow, I can take you to the airport."

"You don't have to. I can get my sister to—"

"I'll take you." He cleared his throat. "That will be a good time for me to fill you in on some things you'll need to know—without the distractions here at the office."

She stood there for a moment before nodding. "Okay, that's fine. I'll have my sister take me to work, so I won't have to leave my car on the street."

"Good idea. Has she asked about the job?"

"Yes. Constantly. Any idea when we'll know something?"

Tony knew they'd been given the go-ahead to hire Christina, but he hesitated because he wasn't sure how Mandy felt about it. "Soon."

She smiled. "Fine. If you don't need me anymore, I have to set up the studio for my next appointment."

The rest of the day was business as usual. He went home after work and made a list of everything he needed to discuss with Mandy.

She came in early looking very professional in a business suit he'd never seen. His heart beat a little harder as he was reminded of how much he cared about what happened to her.

"You look nice," he said, trying his best to keep his tone professional.

She shuffled and blushed. "Thank you."

When it was time to go to the airport, they made sure the part-timers had everything under control. During the drive, Tony checked things off his list as he addressed them. "Just remember that you'll be asked your opinion, and you need to be open and honest."

"I wouldn't know how to be any other way," she said.

"Good." He pulled up to the departure section of the terminal and popped his trunk.

Once the curbside airline employee had her bag checked, she thanked him. "I appreciate everything you've done for me, Tony."

"It's my job. Call if you need anything."

"I will."

He sat and watched her as she disappeared into the building. The security person gestured for him to leave the curb, so he obeyed. All the way to the studio, he thought about how professional yet stunning Mandy looked. No doubt in his mind, the people in the home office would be as impressed as he was. And she clearly had no idea of the impact she had on people, which made her even more appealing.

Tony went straight back to work and relieved Steve, the part-time photographer who'd come in with the understanding he wouldn't have to stay long. A couple of hours later, the counter employee stuck her head into his office and said her shift was over, so she was leaving. He juggled photographing clients with walk-ins. This gave Tony a taste of what Mandy had dealt with over the past couple of months.

He'd finally finished up with the last proofs when the phone rang. It was Christina, sounding frantic.

"I've tried to call Mandy's cell phone, but it goes straight to voice mail."

"I'm sure she's okay," Tony said. "She probably just forgot to turn it on after her plane landed. Want me to give her a message?"

"Mom's in the hospital. She had a heart attack."

Chapter 10

Tony didn't waste a minute. As soon as he got the information, he called the Atlanta office. Uncle Ed's executive assistant, Tony's cousin Sharon, answered on the first ring.

"It's great to hear from you, Tony," she said. "Dad—"

"Is Mandy there yet?" he said.

"That's what I was trying to say. She's in with Dad." Her voice softened. "Why didn't you tell me how pretty she is?"

Tony cleared his throat. "I need to talk to her now."

"What's wrong, Tony?"

"Her mother had a heart attack. She'll need to come back right away."

"Hold on. Let me go get her."

"Wait. Sharon, why don't you get her and show her to the conference room—the one with the sofas? Then you can call me right back and put her on the phone."

"Good idea. I'll go do that now."

✣

Mr. Rossi had sent a stretch limo to the airport to pick Mandy up. And here she was sitting in his office, listening to the details of a job better than she ever imagined.

Someone knocked on the door, and Mr. Rossi cleared his throat. "Yes?"

Sharon, the woman from the front desk, walked in and offered Mandy a sweet smile. "I need to see Mandy for a moment, if you don't mind."

"But we were—"

Sharon interrupted him. "It's important."

Mandy glanced over at the head of the company, who looked as perplexed as she felt. "Okay, if it's that important, go ahead. I'll be right here when you're done with her."

"Follow me," Sharon said. When they reached a room at the end of the long hall, she opened the door, switched on the light, and gestured inside. "Have a seat on the sofa over by the phone. I'll be right back, okay?"

"Um, sure," Mandy said, doing as she was told.

A moment later, Sharon was back. "Tony needs to talk to you, so let me get him on the phone." Without another word, she reached over, punched in the number, and handed the phone to Mandy. "I'll be out front when you're done."

"Tony?" Mandy said as soon as he answered. "What was so important to

317

pull me out of my meeting?"

"Are you sitting down?" His voice was gravelly, unlike she'd ever heard it.

"Yes." Her heart suddenly started hammering in her chest. "What's going on?"

"Christina called. Your mother's in the hospital. She had a heart attack about an hour ago."

Mandy gasped. "I have to come home."

"I know. Sharon's booking your flight as we speak. I'll talk to my uncle and reschedule your meeting for later."

Within seconds after she hung up, Sharon was at the door of the conference room with her coat and handbag. "The driver is out front waiting. I'll ride with you to the airport."

"That's okay," Mandy said. "I'll be fine."

"I'm going with you," she insisted. "My dad's giving me the rest of the day off so I can make sure everything's all set with the airline."

As Sharon coordinated the return trip, Mandy pulled out her cell phone, turned it on, and called her sister.

"She's doing a little better," Christina said. "It was scary at first, though."

"Where was she?"

"In the kitchen," Christina said, her voice cracking. "I was arguing with her about needing to borrow her car, when she passed out." She let out a sob. "It's all my fault."

"It's not your fault," Mandy said.

"If I hadn't promised my friends I'd drive, none of this would have happened. Ashley said she'd pick me up, but I told her I could use Mom's car."

"If you'd left, Mom might have passed out without you there to call the paramedics," Mandy reminded her.

"I didn't think about it like that. At any rate, I need to go back in the room. Dad's coming out, and I think he needs some coffee or something."

"Tell Mom I love her, and I'll be there soon."

After she clicked the Off button, Mandy blinked. Her body was numb and she stared straight ahead.

As soon as the limo driver had all the bags and got into the driver's seat, Sharon took Mandy's hands. "Let's say a prayer."

Mandy bowed her head and listened to Sharon's soothing words of petition for her mother's healing and a safe trip back to West Virginia. When she opened her eyes, Mandy looked into Sharon's kind eyes.

"Thank you."

Sharon squeezed her hands. "Tony told us you were a Christian. Dad was relieved, since we like our management team to be of like mind. Faith in Christ has gotten my family through some trying times."

Mandy swallowed hard. "Yes, me, too."

To Mandy's surprise and relief, Sharon got out of the car, checked Mandy's bags at the curb, and walked her as far as she was allowed. She handed Mandy an envelope, leaned over, and gave her a hug. "We'll keep a prayer vigil going in the office. Let us know if there's anything we can do."

After Mandy found her gate, she opened the envelope and saw her boarding pass and a couple hundred dollars cash with a note to use it for incidentals. The folks at Small World were nicer and more generous than she ever realized before. Everywhere Mandy turned, she saw the Lord's gracious hand. Tears once again sprang to her eyes.

Lord, I pray that You spare my mother and show me how to let go of my need to make things like I want them. Your ways are so much greater than anything I'll ever think of on my own.

She opened her eyes, shoved the envelope into her purse, and pulled out her cell phone to call her dad. He explained that her mother's heart attack wasn't a complete surprise to him because she'd been having heart issues for a while. Mandy listened as he told her how her mom wanted to keep this a secret in order not to worry her and Christina. After she hung up, she sat there in stunned silence until she heard the announcement that her plane was ready for passengers.

Mandy was one of the last people to board, so she was stuck having to climb over the person who'd chosen the aisle seat in her row. But once she was buckled in, she closed her eyes and tried to shut out everything around her.

The flight was miserable as Mandy imagined all sorts of scenarios she might encounter when she got back. She prayed that her sister was right about their mom doing better.

After the plane arrived and she walked out into the terminal, she saw Tony at the closest point security would allow. He extended a hand to take her carry-on bag then placed his hand in the small of her back to guide her toward baggage claim.

"I'll take you straight to the hospital," he said. "And I can stay as long as you need me."

"That's okay. You have a studio to run."

"It's covered." His tone was firm but kind. "Family has always come first with me, and I understand what you're going through."

Mandy didn't know what to say. However, she wondered what he meant by understanding what she was going through.

She didn't have to wait long to find out. Once they had her bags in the car, he opened up.

"Both of my parents have had health issues. My dad passed away when I was younger, but he'd been sick for a very long time. My mother broke down after he died, and she hasn't been the same since. Uncle Ed was the one who lifted the family. His faith kept him focused, and that's why I see the only way to true joy and contentment in life is through Christ."

"I had no idea," Mandy said softly. "I mean, I understand the part about faith in Christ, but I didn't know about your parents."

He offered a gentle smile. "There was no way for you to know until I told you. Now let's pray for your mom."

Mandy closed her eyes as Tony asked for strength for her family and healing for her mother. By the time he finished praying, any sliver of doubt she ever had about him had vanished. Tony was a true believer who genuinely cared about others.

Mandy studied Tony's profile as he drove. When he stopped for a red light, he turned and offered a sympathetic smile. "I'm sorry this is happening, but she's in very good hands."

"I know. Thank you for all you're doing."

"Would you like to hear some unrelated good news?"

Mandy nodded. "Yes, good news is always welcome."

"Everything checked out with Christina, and we can hire her. I just wanted to make sure you were one hundred percent okay with it."

"Why wouldn't I be?" The reservations Mandy had earlier had faded.

He shrugged. "I don't know. I just wanted to make sure you felt like she'd be a good fit for the office."

"She's good with people." Mandy thought back to one of the babysitting jobs they'd shared and how the little ones adored her sister. Deep down, Christina was a good person. Mandy now realized that part of her sister's immaturity had been caused by how the family had treated her. "Kids like her."

"That's important," he said.

Mandy turned back and faced the road as she thought about how much impact Tony had had on her life in such a short time. Her irritation over his sudden arrival had faded.

He pulled up in front of the hospital. "I'll let you out here. After I park the car, I'll join you. Your mother's room is in the cardiac unit on the second floor." He touched her arm and looked at her with a tenderness that showed his sincerity.

"Thanks," she whispered as she got out.

✧

Tony thought about the irony of the situation. Mandy had to return home because her mother's heart was failing, and when he picked her up at the gate, just seeing her made his heart pump harder than a sprint.

He parked the car, jogged to the hospital entrance, and took the elevator to the second floor. The nurse on duty advised him that since he wasn't family, he couldn't go into Mrs. Pruitt's room. He knew that, so he was prepared to wait as long as it took for Mandy to visit with her mother.

Christina appeared a few minutes after he sat down. "Hey," she said.

"Thanks for picking my sister up at the airport."

"No problem," he said. "I wanted to do it. So how's your mother doing?"

"Stable—at least for now." Christina's chin quivered. "When she dropped to the floor, I had no idea what was happening. I wish she'd told us she had a heart problem."

"She probably didn't want to worry her girls," Tony said. "I'm glad she's stable."

"I talked to the doctor about how I thought I might have caused her heart attack." Christina looked him in the eye as she paused. "He said the same thing you and Mandy did. It's a good thing I was there to call 911."

As silence fell between them, Tony noticed Christina fidgeting with anything she touched. She picked at a loose thread on her sleeve, and then she peeled one of her fingernails. He decided to give her the news.

"Looks like we might have an offer for you soon," he said. "You did quite well on the test."

Her eyebrows went up. "I did?"

He nodded. "We have a few more things to do, but it looks good."

Christina's face lit up with a smile, but then she slowly looked at the floor as the corners of her lips turned downward. "Does my sister know this?"

"Yes, she knows."

"And she doesn't mind?"

"Of course not. In fact she pointed out that you're very good with children, which I'm sure you know is a plus."

She looked back up and into his eyes as a smile slowly spread over her lips. "Thank you, Tony. I'm sure this will be good for my mother's heart."

"Maybe," he said, "but don't take responsibility for causing her heart attack. I'm sure you had nothing to do with it."

"I guess we'll find out soon."

"Why don't we say a prayer?"

Christina swallowed hard then nodded. "Good idea."

They'd just lifted their heads when Mandy rounded the corner and joined them. Tony stood up. "How's she doing?"

"Mom seems to be in good spirits, considering all the tubes in her arms and machines everywhere." Mandy hugged Christina. "I'm so glad you were there, or she might not have made it."

Tony took a step back to give the sisters some space. He wanted to be there if needed but not get in the way.

When Mandy glanced in his direction, he felt his pulse quicken. "Would you mind taking me home so I can change clothes? Since Mom's resting, I figured this would be a good time."

"I'll be glad to," he said. He turned to Christina. "You have both of our cell phone numbers, right?"

She nodded. "If anything happens, I'll call right away."

Mandy thanked Tony as he placed her bags by the door. "I should be able to come to work tomorrow if you need me."

"No. I made the schedule thinking you'd be at the home office, so you don't have to come in. You need to be with your family." He touched her cheek with the back of his hand but quickly pulled away. Mandy was again comforted by his presence and understanding of what she was going through.

After he left, she lowered her head and sent up a prayer of thanks—for her mother surviving the heart attack, for her sister being there, and for Tony's support. She changed out of her interview outfit and into more comfortable clothes. Then she made some sandwiches for her dad, her sister, and herself before heading for the hospital. On the way, she called her sister's cell phone.

"How's she doing?" she asked.

"She's napping right now," Christina said. "I'm worried about Dad. He's terribly distraught. I think he blames himself."

"I've been doing that, too," Mandy said. "We have to stop blaming ourselves. Instead we should be thankful for the blessing of Mom surviving and getting the medical care she needs."

"They're planning to do an angioplasty soon. Oh, wait a minute. The doctor just came out, and he wants to talk to me."

"I'll be there in a few minutes."

After they hung up, Mandy focused on her driving. She wanted to hear what the doctor had to say, so once she found a parking spot, she ran to the hospital entrance. By the time she reached the second floor cardiac unit, she was out of breath. Fortunately the doctor was still talking to her sister and dad.

The man in the white coat turned to her with a smile and extended his hand. "Dr. Jacobs," he said. "Your mother is fortunate to have had your sister right there with her. It was touch and go for a while, but I think we've got her stabilized enough with medications to do the procedure."

He explained how he planned to unblock a couple of her clogged arteries. "She'll be here for a week or so, depending on how well she does, and after she goes home, she'll need to take it easy for a while. Does she have someone there to take care of her?"

Mandy glanced at Christina, who nodded. Then she thought about the job. "We both work for Small World Portrait Studio, so I think we can arrange our schedules to make sure someone is there at all times."

Christina's eyes widened, and she opened her mouth to say something. Mandy gestured for her to keep quiet for now.

Chapter 11

After the doctor answered their questions, Christina turned to Mandy. "I got the job for sure?"

"I think so."

Christina settled back in her chair with a smile on her face. "Mom will be so happy about that. Now she and Dad won't have to worry about me, and I can find a place of my own so they can have peace and quiet again."

"Can you stay with them until Mom can get up and around again?" Mandy asked.

"Of course." Christina shook her head. "I'd never leave them stranded."

"I know." Mandy placed her hand on her sister's shoulder. "I'm so happy you're back. Everything is going to be just fine."

"I still feel like this is all my fault," Christina said.

"It's not your fault." Mandy gave Christina's shoulder a gentle squeeze.

"Thanks for trying to make me feel better, but I feel so guilty about arguing with her. If I had known. . ."

Mandy shook her head. "Mom hasn't felt good in years. On the way here, I talked to Dad and found out that she's been seeing a cardiologist since before you left. He recommended surgery a long time ago, but she was scared, so he prescribed some medication, hoping it would improve her condition."

"You're kidding. Why wouldn't she say anything?"

"She didn't want to worry us. Dad said she thought she had everything under control. Another thing is she didn't follow the diet the doctor put her on. That's going to change now."

"I had no idea." A bit of color returned to Christina's face. "I'm glad you told me because I've been beating myself up over this."

"I know. But don't. Mom is in good hands now."

"I'll do everything I can to help her, including make her eat right."

Mandy smiled at her younger sister. "There's no doubt in my mind that you will."

"So how was your trip to Atlanta?"

It seemed like days since she'd been in Edward Rossi's office discussing her future with Small World. "I didn't have much time there, but Mr. Rossi had just told me that I'm being offered a promotion. I'll be the regional trainer for all new photographers."

Christina's face lit up. "Will you be my new boss?"

"No, but I'll probably teach you to work the equipment when you're ready.

They're working on systems for new employees, and I don't think they've ironed everything out yet."

"I just hope I don't embarrass you."

Mandy felt a tug at her heart. "You've never embarrassed me, Christina. I'm proud of you, and I want to see you happy."

Christina was about to say something when their dad appeared at the door looking disheveled. Both sisters jumped up and ran over to him.

"How's she doing?" Mandy asked.

He raked his fingers through his hair. "She's stabilized, and they're getting her ready for surgery."

"Why don't we say a prayer?" Mandy said as she took hold of her sister's and dad's hands.

Mandy began, and then their dad added his prayer. When he paused, Christina cleared her throat and said a few words. After they said "amen" Mandy fought back tears and squeezed her sister's hand before releasing it. She still had the desire to control everything, but at least she was aware of it. With the Lord's help, she'd continue to work on letting go.

"There's nothing we can do now but wait," Mandy said. "Why don't we go on down to the cafeteria? I'll leave my cell phone number with the nurse so she can call us if we're needed."

Tony waited a couple of hours before calling Mandy to ask about her mom. He wanted to be there with her, but he didn't want to impose on her family while they stood vigil during Mrs. Pruitt's surgery. The employees at Small World obviously loved Mandy because as soon as he told them what had happened, everyone was concerned and offered to work more hours so she could be with her mother. Bella said she'd do whatever she could, and Steve offered to help with anything. He encouraged them all to pray.

After he felt like he'd waited long enough, Tony picked up the phone and punched in Mandy's cell phone number. She answered right away.

They had a short conversation. He told her everyone in the studio was praying for her family, and she gave him an update on her mom who had just gone into surgery.

After they hung up, he called his uncle in Atlanta. "Let us know if there's anything we can do," Uncle Ed said. "We've already ordered a card and fruit basket."

"Thanks. I'll keep you updated."

Tony went through the motions of making sure all the customers were taken care of, while the part-timers snapped shots of the children who came in. He kept watching the clock, wishing it would move faster so he could leave and go check on the Pruitt family.

Finally it was time to say good-bye to his employees. After he got the night deposit together, he closed out the register and shut down the computer. They banked nearby, so all he had to do was walk a few doors down and drop the wallet in the night deposit box before leaving for the hospital.

He arrived shortly before ten o'clock and went straight up to the waiting area. Mandy was there with her dad, but Christina had left for the evening.

When Mandy looked up at him, she smiled. "Mom got out of surgery a few hours ago. Looks like everything will be fine."

Tony blew out a breath of relief. "I'm glad." He had to resist the urge to reach for her and pull her into an embrace, so he shuffled his feet and turned toward Mr. Pruitt. "You have two very strong daughters. I bet you and your wife are very proud of them."

Mr. Pruitt nodded. "They've always been good girls but a little spirited at times."

Mandy blushed, which Tony thought was sweet. "I'm sure I gave my parents plenty of. . .spirited behavior." He turned and winked at Mandy. She smiled.

"Thanks for giving Christina a position with your company," Mr. Pruitt said. "Once she learns what she needs to know, she'll do a good job."

"No doubt," Tony said. He wasn't sure if Mandy had mentioned her promotion yet, so he decided not to bring it up. "We've found that once we have an employee who exceeds expectations, other family members often do well, too."

"To be honest, I was a little surprised you didn't have an antinepotism policy. But her mother and I are very happy."

Mandy touched her dad's arm. "You told her already?"

Her dad nodded. "After she came to, her first question was how you and Christina were holding up. I told her you flew back from an important meeting to be with her, and Christina got a good job with your company. That made her happy."

"Good," Tony said. "Looks like everything will be just fine. If there's anything I can do for any of you, let me know, okay?" He paused as his gaze met Mandy's. "Take the time you need. You haven't used any of your paid time off, and if you need more, I'll see what I can do."

"Thanks, Tony."

"I better go." Tony extended his hand to Mandy's dad. After they shook, he hesitated before reaching for her hand. As his grip tightened on hers, she felt an odd sensation fluttering around in her stomach. He quickly let go and shoved his hand into his pocket. "Call me tomorrow if you have time." Then he turned and left.

After he turned the corner, Mandy's dad stepped up beside her and put his arm around her. "Your boss seems to be a good man."

Mandy nodded. "Yes, he really is."

"Ya know, back in my day, portrait studios were run by people who studied a long time to become photographers. I have to admit I'm surprised he wanted to hire Christina."

"I didn't have photography experience when they hired me, remember?"

"Yeah, seems I do remember, but somehow you never surprise me. You've always succeeded at everything."

"Not everything."

"Pretty near everything. How will your sister know how to take pictures? She's always been in front of the camera, not behind it."

"We have great equipment that's easy to use with the right training. My new job will be to teach people how to operate the equipment and what to do to get the best shots of children."

"That's good. I hope she catches on fast."

"She will." Mandy slipped her arm in his and kissed his cheek. "She has good genes."

"So tell me more about Tony. Is he single?"

"Da—ad." Mandy laughed. "I can't believe you just asked me that."

"You can't blame me for looking out for my two daughters." He tilted his head and looked at her from beneath his heavy eyebrows. "My two *available* daughters. I want you and your sister to be happy and have fulfilling lives."

"I can't speak for Christina, but I don't need a man in my life to be fulfilled."

"I know, but it's always nice to have someone to share your experiences with."

Mandy couldn't argue that point. She had to admit, if only to herself, she'd experienced some loneliness. There were times even Brent from the electronics store from across the street seemed appealing. Then she came to her senses.

"If some nice young man just happens to cross your path, I hope you at least consider getting to know him."

"Okay, Dad, I promise I'll give someone a chance—as long as he's a Christian man."

"That goes without saying." He glanced at his watch. "I wonder how your mother's doing."

"Why don't we go see?"

The next morning, Tony arrived at the studio and was surprised to see Mandy there. "Why aren't you at the hospital with your mom?"

"She's doing much better, and I thought it would be better to take time off after she gets home."

"Excellent point." Tony had scheduled around Mandy, figuring she'd need at least a week or two. "Let me call the part-timers and let them know they don't have to come in."

After he finished calling people, he came back out to the reception area and saw Mandy looking over the schedule. "Looks like we'll be busy today. Good." She came around the counter and straightened up some of the displays on the table then walked toward the studio before she stopped and turned to face him. "When do you think Christina will be able to start?"

"I have the paperwork in my office. When do you think she'd like to start?"

"As soon as possible. I think she's excited about working here."

"By the way, my uncle said he'd like to talk to you. He's planning a trip here so you won't have to go back to Atlanta. He's bringing his wife and making a little vacation of it, so I thought maybe you could give them some ideas of things to do while they're here. I thought he might want to stay at Oglebay Park in the Wilson Lodge."

"Sounds like a nice vacation. Does he play golf?"

"He loves it. My aunt will have to find something to do while he's working though." He thought for a minute then added, "You'll like my aunt."

"I'm sure I will." Mandy smiled. "Your whole family has been nice to me."

"Maybe you can show her around one afternoon—that is, if your mother is doing okay and you have time."

His heart warmed at the smile that spread over her face. "I'd love to. Just let me know when," she said softly before disappearing into the studio.

Tony did his paperwork then stuck his head in the studio. Mandy glanced up. "Need something?"

"I'd like to have Christina come in sometime tomorrow if she's available."

"Want me to call her?" she asked.

"If you want. Or I can."

She pulled her bottom lip between her teeth as she thought about it, and then she smiled. "Why don't you call her? It'll mean more since you'll be her supervisor."

Mandy finished setting up the photography area then went back to the counter to make some calls. She wanted to stay as busy as possible while at work to keep from thinking about her mother. She knew Tony would understand if she needed to drop everything if her family needed her. As long as her mother was still in the hospital, Mandy could visit without having to worry too much.

Tony appeared at the end of the counter about fifteen minutes later. "I had a nice conversation with Christina. She's excited about working here, but I understand that she's needed at home, so I told her she could start whenever she wanted to. She wants to start as soon as possible, so I told her she could come in now or wait until after your mother was settled."

"What did she say?"

"I'm waiting for her to call me back. She said she needed to talk to your dad and the doctor."

Mandy was impressed. Her sister had obviously been jolted into another burst of maturity. "Since I'll be doing the photography training, I'll have to be here with her."

"That's another thing I wanted to discuss with you. We're hiring her into the management training program. One of the things they're working on at the home office is a manual with self-administered tests. I'll work with her on company systems and some management policies. After we get past the first part of the training, which should last a couple of weeks, I'll turn her over to you. We haven't done the photographers' manual yet, and we'd like for you to be involved."

Mandy's ego jumped up a couple of notches. "Thanks, Tony."

"I mean it. You have skills that we need to teach others. I just hope we choose the right people who are willing to learn."

"It's really not all that hard." She'd never gotten so many compliments in her life.

"It took me three weeks to master the camera and poses," Tony said. "How long do you think it'll take someone like your sister who doesn't have much experience with a camera?"

She looked pensive for a minute as she stuck a card back in the file drawer. "There's more than just learning the camera and poses. I'll want to work with her on behavior modification for the kids who are—well, rather difficult."

Tony grinned. "She couldn't have a better teacher."

Mandy felt her face heat up. "I remember what it's like to be a kid wearing miserable clothes and being told to sit still when I wanted to get up and run."

"Yeah, I remember that, too." He chuckled. "I think most people forget what it's like to be a child."

"Probably." She finished her filing and pushed the drawer shut then turned to face Tony. As soon as their eyes made contact, she felt a giant thud in her chest.

He blinked and took a step back. Had he felt it, too?

❦

Tony felt like he'd been hit head-on by a tidal wave. The warmth of Mandy's hazel eyes with the gold flecks caused a sensation unlike anything he'd ever experienced.

He cleared his throat and shuffled his feet. "Um. . .when your sister comes in, I'll get her started on the training manual. I think we'll have a better idea of when she's ready for you after she gets started."

She slowly nodded. "I think that's wise."

He remembered his new hire was due in a couple of hours. "While you were out, I went ahead and hired a new part-time photographer. I wasn't sure when you'd be back, so I told her I'd work with her until our crackerjack photographer returned."

"Crackerjack, huh?" She looked amused.

"Well, you're much more than that."

Her smile widened. "Thanks."

Tony was relieved when the phone rang. He gestured toward it. "Want me to get that?"

"No, I've got it." She lifted the receiver and gave him one last smile before she turned her full attention to the caller.

Tony went back to his office to get the paperwork ready for the new photographer to sign. His cousin had encouraged him to get to know Mandy better outside of work, and he understood why. He had no doubt that they'd make a great team—both at work and as friends, or more. When Mandy appeared at the door, he motioned for her to come inside.

As soon as she did, he leaned forward. "How would you like to go out to lunch after church on Sunday?"

Chapter 12

Mandy's heart rate doubled. Had Tony just asked her out on a date? He held up his hands. "Don't feel like you have to. It's not like a date or anything."

Okay, so it wasn't a date. "That would be nice."

"I haven't been in town long enough to know the best places. Any suggestions?"

Mandy didn't normally go out to lunch on Sundays, so she wasn't sure. She shrugged. "What kind of food do you like?"

"Anything I don't have to cook," he replied. "We can decide then."

"Sounds good."

Tony put down his pen, leaned back, and folded his arms. "Okay, so what do you need?"

She tilted her head. "Um. . ."

"You came in here, remember?"

Mandy shuffled her feet as she tried to remember what she wanted. "Must not have been very important."

"If you remember, you know where I am." She started to turn and leave, but he called her name. "I almost forgot to tell you, we're planning a regional campaign that should start in about three months."

"What kind of campaign?"

"TV, radio, newspaper, and magazine ads. We've been working on it for a while, and we about have everything nailed down."

"Anything I can do to help?" Mandy asked.

"Yes, as a matter of fact, everyone on the management team will be asked to look over the package before it goes out."

Management team. That sounded nice. "I'm sure it'll be good."

"The biggest holdup is getting the actors for the TV ads. Ricco isn't happy with what they've done."

"How about using real people?"

"Real people?" he asked. "Like customers?"

Mandy nodded. "Yes. I can think of several customers who'd love to be involved in something like this."

"Not a bad idea. Let me run it past Ricco and see what he thinks. The kids they've filmed are already overexposed, and we're concerned about the credibility of using them, so I think he just might go for it."

"You know my sister went to Hollywood to be an actress," Mandy reminded him.

"Yes, I know." He pursed his lips. "But I'm not sure it would be such a good idea to have her in a TV ad just yet. We need her to focus on her job here and not see this as a stepping-stone back to where she wanted to go."

"If you want me to talk to her about that, I will," Mandy offered.

The buzzer on the door sounded, alerting them that someone had entered. "It's up to you," Tony said.

⁂

The next several days, Mandy spent most of her time either at the studio or with her mother at the hospital. Each day seemed to be better than the one before.

"The doctor says I can go home Monday," her mother said when Mandy entered the room on Saturday. "Would you mind helping Christina get rid of all the unhealthy food? I'm afraid I won't be able to resist it if it's there."

Mandy laughed as she patted her tummy. "Oh I'll get rid of it."

"Please eat healthy," her mother said. "I don't want you to wind up like me. Between the high-fat food and worry, I'm afraid I've been a bad example."

Mandy stroked her mother's hair. "You've been a wonderful mother. But you do need to stop worrying about Christina and me. We're adults now. You've done your job."

"I know." Her mother smiled and reached up to take Mandy's hand. "It's just so hard, though, to turn off what I've been doing for twenty-some years."

"Now that Christina has a job, there's nothing left to worry about. She said she wants to live with you and Dad for a while so she can help out until you get your health back. And you know where I am."

Her mother nodded and smiled as tears sprang to her eyes. "I'm so blessed."

"Our whole family is," Mandy said.

"I'm glad Christina's back. When she left, I felt like my heart would break in two."

Mandy stilled as she remembered Christina expressing guilt over causing their mother's heart attack. "Did you tell her that?"

"I was so upset, I probably did." A stricken look came over her face. "You don't think she's blaming herself for what happened to me, do you?"

Bingo. "Don't worry about that now. Just do whatever it takes to get better. But no more health secrets, okay?"

Her mother nodded. "I'll talk to her."

Mandy gave her another hug. "I have to go to work today, but Tony's encouraging me to take some time off to spend with you."

"I don't want you to risk your job for me."

"Don't be silly, Mom. I wouldn't want to work for a company where they didn't value family."

Her mother smiled. "Christina says Tony's a very sweet man."

Mandy felt heat rise to her cheeks as her mother studied her. "He is nice."

"So do you like him?"

"He's a very good boss."

"You know what I mean, Mandy. Christina thinks he's interested in you."

Mandy tried hard not to smile. "Don't pay any attention to that. He's a very nice, caring boss who knows he needs to treat his employees well to keep them happy."

"I don't want you missing out on an opportunity to find love, Mandy. Even if he is your boss."

Mandy forced a laugh. "That's just it. Because he's my boss, I need to respect him as my supervisor. Period."

"Okay, okay, I hear you. Just don't ever put a job ahead of true love."

"I love you, Mom." Mandy bent over to kiss her mother on the cheek then backed away. "If you need me, just call or tell Dad to call me, and I'll be here."

Her mother lifted a hand and wiggled her fingers in a wave before turning to face the window on the other side of the room. Mandy left the hospital room and nearly collided with her sister as she rounded the corner to the elevator.

"How's Mom?" Christina asked.

Mandy grabbed her sister by the arm and steered her toward the waiting area. "I want to make sure you understand that you had nothing to do with Mom's heart attack."

"What made you say that?"

"She said she told you that her heart would break if you left. You do realize that's a figure of speech, right?"

Christina's shoulders sagged as she expelled a breath. "I don't know. It seems like everything I've ever done has upset Mom and Dad. Back in high school when I made cheerleader, Mom got frustrated over my uniform."

"That's because you didn't tell her you needed it until the weekend before the first game."

"She should have figured it out, since I made the squad. Then there was the play when I needed to color my hair purple."

Mandy laughed at the memory. "Well I have to admit, it did look permanent. You should have told us you were doing a temporary rinse."

"See?" Christina lifted her hands then dropped them, slapping her sides. "You would have known all that stuff. I've just been such a loser all my life."

"You are not a loser. You've had so many things going on, you forgot to communicate." Mandy put her arm around Christina and hugged her. "You were very busy back in high school, but that was then. Now you're all grown up, and you're about to start a wonderful career."

"What if I mess up on the job?" Christina asked. "It'll be hard if they expect me to measure up to you."

"Don't worry about that. Tony's a very smart man who knows we're two separate, very different people."

"I hope so. I sure don't want to disappoint another person."

Mandy gently turned her sister toward their mother's hospital room and gave her a little push. "Go see Mom. I have to go to work so I can relieve you next week. Tony's been working on a training program for you."

"I'll try to make you proud, Mandy." Her eyebrows went up as she reached into her pocket and pulled out an envelope. "Oh, I almost forgot. I went to a consignment shop, and they sold some of my LA clothes that I couldn't use here, and now I can pay you back for the plane ticket."

"You don't have to pay me right now if you need the money for new clothes," Mandy said.

Christina firmly handed it to her. "Yes I do. It's part of my growing up and taking responsibility."

Mandy thought about her need to let go and stop trying to mother her sister. She put the envelope into her purse. "Thank you, Christina. I'm really proud of you."

❧

Tony had just walked out of the back part of the studio when Mandy walked in. "How's your mom?"

"She's doing much better. They're releasing her on Monday."

"Good. I'll call Steve to come in." As he talked, he noticed Mandy's look of concern. "What's wrong?"

"Nothing." She cleared her throat.

He'd been around her enough to know better. "If you need to talk, I'm all ears. I might not know how to fix whatever the problem is, but I can at least listen."

"Thanks." Mandy headed off down the hall to the office where she kept her handbag then came out, brushing her hands together. "I'm ready to work."

He chuckled. "I can tell." He started to go into his office, until he heard her clear her throat, so he turned around to see her looking at him.

"Tony?"

"Yes?" As they held their gaze, everything else around them seemed insignificant. "Did you need something?"

"Thank you for hiring my sister."

Tony sat back as she paused. "You don't have to thank me."

"No one realized how smart she was, but I knew. It's not that easy being so popular and juggling such a busy schedule."

"I can imagine," Tony said. "Somehow you did just fine."

"We hung out in different circles. Mom and Dad always thought of her as the fragile sister, while I was sturdy and capable. Then when she informed us that she was leaving for Hollywood without a single prospect for a job, Mom and Dad hit the roof."

"Must have been rough on them." He'd already figured most of this out, but Mandy obviously needed to talk.

Mandy nodded. "Oh it was very rough. They called me every day after she first left, wondering if I'd heard from her. Most of the time, I hadn't. So I started calling her. She was always in a hurry and needed to go."

Tony nodded. "I remember being her age—too busy for people who cared the most. But I bet you never felt that way."

"I did, but I never had the nerve to act on it or say what Christina said." She paused. "When she finally called and said she was stranded, I have to admit I was annoyed."

"Understandable."

"But I wasn't about to leave her in the lurch. I had some hard feelings about her expecting everyone to drop everything, but once she got home, I realized that was my problem, not hers. She was just finished testing her wings, and now she was ready to come home."

"So how do you feel about her working here?"

"That's what I'm getting at. I have no doubt my sister can do a fabulous job, once she gets into it."

"With you as her trainer, she'll be an excellent photographer."

Mandy smiled. "Thank you. I hope you're right."

"Don't sell yourself short, Mandy," Tony said. "You're an amazing woman."

He waited for her to say something, but she just stood there.

"I appreciate you telling me all this. I know how difficult it must have been for you."

"It was extremely hard," she agreed as she stood. "I need to set up the studio for my next customers now."

After she left the office, Tony prayed that he'd be able to do whatever it took to bring out the best in both of the Pruitt sisters.

At the end of the busy afternoon, Mandy stopped by his office, where he was putting the final changes in Christina's training manual. "Thanks for listening, Tony. I wanted to make sure you understood that my sister and I are completely different."

"You made your point, but I already figured that out." And he admired Mandy now, more than ever.

"Thanks."

Tony shut down the computer, while Mandy got her personal belongings from the other office. They met in the reception area as they were about to leave for the day.

"Wanna do something tonight?"

She stopped and turned to face him. "Do something?"

He lifted a shoulder and tried to appear casual. "Yeah, like go out or—I don't know—eat dinner and maybe take in a movie."

The slow smile that spread across her face warmed his heart. "Yes, I'd like that."

"I'll pick you up in an hour, okay?"

"Sounds good."

✢

The evening was delightful and would have been even better if Tony had gotten the nerve to kiss her good night at her door. But instead he stood there, shuffling his feet, telling her how much he appreciated working with her. This was the first time in his life he hadn't known what to say to a woman he cared about. But it was also his first time to go out with someone he worked with. Finally he just reached up and squeezed her shoulder.

"I had a nice time," she said, her voice barely above a whisper.

"Want me to pick you up for church in the morning?"

She looked directly up at him and nodded. "Sure."

✢

The next morning, Mandy stared straight ahead as the pastor delivered his sermon. Her sister sat on one side of her, and Tony was on the other side. It felt right.

Tony escorted both of them to the parking lot, where he turned to Christina. "Mandy and I are going to lunch. Would you like to join us?"

Christina lifted an eyebrow and glanced back and forth between them then grinned and slowly shook her head. "Nah, I don't think so. I'll go hang out at the hospital and give Dad a break."

"We won't be long," Mandy said quickly. "As soon as I get back, I'll join you."

Christina touched Mandy's arm and snorted. "No, go have some fun. Your work will be cut out for you once I start at Small World."

On their way to the car, Tony leaned over and whispered, "Your sister is very smart and funny."

Mandy nodded. "Where are we going?"

"I wanted to go to Figaretti's, but they don't open until four. Where would you like to eat?"

"Why don't we go across the bridge to Ohio Valley Mall? I'm sure we'll find something there."

"Great idea. We've been thinking about putting a studio in that mall, so I can check it out."

Chapter 13

Mandy got to the studio before anyone else on Monday morning. She promised her dad and sister she'd be at the hospital when her mother was released at ten o'clock, but she wanted to make sure everything she'd scheduled at work was in order.

Tony arrived fifteen minutes later. "I didn't think you were coming in today."

"The Phillips twins have the first appointment, and they're rather difficult." She arranged some of the props on the table by the camera. "Jonathan likes the monkey, and Jason always tries to take it away from him, even though he's more interested in the model cars." She held one up to demonstrate her point.

"Mandy!" Tony crossed the room and took the model car from her then set it down on the table.

"Sorry. I know you can handle them. It's just that—well, I don't want anyone to struggle."

"I know you don't." Tony pointed to the stool behind her, and then he pulled one up and sat down. "Listen. You're going into management soon, and that means you'll have to delegate. If you try to do it all yourself, you'll go crazy, not to mention the fact that you'll wind up building weakness in your trainees."

She pondered that for a moment. "I didn't think about it that way."

"I understand. In fact when I read over the management training stuff for Uncle Edward, I realized how important it was to back away at some point and let people practice what you taught them."

Mandy knew he was right. "Okay, here's my bag of tricks. If one toy doesn't work, try another until you hit on something that keeps the kids' attention."

He laughed and stood up. "Attagirl. Now go help your family. If you need me, I'll be glad to do what I can. Steve will be here around noon, and Bella said she's ready to take on more hours."

"Thanks, Tony." She started toward the door then stopped. "Oh, I almost forgot. Christina said she could start this afternoon if you want her to."

"I think tomorrow morning will be soon enough. I'll have all her books ready in the office. The first thing I want to teach her is how to answer the phone and deal with walk-ins."

Mandy turned to leave but stopped and smiled at Tony. "Thanks for lunch yesterday. I had fun."

"Me, too," he said. "I think Ohio Valley Mall is the perfect place for a Small World Portrait Studio. In fact we're considering relocating this one if the rent keeps going up on Market Street."

"I'd hate to shut this place down."

"But then again, we might not. We like it here, too, and you've built a nice base of steady customers."

"Good. I guess it's time to go now."

Tony laughed. "Yes, I guess it is. Now scoot."

When Mandy arrived at the hospital, she headed straight for the elevator. The door opened on the second floor, and she saw her sister and dad standing outside her mother's room, talking.

"What's going on?" she asked as she approached them.

"The doctor got here early," her dad said. "They're getting her ready to leave, so we should be out of here in a few minutes."

Mandy let out a sigh of relief. Her sister arched an eyebrow and gave her a once-over. "Are you okay?"

"Sure, I'm fine." Mandy self-consciously ran her hands down the front of her blouse and pants. "Why?"

"You just look—well, different." Christina tilted her head and grinned.

"Hey, y'all, they're letting me go home. Finally!"

All heads turned to Mandy's mother as the nursing assistant wheeled her out of the room. "I'll wheel her down to the lobby. If you can pull your car up to the loading area, I'll help her in."

Mandy and Christina stayed behind while their dad went to get the car. Their mother wore a huge smile. "I can't believe I'm finally able to go home and sleep in my own bed."

"Don't you like the service here?" the assistant teased.

"It's great if you like getting prodded, pinched, and awakened at all hours of the day and night." She snorted. "The night nurse woke me up to see if I needed a sleeping pill."

Mandy laughed. "It can't be that bad."

"You're right," her mother agreed. "But I do miss my own bed."

Christina winked at Mandy. "I went through the cupboards and fridge and got rid of all the cookies, ice cream, and other unhealthy foods, just like you told me to."

Their mother groaned. "Looks like I'll have some adjusting to do, but at least I have someone to help me through it."

By the time they got her home, she was out of breath. "Easy does it," their dad said as he lifted her and carefully placed her on the sofa.

"I'm not an invalid," she said. "I can walk."

"I know," he replied. "But let me spoil you a little bit. It makes me feel good."

Christina nudged Mandy toward the kitchen. "We'll fix you something yummy and healthy to eat. Be right back."

Once they reached the kitchen, Christina leaned against the counter and chuckled softly with her hand over her mouth. "Dad was so worried, and now he's treating her like fragile glass. I never realized how lost he'd be without her until this."

Mandy nodded. "Sometimes it takes a scare to snap people's attention back to where it should be."

"You got that right. This whole thing reminded me how important it is to lean on the Lord. I never stopped believing, but I have to admit there were times when I didn't think about His hand in my life."

"I know exactly what you're saying," Mandy admitted. "He's shown me that I can't control everything around me."

Christina smiled. "I guess we'll always be works in progress."

They worked on a vegetable platter with the produce Christina had bought. She held up a small container of low-fat yogurt. "I have a great recipe for dip that is actually heart healthy."

"Great! I could use some of that myself. I think this is a wake-up call for all of us."

"Ya know, I've never had my cholesterol checked," Christina said as she dumped the ingredients into a bowl and stirred. "Mom isn't overweight, so I assumed she was healthy. Who would have thought she had cholesterol as high as hers?"

"I know. I think all of us will be healthier now." Mandy plunged a stick of celery into the yogurt dip then tasted it. "Yum. That's delicious. In fact, I think I like that better than the high-fat stuff we used to eat."

Christina picked up a cookbook and showed it to Mandy. "I found this heart-healthy cookbook with easy recipes, so I don't think this will be too hard. Dad and I have been experimenting with a few things so we'd at least have something to fix for Mom when she got home."

"You're kidding. You got Dad in the kitchen?"

With a nod, Christina chuckled. "Yeah, can you believe it?"

"Now I know he must have been scared."

They fixed some iced decaf green tea and put everything on a tray that Christina carried out to their parents. "Here's a snack to enjoy while Mandy and I fix lunch."

By the time Mandy went back to her own place that night, she was certain that her sister had everything under control. To Mandy's amazement, Christina had a week's worth of menus and exercises lined up for their mom. And even more surprising, their mom seemed perfectly content following orders.

The next morning, when Mandy arrived back at her parents' house to relieve her sister, her dad said Christina had already left for work. "She was pacing and acting all nervous," he explained. "I figured we'd all be better off if she went on over there."

"You're probably right. How was Mom's night?"

"She was a little restless, and I couldn't sleep, so we spent about an hour talking."

"Doesn't she need sleep?"

"Yes, but I think it was good to get everything out."

"Are y'all talking about me?"

Mandy and her dad looked up to see her mother standing in the doorway of the living room. She was dressed in a jogging suit and had her makeup on.

"You look nice, Mom," Mandy said as she crossed over to give her a hug. "Are you planning to go out?"

"Maybe a walk around the block." She cut her gaze over to her husband before adding, "I need to work up to a couple of miles soon, but I figure the block is all I can handle just yet."

"What can I do?" Mandy asked.

"Wanna go for a walk with us?"

"Sure, Mom. Let me go out to my car and get my sneakers. I'll be right back."

Mandy was pleased that her mother was willing to do whatever it took to get healthy. That meant everyone's life would get back to normal more quickly. She spent the remainder of the day helping and watching her dad cater to her mother's whims.

Christina came home at dinnertime. "I am exhausted," she said as she dropped onto the sofa. "There is so much to learn, I feel like my head is swollen ten times its normal size."

Mandy took a step back and studied her head. "Nope. No swelling that I can see."

"How long did it take you to learn how to do all that stuff?"

"Not long. And I didn't have a manual. I'm glad they have some training materials now. It'll be so much easier if you can look stuff up."

Christina's face suddenly lit up as she straightened. "Tony said I can actually start working tomorrow, since I spent the whole day studying."

"Working?" Mandy asked. "As in taking pictures?"

"Ya know. . ." Christina tapped her chin with her index finger. "I'm not sure what I'll be doing. All I know is I'll be glad to move around a little. My back is killing me from sitting all day."

"Dinner's ready. Mom is in the kitchen right now. She and Dad have gone for two walks around the block. She's gradually working up to her two miles per day."

"Looks like we're all learning new stuff." Christina stood up and stretched.

"God has a way of making us learn what He wants us to know."

Christina frowned. "You don't think God actually caused Mom's heart attack, do you?"

"I don't think so. But I do think He's using it to bring all of us closer and showing us how fortunate we are."

After dinner, Mandy went back to her place. Her parents asked if they could be alone the next day, so she called Tony's cell phone to let him know she wanted to work.

"That's fine with me. At least they're not far, so if you're needed, you can be there in a few minutes."

Mandy arrived early on Wednesday then Tony followed. Christina walked in five minutes before they opened.

Grinning, she looked at Tony. "You said I could start working. What do you want me to do?"

"Remember the phone section in the manual? I'd like for you to answer calls and receive walk-ins." He handed her a stack of cards. "Between calls, you can file these prospect cards. After you're comfortable with the reception area, I'll teach you how to follow up on some of those folks who have called or expressed interest in having portraits done."

Christina frowned but took the cards. Mandy knew her sister was unhappy, but she needed to get over it. So Mandy left the front desk and went into the studio, where everything had been neatly put away.

"I tried to leave it like you do," Tony said from behind her. "Does it pass inspection?"

Mandy spun around to face him, and she lost her breath when she realized he was less than two feet away. "Yes." Her throat tightened. "It looks very nice."

He closed the distance between them and took her hands. "Mandy, I—"

"Excuse me," Christina said from the door. "I have a question."

Tony took a quick step back and turned toward the door. "What do you need?"

"How long do I have to stand at the front desk? I have all the cards filed, and no one has walked in yet."

Mandy glanced up at the big clock on the studio wall. They'd been there for less than half an hour, and her sister was already bored. She started say something, but she held back. This was Tony's deal. He needed to handle the situation as he would for any trainee.

"Would you rather go back to the office and study some more?" he asked.

"Um. . ." Christina glared at Mandy, but Mandy looked away. "Would it be okay if I brought my study materials up to the front desk? At least I'd have something to do when I'm not talking on the phone."

"Sure, that would be just fine," Tony replied. "Just remember the customer always comes first."

"I know that." Christina turned and left them alone again.

When Tony looked at Mandy again, she had to hold back the grin that threatened. His shoulders shook with silent laughter. "I can't say you didn't warn me."

"I never said anything about what she just did."

"No, but I'm good at reading between the lines. Your sister is sharp, and she needs to be constantly challenged. I'm thinking we might speed her through the management material in the book and move her into some photography a little sooner than originally planned. Are you up to that?"

"Of course," she replied. "I'll do whatever I need to do."

"Do you realize how much more walk-in traffic we'd get in the mall?"

Mandy reluctantly nodded. "I suppose we probably would."

"Right now our rent is much lower than mall rent, but the paperwork for renewing our lease just came in this morning, and it's worse than we thought. Ricco said it's sky-high—close to mall rent, and they're not budging because other businesses want this space."

"When do we have to sign the lease?" Mandy asked.

"The current lease is up in six months, but I think we have another ninety days on a month-to-month."

Nine months. At least they had that long before they had to move. Besides, it wasn't like they'd be going far. Ohio Valley Mall was just on the other side of the bridge. Fifteen minutes away. But still. . .

"We'd need to assess other aspects besides the rent, though. Like I already said, we have a solid base of customers, and we need to see if they're willing to go to the mall. If not, we need to evaluate cost versus income—or at least potential income."

"Mandy," Christina hollered from the front. "I need you."

"Sorry," Mandy said as she ran toward the front. "I'll have a talk with her after work."

Chapter 14

M andy braced herself to face her sister. "Whatcha need?"

Christina glared at her. "You never told me how boring this job was. I hate standing here, waiting for nothing to happen."

"Then don't just stand there," Mandy said. "Be proactive. Study your materials."

"I've studied them until my brains felt like they'd implode. Is this what you do all day?"

Mandy thought for a moment then gestured toward a stool. "Have a seat, Christina. We need to talk about this whole situation."

Christina did as she was told and sat. "Okay, now what?"

"Small World is currently in a transition. Until recently, there were no training manuals. People got hired and trained on the job. They were thrown into a situation, and they had to swim or they'd sink fast."

"You did just fine with that."

"Not really." Mandy thought about how in-the-dark she'd been since she'd started. "Once I started working here, I was determined to make it work. I enjoy taking pictures of the children, so I focused on learning everything I could about how to do the best job at it."

"Why can't I do that?"

Mandy took her sister's hand. "You can. But don't expect this to be an exciting job right off the bat. Tony already mentioned that we need to speed things up a bit with you, and once we do that, brace yourself."

A myriad of expressions crossed Christina's face, from consternation to contemplation and then satisfaction. "Okay, I think that'll be good. I understand everything so far, so there's really no reason I can't jump into the next step."

"Okay. Perhaps Tony will let you come back and observe the picture taking process. We'll have to have someone at the desk, though."

Christina seemed satisfied with that. "Thanks, Mandy. I'm glad I have you going to bat for me."

"I don't mind doing it now, but I won't always be here to deal with stuff like this."

Suddenly a look of panic shot across Christina's face. "You won't?"

"No, because I'll be traveling after I start the training."

"Oh." Christina frowned. "I guess I'm your guinea pig, huh?"

Mandy laughed. "Yes, but a very cute guinea pig."

Tony walked up with his hands in his pockets. "Are you two okay?"

"Christina would like to move a little faster in her training, and I think she's ready for the next step."

"I agree." Tony looked at Christina. "We don't have the photography training nailed down yet, but I think Mandy will know what to do."

Mandy nodded. "I'd also like to teach her to call prospects who requested more information. She doesn't like standing here waiting for walk-ins."

"Did you tell her about the mall?"

Mandy shook her head. "I didn't know if I should say anything."

Tony turned to Christina. "We've been looking at moving to the Ohio Valley Mall."

She crinkled her forehead. "We are? Why?"

He explained the rent situation. "Sometimes it just comes down to economics."

Christina pondered what he said for a moment then her eyes lit up. "Cool! I love the mall!"

"I know you do," Mandy said as she and Tony exchanged an amused glance.

"I can go shopping at lunch and maybe even get my nails done at the salon."

Mandy groaned. "You'll just need to put yourself on a budget, so you don't spend your whole check in the other stores."

Tony chuckled as he walked away. "I'll leave you two to work this out. But do whatever you think about the photography training, Mandy."

After he closed his office door, Christina made a face. "Am I annoying him?"

Mandy shook her head. "I doubt it. He's just really busy with all the changes."

"Okay, so what should I do next?" Christina hopped off the stool and walked back to the front part of the counter.

"Have you gotten to the section in the manual where it tells how to contact people from the mail-in forms?"

Christina nodded and scrunched her nose. "I hate phone solicitation."

"It's not really phone solicitation since they filled out the forms and requested information. All you have to do is call, tell them you're available for any questions, and invite them in. Make sure you have a price list nearby because a lot of people want prices."

"It's okay if I quote prices over the phone?"

Mandy tilted her head. "Of course. Why wouldn't it be?"

Christina hung her head. "I guess I must not have told you that I worked as a phone solicitor for a company in Hollywood that wouldn't allow us to mention price. I hated that job."

"You definitely didn't tell me about that. How long did you work there?"

"About three hours. After getting hang-up after hang-up, I finally just grabbed my handbag, marched right into my supervisor's stuffy office, and told him I quit." She frowned. "He had the nerve to laugh right in my face. He said I'd never amount to anything."

An alarm sounded in the back of Mandy's mind, but she tried to squelch it. "You've been with Small World longer than that." She pointed to the date on the calendar. "It must not be too bad here."

The color in Christina's face drained, and she grabbed Mandy's arm. "I don't want you to think I'd do that to you. I'd never just walk out of here."

"I hope not."

"You mean too much to me," Christina said. "Besides, before I accepted this job, Dad had a talk with me. He said I couldn't just think about myself this time. I had to consider the fact that we're sisters, and anything I do might reflect on you."

"Dad said that?"

Christina nodded. "And that's not all he said. It'll take me hours to tell you everything I had to go through with him before I agreed to work here."

"I want you to be yourself. If you ever feel like this isn't the place for you, please let me know."

Christina shrugged then nodded. "I can see where he's coming from. After all, I don't have the best employment history. And I have to admit I hesitated at first. Then I decided to do whatever it took to stick it out, no matter how much I hate the job."

"You hate it?"

"Not yet." Christina smiled and playfully shoved Mandy. "Just kidding. No, I actually like it here, even though standing at the counter is boring."

"All jobs have something not to like," Mandy said. "It's up to you to turn that around. I don't like standing here without something to do, either, which is why I use my time to call people."

"That makes sense." Christina glanced over at the stack of cards that had recently come in. "Do you have a script?"

"Not a script, but the guidelines should be in your training manual." Mandy reached for the manual that Christina had stuck beneath the counter, and she flipped through until she found the section on follow-up. "Here it is. Read this a couple of times, and then we can practice before you place your first call."

"Is that your job?" Christina asked. "I mean, you're the photography trainer, not the phone-call trainer."

"I think it's okay for me to do this for you. Our goal isn't to stay in some narrow job description. We want to provide the best service and product to keep our customers happy."

Tony heard every single word between the sisters, even behind the closed office door. He grinned as Mandy helped Christina work through her concerns.

From the moment he saw them interact, he could see the love between them, but he also saw that there were issues, too. Christina had quite a bit to learn about business, but Mandy needed to learn to delegate and not try to do everything herself. *She'd make an awesome mom.* He quickly dropped that thought and forced himself to concentrate on work.

He got up to take over from Mandy. As he opened his office door, both women were standing close, looking at the training manual. His pulse quickened when Mandy turned around and smiled at him.

"I was just showing her some stuff to do when it's slow," Mandy said.

"Good idea."

Christina picked up a card and turned to Mandy. "How about we start now?" She looked at the name on the card. "You can be Mrs. Fielding."

Tony lifted an eyebrow as he looked at Mandy. "We get to see if acting runs in the family."

Mandy rolled her eyes as she laughed. "I'm afraid my sister got all the acting genes."

He hung around and listened as they rehearsed the first time. Christina was actually pretty good at answering the objections Mandy tossed at her.

"You can do this," Mandy said. "Would you be more comfortable with me here, or would you like for us to leave you alone for your first call?"

Christina chewed her lip for a few seconds. "I'm sort of embarrassed to make a fool of myself in front of you, but if I need help, it'll be nice to know you're right here."

Tony made a quick decision. "I'll go check some bulbs in the studio. Let me know if you need me."

He hovered close to the door during the first part of Christina's call. She stumbled at first, but within seconds she found her footing. The second call she made came across much more confident.

After he turned on all the lights to make sure the bulbs worked, he joined the women at the counter. "So how's it going?"

Mandy lifted her hands. "My sister is a natural at this!"

"I never doubted that a minute," Tony said.

Christina did a pretend curtsy, flashed a wide smile, and nodded. "I'd like to thank all the little people who believed in me."

Mandy rolled her eyes. "Looks like we've created a monster."

Tony laughed. "I've always liked monsters."

"Such a guy thing to say," Christina said.

"If it quacks like a duck. . ." Tony wiggled his eyebrows. "Okay, you two.

Now that you're an expert on follow-up calls, Christina, I need to see Mandy in my office for a few minutes." He turned to Mandy and winked.

"You two run along. I'll be fine," Christina said as she laughed and waved them off. "I'll book as many appointments as I can."

Once he had Mandy behind a closed door, Tony had a chance to observe her without any distractions. She exuded confidence in a quiet sort of way, and she made him feel all was right in the world.

"You needed me?" she asked.

Her choice of words struck him hard. There was no doubt in his mind that God had placed Mandy in his life for a reason, and Tony suspected it wasn't just to have someone nice and trustworthy to work with.

"I talked to Ricco early this morning, and he wants you to clear your schedule the week after next. We're going ahead with your promotion immediately, so you'll get paid for training."

When she opened her mouth, he thought she might argue with him, but she quickly closed it and smiled. His heart pounded and warmth filled his soul.

"I appreciate how you've shown your sister some phone techniques, since it's vital to company growth. While she gets comfortable with that, I'd like for you to work with a couple of new part-timers I just hired."

"When do they start?" she asked.

"The day after tomorrow."

Christina tapped her fingernails on the counter. "Are they management trainees, too?"

"No, they're part-time photographers. You can work with them together, and once they catch on, you can spend some time behind the camera with Christina."

After Tony left them alone, Mandy started to say something, but the phone rang. She instinctively reached for it, but Christina beat her to it.

"Small World Portrait Studio, this is Christina, how may I help you?"

Mandy was impressed. Her sister had the spiel down pat, and she had a friendly lilt to her voice.

"Please hold," she said. She punched the HOLD button. "How do I let Tony know he has a call?"

Mandy showed her how to buzz Tony to let him know which line to pick up. Once that was done, she complimented Christina on her phone skills.

"I said what was in the manual. It's easy." Something caught her attention, and she diverted her gaze to something behind Mandy, smiled, and waved.

Mandy turned around and saw Brent from the electronics store. "Be careful with that guy, or you'll never get rid of him."

"Why would I want to get rid of him? I already told you I think he's cute."

"Remember, he's a little nerdy."

Christina giggled. "Nerds are cool. I like the smart guys."

Mandy wasn't so sure how smart Brent was, but if Christina liked him, what did it matter? "So have you had a chance to talk to him?"

"Yes, and we have a date for tomorrow night."

That was a shock. "Why didn't you tell me?"

Christina groaned. "You're acting just like Mom and Dad. I'm a grown woman. I shouldn't have to tell you about everyone I go out with."

"True."

The next appointment came in, so Mandy left Christina in Tony's care. By the time she finished, it was almost time to close up shop.

Brent stood by the door waiting for Christina. Tony saw that, so he offered to walk Mandy to her car.

"Are you okay?" he asked.

She nodded. "Yeah, why?"

He gestured toward Christina and Brent who stood about a foot apart facing each other, with Christina leaning against their mother's car, looking like a flirty teenager. "When Brent showed up, you started acting different."

"I'm just disappointed she didn't tell me about Brent."

"You're not jealous, are you?" he teased.

"No, of course not!"

"Whoa, don't get all worked up. I was just asking."

"Sorry. I guess I was being overly protective of my little sister."

Tony made a humorous face. "I don't think you have to worry about Brent. He seems pretty harmless."

"I'm sure he is."

He backed away from her car. "See you tomorrow, Mandy."

As she pulled away, she thought about how everything in her world changed and how the Lord had such a sure hand in her life.

She rounded the last corner to her house, when her cell phone rang. It was Tony.

"I forgot to ask you something. What are you doing for dinner tonight?" he asked.

"Um. . ." She racked her brain and couldn't think of anything. "I don't know, why?"

"Would you like to go out to dinner with me?"

Chapter 15

Um. . ." Mandy thought about the alternative—a microwaved frozen dinner. "Sure, that sounds good."

"Can you be ready in an hour?"

"Absolutely."

As soon as they hung up, Mandy headed straight for her closet. She wanted to look nice but not like she'd put too much effort into it. After skimming her closet for about five minutes, she chose a knee-length pencil skirt and a teal silk blouse Christina had talked her into buying—nothing elaborate, but nice enough to go anywhere.

Tony arrived on the dot, looking more handsome than ever. Even though she'd been with him outside of work before, this felt different—more like a date. That realization alone made her tummy flutter.

"Very pretty," he said. "I like that color on you."

"Thank you." She felt the heat rise to her cheeks. "You look nice, too."

He laughed. "I do clean up well—or so I've heard."

To her surprise, they drove straight to Figaretti's, one of her favorite restaurants in town. The cozy atmosphere added to the intensity of how she was starting to feel toward Tony.

After they ordered, Tony leaned toward her. "I wanted to discuss some things. . . ."

Her heart hammered in her chest, but he'd quit talking. Instead, he studied her face like he'd never seen it before. "What do you want to discuss?"

"I want to talk about—" He glanced away and pursed his lips before turning back to her. "I thought we'd talk about Small World, but I thought it would be better to talk away from the studio."

Mandy's heart sank. So this *was* a business dinner. She had to look away to cover her disappointment.

"I've been talking with my uncle about a strategy for the future, and he agrees that we need to work on building more business skills in our managers and encouraging them to hire more part-time photographers. That will take care of two issues—burnout and being able to see who has a knack for the job."

She tried to focus on his words, but her ears rang with embarrassment over her misperception of his intentions. "That makes sense."

He continued. "I'm thinking that I'll probably put Christina in an assistant manager position until I'm sure she's ready to run the studio as a full manager."

"The one here?" Mandy asked. She'd assumed Christina would get her own studio but somewhere else.

"Yes. I think she likes it here, and there's no point in moving her into a situation she's not comfortable with."

"So. . ." Mandy said slowly, "where will you go?"

He shrugged. "Wherever they need me. After I agreed to work for the family business, they made it very clear that I'd most likely have to move around a bit and travel a great deal more before they settle me in a long-term position."

"Oh." Mandy hated the feelings that bubbled inside her.

"Did I say something wrong?"

She dared a look into his eyes but instantly regretted it. "No." Her throat constricted, causing the word to come out in a squeak.

"Your new position is still on the drawing board. We're trying to decide how we want to use you. Ricco was thinking that we'd bring the full-time photographers here for training, and they could go back to their studios and work with the part-timers."

Mandy nodded. "That makes sense." She felt like she was going through the motions, while all she wanted to do was jump up and run away from Tony.

"It does, but I like my idea better."

At least he was giving her cues to keep her in the conversation. "What's your idea?"

"Since you'll be a regional trainer, you can go to each studio and work with the photographers as a group. That way, the instruction will be consistent." He paused and smiled before adding, "That is, if you don't mind traveling."

"I don't mind. I figured I'd have to travel some."

"Good. You and I are on the same page then. Fortunately Ricco is open to our suggestions. It's important to him and my uncle that our management team is happy. That's the only way we'll keep skilled and committed people with the company."

At least her career seemed to be going well. Mandy took a couple of deep breaths and forced a smile. "I'm happy with Small World, and I'm grateful for your confidence."

"But?" He tilted his head and studied her.

"No *buts*. Everything is going even better than I ever imagined."

"I'm glad."

Their food arrived, so Mandy was able to divert her attention away from Tony's warm brown eyes that melted her insides. He bowed his head, and she followed. He softly said a blessing before they started eating.

They made small talk for a few minutes until he asked about her mother. "Christina says she's doing well. Have you had a chance to see her?"

Mandy nodded. "She's been busy lately, between all her long walks and the fact that Dad has suddenly turned all his attention toward her. I think it scared him to think he might lose her."

"I can see how that would happen. Sometimes it takes fear to make us realize the importance of something we have."

The way he said that gave Mandy the impression he understood firsthand. "She's lost a few pounds, and Christina said Mom fusses at her when she brings junk food into the house."

"That's understandable."

"Mom used to bake cookies, pies, and cakes all the time. We had dessert after every meal. Now Mom keeps a big bowl filled with fresh fruit."

Tony laughed. "I'm afraid there would have been a mutiny in our house if my mom did that."

"There probably would have been when we were younger, but after our scare and finding out how high her cholesterol was, we're happy she's making these changes."

"I'm glad to hear your mother's doing better. She's been on my family's prayer list."

"Thanks, Tony." Mandy took a sip of her tea as she thought about how nice Tony was. He couldn't help it if she'd developed a crush on him.

When she put her napkin on the table beside her plate, he gestured for the server to bring the check. "I had a wonderful time, Mandy. I think it's a good idea for us to get to know each other better, since we're working on the same team. I think the timing on company growth is perfect, and with you on board, there's no doubt we'll have the best children's photographers in the industry."

Tony had just given her one more reason she couldn't let him know how she felt. His focus was on company growth, nothing else. But when he looked at her again with such a tender expression, she couldn't help the sensation of swirling into an abyss.

❧

The following Sunday, Mandy arrived at church early, so she sat toward the front and saved Christina a spot. When she turned around to watch for her sister, Mandy spotted Tony, who made eye contact right away. He waved then walked toward her as though on a mission. She scooted over more to make more room for him.

"Mind if I join you?" he asked.

"Of course not."

She kept glancing around, looking for Christina, while Tony chatted with the man next to him. Finally her sister arrived, arm in arm with Brent.

"I cannot believe what I'm seeing," Mandy said.

Tony turned around and waved. Brent's deer-in-the- headlights expression changed to one of relief. He and Christina made a beeline toward their pew.

Everyone scooted to make room. It was a tight squeeze, so Tony lifted his arm and rested it on the pew behind Mandy. She wanted to snuggle into him, but that obviously wasn't suitable for two very strong reasons—this was church, and he was her boss. Her face flushed.

With so many people in the pew, Mandy and Tony had to share a hymnal for the traditional songs, and they put their heads together to see the contemporary lyrics on the screen in the front of the church. As the tall man on the front row swayed to the music, Tony and Mandy had to move in the opposite direction. After a few times, it became comical, and Mandy let out a giggle. Tony winked and smiled down at her.

After church, Tony walked out to the parking lot with Mandy. "What are you doing this afternoon?" he asked.

"I'm stopping by Mom and Dad's house. They've been so busy, it's hard to catch them home."

Tony grinned. "I'm happy your mother is doing so well."

"I know. We used to think she was content cooking all day, but after her heart attack, she said it was time to really live while she was able to."

"Well, I was going to ask if you wanted to do something."

Mandy wondered if she should risk asking if he'd like to join her. She hesitated for a few seconds before deciding to just go for it.

"Would you like to join me?" she asked. The minute she said that, she second-guessed herself and wanted to take back the invitation. "I mean, my parents really appreciated how much you helped when Mom was in the hospital and all. . . ." She felt like crawling into a hole.

"I'd love to, if you don't think they'd mind."

Mandy's heart raced. "They wouldn't mind in the least."

He nodded. "I miss my family, and the opportunity to spend some time with yours would be nice."

"They used to always have a big spread of food on Sundays, but I'm not sure now."

"I don't want to impose on them at mealtime."

"Trust me, Tony, if there's food, there will be plenty for you and leftovers for a week."

"If you're sure. . ."

"I'm positive. Why don't you come to my apartment in about an hour?" she said. "I can drive us to my parents' house."

"Sounds good."

As soon as Mandy walked into her apartment, she called her parents. Her dad answered. "I wanted to make sure we were still on for this afternoon," she said. "And if you don't mind, I'd like to bring Tony."

"Absolutely." His voice sounded more cheerful than she remembered since she was a little girl. "We went to the early service this morning so we could come home and start cooking."

"You said 'we.' Does this mean you cooked, too?"

"Yep. Your mother told me she doesn't think it's fair that she has all the fun. Just wait until you taste my fruit salad. In your mother's words, it's heavenly."

Mandy laughed. "Can't wait. I'm glad you and Mom are enjoying yourselves."

"After the scare, both of us realized we'd been on a treadmill, doing things we'd always done, and not truly enjoying God's blessings."

After they hung up, Mandy rocked back on her heels and thought about what her dad had said. She'd never thought of her parents as unhappy, but they didn't exactly exude joy, either. Now they sparkled with laughter and happiness every time she saw them. Her mom even said that her heart attack was the best thing that could have happened to their marriage.

The more Mandy thought about her parents, the more she pondered her own life. Basically she was guilty of doing exactly what her parents had always done in the past—running on a treadmill and hoping nothing bad would happen. She'd wanted to be promoted to manager of the studio, but other than that, she never put much thought into anything else she might want.

Now that she had the surprise promotion to photography trainer, Mandy decided it was time to take stock of what she had, decide what she really wanted in life, and make plans based on what was in her control. She couldn't do any of that without His help, so she bowed her head and prayed for guidance, wisdom, and the ability to recognize opportunity—both professional and personal.

The first thing Tony noticed when Mandy opened her door was a sense of self-awareness he hadn't seen before. She smiled and invited him in.

"Mom and Dad know you're coming. I hope you're hungry."

He lifted his eyebrows. "I didn't mean to invite myself for lunch, but I never turn down good food."

Her smile was warm but filled with amusement. "This will be good, as in *healthy*, for you. I have no idea how it'll taste without Mom's trademark butter, salt, and sugar."

Tony patted his belly. "I could stand to eat a healthy meal, so I won't complain." He gestured toward the door. "Ready?"

"Yeah, let's go."

"Mind if I drive?" he asked.

She shrugged. "It doesn't matter to me."

He pointed his remote toward his car to unlock it. "Good. I have to admit I'm a little nervous, and driving will give me something to do with my hands."

Her eyes twinkled as she smiled at him. "That's cute."

On the way to her parents' house, Tony asked questions about her up-bringing. "Christina doesn't seem like the domestic type. How about you?"

"Neither of us has a domestic bone in our bodies. Mom took care of everything, from food to cleaning. We just had to maintain our rooms and help out with one chore a day."

As they came to a light, he contorted his mouth and cut his gaze to her. "I hate to admit this, but until I went into the army, I didn't even do that. All I had to do was make my bed every morning."

"So you were spoiled, huh?"

He shrugged. "I don't know if you could call me spoiled. I always appreciated everything, and I found ways to make my spending money. My parents didn't believe in unearned allowance."

"Same here. We didn't get a dime until Mom checked our chore list to make sure everything was done." She sighed. "I just wish I'd learned how to cook."

"It's never too late to learn."

"True. My dad's proof of that."

She turned her head to look out the window, giving him a nice view of her profile. Mandy was very pretty, but what he liked most about her profile was the way her chin jutted when she was deep in thought.

Before the light turned green, she turned and looked him directly in the eye. Everything around him seemed to swirl out of focus—everything but Mandy. At that moment, he knew he was falling in love.

She pointed to the light. "You can go now."

"Oh, yeah." His voice came out scratchy. "I was distracted."

Out of the corner of his eye, he noticed her every movement. He wanted to reach over and take one of her hands in his, but he didn't dare do it—not until he had some idea how she felt about him. The last thing he needed was to make their situation awkward as long as they had to work together.

As they walked up the sidewalk to the Pruitts' house, Christina flung open the door. Brent was right behind her, grinning.

"Hey, you two," Brent said. "Don't tell me you're an item now."

Tony felt like someone had stolen the air out of his lungs. He stopped in his tracks and waited to see Mandy's reaction. To his dismay, she let out a nervous giggle but didn't say a word. Instead she walked right past Christina and Brent.

Not knowing what else to do, Tony followed her through the house to the kitchen, where her parents stood on either side of an island. Her dad was peeling fruit, and her mother was garnishing a vegetable platter.

"We're just about ready to eat," her mother said as she pointed to the counter behind her. "Why don't you each grab one of those bowls over there and carry them into the dining room?"

Mr. Pruitt chuckled. "This is the first time Mandy's young man has been to the house, and you're putting him to work already?"

Mandy wanted to crawl into a hole and never come out. Her young man? How could her dad do that to her?

Tony reached for a bowl. "I don't mind."

Avoiding his gaze, Mandy grabbed a bowl and led the way to the dining room. Once they were alone, she turned to him. "Sorry about that, Tony. I don't think my dad meant anything by that."

"Too bad." He set the bowl down on the table and closed the distance between them. The only thing in their way was the bowl in her hands. "I was kind of hoping he knew something I didn't know."

"Huh?" She tilted her head as she waited for him to explain.

For the first time since she'd met Tony, he looked ill at ease. After shuffling his feet and looking around the room for a couple of seconds, he blurted, "Mandy, my feelings for you are growing. I'm sorry if this makes you uncomfortable, but no matter how hard I try to keep our relationship strictly professional, I feel myself falling in love with you."

Chapter 16

Mandy stood there and stared at Tony, not believing what she just heard. Here he was, one of the best-looking guys she'd ever seen in her life, his future mapped out by the good fortune of being born into a family with a growing business, exuding kindness like she'd never seen before. Why would he be interested in her?

"Um. . ." She nervously glanced over her shoulder to see if anyone else was behind her. When she turned back around to face Tony, she didn't know what to say.

He shoved his hands into his pockets and looked down at his feet. "Well, I guess I just got my answer."

"Your answer?"

Emotion sparked in his eyes as he met her gaze. "You don't feel it, do you?"

"I—I just don't know what to say."

He let out a small snicker of resignation. "You don't have to say anything, Mandy. I just took a big risk that didn't pay off."

Mandy set the bowl on the table and turned back to face Tony. She was about to let him know that she felt the same way when her sister and Brent burst into the room.

"Hey there!" Brent made a snorting sound. "So they put you to work, huh?"

Mandy's heart sank. She couldn't very well discuss her feelings for Tony with other people around.

Tony nodded and motioned for everyone to follow him. "Let's see what else we can do to help."

After all the food was on the table, everyone bowed their heads. Mandy's dad said the blessing. When she lifted her head afterward, she thought about how cozy they were—her whole family here, and everyone part of a couple.

"Mom, this looks and tastes wonderful," Christina said after she ate a couple of bites. "I didn't know healthy food could be this good."

"I know," their mother replied. "When the doctor first told me I needed to change my lifestyle, I wondered if it was worth living for." When everyone groaned, she gestured for them to quiet down. "But once I found some fun activities and your father brought me some new cookbooks, I see how much better life can be."

"I need to start eating like this," Tony said. "Maybe you can share some recipes."

Mom smiled and tilted her head as she looked at Tony. "You cook?"

"Not much, but I think I should probably start."

"I didn't cook before," Dad said. "But now I like to putter around in the kitchen, and it's kind of fun."

If someone had told Mandy about this conversation a year earlier, she never would have believed it. In fact, this whole scenario seemed unreal—with her sister coming back from Hollywood and fawning over geeky Brent, her boss having dinner with her family after admitting he had romantic feelings for her, and her parents eating fresh, natural food that they cooked together.

Christina clearly hung on every word Brent said, which obviously pleased him to no end. Mandy studied them with interest. When she turned to Tony, she saw that he'd been observing her.

"Want some applesauce cake?" her mother asked after everyone put down their forks. "It's low cal, low fat, and delicious."

"I'm stuffed," Mandy said. "But I'll be glad to take some home for later."

Everyone pitched in to clear the table. Tony volunteered to do the dishes so Mandy could spend some time with her family. Brent took a hint and joined him in the kitchen.

"Your young men are certainly thoughtful," their dad said as they settled in the family room.

Christina beamed. "Brent is the sweetest, most wonderful man I've ever met."

"He certainly seems to be into you, too," Mandy said.

"Just like Tony is into you." Christina grinned. "Looks like we both found love at the same time."

Before Tony's admission before dinner, Mandy would have argued that point, but now she wasn't sure what to say. She didn't want to discuss it with Christina yet.

Mandy decided to change the subject. "Mom, dinner was wonderful."

"Who knew healthy food could be so delicious?" Her mother beamed. "And you'll be happy to know that your father and I have joined the Hundred-Mile Club."

"Hundred-Mile Club?" Christina grimaced. "That's a lot of miles. Are you sure you can do that?"

"Of course we can. We just had to sign a statement that we walked, ran, biked, or swam a hundred miles per quarter. It's through our senior group. As long as we do that every three months, we can stay in."

"Cool. Maybe I should do that," Christina said.

"Sorry, sweetie." Their mother gave her an apologetic look. "You have to be over fifty-five."

Christina frowned. "That's discrimination."

The rest of the family laughed. Tony and Brent appeared at the door.

"We've been thinking about a way to start a fitness program for Small World," Tony said. "It's been a challenge since we're spread out all over the country. Maybe we can start something similar."

Christina's eyes lit up. "I'll be the first to join." She turned to Mandy. "You'll do it, too, right?"

Mandy shrugged. "If you can do it, I'm sure I can."

"What's that supposed to mean?"

"Girls!" Their dad lifted a finger. "I'm sure your sister didn't mean anything by her comment, Christina. And, Mandy, be more careful about how you word things, okay?"

Mandy looked over at Tony, who was obviously trying to hide a grin. "Okay, Dad."

"All the dishes are done," Tony said. "Anything else you need while we're here?"

Mandy's mom got up. "You boys are very sweet. Our daughters sure know how to pick 'em."

Christina beamed at Brent, while Mandy felt her cheeks flame. She stood and walked over to the door. "We really need to go. Thanks for everything, Mom and Dad. Dinner was delicious."

"Don't forget your applesauce cake. I'll get some plastic containers so y'all can take some home."

Mandy and Tony waited for their cake then left. As soon as they pulled up to the stop sign at the end of the street, Tony glanced at Mandy. "Your family reminds me of my own. Very loving and fun."

"And centered on food?"

He laughed. "Yeah, that, too."

"Sometimes God lets things happen to get our attention."

Tony slowed down for the stop sign, looked to see that there were no cars coming, and turned to Mandy. "Yes, I know—things we never expected." He reached for her hand and lifted it to his lips for a light kiss.

Mandy gasped. She wanted to say something, but her brain wouldn't cooperate. Her breath caught in her throat.

After Tony accelerated past the stop sign, Mandy studied his profile as she thought about what he'd said earlier. "Mandy?" He let go of her hand, sending disappointment surging through her. "I hope my admission of my feelings didn't make you too uncomfortable."

She cleared her throat. "You surprised me."

"I know, and I'm sorry."

"Oh, don't be sorry. Please. I sort of, well. . ." Mandy had never told a guy she loved him. The very thought of doing so made her palms sweat.

"You don't have to say anything. I understand."

"No, I want to say something. It's just that I've never been like this before."

"Been like what?" he said, cutting his gaze over to her for a split second before turning his attention back to the road.

She sucked in a breath before blurting, "I've never been in love before."

Tony immediately pulled into a business center parking lot and parked before completely turning around to face her.

"Are you now?"

Her ears rang and her heart pounded as she nodded. "Yes, I'm pretty sure I am."

He leaned back. "With me?"

She nodded.

"This is great news!" He reached for her hand again and dropped a kiss on the back of it.

"I hope it's okay, though," she said. "I mean, I love my job at Small World, and I don't want to do anything that isn't—"

"It's fine, Mandy. We obviously don't have a problem with family members working together. This is different. I'll talk to Ricco and Uncle Ed about it, but I'm sure they'll be happy."

"What if they're not?"

"I'll be surprised, but we'll deal with it then. Right now, I just want to enjoy knowing you feel the same way I do."

She opened her mouth to thank him, but that seemed awkward, so she clamped it shut. Even during her last relationship, she knew the guy wasn't *the one*. She liked him quite a bit, but she never felt that she was in love like she was now.

He pulled up in front of her apartment and got out to walk her to her door. "You weren't kidding about there being plenty of food. I haven't eaten this much since the last time I went to a family reunion. My mother and her sisters like to outdo each other." He patted his belly. "At least after today, I don't have to worry about all the cholesterol."

"Would you like to come in?" she asked.

Tony hesitated then shook his head. "Maybe some other time. I need to get back to my place and clean up a bit then call my mother." He took a couple of steps back. "See you tomorrow, Mandy."

❧

Tony had been tempted to abandon everything just so he could spend more time with Mandy, but it was time to call his mother. He hadn't missed a Sunday afternoon yet. One thing he knew was that he needed to clean his apartment before the call because the first question out of his mother's mouth was if he was living in a pigsty. It was funny, but he also knew she was serious. His mother had always been a neatnik. Her motto was "A cluttered house means a cluttered mind, and you can't get anything done in either."

Since he hadn't been home much, it didn't take long to straighten up, dust, and vacuum. Before he punched in his mother's phone number, he prayed that he'd be able to say the right things that would ease her mind. After his last move back to Atlanta, she'd begged him to stay. When his uncle asked him to work in West Virginia, she'd been upset until he assured her Tony would likely be back in a year or two.

He expected that she'd be waiting by the phone, so he was surprised when she didn't pick it up until after the third ring. "What took you so long?" he asked.

"You think I wait by the phone every Sunday?"

"Um—yes." He laughed.

She clicked her tongue. "Maybe I do sometimes, but today I'm busy. I had a bunch of people over for Sunday dinner. I heard some good news from Ed and Ricco."

"You did? Wanna share?" He expected to hear something about their opinion of Mandy, since she'd made such a good impression during her trip to the home office.

"I don't know if I'm supposed to tell you this, but they didn't say not to, so I might as well." She paused for a few seconds to catch her breath before blurting, "You're coming home soon!"

"I'm what?"

"You heard me. Ricco said he thinks you'll have someone to take over the studio in West Virginia, and he needs you in the home office."

"But. . ." Several months ago, before he had a chance to develop feelings for Mandy, Tony would have been elated. But now West Virginia was beginning to feel like home to him.

"I'll be so happy to have you back home where you belong."

Tony didn't want to upset his mother, but he also needed to let her know how he felt. "Mom, I really like it here."

He expected an argument or at least one of her signature gasps. Instead he got a giggle. "It's that girl, isn't it?"

"What girl?" So Ricco or Ed *had* mentioned Mandy.

"You know exactly what girl I'm talking about. I hear she's very pretty."

"She is, Mom. Very pretty. But more important than that, she loves the Lord."

"I wouldn't expect otherwise, Tony. You have a good head on your shoulders."

"I had dinner with her family today. They remind me a lot of our family."

He could practically hear his mother smiling through the phone. "So tell me all about them."

Over the next five minutes, Tony talked nonstop about Mandy's family, the food, and how her parents drew closer in the kitchen after her mother's heart attack.

"They sound very sweet." She sniffled. "I wish your father were still alive. I think he would have enjoyed something like that."

Tony knew that once his mother got on the subject of his dad, she was likely to wind up in a full sob. Sometimes that was fine because she needed the release, but he wanted her to be happy now.

"Mom, is there any way you can come up here for a visit soon?"

"Now that you're inviting me, yes. Ed said I could come with him and Cissy next week—that is, if it's not too soon."

Tony laughed. "I'm fine with that. I'd love to have you."

"So, is your apartment a pigsty?"

"I'm keeping it clean. Not as clean as you would, but I think you'll be pleased."

"As long as you don't leave your underwear on the floor and dishes in the sink overnight." She paused before adding, "You don't, do you?"

"No, Mom, I'm good about picking up after myself."

"So tell me more about your girlfriend."

"Haven't I told you enough?"

"You told me about having lunch with her family, but I want to know more about *her*. You said she loves the Lord. You've been to church with her, right? What is her church like?"

"It reminds me a lot of the church I went to when I was in Atlanta."

"The one you took me to?"

"Yes," he replied.

"Good. How about her cooking skills? Is she a decent cook?"

"I really don't know, but that doesn't really matter to me."

"Ya know, I couldn't cook when I first married your father."

He'd heard this story many times. "Yes, Mom, I know."

"But he married me with the understanding that I'd learn from his mother because my mother was German, and she couldn't cook the kind of food he liked."

"So what are you saying?" he teased.

"I'm not saying anything you can't figure out for yourself. Just make sure she's willing to bend a little before you get too serious."

"Don't rush this thing. I just told her how I felt this afternoon."

"Your father and I got engaged three months after we met. How long have you known this girl?"

"Four months."

"How much do you see her?"

"Almost every day." He smiled as he pictured his mother calculating the amount of time they spent together.

"And you're with her all day at work. That's long enough."

"Long enough for what?"

"This mother didn't raise a fool, Tony. You know exactly what I'm talking about."

Chapter 17

Tony had to hand it to his mother—she didn't hold back. After he got off the phone, he sat and stared at the wall, thinking of what to do next. Even though Small World didn't have a policy against their employees marrying, there was the matter of logistics. He couldn't very well ask Mandy to give up the career she clearly wanted, just to make him happy, and their positions were likely to take them to very different places.

Finally, after pondering it as long as he could without obsessing, he got up and headed to the kitchen. He'd kept his place neat, but since his mother was coming, it had to be better than that. He opened the refrigerator and started tossing stuff he knew he'd never finish—mostly leftovers from restaurants.

Mandy went to work the next morning with some trepidation. Now that she and Tony had opened up and said they loved each other, she worried that work might be awkward.

As soon as she opened the door, her sister looked up from her notebook and greeted her with a smile. "I love this job!" Christina exclaimed.

Mandy grinned. "What brought that on?"

"Tony told me I'm doing really well, and he wants me to move on a fast track."

"Wow, Christina, that's wonderful." Mandy walked past her toward the spare office to put her purse down. She passed by Tony's office and heard him talking on the phone. When she came back out, her sister was still busy reading the notebook. "When did he tell you this?"

"First thing this morning. He was here when I got in"—she glanced at her watch before looking back at Mandy—"about half an hour ago."

"Why so early?"

Christina's cheeks flushed. "Brent offered me a ride to work, and since he had to get in early, I figured I could get ahead on my studying."

Mandy had never seen her sister so happy about a man or a job. She'd had more than her fair share of guys stumbling all over themselves when she was younger.

"You really like Brent, don't you?" Mandy asked.

Christina nodded. "He's the sweetest, smartest, and most caring guy I've ever dated." She shrugged and added, "It doesn't hurt that he's cute, too."

Cuteness, like beauty, was definitely in the eye of the beholder, Mandy thought. Tony was cute. Brent was—well, simply okay.

"Would you mind handing me the appointment book? I know we have several scheduled sessions today, but I don't know the specific times."

Christina pulled out the book and passed it to Mandy. "Tony wants me to observe at least one of the sessions."

"That's fine." Mandy caught sight of Tony out of the corner of her eye as he appeared at the door. "Hi." Suddenly she felt awkward and didn't know what to do with her hands.

He smiled. "So, do you mind working with Christina on the cameras a bit today?"

"I'll be glad to." Mandy cleared her throat. "I can show her some camera basics between appointments, too."

"Perfect." He glanced at Christina. "You can practice taking pictures of Mandy."

"No." The word came out automatically. "I mean, I'm sure we can find something else to photograph—maybe a stuffed animal grouping."

Tony folded his arms, tilted his head, and looked at her with curiosity. "That's nothing like having a real, live subject. Especially a reluctant subject. You know that, Mandy."

"Yeah, but—"

Christina spoke up. "My sister has never liked having her picture taken. She's been like that all her life."

Tony's lips quirked into a smile. "I can't imagine why, as pretty as she is."

"I know," Christina said as she turned back to face Mandy, who wanted to crawl into a hole from way too much attention.

"Okay, whatever," Mandy said. "But now I need to get the props in place for the first appointment."

Tony walked around behind the counter. "Why don't you help her, Christina? You need to know every aspect of how to run this place, since I hope to have you in charge soon."

On their way to the back part of the studio, Christina let out a faint squeal. "I have to pinch myself. I can't believe how perfect this job is for me."

Mandy nodded. "You do catch on quickly."

Christina frowned as she stopped, grabbed Mandy's arm, and turned her around. "You didn't think I could do this, did you?"

"I had no doubt you could do it," Mandy said as she tried to think of the right words that wouldn't upset her sister. "The only concern I had was how committed you were to the job. Your whole life, all you talked about was how much you wanted to be famous." She held her breath until Christina smiled then let it out.

"I think most girls want to be famous at some time or other. After I got to Hollywood, I saw that it wasn't everything I thought it was. It's a lot of hard work, and there's always someone who wants to drag you down."

"I can imagine," Mandy said.

Christina shook her head. "Not to mention the faith issue. I can't even begin to tell you how difficult it is to hold on to Jesus in the midst of all those distractions."

Mandy thought her heart would burst, she was so proud of her sister. "You were smart to come back." She took a couple of steps toward the cameras then stopped again and turned back to Christina. "I have complete confidence in you, now that you've grown up and taken charge of your life."

Tears formed in Christina's eyes as she pulled her lips between her teeth. Mandy hugged her then gave her a gentle push toward the cameras.

"It's time to learn the parts of the camera and how they work."

"I'm ready." Christina rubbed her hands together. "So show me your stuff."

They spent the next half hour going over the different aspects of the camera—all things Christina needed to know before taking pictures. When the first appointment arrived, Christina stood beside Mandy and helped with the props. Mandy was delighted by how well her sister related to the children.

Mandy showed Christina the card she kept with notes about the family. She pointed to the comment, *Treats allowed*. Christina nodded and picked up the basket filled with candy.

After they had all the pictures organized on the computer, Mandy let Christina help the family choose the shots they wanted. At first she disagreed with the parents, saying their choices weren't the best, but Mandy pulled her aside and explained that the ultimate choice wasn't hers. The parents were delighted with the pictures. They left smiling.

"Now let's go back and practice," Mandy said. "If I'd known I was having my picture taken today, I would have worn more makeup."

Christina made a face and waved off her comment. "You've always been gorgeous without a speck of makeup. I'm the one who had to cake it on."

"You're kidding, right?" Mandy laughed. "You were always the pretty one, and I was the smart one."

"Well, I just happen to think we're both pretty and smart. I think a better way of putting it would be that I'm the confident one, and you're the one who needs a better self-image."

Mandy couldn't argue with her there. "Whatever."

"So show me what to do again," Christina said as she inspected the camera. "I turn this little thingy then I press this?"

She might not have grasped the terminology, but she quickly caught on. Over the next half hour, Christina took dozens of pictures of Mandy.

By the time they finished putting everything away and got back to the front counter, Tony already had Mandy's pictures up on the computer screen. "Nice," he said in a low, appreciative tone. "Very nice." He grinned at Mandy.

"You're an excellent trainer."

Mandy felt her cheeks flame as Christina joined him and started talking about how good she looked. "Look at the skin tone in this one. She looks like a professional model."

"Better," he argued. "I've never seen a professional model with such great proportions."

"Hey, you two," Mandy said from the back of the counter. "I'm right here."

"Come look at this." Christina gestured her over. "If you don't mind my saying so, I'm an excellent photographer."

Mandy took a chance and glanced at the photos. Her eyes widened. "Is that me?"

Christina did a double take before laughing. "Yes, who did you think it was? The Cookie Monster?"

Tony cast a silly look at Mandy. "The Cookie Monster wishes. Seriously, these are some great shots. Mandy, you did a great job of showing Christina how to take good pictures."

As Mandy studied the shots, she realized that Christina really did have a natural eye for photography. Not everyone knew when to snap the picture. Obviously Christina did. After Tony clicked onto the next page, and the shots got even better, she nodded.

"Good job, sis." She was still embarrassed about being the subject, and she didn't know what else to do, so she rolled her eyes.

Tony backed away from the counter. "I think I'll go to my office now and let the two of you discuss photography."

As soon as he was out of hearing range, Christina planted her fists on her hips. "What is going on?"

Leaning against the counter, Mandy slowly shook her head from side to side. "Things are so different now. They're happening so fast. I'm not sure how to deal with them. I have no idea what to do."

"Wanna discuss it later?"

✻

After seeing the amazing pictures Christina took of Mandy, two important thoughts hit him hard. Christina could wind up being as good a photographer as her sister with the training she was getting, and the photographs had captured the inner beauty he'd seen in Mandy since he first met her. Her eyes sparkled with joy, and the slight tilt of her head showed a playful side that not everyone could see. Her smile could brighten the darkest of rooms.

Tony called his mother to find out what time she was arriving at his apartment on Friday. She said she was coming to the studio first, and then she'd go to the apartment with him.

He had a good idea why she wanted to come straight to the studio.

"That's fine," he said.

"Don't worry about cleaning for me," she said. "I can do that while I'm there."

"Don't be silly, Mom. I'm a grown man, and I can clean my own apartment."

She laughed. "You might be grown to the rest of the world, but you'll always be my sweet boy, Anthony."

"Shh. Don't say that again." He lowered his voice. "Someone might hear you."

"Oh trust me, Tony, I won't tell Mandy that."

"I didn't say anything about Mandy."

"No, but I can't wait to meet her." She paused before asking, "She will be there Friday when I arrive, right?"

His suspicion had been confirmed. "Yes, she'll be here. Uncle Ed is meeting with her, remember?"

"Good." He could practically hear his mother grinning over the phone.

He hung up and went back out to the front desk, where Christina was studying her books. She glanced up and gestured for him.

"Need something?" he asked.

She nodded. "What if someone either doesn't order pictures or they want to add to their package later? Can they come back and order them later?"

"Yes, we try to get them to place an order, but we don't like to pressure people."

"Okay, good. I'm thinking that someone might start out wanting the special then change their mind and want a bigger package after they see how cute their kids are."

"Happens all the time," he said. "We keep the pictures in the system for at least a year."

A woman stepped out of the studio and approached the desk. "Are you Christina?" she asked.

Christina nodded. "May I help you with something?"

"Mandy wants to see you."

Tony nodded toward the back. "Go see what she wants. I'll watch the desk."

As soon as Christina left, Tony glanced down at the notebook page Christina and saw the copious notes she'd jotted in the margins. He smiled at how thorough she was and how seriously she seemed to be taking this job.

⚜

Mandy stepped away from the camera and motioned for the children to be still. Their mother stood to the side, smiling.

"Christina, would you like to give me a hand?"

"Sure, what do you need?"

Mandy waved her hand toward the camera. "You can take their pictures." Christina's eyebrows shot up. "You mean, like, for real?"

Both Mandy and the children's mother cracked up laughing. "Yes, for real. I've already discussed it with Mrs. Martin, and she's more than happy to let you work with her kids."

"That's right," the woman said. "We're regular customers, so you'll be seeing us again in a few months."

"Oh, okay." Christina tentatively stepped behind the camera and made a couple of adjustments. She was tentative at first, and she asked for Mandy's help.

"You'll do just fine as long as you do what I taught you," Mandy assured her as she took a step back. "If you mess up, we'll just do them over."

Within minutes, Christina had taken several pictures and adjusted the children's positions for more shots.

"She's very good with them," Mrs. Martin whispered. "Where did you find her?"

Mandy grinned at her favorite customer. "She's my sister."

"All done," Christina said. She grabbed the goodie basket and passed out stickers and candy. "Y'all were great! Have two—" She glanced over her shoulder at Mrs. Martin, who nodded before she pulled more candy from the basket.

After Christina finished with the children, they joined their mother and Mandy. Christina was right behind them.

"Your sister, huh?" Mrs. Martin said.

Christina took a couple of steps toward Mandy until they were side by side. "I'm the baby."

Mrs. Martin laughed, tilted her head, and looked back and forth between Mandy and Christina then slowly nodded. "Yes, as a matter of fact, I can definitely see the resemblance. It's nice that you work together so well."

"She taught me everything I know," Christina said as she put her arm around Mandy and squeezed. "I still have a lot to learn."

"Don't we all?" Mrs. Martin said as she walked toward the reception area. "I'll take the kids to the sandwich shop while you get the pictures ready."

The second the Martin family left, Tony lifted a finger. "I need to talk to both of you before you work on the pictures."

"Okay," Mandy said. "One at a time or together?"

She watched as he made his decision. "Why don't I talk to you first, and Christina can watch the counter. You know how to pull the proofs up, right?"

Christina nodded. "Sure. I'll get them arranged how I think they should be while y'all talk."

Mandy followed Tony into his office. He went around behind his desk and told her to close the door.

"You know my uncle's coming, right?"

She nodded. "Yes. I have everything ready to discuss my new position."

"Good." He leaned back in his chair and took a deep breath. "My mother will be with him."

"Your mother?" Mandy asked. "I didn't know she worked for the company."

"Oh, she doesn't. She just wants to spend time with me and—well, to meet you."

Chapter 18

Mandy gulped and forced a smile, hoping Tony wouldn't see her distress. "I'm looking forward to meeting her, too."

Tony laughed. "She's not too bad."

"What's that supposed to mean?"

"She doesn't bite." A grin remained on his face as he shook his head. "My mom is one of the sweetest women I've ever met. Very capable, too. In fact she reminds me of you."

Mandy pursed her lips before retorting, "So you like me because I remind you of your mother?"

"Maybe some." The corners of his lips twitched.

"At least you admit it."

Tony reached out and gently glided his hand across her cheek, sending shivers throughout her body. "You're both Christian women who are capable of doing anything you want to do. However, your goals are completely different from hers."

Mandy folded her arms and tilted her head. "How so?"

"She's always been perfectly happy staying home, baking, and telling us kids what to do. You, on the other hand, are career focused."

"I like what I do," she said. "The kids are great."

With a chuckle, Tony backed away. "Maybe you and my mother are alike on that point, too. She loves children with every fiber of her being."

"Mandy, I need your help!"

The sound of Christina's voice burst the invisible bubble that had formed around Mandy and Tony. "I'll be right there."

As Mandy helped Christina set up for the next photography session, she thought about the conversation with Tony. He'd always been open—even in the beginning when they'd first met—and he let it be known he didn't even want to be in Wheeling. And as he gradually accepted his position, he admitted how he'd misjudged everything.

As the next few days passed, Christina grew more and more competent with the camera. Mandy and Tony were both impressed.

"Do you really think she'll be ready to manage the studio soon?" Mandy asked.

He rubbed his chin as he thought it over. "She could probably do it now, if we let her."

"I don't know about that."

"You're her sister. At some point, you need to let go and allow her to make some mistakes."

Mandy nodded. "True. I certainly made my share of them."

"You've done a good job of training her."

"Thank you."

Tony licked his lips and stared at her for a moment before doing an about-face. As he walked away, Mandy wondered what he'd been thinking.

Friday morning, Mandy stood at the counter going over the day's schedule. She was about to tell Christina that Tony's aunt, uncle, and mother would be in, but before she had a chance, her sister's eyebrows shot up and her eyes widened.

Mandy glanced over her shoulder to see what her sister was looking at. Through the glass window, she spotted a couple of women standing on the sidewalk beside a shiny red convertible. One woman was smoothing down her hair, while the other was looking up and down the street as if trying to find something. Edward joined them on the sidewalk. As he guided the women toward the front door, Mandy felt her mouth grow dry and her stomach flutter.

"That's Edward Rossi, his wife, and Tony's mom," Mandy whispered.

"Oh," Christina said, nodding her head. "No wonder your face is bright red."

Mandy groaned. She couldn't play it cool if she tried. She took a couple of deep breaths, trying to relax before Mr. Rossi opened the door for the others.

The first woman in the door zeroed in on Mandy. "Oh, you must be the girl I've heard so much about."

Mandy heard her sister snickering behind her. She cleared her throat.

"I'm Maria, Tony's mother," the woman said as she approached Mandy with open arms.

"I'm Mandy."

Mr. Rossi and his wife, Cissy, introduced themselves to Christina, who was the epitome of professionalism. She shook their hands and offered them a tour of the studio. As soon as Maria let go of Mandy, the sisters followed the others to the back. Tony joined them.

"You've got good reports, Tony," Mr. Rossi said. "I'm sure it must have something to do with these lovely ladies."

Christina spoke up. "It's probably because of my sister's hard work. She really knows her stuff."

Mandy appreciated Christina's efforts, but she was embarrassed. "It's all of us."

"Where are the part-timers?" Mr. Rossi asked.

"They're not able to work the hours we need, and the last one I hired didn't show up," Tony replied. "That's why I've been looking for more people."

Mr. Rossi nodded. "It's tough to keep a solid staff of part-time help."

Christina cleared her throat, and all heads turned to face her. "I've contacted one of the local senior citizen groups to see if anyone wants to supplement their social security income. Of course I asked my sister first, and she said I could give it a try."

Mr. Rossi rubbed his chin. "What a great idea. They're more likely to stick around than a student, and if they need the money, they'll work the hours you ask them to."

"Plus they don't need to worry about child care, and they won't expect too many hours," Christina added.

Tony tilted his head. "I had no idea you did that, Christina. I agree with Uncle Ed—it's a great idea. Why didn't you say something to me about it?"

"I just called them late yesterday. I was gonna talk to you sometime today, and. . .well, the opportunity just presented itself." She cast a sheepish glance Mandy's way then turned back to Tony. "I hope you're not too upset."

"Oh, I'm not upset in the least," Tony said. "I'm just glad you took the initiative."

"Which brings me to a very important announcement," Mr. Rossi said. "We've decided it's time to bring you back to Atlanta, now that you have capable people to run this place."

Mandy felt like her heart had dropped to the floor and someone had stomped on it. She pulled her cheeks between her teeth to keep from showing a reaction.

"That is, if my son wants to come back to Atlanta," Maria said softly.

Christina looked at Mandy with concern, but she didn't say a word. Everyone grew quiet until Mr. Rossi spoke up again.

"Mandy, do you have some time to discuss your new position?"

She nodded. "Yes."

Mr. Rossi asked Maria and Cissy to go shopping for a little while and come back for him later. "Or you can go to the hotel," he added.

"Shopping sounds great to me," Maria said. "Too bad these girls have to work, or they could go with us."

"My sister isn't much of a shopper," Christina blurted. "But I love it."

Maria winked at Mandy. "To be honest, I'm not all that much of a shopper either. I'd much rather be in the kitchen cooking for my family."

Mr. Rossi patted his belly that hung over his belt. "Cissy doesn't mind cooking either, but she used to be quite a shopper before we had kids." He quickly resumed his professional stance and gestured toward the office area. "After you, Mandy."

Mandy was about to sit closer to the door, but Mr. Rossi encouraged her to go behind the desk. "I don't want you to be uncomfortable," he said. "Now that you're on the management team, you're like family."

Her lips twitched into a smile. "Thanks."

"So have you thought about some of the things you'd like to do in your trainer position?"

She nodded. "I've made some notes."

"Okay, let's discuss them." He gestured for her to go ahead of him. "By the way, I'd like you to call me Edward or just Ed. This Mr. Rossi thing makes me feel old."

Mandy grinned. "Okay. . .Edward."

Two hours later, they'd finished talking about how she'd do her job. He'd asked if she preferred traveling or having new photographers come to her. She said it didn't matter—that she'd do whatever was needed in each specific case.

"That's good," he said. "It's hard for some people to leave their families. How about you come to Atlanta again? Is your mother healthy enough for you to leave?"

"She's doing great," Mandy said. "I'm proud of how she's changed her lifestyle, so it won't happen again."

"Yeah, Tony told me she's a great cook."

Mandy was dying to hear what else Tony had said, but she didn't want to come right out and ask. Instead she just smiled.

"Okay," Edward said as he stood. "That about does it. I'll come in tomorrow and on Monday to handle some issues with Tony and get to know Christina a little better, since we're turning this place over to her. The two of you need to start interviewing some more photographers."

"When will we need to do this?"

"Right away. I want to bring Tony back to Atlanta in a month to six weeks."

Mandy looked down to keep him from seeing her expression. When she felt like she could look at him without showing how she felt, she saw the tenderness in his expression.

"We also need to discuss where we place your office, too, Mandy. Since this is such a new thing for us, we're not sure if we want you to remain in a studio or if you should be in the home office. Of course, we wouldn't want you to leave your mother if she needs you."

Mandy licked her lips. "Thank you."

After he left the office, she remained sitting there staring at the blotter on the desk. Before her mother's heart attack, she wouldn't have minded moving for her job, but after the scare with her mother, she felt the tug to stay in West Virginia. Besides, she and Christina had just begun to forge a new, more adult sisterly relationship, and the experience was amazing. After the great news of her promotion, she should have been in a much better mood.

Tony appeared at the door. "Uncle Ed wants to meet with me. He said it won't take long, so you and Christina can go to lunch as soon as we're done."

Mandy took a few minutes to gather her thoughts before she got up and joined her sister at the front. Christina looked up with a broad smile.

"Isn't this the best company ever?" Christina said. "I'll never be able to thank you enough for finding this place."

Mandy forced herself to smile back. "Yes, it's a very good company."

Christina leaned toward her with a look of concern. "What's wrong, Mandy? Did I do something?"

"No, you didn't do a thing."

With a tight jaw, Christina looked around the corner then whispered, "Did Tony say something to upset you?"

"No."

"Okay, I give up. Tell me what's got you all upset."

Mandy was tempted to tell her nothing and pretend everything was fine. But she couldn't. She needed to vent.

"Just when I fell in love with someone who loves the Lord, loves me, and is everything I want in a guy, things go haywire."

"You mean like Tony going back to Atlanta?" Christina asked.

Mandy nodded. "He's never made it a secret about his plan. In fact when he first got here, he openly resented being made to work at the studio level. He wanted to work at the home office as soon as possible, and now he has his chance."

"Yeah, that makes things tough for you," Christina agreed. "But there's nothing you can do. We need to pray about it."

Christina had just placed her hand on Mandy's shoulder when they heard the sound of Tony's office door opening. Both of them glanced up.

"Thanks, Uncle Ed," Tony said. "I'll think about everything and get back with you soon."

"Don't wait too long, Tony. In fact, I need an answer by the end of the month."

"That gives me two weeks."

Edward grinned at Mandy and Christina. "I'm happy to see that Small World is able to attract such good people. You made it easy for us to do what we need to do for company growth."

Tony spoke up. "Why don't you ladies go grab some lunch?" He pulled out his wallet, opened it, and handed Mandy some money. "If you don't mind, I'd like for you to bring me something back."

Mandy pushed the money back at him. "I'll treat."

Edward laughed as he whipped out some money. "No, I'll treat. Every-one, put your money back. This is on me."

"You don't need to buy our lunch," Mandy said.

"No, but I want to," Edward said as he took Mandy's hand and folded it around the money. "In fact I'd like to join you ladies, if you don't mind. Cissy and Maria called a few minutes ago and said someone told them about a charming restaurant called Stratford Springs."

Mandy nodded. "They'll enjoy it."

Edward tilted his head. "Would you ladies like for me to take you there now? Cissy said they were heading there now, so we can join them."

"Um. . ." Mandy had some work to do, and it might take awhile, but she didn't want to turn Edward down. She turned a pleading look toward Tony.

"I need her back here in less than an hour, and it might take awhile to get there," Tony said.

Edward folded his arms as he made a contemplative face. "I understand. Maybe some other time."

"Sounds good," Mandy said.

"Why don't you join Mom and Cissy?" Tony asked. "I'm sure they'd like that."

With a nod, Edward walked toward the door. "Since you three have so much to do around here, I think I will."

After he left, Mandy let out a sigh. "Christina, let's go get some food." Then she turned to Tony. "What would you like us to bring you?"

He shrugged. "I'll eat anything you get."

※

Tony couldn't help but notice the change in Mandy's attitude. She'd been so happy about the promotion, but now she was more subdued. He had a pretty good idea of what was bothering her. He'd have to talk to her after she and Christina finished with their afternoon appointments.

He was surprised when they walked in the door twenty minutes later. Mandy handed him one of the two bags she was holding. "We decided to eat here, since there's so much to do."

"All the more reason to get more people in here. That was a brilliant idea Christina had to hire seniors to make calls and staff the desk."

Mandy agreed. "My sister is very smart."

"It obviously runs in the family."

"Thank you." Mandy avoided his gaze as she backed out of his office.

After lunch, the photo sessions went smoothly. Tony took calls from people interested in working, and he booked some interviews. At the end of the day, he asked Mandy to stick around for a few minutes.

Chapter 19

Come on in," Tony said.

Mandy hesitated at the door before going into his office. "You needed to see me?"

"I noticed how you changed after Uncle Ed mentioned bringing me back to Atlanta."

Bull's-eye. "Sorry." She swallowed hard. "So when are you leaving?"

"I'm not sure I am," he replied. "It all depends."

After waiting a couple of seconds, and he didn't answer, she decided to probe. "What does it depend on?"

He stood up, came around from behind his desk, and took her hand. "On us."

Mandy's heart thudded so hard, she was sure he could hear it. "What about us?" Her voice came out low and airy.

Tony let go of her hand. "This isn't the time or place to do this."

"Do what?" Mandy asked.

He narrowed his eyes and grinned. "You're good."

"Whatever. When do you plan to open up and tell me?"

He lifted her hand to his lips and kissed the back of her knuckle. "How about tonight?"

"What if I have plans?" She shot him a playful grin. "After all, it is rather short notice."

"If you have plans?" He gave her a mischievous look right back then set his jaw and narrowed his gaze. "Break 'em."

"Oh." Mandy couldn't think of a witty retort, so she dropped the act. "I don't have plans. Would you like to come over?"

"I have a better idea. I'll pick you up at seven. Wear something nice."

"Where are we going?"

Tony winked. "You'll find out soon enough."

Mandy realized she wasn't going to get anything out of him then, so she nodded. "I'd better get moving, since I have to change into something nice."

Tony glanced at his watch. "Yeah, you'd better hurry up. I'll be at your door in forty-five minutes."

All the way to her apartment, Mandy thought about the possibilities. If she had her way, Tony would tell her he'd never be able to leave her, and he'd remain in Wheeling to be near her. Then her thoughts drifted back to when she first met him. He'd made it very clear that Wheeling, West Virginia, was a temporary stop for him on his way up the career ladder of his family's business. His very words were, *"If I hadn't taken time out to join the army, I'd be where I want to be right now."*

As the memory sank in, Mandy's hope diminished. She'd known Tony long enough to fall in love with him. And long enough to know that when he wanted something, he'd do whatever it took to get it, as long as it didn't go against his faith. He most likely wanted to celebrate his dream job with Small World.

After Mandy got home, she forced herself to pull on her favorite dress and refresh her makeup. He'd said to wear something nice, and this was the nicest thing she owned. Too bad that after this, she'd be sad every time she wore it.

Tony arrived five minutes early. Mandy thought about how he was probably eager to talk about his promotion and ultimate move. She wanted to be happy for him, so she put on her best smile and opened the door.

He reached for her hand and slipped a corsage on her wrist. She tilted her head. "What's this all about? Are we going to a prom?"

With a chuckle, he shrugged. "Maybe." With a sweeping gesture, he said, "Ready to go?"

"Let me grab my purse."

As soon as they got in the car, he put a CD into the car stereo. As strains of instrumental Christian music played, Mandy studied Tony's profile in the dim light of dusk. Was it her imagination, or was he nervous?

"Where are we going?"

"You'll see." He made a couple of turns then headed straight for Oglebay Park.

"Why are we going to a park?" she asked. "You told me to dress up."

He lifted a finger to her lips. "Just relax, okay?"

She clamped her mouth shut and nodded. After all, she didn't see that she had any choice.

He found a parking spot and helped her out of the car. "Let's go over there," he said. "I'd like a nice view."

Mandy did as she was asked, being very careful with each step, since she'd worn her heels. "I just wish you'd warned me that I'd have to walk in the grass. I would have worn sneakers."

Tony smiled as he bent over and scooped her into his arms. He didn't say anything until they'd reached a place with a garden view, and he gently set her down. "I thought this would be perfect since you're prettier than any flower that has ever grown here."

Mandy playfully swatted at his shoulder. "Stop that. You're being silly."

Without another word, Tony turned her to face him, a serious look on his face. "Mandy, I've already told you I love you."

Her mind went blank. She wanted to say something, but nothing would come out.

"As you know, this opportunity with Small World is something I've wanted since I came back. Seven months ago, before I met you, I wouldn't have hesitated. But now, I can't imagine life without you."

Mandy swallowed hard as her thoughts swirled. "What are you going to do?"

He hesitated then reached into his pocket and pulled out a small black box. As he got down on one knee, Mandy's knees started to wobble, and she swayed.

Tony reached out to steady her and smiled. "I don't care where I live or what I do as long as I have you by my side. Mandy"—he opened the box, and a flash of brilliance defied the darkening sky—"will you be my wife?"

Mandy reached out and touched the ring then quickly drew back. "I—I don't know what to say."

He frowned and started to stand. "Um, I thought you might—"

Mandy gently pushed him back down. "Yes, I'll marry you, but what about the promotion? Both of our promotions?"

Tony remained on one knee as he placed the ring on her finger then stood to face her. "Ricco, Uncle Ed, and I discussed it. He said I can remain in Wheeling as a studio manager, and you'll work out of the office in this area."

"But I thought you had to go back to Atlanta. Your mom—"

He laughed. "I called her. When I told her what I planned to do, she said that was even better than having me back in Atlanta."

"Oh." Mandy couldn't help but smile, but then she remembered something. "What about my sister? Wasn't she supposed to manage the studio?"

"That's the best part. I talked Uncle Ed into keeping the Wheeling studio open—at least for the time being. Christina has agreed to be the first manager in the new studio in the Ohio Valley Mall."

Mandy frowned. "Does she know about—this?" She held up her finger and pointed to the ring.

A sheepish look crossed his face. "Well…yeah. You're not mad, are you? I mean, I wanted to talk to your parents, and she was right there, and—"

She slowly shook her head. "No, I'm not mad at all."

Tony leaned over and kissed Mandy and then they turned to look at the flowers. After a couple of moments of silence, he tugged her toward the car. "C'mon. I have reservations for dinner at the Ihlenfeld Room." He chuckled as she wobbled toward the car. "If I'd known how difficult this would be for you, I wouldn't have asked you to dress up."

She lost her balance, and he caught her. She laughed. "Looks like I'm literally falling for you."

"And I'll always be there to catch you."

A Letter to Our Readers

Dear Readers:

In order that we might better contribute to your reading enjoyment, we would appreciate you taking a few minutes to respond to the following questions. When completed, please return to the following: Fiction Editor, Barbour Publishing, Inc., P.O. Box 719, Uhrichsville, OH 44683.

1. Did you enjoy reading *Appalachian Weddings* by Debby Mayne?
   ❑ Very much. I would like to see more books like this.
   ❑ Moderately—I would have enjoyed it more if _____

   _____

   _____

2. What influenced your decision to purchase this book?
   (Check those that apply.)
   ❑ Cover   ❑ Back cover copy   ❑ Title   ❑ Price
   ❑ Friends   ❑ Publicity   ❑ Other

3. Which story was your favorite?
   ❑ *Noah's Ark*   ❑ *Portrait of Love*
   ❑ *Special Mission*

4. Please check your age range:
   ❑ Under 18   ❑ 18–24   ❑ 25–34
   ❑ 35–45   ❑ 46–55   ❑ Over 55

5. How many hours per week do you read? _____

Name _____

Occupation _____

Address _____

City_____ State _____ Zip_____

E-mail _____